ACP 8533

Lawless

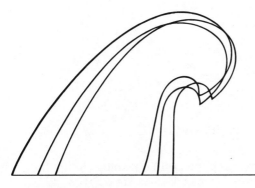

LOVESWEPT®

Patricia Potter

Lawless

DOUBLEDAY

NEW YORK LONDON TORONTO SYDNEY AUCKLAND

LOVESWEPT®

PUBLISHED BY DOUBLEDAY
a division of Bantam Doubleday Dell Publishing Group, Inc.
666 Fifth Avenue, New York, New York 10103

DOUBLEDAY and the portrayal of an anchor with a dolphin,
and the word LOVESWEPT and the portrayal of the wave device
are trademarks of Doubleday, a division of
Bantam Doubleday Dell Publishing Group, Inc.

Library of Congress Cataloging-in-Publication Data

Potter, Patricia, 1940–
    Lawless / Patricia Potter. — 1st ed.
      p. cm.
    I. Title.
PS3566.O718L39   1991
813'.54—dc20   91-12078
                            CIP

ISBN 0-385-42146-X

To Beth de Guzman, whose enthusiasm and support contributed so much to Lawless and meant so much to me

One

"A woman!"

The gunfighter stared at his would-be employer with as close to outrage as his unemotional nature permitted.

"You brought me here to frighten a woman?" The words were said quietly, but the speaker's anger was evident in the twitching of a muscle in his cheek. His voice was low, as deep and ominous as distant thunder, and his glittering eyes never blinked.

They were the strangest, coldest eyes Alex Newton had ever seen, and he uncharacteristically fidgeted in his wheelchair. He wondered if he'd made a very bad mistake in sending for the gunman named Lobo. He sought frantically to pacify the man who, by his very presence, dominated the richly furnished room which was Alex's sanctuary. "She isn't alone. There's also a man who helps her—"

Lean and predatory, Lobo had begun pacing Alex's study like the restless wolf for which he was named. But at Newton's words, he turned abruptly. "Tell me about the woman," Lobo interrupted.

Alex stifled his conscience. He would do anything to destroy his hated enemy, Gar Morrow. Anything. "An old man left her his ranch after she visited him a number of evenings. By rights it should be mine."

The gunman's eyes narrowed. The man was holding something back. He knew it. He could feel it. Yet, Newton's explanation satisfied him. He had never held women in very high esteem. He had found their capacity for cruelty greater than that of a man. He would never forget the old Apache woman to whom he had been given as a slave when he was little more than a tad. He would never forget wakening in the cold to her kicks in his ribs, or to the rope pulling around his neck. When he wasn't fast enough, she would tug it until he choked, and then she and the other women would laugh as he struggled for breath, his hands frantically trying to free himself. Nothing he had experienced since had changed his view of women. They were useful for one thing only.

He had few scruples now. But it irritated him that he had come all this way for such a job. It was insulting. A woman, for chrissakes. His mouth tightened.

"Five thousand dollars if she sells the ranch," Alex Newton said.

"For scaring a woman?" Lobo sneered. "Isn't that rather high?"

"There's another factor. The man who stays on her ranch is an ex-sheriff named Thomas."

For the first time, Lobo's interest was pricked. He had been ready to walk out, but now he hesitated. The name tugged at his memory.

Lobo continued to fix Newton with an unblinking glare that would give credit to a rattlesnake. "What's the first name?"

"Brady. Brady Thomas."

"From New Mexico?" Lobo growled.

"At one time, I've heard," Newton replied.

"Why is he there?"

Alex twisted uncomfortably again. He hadn't expected the guilt he was experiencing. He had been very angry when he had sent for this man. For the tenth time, Willow Taylor had turned down his offer to purchase her run-down ranch, even at several times its worth. But now that he had gone this far . . .

Lobo interrupted impatiently. "I asked you why he's at the ranch? Why he's an *ex*-lawman? Last time I heard, he was one of the best."

"Why do you need to know?"

"I want to know everything. I never do a job blind. That's why it's always done right. I know Thomas's reputation in New Mexico. It was a damned good one."

"He's a drunk now," Alex said reluctantly. He was committed to action, but that didn't mean he wanted to have this man in his house one second longer than necessary. He remembered all the stories about the renegade killer, that he was a white man who had fought with Apaches against his own kind, that he was a gunman without pity or scruples. He shivered inside again, fighting to keep his fear from showing. Alex Newton had always considered himself a strong man, brave and self-reliant until a bullet had doomed him to a wheelchair, had made him helpless. He hated his feeling of impotence, particularly in the presence of this dangerous, powerful animal. Lobo. The name fit.

"Since when?" Lobo's question shattered Alex's thought, and it took him a moment to realize the gunman was still asking about Brady Thomas.

"About three years."

"Why?"

Alex looked at the lean gunman with anger. It was as if *he* were being interviewed, not the other way around.

"Why?" The gunman's voice was like a pistol shot.

Alex shrugged, hoping to display an indifference he didn't feel. "I've just heard rumors about it. He stops drinking for a while, then starts again. Town fired him. He puts up at Willow's ranch."

Lobo began stalking the room once more. He didn't like Newton. He didn't like the job, though the presence of Brady Thomas did lend it a certain interesting aspect.

"Tell me more about the woman."

"I just want you to frighten her."

"Thomas won't frighten easily."

"He might now," Alex said.

Lobo didn't believe it. He'd known men like Brady Thomas. They never backed down.

But his interest was caught now, and he knew it showed from the feral look in Alex's eyes.

"I won't do anything illegal," Lobo warned. "I won't go to jail for you. I always stay within the law." He didn't add he was often able to twist the law to his own use.

"I just want you to scare her off," Alex reiterated.

"Why me?"

"Your reputation," Alex said frankly. "I'm hoping your name in itself will frighten her into selling. She has no right to the ranch anyway. She'd be better off without it. A woman can't run a spread by herself. And I've offered her several times its worth."

"Why then . . . ?"

"Probably thinks she can get more," Newton said, once more holding his tattered conscience in check. "Another . . . rancher wants it too. But I ain't going higher, and the other man can't afford more."

Lobo uttered a brief oath. Damn the man. Still he was already there, and it sounded simple enough. He had nothing else at the moment, and the woman was apparently unscrupulous herself, taking advantage of a dying man.

"And what if they don't scare?"

Alex was confident they would, even stubborn Willow Taylor. He did not consider himself a coward, yet looking at Lobo's hard eyes, he felt himself tremble.

"Then two thousand for your trouble, no questions asked." It was a bad bargain. Alex knew it. But he wanted Willow gone and this man was the most likely one to drive her away.

"In advance." The gunman's voice was curt.

Alex wheeled his chair over to the safe in the corner. After he opened the door, he carefully counted out a stack of bills and gave them to Lobo.

"You can stay in the bunkhouse," Alex said uncomfortably, hoping the man would refuse. He had a daughter. Thank God, she was away from the ranch at the moment. Marisa enjoyed danger, and this man radiated it. For a moment he tried to see the gunfighter as a woman would.

Lobo was tall and lean but well-muscled. A hank of sandy hair fell over a high forehead, emphasizing striking glacial eyes that were a light blue-green color. The nose was straight and well-proportioned, and the chin willful. Some might call him handsome, Alex supposed, despite the intimidating coldness in that face. There was no sign of Indian blood in him, although Alex had heard that he had lived with Apaches for a number of years. Alex had seen captured Indians who were hostile, and was familiar with the impassive expression they showed to the world. Lobo bore the same hostile indifference and arrogance. It was obvious he didn't give a damn what Alex, or anyone else, thought.

Lobo watched Newton's appraisal with amusement, then glanced around the large, gracious room with contempt. "No," he said. "I'll camp someplace on the ranch."

Alex shrugged, relieved. "Keep me informed."

Lobo gave him a curt nod and disappeared out the door, leaving a measure of tension and violence hovering in the room.

The Gunfighter!

The whole town was buzzing about The Gunfighter.

Willow George Taylor had heard nothing else all day, and now she looked up into the worried eyes of her friend, Dr. Sullivan Barkley.

"Not just any gunfighter," Sullivan said. "One of the worst of the breed. A man named Lobo."

Willow had heard of him, of course. Who hadn't? She had a classroom full of children, and the boys talked frequently of gunfighters and famous lawmen and shootouts.

"But why would Alex . . . ?"

Sullivan looked at Willow with affection *and* mild exasperation. Willow always went her own way, stepping on toes here and there in pursuit of whatever she believed was right, never thinking about the consequences. He had never met anyone like Willow. The town of Newton had never met anyone like Willow.

And no one ever quite knew what to do about Willow.

From the first moment she had stepped off the stagecoach and pronounced herself the George Taylor the town had hired to be its teacher, she had been like an earthquake, shaking the foundations of the ranching and farming community whose only excitement until then had been the ongoing feud between Alex Newton and Gar Morrow, onetime friends and cofounders of the Colorado town.

The problem now, Sullivan thought ruefully as he looked into Willow's blue eyes, was that Willow didn't take the new threat seriously, not after all the other crises she'd weathered.

"You must take care," he warned her as his gaze traveled around the schoolgrounds. He had hurried over from his office to catch her at the end of the day. He'd discovered she'd already heard the news, but the impact appeared slight. There was perhaps the slightest tremor on her lips, but it had disappeared quickly as she announced her intention to return home with the twins.

Sullivan shook his head. Jimmy and Jeremy were little protection, though the Lord knew they cared enough and would try to keep her from harm. All of Willow's little band of orphans and misfits would, but none were a match for a man of Lobo's reputation. A drunken ex-sheriff who acted as a ranch hand when he was sober; Estelle, a retired soiled dove who was afraid of her shadow; Chad, a thirteen-year-old boy who'd seen more bad times than most people in a lifetime; eight-year-old twins, and tiny Sallie Sue—they could do nothing against a killer like Lobo.

Sullivan shivered. "Alex's men say Lobo's arrived. Why don't you move back into town for a while?"

Willow's back stiffened. "There's no place large enough for all of us."

"I'll take the boys. You can stay with Sallie Sue in your old house."

"And Brady and Estelle? I couldn't leave them there alone. And there are the horses and the garden and . . ."

Sullivan sighed. Willow was the most stubborn woman he had ever met. Jake's place had been hers for a year, and she loved it, dilapidated as it was. Disapproving town officials had not scared her off; a schoolroom full of unruly, undisciplined boys had not scared her off; censure had not scared her off when she took in Estelle; and he knew Alex Newton would not scare her off.

Or even a man called Lobo.

"I'll ride back to the ranch with you," he said with a smile that warmed her heart. When she'd first come to Newton, she'd thought she might come to love him. But although there was warmth and liking between them, there was no passion or excitement, or any of the feelings she had read about but never felt. She had, however, seen his eyes rest on Marisa Newton with more than passing interest, although he had never tried to court her.

"I would like that," she said softly. No matter how much she tried to brush the worry away, a nagging fear whispered in the back of her mind.

Sullivan tied his horse to the back of the buckboard, then helped Willow up on the seat and the twins to the back before jumping in. He was lean to the point of thinness, and fought occasional bouts of malaria. They came at unexpected times and Willow had nursed him more than once.

They rode along in companionable silence, listening to the twins chatter. Finally, Willow asked in a low voice she hoped would not carry, "What have you heard about *him?*"

Sullivan shrugged, wanting to reassure her and yet make her realize the danger. "You know I don't put much stock in what people say. But he *is* a gunslinger."

"You don't think he would hurt the children? You don't think Alex would permit that?"

Sullivan knew Alex Newton was a man out of control. He had visited Alex and tried to talk to him, but to no avail. Willow Taylor, Alex had said, his face red, had no right to Jake's ranch. Willow had bewitched the old man.

"I don't know," he told Willow now.

"No one would hurt a child," she protested.

What about a woman? he wanted to ask. But he didn't

think his words would do any more good with her than they had with Alex. She saw the world through different eyes. She firmly believed that everything eventually turned out exactly as it should. And so far she had been right. The town had succumbed, however reluctantly, to her.

But Lobo was an entirely different matter.

Sullivan had seen the cruelty of human beings during four years of war. He had seen it again as an army doctor when communities had been ravaged by Indians and Indian villages by soldiers. Unlike Willow, he had lost much of his idealism. He was only too aware of what some men were capable of. And from everything he had heard of Lobo, it was a great deal.

Lobo looked from the top of a hill to the lonely-looking ranch house. It was in great need of paint, but its shabbiness was somehow diminished by the flowers bordering it. There was a fat horse in one corral and a bull in another. Beyond the house he saw the gray-green color of things struggling to grow in a garden. The fences badly needed repair though, and the barn didn't look much better. The hen house seemed ready to fall over.

The ranch didn't appear worth the trouble Alex Newton was taking, and probably wouldn't be were it not for the section of the river it bordered.

Lobo turned toward the sun. It was late afternoon, and the bright golden ball was as he liked it—at his back. Hooking one leg over the saddle horn, he faced the ranch again.

He had surveyed the entire area after leaving Newton's place, even though this didn't seem like the kind of job where caution was a primary concern. But he had found it wise in the past to scout out routes of quick departures. It was simple habit. He never overlooked the possibility of complications.

He saw three figures emerge from the house. The grown-up wearing a dress must be the Taylor woman. The other two looked like children, the smaller not much more than a babe.

Alex Newton had said nothing about children! Anger rose

in Lobo's craw, and as he debated whether to ride off with Newton's money in his pocket, he heard a distant scream. It reminded him of the screeching of a rabbit when it had been grabbed by a fox, and he felt a sudden surge of pity. An echoing cry rose from deep inside him, a cry from the past that was as sharp as an arrow, a cry that was his own. The last he remembered making as his brother's shouts of desperation rang in his ears.

He spurred his horse as another scream tore through the blast of hot wind. As he neared the house, he saw a boy stretched out on the ground. At the sound of the pinto's hooves, the boy glanced up, panic in his face. The woman was nearby, a pale wisp of a thing who clutched her hands together in despair and fear.

"M-my . . . sister," the boy stammered. "She fell into a hole."

From down below, Lobo heard a childish wail that ended in a whimper.

Remembering only briefly that he had been summoned to frighten the occupants of this ranch into submission, he slipped from his horse, the lariat he always carried with him clutched in his hand. Lobo quickly tied one end to the saddle horn, then moved toward what appeared to be an abandoned well shaft. The cries were growing weaker, like the haunting cries of his brother so long ago.

Don't care, he warned himself. *You can't hurt if you don't care.* But the sounds were eating into him like red ants on bare skin. He tried to look down into the hole, but it was too dark. With his gloved hands he tore away the rotten wood partially covering the top. Even then he could barely see within. There was only a flash of white skin.

He judged the size of the hole. He would barely be able to fit inside. The walls looked as if they were crumbling, and he could hear rustling sounds. He stiffened as he thought about the possibility of snakes.

"What's your name?" he asked the boy roughly.

"Ch-Chad," the boy stammered.

"Get another rope," Lobo said. "Fasten it to that tree and drop it in when I tell you."

Chad didn't question him; he immediately headed for the barn. But he turned around when he heard the stranger call out unintelligible words. The man had tied his rope around his waist and had started lowering himself into the well. At his commands—that's what the words were, Chad quickly figured out—the horse moved forward, one step at a time. Chad watched one more second in amazement before entering the barn.

Rope in hand, he returned to the well and quickly did as he'd been told. The horse had stopped moving, and the line from the saddle horn was taut. He heard the stranger utter what sounded like a curse. He had heard plenty in his life, and although he didn't understand what the man had just said, he recognized its intent.

Sallie Sue's whimpering had stopped. Chad leaned down and hollered. "Is she all right?"

"I don't know yet," the man snarled, then cursed again, this time in very distinct English. When he finished, he said more calmly, "Drop that second rope."

Chad did so with alacrity, and heard another curse. "Not so damned fast. There's snakes right below me. Your sister's caught on a ledge between them and me. She's not more than three feet above them."

The boy slowed the descent of the rope considerably and started praying, although he had little experience at that particular endeavor.

"Tighten it," came the voice again. "I can squeeze against the wall just enough to get her past me, but you'll have to pull her up on your own. We can't come up together, not without knocking down the walls. I'll climb up under her in case she falls."

"Yessir," Chad said.

"Start pulling."

Chad did, and he thought his arms would break or come loose from their sockets. He heard rock hit bottom as the sides of the well started crumbling.

"Slow down, boy," came the rough command. "You're doing fine."

Chad felt himself swelling with determination and pride.

There was something about the man's voice that gave him more strength than he knew he had. And then two other hands grabbed the rope behind him and he knew they were Estelle's. Together they pulled, and the man commanded the horse to slowly back away, pulling the weight of his master up.

There was the sound of another wall collapsing, and it was all Chad could do to keep from pulling fast.

A dirt-covered Sallie Sue started to emerge, and Estelle let go of the rope and ran to pull the child into her arms. Several seconds later, the stranger appeared, his body also coated with dirt.

Chad started to thank him, but he stopped when he saw the man's eyes. They did not invite thanks; they even commanded against it. Chad couldn't help stare at them, at the unusual color. Like winter frost skimming a mountain pool. Chad felt himself shiver in the blistering hot afternoon.

But Chad was filled with curiosity, and there was a question he had to ask. "How did you get your horse to do that?"

The stranger ignored the question and stared at Estelle, who was squeezing Sallie Sue so tightly Chad thought the girl was in more danger now than she had been minutes before. At the unblinking, appraising look of the man, Estelle fled to the house.

Chad watched as the man took one step toward Estelle, and then turned back to him. "Miss Taylor?" His voice carried puzzlement.

"Naw, that's Estelle," Chad said. "Willow's not here. She hasn't come back from school."

Lobo's eyes ranged over the ranch. His brow furrowed. "School?"

"She teaches school, didn't ya know? Everyone knows that."

"You her kid?"

Chad shrugged. He guessed he was. "One of 'em," he said.

"Why aren't you in school?"

"Willow needs me here during the day." Chad was too ashamed to say he'd flatly refused to go because he'd been so far behind the other kids his age. Willow taught him privately.

Lobo's senses were reeling. *One of 'em,* the boy had said. "There's more of you?"

"Two," Chad said, watching surprise register in the stranger's cold eyes. He fought to keep his own eyes from going to the well-worn gunbelt on the man's hips, the holster held tight against his body by a leather strap around his thigh. There was a tension about the man, an aura of danger that fascinated Chad.

"Goddamn," the stranger said to himself.

"Willow will be here pretty soon," Chad told him. "She'll want to thank you. Sallie Sue's her baby. She was chasing Brunhilde."

"Brunhilde?"

"One of the chickens. Sallie Sue's pet," Chad explained. His expression changed to one of disgust. "Now I'll have to catch her."

Lobo found himself blinking. Sallie Sue, for God's sake. What a name for a kid. And Brunhilde. A chicken?

Chad suddenly found his manners. "Why don't you come inside. There's some cookies," he offered.

Cookies, for chrissakes.

Lobo winced. He had been hired to scare the hell out of the woman who lived here, and now he was invited for cookies! Filled with unaccustomed confusion, he ignored the boy and untied the rope from around his waist, circling it in loops and tying it back on his saddle.

Lobo leapt into the saddle and leaned down to speak to the boy. "Get that damned well fixed." Only after he said the words did he realize how ridiculous they were. These people would be gone shortly. Very shortly.

Before Chad could utter a word or even ask for the stranger's name, the man was gone in a swirl of dust. Chad thought that the whole episode was just like one of Willow's stories, and wondered whether he had imagined the whole thing.

But then he saw the last of the dust settling down in the distance, and he grinned to himself.

God's whiskers, but did he have a story of his own to tell.

Thoroughly disgusted with himself and his incomprehensible behavior, Lobo finally found a clearing alongside the river that ran through the ranch. It was nearing dusk, and he was filthy from his venture into the hole. He washed in the river, not much more than a trickle of water because of the hot, dry weather, and he started a cooking fire.

Sitting under a tree, watching the flames flare and lick the coffeepot, he felt an unusual disquiet. Nothing was as he expected it, and he didn't like the feeling of not having control.

Nor did he like being lied to. Even if Newton hadn't actually lied, there was a hell of a lot he'd left unsaid.

Not only a woman, but children were involved. What in the hell had Newton expected him to do to kids?

And he was supposed to believe that the woman had seduced and cheated an old rancher. After bearing four children, how could she entice anyone? He had seen enough worn women in his life, old before their time because of childbearing. And every woman teacher he'd ever seen had been as homely as sin.

Goddamn Newton.

Lobo recognized only one weakness in himself. Young things. He had no pity, no mercy, no compassion for those who should be able to take care of themselves. *He* had survived. Others could well do the same thing.

But the young . . . like the small girl . . .

When he allowed himself to think about it, he knew those feelings reached back to when he had been only seven and the Apaches raided the wagon train. He remembered the agonized cries of the adults as they were killed, and those of children too young to travel. Imbedded in his mind were the sobs of the survivors, the children taken as slaves, the way they weakened day by day until only he and his brother survived. And then his brother, broken by lack of food, by exhaustion, by fear, gave up too, and had been left in the desert to die. Lobo would never forget his brother's terrified cries for him.

Lobo had tried to stay with him, but he had been roughly pulled away by a brave who tied a rope around his waist and dragged him behind a horse until he struggled to his feet. Every step he'd trudged for a mile, he heard his brother crying his name. He still heard that sound sometimes in the night. He'd heard it today when the child fell in the well.

Damn Alex Newton. He would see the man in the morning and tell him exactly where he could stuff his job. And Lobo would keep the two thousand dollars. For his trouble.

He settled down on the blankets, his head against his saddle, and watched. Sunsets were one of the few things that gave him pleasure, and more important, a sense of freedom that had been denied him as a boy and young man. Now he roamed where he wished, answering to no one, setting no rules for himself, no limits.

He stretched, taking satisfaction in feeling each muscle respond. His body was whipcord lean through both conditioning and purpose. No one who lived with the Apaches had excess fat, especially a white slave. By the time he'd left them, he needed little food to survive, and could go days without water. He could run twenty miles without breathing hard, and could ride any horse. He could kill in a dozen ways and do it without regret.

And while he hadn't sought the reputation that had inevitably come to him, neither did he do anything to soften it. His reputation kept people away. Sometimes just his eyes, the icy-cold blue-green eyes, made them shiver and keep their distance.

That was exactly the way he liked it.

The fire in the sky was being doused now by the softer hues of twilight, and the scene lost its interest for Lobo.

He turned over, but sleep wouldn't come. He thought of the boy and his offer of cookies. Christ, wouldn't the . . . teacher be horrified!

Two

"And he could make his horse do anything. You should have seen him."

"Slow down, Chad," Willow said with a smile as Sullivan tended Sallie Sue's scratches in the small bedroom Sallie Sue shared with Estelle.

It was obvious Chad had a hero.

Sullivan looked up, pronouncing Sallie Sue fine despite the harrowing experience. Then he turned to Chad. "What did he look like?"

"Tall . . . taller than you, Dr. Sullivan," Chad said. He'd endowed him with all the heroic features of the gods in Willow's books. He'd also marveled at how the horse walked back and forth at the sound of words. "You think he'd teach me how to do that?"

"Who is he?" Willow asked with some exasperation.

Chad shrugged. "He didn't say."

Sullivan tweaked one of Sallie Sue's braids. "I'll fix that well covering before I go. Where in the hell was Brady?"

Chad shrugged again, and Willow was afraid of what that meant. She had hoped—

Sullivan's voice broke into her thoughts as he continued to question Chad. "Tell us more about this stranger."

Chad tried to remember, but he could recall only the whole, not the parts. The stranger had been too overwhelming in his entirety, but Chad tried. "Sort of sandy hair, sort of blue eyes . . . and tall," he repeated.

Willow raised an eyebrow at Sullivan. The stranger had had to be very tall indeed to make that kind of impression on the usually unimpressionable Chad. The boy had worked in a saloon since he was eight, and he had few illusions about men. He normally viewed the world, including Willow's Greek heroes, with a skeptical eye.

Sullivan shook his head. "No one I recognize. Could have been a cowhand, I guess. All of them are pretty good with horses and a rope. Or a drifter."

Chad shook his head. *His* stranger had certainly been no ordinary cowboy. He took exceptional pride in the fact that he had helped in the rescue, that he had been partners with the man who spoke to horses.

"I wish I could thank him," Willow murmured wistfully.

"I asked him to stay . . . even offered him some cookies," Chad said.

"And he didn't say anything about where he was going?" Sullivan's voice was insistent.

Chad shook his head.

Sullivan's eyes caught Willow's, and she knew what he was thinking. But that couldn't possibly be. The only stranger they'd heard about was the gunfighter, and he certainly couldn't be their Good Samaritan. She tended to believe Chad's stranger was just that—a stranger who happened to be passing through and was kind enough to stop to help.

Willow hadn't told Chad about the threat, although she feared the twins probably heard the news at school. Was that why Brady had disappeared? He had intended to go into town for supplies that day. Perhaps he'd heard about the gunfighter.

"You'll have supper with us tonight?" she asked Sullivan.

He shook his head. "I have to get back," he said as he

turned toward the door. He grinned suddenly. "There's another town meeting."

Willow lifted her eyes heavenward. She didn't have to ask what about. They were always about her.

Chad rushed ahead of both of them through the door. "I'm going to tell the twins what happened."

Sullivan looked at Willow. "I wonder how tall the stranger's going to be before Chad gets through telling everyone tonight."

"He'll reach the heavens, no doubt." Willow grinned.

"I wish to hell I knew who he is."

"Well, he obviously meant no harm."

"No," Sullivan said slowly, his gaze lingering on Willow. She was a pretty woman. Not as beautiful as Marisa Newton, but she had a glow that warmed those around her.

A few wisps of auburn hair framed her face browned by the sun. Her vivid blue eyes were always alive and smiling, refusing to see the darkness in life, the evil, even the indifference that was often a part of evil. If she did believe such a thing really existed, she probably felt it could be overcome. This attitude was what frightened him, for she had no idea of Alex Newton's determination, or his capacity for violence.

"Be careful, Willow," he warned her, willing her to listen. "Alex is obsessed. I honestly don't know what he's capable of now. He holds Gar responsible for Mary's death, and it's been eating at him all these years. He sees you as his enemy now that you allow Gar to use your land."

"But Jake did."

"Jake once saved Alex's life."

"That shows Alex has some honor."

"I'm not sure, not anymore," Sullivan said reluctantly.

Willow frowned, her whole face creasing with concentration. "There has to be a way to solve this, to get the two of them together again."

Sullivan smiled. That belief was the ultimate optimism, and he no longer believed in miracles, not after the war, not after the deaths of his own family.

"You'll need your Odysseus to solve that one," he said with a dry smile. The children had told him some of the stories

Willow read to them. Odysseus, the warrior who was crafty and wise and brave and resourceful. The whole town needed him now, Sullivan thought. He feared the valley would explode into war if Alex persisted in trying to ruin Gar Morrow.

"Perhaps," Willow replied with a complacent smile as she thought of Chad's hero.

The stranger did indeed grow taller during dinner, chasing from Willow's head all thoughts of the gunman named Lobo.

Dinner was the meal Willow loved best, even when Estelle cooked. It was then she felt the full measure of companionship and warmth and security. She would stay and she would make the ranch work. Drought or no drought. Gunfighter or no gunfighter.

This was her home, the only home she'd ever really had. In Boston, where her father was a schoolmaster, they'd lived in a pair of small rooms in a large hall with boarding students who came and went. Now she owned this ranch, and this was her family, the big family she'd always wanted so fiercely.

They were finally comfortable together. Even Chad, who at thirteen was the oldest of the children. All too grown-up for his age, Chad had become her confidant, friend, and ranch hand, and at last he even permitted her to touch him with affection. In the beginning that had not been so.

Touching was natural to Willow. Her father had been an affectionate man, and she had been raised to express affection openly. But she had understood quickly that touching, for Chad, had meant brutal beatings for most of his life. He had flinched when anyone came close to him, even after his father had been knifed to death during a drunken brawl.

Chad had been ten then. He had never been to school and barely made enough to eat by cleaning the saloon—if his father didn't find the money first.

When Chad's father died, the sheriff intended to send the boy to an orphanage in Denver, but Willow knew about orphanages. She and her father had been patrons of one in Boston, and she knew it could well kill what spirit Chad had left. She volunteered to take the boy.

Chad was the first of several orphans to come to her. Willow's small house, provided by the town for its teacher, had suddenly started to fill up. Two boys, twins, were left with the sheriff by the master of a wagon train. Their parents had died of cholera on the way west.

And then Sallie Sue, who was little more than a baby, came to Willow when the child's mother died giving birth to a stillborn. The father had disappeared.

Estelle was her responsibility too. She was not a child, but was just as needy. She had been a saloon girl, a prostitute, until one customer beat her half to death, blinding her in one eye. After that she couldn't stand the touch of a man, and she had no skills. Much to the disapproval of the townspeople, Willow had taken her in.

Brady had been the last. He was one of the town drunks, an ex-sheriff who had fought one battle too many and buried himself in a bottle. Willow had found him half dead of pneumonia in an alley, and had called Sullivan. Homeless and alone, Brady needed someplace to recuperate. By then, Willow had the ranch, and Brady had temporarily moved into the barn, doing chores for his keep.

Willow had to grin now at Chad's tales of the stranger, which grew more mythical by the moment. At least, they kept everyone's mind off Estelle's cooking.

Estelle, an outcast nearly all her life, had wanted so badly to become a part of the family that she had taken over the cooking. No one was cruel enough to point out exactly how badly she fulfilled that function and they all did their best to eat.

With the puckish humor that endeared her to her students if not to their parents, Willow thought that perhaps she should challenge Newton's gunfighter to one of Estelle's meals.

Then she immediately felt guilty as she looked at Estelle's anxious face.

"Is it really all right?" Estelle asked as she had each time she'd cooked for the past month.

Heads nodded. Lies came easier that way.

Sallie Sue was the most vocal, particularly about the gravy

and biscuits. "Like my pies," the girl observed. At three, she was very proud of her mud pies.

A choking noise came from Chad, a gargled sound from one of the twins.

"Story tonight?" Sallie Sue demanded after Chad had completed his fourth recital of the afternoon's events.

Willow forced another piece of incinerated beef down her throat, and nodded, her eyes twinkling. Stories were usually told on Friday and Saturday nights, so she could work with Chad on his studies during the week. But Sallie Sue's bruised face was irresistible. "After dinner," she conceded. "Does anyone remember where we left off?"

"The wooden horse," Jeremy, one of the twins, said quickly. He was completely intrigued by war and the resourcefulness of Odysseus.

As the daughter of a schoolmaster, Willow had grown up with the tales of Odysseus's travels, had even taught them in the prestigious Boston boys' school where her father also taught. As a child, mythology had been her escape, as a scholar her expertise, as a foster mother her gift.

After dinner, Sallie Sue sat, as usual, on Willow's lap. The other children sprawled on the floor. Willow looked at the corner where Brady often sat in the shadows, an unlit pipe in lieu of a drink. She missed him and worried about him.

"Once upon a time," Willow started as she always did. Any other beginning brought forth objections from Sallie Sue.

"In an ancient land far away," she continued softly, "there was a young prince named Odysseus. He was brave and wise and good, and—"

"There was an evil city named Troy," Jimmy interrupted eagerly.

Willow hoped Homer would forgive the liberties she took with his tales. "And Odysseus knew he could never get his soldiers inside its tall walls, so he and his fellow warriors started building a big wooden horse. It was to be a gift, you see. . . ."

* * *

Reverend Cecil Mooney opened the town meeting with a prayer. Mayor August Stillwater then took over as nearly eighty people stirred nervously in the rough wooden pews of the church.

There had not been very many town meetings prior to Willow George Taylor's arrival.

And then there was the biggest one of all.

The first town meeting had been held four years earlier to discuss the establishment of a school. The valley population had grown. Civilization was coming to Newton. A school was needed.

A collection was taken up to build a school and advertise in an eastern newspaper for a schoolmaster.

There was collective relief when the advertisement was answered by one Abner Goodbody. A fine, stable-sounding name. A responsible name. The town sent fifty dollars for traveling expenses.

Abner Goodbody arrived, and was gone three months later to the gold fields.

The second applicant also had the solid name and credentials that warranted a town celebration. Samuel T. Morgan. A graduate of Harvard. No one asked why a Harvard graduate would come to a small plains town of some three hundred people. But they began to wonder two weeks after he arrived. He couldn't remember the alphabet, much less figure how much money a herd of one hundred cattle would bring. One month later he, too, left—for the silver mines.

And then came the application from W. George Taylor, who had taught for three years at a prestigious school for boys. Stable. Obviously qualified. Money was sent. The fund was reaching sock bottom.

Much of the town gathered to welcome the coach bringing the new schoolmaster. High hopes changed to horror when a young woman stepped off and introduced herself as Willow George Taylor.

The pronouncement precipitated a crisis. The advertisement, the mayor thought, had been quite clear that a man was required. Who else could handle half-wild boys? The town had been deceived and wanted its money back.

"Not at all," Miss Taylor had countered. She had given them her legal name and rightful credentials. She was a competent teacher. If they wanted her to leave, she would, but the money was gone. Or they could give her a chance.

After a long, acrimonious meeting, the town decided to do just that: give her a chance. The decision wasn't reached out of tolerance or kindness. There was simply no more money to send for another teacher.

Much to everyone's surprise, the new schoolmarm did know how to calculate the price of a hundred head of cattle. More important, the students almost instantly adored her, and her stories, and her special ability to make learning fun. Boys who wouldn't go to school before seldom missed a day if they could help it. When the term of her employment expired, it was grudgingly renewed. There was still a residue of resentment at being gulled.

And then there was another town meeting when she decided to adopt Chad. A single woman certainly shouldn't adopt a boy, even a young boy. It just wasn't proper.

Sullivan Barkley stood up and asked if anyone else would take the boy. When there was silence, he merely looked from one woman's face to another until heads hung and gazes lowered.

There was an even longer meeting when Willow took in Estelle. What kind of example was she for children? Taking in a soiled dove, which was the kindest description of Estelle offered that night.

"Cast not stones," the doctor said as he studied each man's reddening face.

And then old Jake left her his ranch, and another meeting resulted. What had the schoolmarm done to merit such a gift? Alex Newton was furious she wouldn't sell the land to him and was pressuring the town to fire her.

By then, Dr. Sullivan was becoming very impatient with the town. If Willow Taylor went, then he would leave also. Faced with the possibility of losing the only doctor within one hundred miles, the townspeople reluctantly agreed to keep her on.

A new crisis loomed now. According to the telegraph operator an infamous gunman called Lobo was heading their way. All because of Willow Taylor's stubbornness.

"We're to be invaded by a notorious gunman," Mayor Stillwater pronounced, his face flushed in the flickering light of oil lamps. "You all know what that means. None of us will be safe. Our womenfolk won't be able to walk outside our homes."

Sullivan stood up. "We all knew this was coming the day Jake died. He was the only one who kept Newton and Morrow separated, and he did the only thing he knew to keep it that way."

"But a woman?" The complaint came from the back of the room. "She has no business running a ranch. She should be teaching."

Sullivan leaned against the wall. "Any complaints in that direction?"

The wife of the mercantile owner stood up. "My Robert just got a scholarship out east because of Miss Willow. She's the best thing that ever happened to this town."

"And the most dangerous," grumbled a man who had no children.

Another man rose. "We all admit she's a good teacher. But why does she insist on keeping that damn . . . darned ranch, specially if old Alex wants it? I say we tell her to sell it to him."

Another voice spoke up. "You think she'd listen? She ain't never listened before."

Sullivan broke in again. "And what do you think will happen if she did sell to Alex, and Gar Morrow was cut off from water? We'd see more than one gunfighter in town. The whole damned range would go up in flames. We'd have more gunfighters in town than citizens."

The mayor turned to the current sheriff, a quiet man who seldom had much to do except jail a drunk or break up a fight between Morrow and Newton cowhands. "Is there anything you can do about the gunman?"

"He ain't wanted anyplace I know of," the sheriff said. "I

checked. Seems he's mighty careful in letting the other feller draw first. Or else there ain't no witnesses."

"You can tell him to get out of town," the mayor suggested.

The sheriff looked down at his badge. "You can have the badge back 'fore I go against someone like that renegade. They say he lived with the Apaches and is meaner than any of 'em."

There was a silence. They all knew no one would take the job, considering the current situation. The town had always been a relatively quiet place, except for the bank robbery four years before when Brady Thomas was still sheriff. And now the damned feud between Alex and Gar.

Everyone at the meeting knew the story. Alex, Gar, and Jake had been close friends when they came to the area twenty years earlier. Alex and Jake had chosen land along the river, but Gar had picked a spectacular piece of rolling acres to the west. The land included a stream, which Gar believed would provide enough water. But the stream dried up during a drought, and Gar became totally dependent on the river. There was no problem for years since they were all friends. But then Mary Newton was killed. . . .

The mayor cleared his throat. "Maybe we should just wait. Maybe this . . . gunman won't even come. Maybe we can talk some sense into Alex."

"And if we can't?" That came from Sullivan.

"She could always sell," the mayor said.

"You know she won't do that," Sullivan countered. "She loves that ranch. And she needs the room."

"We didn't ask her to take in all those—"

"Fact is," chimed in another voice, "we advised her not to."

Sullivan stared at the gathering. "If anything happens to her, it will be on all your heads."

The meeting ended on that discordant note.

Lobo slowed, forcing himself to relax as he rode toward the Newton ranch house at daybreak.

During the night, he had reached a decision. He was going

to shove this job down the man's throat. And keep the money for his trouble.

When he arrived at Newton's ranch, he strode in the house without knocking, his anger visible in his clenched jaw and the icy glare of his eyes. He half expected Newton to still be abed, but the man was up, eating breakfast.

Alex was startled when the gunman burst into his house. He looked up, certain his objective had been accomplished, that Lobo had, indeed, frightened the woman into selling.

"Why in the hell didn't you tell me the woman had kids? Four of them. What else didn't you tell me?"

Alex stared at the man in confusion. He hadn't told him because he hadn't thought it important.

"I . . . didn't think it mattered," Alex said. "I was told—"

"That I frighten kids?" Lobo said with cold fury.

"Just the woman. Did you see her?"

"No," Lobo said with satisfaction. "But I rescued the little girl from an old well she fell into."

"You did what!"

Lobo grinned. Alex thought it a wolfish grin. Or something the devil might display before grabbing a soul.

"You're going to have to find yourself another hobgoblin," Lobo said. "I just became a hero."

"Who else was there?"

"A boy, about twelve. A thin woman who seemed terrified of me."

"That had to be Estelle."

"Who in the hell is Estelle?"

"Used to work at the Golden Slipper Saloon. Saloon girl."

"That was a whore?" He found it almost beyond belief as he recalled the woman's terror, the thin form, the hair bound in a straggly knot.

Alex nodded, amused at the gunman's reaction.

"Christ, what else?" Lobo queried. "A saloon girl. A passel of kids."

"I told you there's no way she can manage that place. It would be a kindness if she's made to realize the benefits of selling."

"I'm not in the kindness business."

Alex couldn't stop a small smile this time. "No, I guess you're not. And did you tell them just what business you're in, who you are?"

"No. What difference does that make?"

"Perhaps," Alex said thoughtfully, "it will still work."

"You didn't hear me, Newton. I'm through."

"I was told you always finished a job."

"Only when I'm told everything. Everything! You left out a lot of details, my friend."

The way Lobo said "friend" made Alex itch. "She did cheat Jake. The ranch was supposed to be mine."

"Sorry, Newton."

"The kids aren't hers," Alex said desperately. He had pinned all his hopes on this man. Not to speak of the two thousand dollars he had already paid.

Lobo was almost out the door when he turned abruptly. "Not hers? What do you mean?"

"They're kids she uses to help farm the place."

"Even a little girl?"

Lobo was trying to grasp Willow Taylor's character. A mother who was not a mother at all. A schoolteacher who made slaves of kids and housed a whore. A seductress and cheat. Newton had more or less accused her of all of that. But none of it fit. It certainly did not fit with the eagerness of the boy who'd asked him to stay for cookies, or the well-fed chubbiness of the little girl named Sallie Sue.

Suddenly understanding dawned in his head. Newton hadn't told him the woman would be away during the day because he had wanted him to frighten the children! Perhaps Newton believed that was the best strategy.

Lobo's fury boiled. He'd done a lot of things he wouldn't brag about, but he'd never harmed a child. "You wanted me to scare the kids," he said, his voice low and deceptively gentle. "That's not a man's job, it's a coward's."

Alex winced. Twenty years earlier he would have killed a man for saying those words. Now he was helpless. And he hated himself as much as he hated Lobo. But he also needed the gunman.

"I'll up the ante. Ten thousand if she sells. No violence.

Just let her know you're just one of many I'll hire if she doesn't sell the land to me."

"I'm through," Lobo said.

Alex played his trump. "If you leave, I'll send for Canton. I understand he's available now."

Lobo's long stare was cold and menacing. He knew exactly what Newton was thinking, and Newton was right. He and Canton *were* competitors, but they were also professionals. Lobo respected Canton because he, like himself, never let emotions get in his way, especially personal likes and dislikes. There was tension between them when they met, because they were each wary of the other, and even warier of the crowds that always gathered, crowds aching for a gunfight between the two, crowds eager to see someone die. But he and Canton had never been on opposite sides, not yet.

"I'll think about it," Lobo repeated, contempt on his face.

"How long?" Alex didn't like the tightness in his throat, the way his words seemed to stick in it.

Lobo narrowed his eyes. "I'll let you know, Newton." He turned and strode out of the room with long, lazy strides just as a pretty girl came flying down the stairs. Out of the corners of his eyes he saw her stop abruptly and stare, but he ignored her and went straight out the front door. He'd had enough of Newtons.

Marisa went into her father's study. "Who is *that?*"

Alex winced. "Just a drifter. Stay away from him."

But Marisa sped to the door, throwing it open to watch the man mount a magnificent paint horse. He didn't use stirrups like other men; he effortlessly used one hand on the saddle horn to propel his body up in one lithe movement.

From his study, Alex saw his daughter's back as she peered out the door.

And he had the terrible feeling he had just caught the wolverine's tail.

* * *

Lobo started back to his camping site, then looked up at the sky. It was still very early. Perhaps he could catch a glimpse of the Taylor woman on her way to school.

He'd seldom been curious about things that didn't concern him and he'd halfway decided the woman no longer mattered. Nothing that Alex said had changed his mind about leaving. But something prodded him on, and that something pricked his insides like the porcupine quills used in Apache torture.

Willow Taylor was a teacher, a teacher who tried to run a ranch. A woman who inspired a powerful man like Newton to hire someone like him. A "good" woman who sheltered a whore, and a drunk, and orphaned children. What in the hell kind of woman was that?

Go, something powerful inside told him.

Stay, something equally as compelling said.

Instead, he found himself riding toward the hills that overlooked the road linking the Taylor ranch to town. He would take one look and then travel on. To hell with Newton.

He found the place he was seeking. He doubted whether he could be seen at this distance, especially half hidden as he was in the high grass.

Lobo didn't have to wait long before he saw a buckboard approaching, the reins held by a slender woman in a blue dress. On the seat with her were two boys.

Much to his surprise, the woman didn't wear a bonnet to cover her face, and her skin was lightly tanned and framed by wisps of dark auburn hair that was confined by a blue bow. She smiled at the boys next to her and threw back her head in laughter. A hot blast of wind caught the sound of warm amusement and carried it to Lobo. It was like none he'd heard before. Gentle, like spring rain. His hands tightened on the reins of his horse, and his knees drew the horse back until he blended into the high buffalo grass on the hill. He couldn't see her eyes, and he wondered about their color. Blue probably, with that shade of hair. She managed the team with competence, and her body was straight and proud.

The buckboard disappeared in a cloud of dust and he continued to sit there, the woman's sweet laughter echoing in his ears, the impression of beauty stamped on his mind. His heart twisted with confusion, with a kind of bewilderment that something had finally seemed to touch him, even as he realized it was something he could never have.

Three

Lobo rode to the edge of the mountains. It was near dusk when he stopped. He was fleeing for his life.

He had never run away from anything before. As the sun started its descent behind the mountains, he stopped to rest his horse alongside a stream. The horizon was a blend of soft colors that night, unlike the burning sky of the prior evening.

Soft and gentle. Like the woman's voice that morning.

To rid himself of the remembered sound, he focused on bitter memories that reminded him of the folly of wanting, of caring, of protecting. He thought of another evening like this one, soft and quiet, that had exploded into fire and blood, a day so many years past, a day he had buried deep within himself.

The wagon train in which he was riding had stopped at sunset. The sky was golden brown, full of cinnamon, he'd told Timothy. He also remembered telling his brother it meant good weather the next day. He didn't know whether it did or not, but the prediction made Timothy smile, and he'd been grateful for that. Timothy seldom smiled.

The Apache had chosen that moment to swoop down on

the poorly guarded train, and there had been no time to fight back. Lobo and his older brother had watched their mother and father die, along with the other adults on the train. Only five children survived, and they were taken as slaves.

The boy Lobo had felt little else other than terror. He and his brother had been regularly beaten by their religiously fanatic father, and neither boy had ever received a kind touch or word from either of their parents. Lobo had been large and strong for his age, and he'd tried to protect and care for Timothy, even doing some of the older boy's chores and shielding him from beatings, often taking them himself.

His harsh childhood, he realized later, had been good training for what came later. He had learned to protect himself from blows, from showing emotion, from sinking under the weight of unending labor and cruelty. It was why he survived and other children didn't. His protection of Timothy, he felt, had also been his brother's death warrant. Timothy couldn't survive the pace and deprivation that was part of the Apache's testing. And so Timothy was left alone in the desert to die.

And Lobo had never again allowed himself to feel or care for anyone again.

He finally gained the freedom he'd always coveted, and that had been enough. There was no laughter, no joy, no peace in him, and he'd never felt need for such elusive feelings. He considered them dangerous at best, for they kept the mind from the most important thing: survival.

Lobo watered his horse slowly, and thought about camping there before pushing on to Denver. He checked the two thousand dollars in his saddlebags and wondered what would Newton do.

Lobo had met men like him before, obsessed men. There had been the tone of madness in his voice, and Lobo had learned to be wary of that particular species. Men like himself, cold professionals, were easier to predict.

Would Newton really hire Canton if Lobo left?

Marsh Canton was very fast with a gun, perhaps even faster than he. Would Canton have the same reservations about children as he did? Never mind the woman. Lobo wouldn't allow himself to think about her.

Lobo thought briefly about the boy at the Taylor ranch. He'd had the same cowlick his brother had, the same straw-colored hair, the same flash of hero-worship in his eyes, for God's sake.

It was none of his business.

Unsaddle your horse, he told himself. *Bed down for the night. Forget today and find another job.*

The advice made a hell of a lotta sense.

You've never left a job unfinished.

To hell with Newton. And his goddamn job.

And Canton?

Let him do his worst. It's not your business anymore.

You can still get them off the ranch. Without bloodshed.

Possibly.

And earn ten thousand dollars.

An honest streak kicked him in the gut. He didn't care about the money. Not now. He hated to think, though, that he cared about anything else.

He sighed. But the decision was made. Tomorrow he would pay another visit, after school hours, on Miss Taylor. He would make it very plain that he, and others like him, were prepared to do whatever was necessary to force her from the land. He hoped like hell she'd believe him.

Once more Lobo surveyed the run-down ranch. It was late—suppertime he judged—and the woman should be home. As if to reassure him, a wisp of smoke curled upward from the chimney of the house.

He had spent the night in the mountains, half hoping the fresh air would brush away the idiotic decision he'd made the prior evening. But it hadn't. Something drove him back to this same hill, the hill he'd watched from before. He had tried to plan what he would say. But he discarded one set of words after another. He had never been easy with them in any event. Chrissakes, he'd never had need of words. A look, a movement were usually enough.

Not that he had that many words to call upon. During his years with the Apache, he had never heard English spoken, and he hardly spoke with members of the tribe, even after he was reluctantly made a warrior. He'd had even less to say to those who had reviled him once he'd reentered the white world, the edges of it, anyway. He had started speaking with his gun and knife, and that had been sufficient.

But now words were needed, convincing words as well as threatening ones. Although he didn't quite understand his newly discovered concern for someone other than himself, he did not want the woman with the soft laughter hurt, nor the boy with the straw-colored hair like his brother's, or the small, chubby kid named Sallie Sue. And he had few doubts that Alex Newton would do whatever was necessary to drive them away.

So it was up to him to frighten them out. That was the best solution for everyone. The woman would have money, Alex would have the land, and he, Lobo, would have ten thousand dollars and could get the hell out of there.

He rubbed the back of his neck, wondering what it was about the scrubby ranch house or dying vegetable field that made the woman reluctant to sell. Most women would take the money and run.

Not that her reasons mattered.

Determined to end the matter, Lobo spurred his horse and trotted down the road toward the ranch.

He heard the roar of the bull, then the terrified yell of a boy. Christ, what now?

His knees pressed the pinto's sides and the horse stretched into a gallop as another screech of pure terror came from the corral. His hand tightened on the reins when he saw that the bull had somehow escaped from the corral and, head lowered and horns aimed, it made directly toward the boy.

The boy darted away, and the animal barely missed him. It turned and began another attack. Lobo could use his pistol, but anger might spur the animal to continue charging after it was shot, if indeed he could even hit the small vital spot from atop a speeding horse.

Discarding that course of action, Lobo urged his pinto to run beside the bull and kicked his feet loose from the stirrups. He leapt from the horse onto the bull's back, grabbing the animal's horns and swinging his weight to force the bull off balance and down to the ground. Lobo twisted around a split second before the bull landed, escaping the animal's weight but managing to hold the beast down. He had a matter of seconds, no more, before the bull recovered and struggled back up.

"Get to the fence," Lobo yelled to the boy, moving once more to keep the bull off balance. He felt the great muscles under him strain to rise, to throw him aside as he saw the boy reach the fence and climb up.

Lobo whistled, and the pinto came within several feet of him. With a speed that bewildered both the bull and Chad, Lobo was up, his hand grabbing the saddle horn and his feet running alongside the horse. Then he swung up and the pinto stretched into a full gallop, quickly outrunning the mad bull.

When Lobo saw the bull head for open range, he turned his horse and trotted back to the corral.

The boy was shaking, and his face was full of awe.

"I ain't never seen anyone do anything like that before," he whispered in awe.

"You all right, boy?"

Chad looked down at himself. "I . . . I think so."

There was so much doubt in the boy's eyes despite the evidence of his wholeness that Lobo's mouth twitched.

Chad visibly tried to control his shaking. "Old Ju-Ju-Jupiter misses Brady, I guess," he said as Lobo studied him with frosty eyes.

Brady. Brady Thomas, Lobo recalled. The ex-sheriff.

Lobo took his eyes from the boy and looked over the rest of the ranch. A woman—Estelle—was halfway to the corral when she stopped, her shoulders slightly stooped, her glance on the boy, apparently reassuring herself he wasn't hurt before she turned away. Lobo glowered at the boy with disapproval. "You and she here alone?"

The boy raised his chin. "I can take care of th-things. . . ."

Lobo raised one eyebrow. "I see," he said dryly.

The boy's face flushed and he glanced down. "I'm . . . beholden to you . . . again," he finally said. "But Willow's gonna be mighty distressed about Jupiter."

"Jupiter?"

"The bull."

"What kind of name is that for a bull?"

The boy flushed again at the criticism.

"Don't answer, boy," Lobo said. It made about as much sense as Sallie Sue and Brunhilde and everything else on this place.

"Can you . . . I mean, will you help me fetch Jupiter?"

Lobo's brows rose in disbelief. But the boy meant it. "No," Lobo said flatly. "He's dangerous. Let him go."

"But he's old, sort of a pet, and Willow—"

"A pet?" Lobo said in a very soft voice. If he had one ounce of the sense he attributed to himself, he would ride off and never come back. He looked out on the dry range beyond the fence, and saw the bull had stopped and was looking around as if bewildered.

He looked back at the boy, who was starting to climb down from the fence, a determined look on his face, as if he would go after the animal himself if Lobo didn't help.

Lobo knew what he ought to do. He ought to ride out there and kill the damn animal, and tell the boy that's what would happen to all of them if they didn't get the hell off the ranch.

Yet he couldn't. Something about the boy reminded him of the kid he'd once been. This one, too, had seen trouble. Lobo recognized it, like a brand, the first time he'd seen him.

Lobo reluctantly rode out to the bull and roped it. The bull obediently, even gratefully, followed him back and went into the corral.

The boy evidently saw his puzzled look and tried to explain. "I think sometimes he just remembers other days . . . and he misses Brady. He doesn't really mean any harm."

"Where's . . . Miss Taylor?"

The boy shrugged. "She's usually home by now, but sometimes she stays late at the school. She'll be real grateful you helped Jupiter."

Chrissakes. Lobo felt his gut tighten again.

"Will ya stay and have dinner with us?" The boy's plea drifted awkwardly in the air. "I know Willow would be real happy."

Damnation.

"Just stay the hell away from that bull," Lobo said in his meanest tone. "Damn fool kid," he muttered.

"Chad."

Lobo raised the eyebrow again.

"My name's Chad," the boy said, obviously expecting a name in return.

Sending the boy a hard, baleful look, Lobo pulled back the reins of his pinto, and the horse moved backward with small dancing movements. When Lobo was well away from the fence, his knees tightened, and the horse exploded into movement, leaving dust in his wake.

Lobo had traveled a mile when he was suddenly struck by fear for the woman named Willow. Why wasn't she back yet? Had Newton hired someone else and ordered an ambush?

He rode back to the grassy hill, his eyes intent on the trail, his mind cursing Newton, when he heard the sound of wheels and hooves. The buckboard appeared, and she was there, looking as fresh as she had the other day, with the two boys playing in the back.

As fresh and innocent and pretty.

With a relief he didn't understand, he backed the pinto until he hoped he was out of sight. The sun was behind him, and its glare would blind anyone looking his way.

He would come back Saturday, when he knew she would be there, and convince her to leave. He would cite the events of the past few days as to why she couldn't stay, even without Newton's threats and determination. He would convince her in a bold, logical way.

He watched until the wagon disappeared down the road, and then he rode slowly back to where he had camped two days earlier, the sight of her haunting him. If he ever wished . . .

But he didn't. Wishing was for fools.

* * *

Willow saw the figure on horseback, just barely visible in front of the glare of the setting sun. Her eyes were very good despite all the reading she did, and they picked out the beautiful pinto and the lean graceful figure that sat so still in the saddle.

She'd never seen the horse before. She would have remembered its bold, striking colors. She couldn't make out the face of the man or the color of his hair.

She thought briefly of the gunfighter, but this man seemed to have no hostile intent. A stranger?

Had Chad described the horse of the stranger who had helped Sallie Sue? No.

Coincidence, she thought. Just coincidence. Still he looked . . . like a guardian sitting there. Like a statue of an ancient and benevolent god.

As she drove the buckboard up to the house, Chad came flying out.

"He was here again," Chad said, his eyes glowing. "Wait till I tell you what happened."

Willow couldn't get the man out of her mind. Not that night or even the next day.

Even as she taught in the classroom, even as she assisted the twins through multiplication. Even as she related Coronado's journey up through New Mexico, even as she led Robert, her prize pupil, through Latin.

What did he really look like?

She had just images, images of strength.

She had tried to get more information from Chad. He was blond, he'd told her. Well, not exactly blond. More sandy, maybe. And his eyes . . . well, he'd never seen anything like them before. A curious color. More blue than green, perhaps. Or more green than blue.

And what did he say?

Very little, according to Chad.

It was odd the way he turned up in times of need and then

disappeared. She wished that he had stayed, or that he'd left his name so she could thank him. Since he'd mysteriously appeared days apart, he obviously wasn't just passing through. Yet when she asked townspeople about him, no one else had seen anyone remotely resembling the description.

Sometimes she wondered if he even existed. And then she saw in her mind, as clearly as she had actually seen him that evening, the man and horse, as still as statues, silhouetted against the sun, and her heart thundered as it never had before.

Willow was not unaccustomed to the attention of men, particularly since she came west. There was scarcity of eligible women, and while not particularly striking in looks, she was reasonably desirable. Out west, almost any single woman with only one head was.

As a result, she'd been nearly trampled by a herd of men callers—from cowhands to the widowed banker—when she first came to Newton. It took months for the word to get around: The schoolmarm was eccentric and cold-natured. She apparently had no interest in men or marriage.

Neither was true. Willow would have liked very much to marry and have children of her own. But not just anyone would do. Somewhere in the back of her mind she knew she was unrealistic in her dreams. She had lived with Greek and Roman gods far too long, with their adventures and their bravery, and even their excesses. Mr. Folley, the potbellied banker, and the often unwashed and rough cowboys couldn't compete.

Willow was not willing to compromise on the matter of marriage. It was white knight or nothing. Nothing, she'd conceded to herself, appeared much more likely.

And then, of course, there was the matter of her position. As a teacher, she had to be above reproach. She was an example, a figure on a pedestal, and, like Caesar's wife, must be spotless in reputation. She had not always succeeded in this, particularly when she had taken in Estelle and Brady, but there had never been any rumor of sexual impropriety.

So at twenty-five she had resigned herself to spinsterhood

and devoted the great well of love in her to anyone or anything in need. She did not feel deprived or unfulfilled. She was determined to live every minute of her life to the fullest, and she took great pleasure in the simplest delights—the touch of a fresh spring breeze against her skin, the smoky flavor of fall, the beauty of a sunset and the smile of a child. She loved gardening, enjoyed listening to the horses neigh in contentment when she fed them oats, and even relished challenging the staid and self-righteous townfolk.

That had been enough—until now. For the first time in her life she was filled with tingling anticipation whenever she thought of a man—the man on horseback.

The paladin.

The protector.

The white knight.

The sun was halfway up in the east when the reluctant paladin heard hoofbeats.

He'd been up since sunrise. He'd curried and fed his horse, made coffee and cooked bacon, and he was considering how best to use the rest of the day when his ears picked up the sound of an approaching horse. His heart stopped when he saw the rider was a woman, but it quickly resumed beating when he recognized the girl from Newton's house. He scowled.

Without giving her the merest sign of recognition, he poured himself a cup of coffee. Only after taking a sip did he look up at her, one eyebrow raised in question.

Her face flushed. "Papa thought you may have left."

His eyes raked her slowly, from the hat that sat jauntily over dark hair to her neatly booted feet. "He send you here to find out?"

The flush on her face grew darker. "No."

He took another sip of coffee. He could almost feel her puzzlement. She was, he guessed, used to getting her way.

"Can I have some coffee?" she finally said, unwilling to surrender to his indifference.

"This is the last of it," he said, taking a long swallow. He wanted her to go. He sensed she was trouble, and he had enough of that already.

Though he didn't look up, he knew she had dismounted. "I heard your name is Lobo," she said.

Lobo continued to sit in silence.

"You're staying, then?" she tried again.

He looked up. She was pretty enough. Her hair was the shade of mahogany and her eyes dark brown, but she didn't interest him. She was obviously very young, young and foolish and willful. He had seen her type before, and it always meant the kind of complications he didn't want.

Lobo stared at her with a studied insolence that was usually effective in driving people away. "What do you want, lady?" he asked.

She flushed even more, and he expected her to say something about going to her father and having him fired. It had happened before.

"To meet you," she said instead. "I've never met a gunfighter before.

"You're not scared?" A grim smile accompanied the question.

"Yes," she admitted.

"You're smart, then. Be smarter. Get on that horse and go."

"Why?"

"Because I eat little girls like you for breakfast."

She looked down at a dirty plate. "You've already had breakfast."

"An unsatisfactory one."

She smiled, her lips slightly trembling. "I didn't know gunfighters had a sense of humor."

"We don't," he replied.

She stood there studying him, and he returned look for look.

"There's a dance tomorrow night. Saturday. In town."

"I don't have time for dances."

"I'll tell Papa you're still here."

He shrugged.

"He's upset."

Lobo shrugged again. "That's his problem."

"Have you met Willow Taylor yet?"

Lobo's back stiffened. His eyes went even colder.

The girl hesitated. "I—I like her. You . . . wouldn't hurt her, would you?"

"Is that why you came?"

The girl bit her lip and nodded slowly.

Lobo rubbed the back of his neck. This was the damnedest job he'd ever had.

"Will you?" she insisted.

"Go home and talk to your papa. Not me."

"Please."

"Go home," he repeated, rising and splashing what was left of the coffee on the fire. Without paying any more attention to her, he saddled his pinto and swung up into the saddle. If she didn't leave, he sure as hell was going to. He didn't look back as he trotted away.

He'd slept uneasily the previous night, but he needed little rest. He'd always been able to snatch a few minutes here, a few there, even on horseback, and be as wide awake as someone who slept for several hours. Another legacy of his time with the Apache.

If he looked at those years objectively, he supposed he should be grateful. He had abilities few other men had or probably wanted.

But as he'd lain awake considering those talents and his life, he'd found them wanting.

He had never realized how much he was missing until he'd heard the Taylor woman's laughter. He hadn't known people laughed like that.

Lobo had heard laughter before, mocking laughter. Cruel laughter. Harsh laughter. But never the kind that made a man want to smile.

Christ, he would be baying at the moon next.

Lobo wandered down to the river that ran by the Newton and Taylor spreads. The water was low, only a few muddy inches, because of the drought.

He had been in fights over water before. Why should this one be different? But it was. And he realized how much when in the late afternoon he found himself returning to the grassy hill. He dismounted and settled himself to watch the road. He saw the buckboard approach, but this time a roan was tied to the back and a man sat beside the woman, his hands holding the reins.

Lobo drew back as if burned. He didn't understand the stabbing pain in the pit of his stomach, or the hollow emptiness that reached from within him and swallowed him whole.

Brady came back that night. Willow heard a horse trot up just after she'd extinguished the oil lamp in her bedroom. She quickly rose and went to the window. She thought about her rifle downstairs, but she doubted whether she could use it against a human being.

With a breath of relief she saw Brady lead his horse into the barn. She thought about going to talk to him, but decided to wait until the next day. His shoulders were slumped, and even from a distance he looked tired and defeated. He had been doing so well. . . . Worrying about him, she went back to her bed.

Brady lit the oil lamp in the tack room. It took him several minutes, for his hands trembled.

He'd heard about the gunfighter, and he knew he was the only one who could protect Willow and the children. For five days he had stood at the base of the mountains and practiced with his Colt. Once, he had been fast and accurate. Now he could barely get his gun from the holster, and three out of four shots went far wide of their mark.

The gun, once his friend, was now like a rattlesnake in his hand. He hated it.

He had not used his Colt in three years, not since he'd killed the last of the murderers of his wife and son, shot him in cold blood as the man pleaded for his life. He'd thought there would be some satisfaction, some peace then, but there was not. He'd discovered he was no better than the men he'd hunted.

Thirst clawed at him as he continued to stare at the hands that betrayed him. He was useless. Worthless. Self-hatred gnawed at his guts.

He opened the one window in the tack room, breathing deeply of the still air. But that didn't help. Almost without thought he went to a box where he stored his few belongings and searched out the smooth form of a bottle. It had been there, untouched, for months now. He hesitated, then drew it out. Why not? He was no good for anything, anyway. He put the bottle to his lips and took a long swallow, and then another.

A cigarette. He needed a cigarette. He never smoked in the barn, but . . . why not. He was careful. He rolled a smoke, and by God, his hands had stopped shaking. He brushed tobacco off his lap and took another pull from the bottle.

He took the glass from the top of the oil lamp and used the flame to light the cigarette. He didn't put the glass back. He finished the cigarette and very carefully put it out, taking one swallow after another from the bottle, regretfully setting it on the table next to the lamp when there was no more.

That's all he'd needed. Just a small drink. His eyes closed, and soft snores filled the room, still alight with the unprotected flame.

Hours later a breeze ruffled the plain cotton curtains of the tack room, pushing them toward the lamp. The flickering flame caught the edge of a curtain and started inching upward, reaching out for additional fuel and finding it in the old dry wood of the barn.

Four

Lobo rose before dawn. It was Saturday, and he had every intention of facing her before she got away again.

He purposely didn't shave. The more intimidating he looked, the better his chance at success. And he knew exactly how intimidating he could look. There had been more than one occasion when potential opponents ran rather than fought after seeing him.

Lobo had spent the night concentrating. He was good at that. He had concentrated himself out of a hell of a lot of bad spots. Now he concentrated on forgetting that damn laugh and red-gold hair. . . .

Goddammit, he was doing it again.

Without fixing coffee or eating, he saddled his pinto, which nudged him for attention. He glared at the horse. Even the animal was going soft. He mounted, and with his temper close to exploding although he couldn't explain why, he spurred the pinto into a gallop.

He reached the small hill, which was becoming altogether too familiar, and he looked once more toward the ranch house. The morning was still gray, the sun just tipping over the horizon, and a hot wind had come with first light.

Lobo felt a sense of satisfaction as he saw smoke. They were awake.

But as he studied the peaceful scene, he saw that the smoke wasn't coming from the house, but the barn. His knees tightened against the pinto's side, and he raced toward the house, shouting.

"Fire!"

Willow heard the warning as she was dressing. Leaving the top buttons of her dress undone, she ran to the window and looked out.

She could see the barn, see the wisps of smoke coming from it, and she sped to the door, throwing it open, yelling as loud as she could to wake the others.

Chad immediately appeared, and so did Estelle and the twins. "Take care of Sallie Sue," she shouted to Estelle as she ran out the front door toward the barn, barely aware of the large pinto and the man swinging down from the nervously sidestepping horse.

He brushed past her without a word and ran into the barn. Willow followed right behind him, terror filling her mind. The man opened the stall gates and flushed the horses out, while Willow ran toward the tack room in the back. She knew Brady was there.

The door was closed, smoke curling out from the crack underneath. She tried to open it, but it was stuck, and she slammed her body against it fruitlessly.

Then she felt herself being pulled away, and she saw the stranger kick the door open. Flames spurted out, and he disappeared into the hole of fire and smoke.

In what seemed like hours but must have been merely seconds, he reappeared, carrying Brady over his shoulder. Brady's head rolled with each movement.

"Get the hell out of here," the stranger roared.

"Jupiter," she cried.

"I'll get him," he said. "Just get out of here before you kill all three of us."

Willow looked around. The hay was on fire, and lit embers were floating everywhere. She could hear the hiss and crackle of the growing inferno, and the heat was terrible. She could also hear the frantic bellow of Jupiter.

"You go out," she said. "I'll get Jupiter."

The man didn't argue any longer, but grabbed her arm roughly. Willow felt propelled along without choice. When they got out of the smoke-filled barn, she was thrust into the arms of Chad, who had just taken out the two cows and had started to go in again.

"Jupiter," the boy yelled. Willow saw the man nod impatiently as he set Brady down on the ground. He said, "Get everyone out of the way. When that old bull comes out, he'll be wild." Then, pulling his bandanna over his mouth, he returned to the barn.

Willow and Chad dragged Brady toward the fence as she yelled at the others to get on the other side. The whole barn was ablaze now, and Willow knew fear like she'd never known before. The man wasn't going to make it out; no one could. She ran toward the entrance to tell him to forget Jupiter, when she heard a yell, then the sound of heavy hoofbeats. There was a crash, and then Jupiter charged through the doorway, his eyes red and his back gray with ashes. The man stumbled behind him, his shirt torn and smoldering, and his gloves scorched.

"Get away from the barn," he yelled. "It'll collapse in minutes."

But Willow couldn't move. "You're . . . hurt."

"Goddammit, get away," the stranger roared as he leaned down and once more picked up Brady's still body. They ran toward the open gate, but when they heard a crash, Willow stopped to turn around. The roof had caved in, and flames and smoke reached up into the hazy sky.

They walked toward the others. Estelle was holding tightly on to Sallie Sue, while Chad was trying to hang on to the halters of two horses. The other horse had disappeared, and

Jupiter was running toward open range as though he were still a young bull.

The stranger dumped Brady on the ground, and Willow flew toward him. "Is he . . . ?"

"Drunk," the stranger said with disgust. "It looked like he started the damned fire."

"Then . . . it was an accident?" She didn't want to think anyone would do this to them.

"He smells like a damned saloon," the man said. "The fire obviously started in his room. What in the hell do you think?"

But she was no longer listening to him. She knelt down at Brady's side, holding his hand, reassuring him as he started to mumble some words. She just barely heard the stranger's grunt of disgust. She did notice his dusty boots moving away, and she suddenly realized she had not thanked him. She looked up to see him striding to his horse.

"No!" she said loud enough to stop him.

He turned, his soot-covered face impassive.

"Please don't go."

Willow stood. She had no doubt that this was the man who had saved them twice before, and somehow she knew that he meant to disappear as he always had. She also knew in some unexplainable way that if he left now, she would never see him again. And she couldn't allow that to happen.

Her gaze locked on him. Chad had been correct in one thing: This man was taller than Sullivan, taller than anyone she knew. His hair, though sprinkled with soot, shone when the morning sun hit it, and his eyes blazed with an inner fire, like rare fine stones.

His face was partly covered with blond bristles, and the strong angular features, though harsh, had a touch of vulnerability. Perhaps, she thought, it was caused by his indecision, a kind of bewilderment as if he didn't really understand what he was doing there.

"Please help me get him inside," she said, using the only excuse she knew would make him stay. She instinctively realized that if she'd used his own wounds as reason, he would continue his escape.

And escape was how he considered it. She could tell from the way he looked toward the horse, and the horizon beyond it, before lowering his head in a gesture of defeat.

"He's not worth your trouble," the stranger said harshly.

"Of course he is," she replied. "He's my friend."

"Then, lady, you sure as hell don't need any enemies." His voice was gravelly and harsh, even condemning, and yet Willow felt an inexplicable attraction to him.

Lobo was caught in the silent intensity that seemed to encompass him and hold him motionless. He closed his eyes against the unwanted, unexpected explosion of need within him, against the strange suspension of time that locked them together. He felt like an actor in a play, a puppet directed and controlled by others. Yet he didn't want to break that hold. Yes, he did, but he didn't know how.

He opened his eyes again and met her gaze directly. Her eyes *were* blue, as he'd thought. But he'd never thought they could be *this* blue. They were like the mountain sky on a warm summer afternoon just before dusk. Deep and rich and glorious, a color that made him ache inside because it was so damned pure.

She continued to level a look at him that seemed to reach straight inside him. For one of the few times in his adult life he saw no fear, no revulsion for what he was. He felt as if a damned twister had invaded his usually disciplined mind and body. His hand went to his gun, as it always did in moments of confusion. His gun was the only sure thing in his life, his only ally.

He saw her eyes follow the movement, but instead of terror, there was awareness and even understanding that his intent wasn't to do harm. His hand fell away.

"Please." Her soft plea broke the silence, and he remembered her request. A damned drunken ex-sheriff, for chrissakes. She wanted him to help a man who years earlier would have run him out of town on a rail.

He looked around. Twins, barely distinguishable from each other, stared at him with wide, awe-struck eyes. The child Sallie Sue struggled to get down from the thin woman's arms. The woman set her on the ground in an unexpectedly graceful movement, and the little girl ran to him.

She looked up from her small height. "Thank you for thaving Jup'ter. And me." She turned and ran back to the woman, who regarded him steadily for a moment before turning toward the house.

The schoolteacher waited patiently by the side of the silent man. He hadn't known women who had such patience. She would have made a passable gunfighter with those level eyes and quiet doggedness. She was waiting for his move, not pushing, just waiting, as if she knew that pleading would drive him away.

His gloved hand went to the back of his neck and rubbed it absently, and he was only barely aware of the burning pain in his fingers. His attention was riveted on the sudden desperation in the schoolteacher's very blue eyes, and something in him couldn't deny her.

He strode to where she still knelt and stooped over who had to be Brady Thomas. Roughly he rubbed Thomas's face, trying to bring some life back into it. Thomas moaned and opened his eyes, squinting against the morning sun.

Lobo put his arm under the man's shoulders and pulled him up. "Walk, damn you," he ordered.

Brady attempted to put one foot in front of the other, often stumbling as they slowly moved to the ranch house. Lobo knew it would have been easier to carry the man, heavy as he was, but he wasn't going to make it easy for Thomas. The man had nearly killed good animals, not to mention destroying the barn. Lobo had no sympathy even though the loss of the barn would make existence on the ranch all but impossible. Brady Thomas had done his job for him, and all he felt was a slow, burning anger against the man.

He didn't understand why the woman didn't feel a similar resentment. As he stole a glance at her, all he saw was concern for Thomas.

They reached the house, and he looked at her for directions. She led the way to a small room with one large bed and two smaller ones. Lobo dumped his burden on the large one and started out the door, more aware now of the pain in one of his arms and both hands.

Just outside the bedroom door he looked down at his hands, the half-burned gloves sticking to the skin, the scorched shirt-sleeve barely covering a red arm. He had ignored the pain; it was another matter of concentration. But he knew he had to do something about the wounds before they became infected.

The woman was studying them too. "Those are bad burns," she said.

He shrugged. "It's nothing."

Her blue eyes filled with concern. It was unsettling, and he moved toward the front door.

"No," she said in an authoritative schoolteacher voice. "We have to do something about those burns."

Lobo didn't know why he stopped.

Her voice softened. "And I want to thank you. You must be our guardian angel."

Guardian angel. For chrissakes!

"Chad has told me all about you," she continued as if she didn't notice the glower on his face. "And I've been wanting to thank you. I'm Willow. Willow George Taylor."

That name wasn't much better than his own or Sallie Sue.

"But everyone calls me Willow," she added with a brilliant smile that could melt snow.

She waited for him to proclaim his identity, but there was only silence.

She appeared unfazed. She stepped closer to him and reached out to take his arm, frowning as she studied the small blisters. He felt something other than pain run down his spine.

She looked up at him and smiled slowly. "I'm not going to allow you to leave the house until I see to those burns."

Lobo hesitated. He didn't want to leave. He didn't want to lose that smile. He wanted to prolong the cool touch of her fingers on his skin, the concern in her eyes for him. *For him.*

He swallowed, knowing he should get the hell out of the house, out of Newton, out of the territory, probably out of the country.

"I'll get some salve for those burns, and you can have one of Jake's shirts."

"Jake?"

Relieved that he had finally uttered a word, she smiled again. "He left the ranch to me. He died eighteen months ago."

"He didn't do you a favor, lady," Lobo said. "This place is a disaster."

She suddenly looked wistful and incredibly appealing. Burns or not, he had an enormous urge to take her in his arms. How would she react when she discovered who he was? A gunslinger. A man decent people crossed the street to avoid. Fool! he called himself.

"I know," she admitted softly. "But we've made it this far."

Lobo raised his eyebrows. Now was the time to make her see reason.

"Lady, two kids and a drunk would be dead if I hadn't shown up."

"But you did," she said with indisputable reason.

Frustrated, he stared at her. There was such complete blind faith in that face, in those eyes. He'd never seen anything like it in all his years. He damned well hoped he never would again.

"Lady . . ."

"Willow."

"Miss Taylor . . ."

"Willow."

His hands clenched. "There are people who want you out of here."

Her smile faltered slightly. "You've heard the stories too. I can't believe Alex Newton really wishes me harm."

He wanted to shake her. He wanted to prove it to her by telling her he'd been hired to do just that. But the words stuck in his throat. It would be like whipping a puppy, he thought. He couldn't bear to see that light leave her eyes. Nor did he want to lose the smile for himself. Not yet. Not until he stored a little more of it in his memory.

Before he could say anything, she was guiding him into the kitchen.

"Estelle," he heard her say in the gentlest voice, "can you get some water and soap for me. And the medicine box."

The two younger boys came in. "Chad's taking care of your horse, Mister," one said.

"Don't know if we'll ever git ol' Jupiter back," the other said.

"He sure was a-running," the first boy said. "I'm Jeremy. He's Jimmy. We're twins," he said proudly. "We thought Chad was lyin' when he told us 'bout you."

"What's your name, Mister?" the other twin asked.

"Don't ask so many questions, boys," Willow said.

"But you always tell us to ask questions. You say that's how we learn things."

"You also learn things by being quiet and listening," she said. "Jeremy, go get a shirt from Jake's trunk in the store-room." She turned back to Lobo as the thin woman with the odd eyes returned and timidly set a box on the large round table that dominated the kitchen.

"Won't you take off those gloves and shirt and sit down?" Willow Taylor's voice was soft.

He hesitated, knowing that of all the things he had done in his life, this was probably the most foolish. Yet the burns must be treated. He didn't want to go to a doctor. He didn't want to go into town. He surely didn't want to go back to Newton's place and explain, not that he minded what Newton thought. He just didn't like asking for help from the man.

"Hell," he murmured, and looked from his hands up to her face, and toward a mouth that was obviously trying not to smile. He tried to take off the gloves, but they stuck to his hands. His shirt pulled easily over his head, though, revealing an arm streaked with red.

"Hell," Jimmy echoed, and received a reproving look from the women.

"Well . . . he said it," he protested.

"Well, small boys don't," Estelle countered.

"Why?"

Lobo scowled at him, and the boy snapped his mouth shut.

"Do you think I can learn to do that?" Willow Taylor said, her mouth twitching even more than it had a moment before.

Then her gaze went to his chest, and he knew from her faltering smile that she had seen the scars. He winced. They were too ugly for her, and he felt naked under her gaze, all the way down to his equally scarred soul. He was about ready to go, burns and all, when a bowl of water and soap were placed next to him. He tried to pull off the gloves again, setting his jaw as the pain became agonizing.

Soft hands clasped his and drew them down into the water, her fingers gently separating the cloth from flesh, her eyes reflecting a hurt of their own as they saw the exposed raw flesh. She washed it carefully, tenderly, then covered it with cooling salve. When she was finished, her lips were trembling and her eyes were glazed with tears. With wonder he actually believed that she was feeling more pain than he.

"You shouldn't ride," she said. "Stay here a few days."

"Do you have something to wrap them with?"

"Yes," she replied reluctantly. "But they would be better open to air."

"I'm leaving," he said curtly. "With or without bandages."

She nodded and bandaged the hands and arm. Every touch, she knew, had to be agonizingly painful, but his expression never changed. It was as stoic as a carving.

Jimmy returned with a shirt, and Lobo pulled it on awkwardly, not protesting when the woman started buttoning it. There was an intimacy about the last few moments, about sitting in her kitchen shirtless, about her fingering the buttons that made him uncomfortable. He had never felt things like this before, never felt the warmth that filled the kitchen, or the gentle humor, or the soft, caring touch.

He'd also never said thank-you before, and the words stuck in his throat. So he merely nodded his gratitude and, without any more words, strode out the door.

Willow walked over to the window and watched him mount. From the way he used his hands, she would never have known he was injured.

The rider's body moved so easily in the saddle, he and the horse seemed a part of each other. His shoulders proud, his back stiff, her stranger looked straight ahead, never turning back even though she wished him to with all her might.

Her hands still trembled from touching him. His shoulders had been wide, his chest strong and covered with crinkly blond hair. His body was perfect, except for what looked like knife scars, jagged and rough. She'd hurt when she'd seen them, just as she had hurt when she caused him pain by washing the burns.

There was so much strength in that body. And so much pain. The physical scars were easy to see, but he was expert at hiding the mental kind. She'd seen only a brief glimpse of them, but they were there in his anger, in his hesitancy to accept her help.

Willow had seen injured wild things before. She had nursed them back to health. She'd held and reassured frightened and lonely students at her father's school. She knew trust and healing took time.

Chad had once shared the same suspicion this man apparently had of other people. She had slowly earned the boy's trust.

She would also earn this man's.

She'd known from the moment he'd first met her gaze that she could not push.

But he would be back.

She knew that too.

Five

Willow had more visitors that afternoon.

She and Chad were out looking at the smoldering ashes of the barn when three men rode up and dismounted.

Gar Morrow, a tall, stocky man, looked with question at the scene before him, his mouth tightening.

"Newton?" he asked curtly.

Willow shook her head. "An accident."

"You sure?"

"Yes," she said. She seldom saw Gar Morrow except when he needed to use her land to get his cattle to water or when they accidentally met in town. Once he had briefly appeared at a benefit picnic for the school. He had stayed only a moment and then left a substantial check.

Gar's gaze went from the barn to Willow. He took off his hat, as did the two men next to him. All three wore guns. "I would like to talk to you. Alone."

Willow stiffened. She didn't like the feeling she was getting. But she agreed, and nodded for Chad to leave. When he was out of earshot, Gar hesitated, looking distinctly uncomfortable. "I didn't want to frighten the boy," he said.

"What is it, Gar?"

"I heard about the gunfighter Alex hired," he said. "You gonna sell?"

Willow's chin went up. "I said I wouldn't.

Gar's expression relaxed slightly. "I've heard of that man . . . Lobo. He won't give a damn you're a woman."

Willow stilled a moment, then her hands busied themselves in the cloth of her dress. "Perhaps not," she merely said.

"Dammit, Willow, listen to me."

"I am listening."

"I've hired someone myself. A man named Canton. I want him to protect you."

"No," she said. "I don't want a hired gunman around here."

"Willow . . ."

"I have Brady and Chad."

Gar looked at the still-smoking ruins of the barn, and furrowed his brows. "A drunk . . . and a boy."

"And I have right on my side."

"Dammit, Willow, right won't do a goddamn thing against someone like Lobo."

"And this man of yours can!"

"Yes."

"I will not have Jake's ranch turned into a battleground," Willow said stubbornly. "Jake didn't want it either. That's why he left it to me."

"Jake was a damned old fool. He didn't know how much Alex has changed."

"Why?"

Gar stared at her with puzzlement. "Why what?"

"Why did he change so much? Why does he hate you? What happened that can't be fixed? Perhaps if you talked . . ."

"Stay out of it, Miss Taylor." He hadn't called her Miss Taylor for months.

"I can't. You two have put me in the middle."

Gar Morrow lowered his head. There was defeat in the gesture, in the face that Willow thought must once have been very handsome. Now it was lined and tired-looking. Yet a determined light still shone in the eyes.

"There's nothing more hopeless than a shattered friendship," he said wearily. "And I'm sorry you and the children are involved. But reconsider about Canton."

"No," she said. "It would just make things worse."

He stared at her. "According to his wire, Canton should be here late this afternoon. But I wanted to talk to you first. Will you at least meet him?"

She shook her head.

"I won't have anything to do with a gunfighter. The boys already talk too much about guns and gunfights and violence. I won't have them exposed to a man who kills for money. I won't let them make a man like that into a hero."

"Willow—"

"But I thank you, Gar, for your concern." It was a dismissal, plain and simple.

Gar shook his head. "If you need any help . . ."

"I know," she replied softly. She wanted to say more. She wanted to say she already had a knight errant, a man who helped not because of money, but because he was a good man. But the images of her stranger were too new and precious to share. And she didn't know what to say about him. She still didn't know who he was, or where he came from. But she knew he would be back.

Gar Morrow gave her a frustrated stare before turning and nodding to his two men. "Just remember . . ."

She nodded.

Willow wished she had never told Sullivan she would go to the dance with him.

But she had, two days before, when he had driven her home. They sometimes went to social events together; it was a kind of protection for each of them.

She could quite legitimately decline when he arrived. She had the best of excuses after that morning's catastrophe, yet she had promised, and Sullivan asked very little of her in return for all he did for them. And she suspected Sullivan had an ulterior motive for wanting to go: Marisa. And perhaps she had had one, too, when she agreed: the stranger.

Willow felt a sudden quickening of her blood, even though she doubted very much he would attend. He didn't seem the type, yet . . . he had to belong someplace.

While she waited for Sullivan, she wandered out to scan the garden. She swallowed as she saw its condition, the baked earth, the scraggly, struggling plants that had once looked so healthy and green.

She swallowed. Except for finally meeting their obviously reluctant knight errant, it had been a disastrous day.

What would they do now? All the hay was gone, all the tack. They still had the buckboard but none of the necessary equipment to hitch the horses to it.

The weather would start changing soon, and they no longer had shelter for the animals. The garden, from which Willow had hoped to supplement their food supply, was dying in the drought.

Willow allowed herself several moments of panic, even of thoughts of giving up. But they fled quickly. Jake had trusted her. The children depended on her.

And Estelle.

And Brady.

Her heart suffered for Brady. When he'd fully recovered from the aftermath of whiskey and smoke, Brady had realized exactly what had happened. He had crumpled with remorse and self-recrimination.

Willow had tried to reassure him. Possessions meant little. Only people mattered, and they were all safe.

But face ravaged, eyes red, he would accept none of it. Brady said he would ride bareback to town and obtain a saddle, then find Jupiter. After that he would leave the ranch, the town, perhaps even the territory. He had caused enough trouble.

"But we need you," Willow had protested.

Brady laughed bitterly. He remembered hearing a voice saying, *You sure as hell don't need any enemies.* The words had pierced his half-conscious mind and had stuck there. They would never leave him.

"Please, Brady," Willow begged.

His head aching, his throat burning, and his stomach cramping, Brady turned and looked at her. "You have enough problems without me, Willow."

"But—"

"And now it seems you have someone to help you." Brady remembered little about the morning, only arms lifting him and dropping him, and those few words. But Chad had filled in some of the blank spots. The boy was bursting with admiration for the heroic stranger who seemed always to appear in time of need. Brady wished like hell he could remember something of the man, but the earlier hours of the day were only painful blurs.

He did ascertain from Chad that the man meant well. He was probably just a cowhand who had wandered onto the farm for water and then had checked back to see if everything was all right. There was a certain code in the West about helping women and children.

Perhaps the man could help Willow against Lobo. Maybe it would be even better if she moved back to town, where Sullivan could watch over her. One thing Brady knew for sure: he himself wasn't of any use, not to her, not to himself, not to anyone. It was time he moved along.

So he shook his head gently at her next protest. "I'll find Jupiter," he said with finality, "and then I'm leaving."

"But where will you go?"

He shrugged. "A drunk doesn't care where he is."

There was so much self-accusation, so much self-hate in his eyes that Willow wanted to cry for him. But she didn't. Pity wouldn't help anything.

"But I'll find Jupiter for you first," he promised.

Willow nodded, her mind working. She would find a way of making him stay. He had been doing so well. He had even been happy in a small way. Sallie Sue adored him, and the twins often followed him around. Only Chad, who'd seen too much drinking in his own father, was wary.

After Brady had left, Willow and Chad went out to the still-smoldering ruins of the barn. There was nothing salvageable, not even a stray piece of lumber. Her credit was already stretched to the limit at the store because of the seed, and if there wasn't rain, she would lose that too.

She thought very briefly about Alex's offer for the ranch, and even Gar's, but a sale to either would mean a bloodbath in the valley. She had to find another way.

As Chad looked after the horses, she thought again about the man who had helped them, and the magnetic force that had flowed so vibrantly between them. He was not handsome in the traditional sense, and yet the face was strong and compelling. She wondered how a smile would look upon it. He seemed to have precious little experience with that. She had never seen eyes quite as protected as his, or a mouth quite as grim.

Yet he had risked his life for them three times now, declining even thanks.

Like Odysseus, he seemed to come from nowhere to confront obstacles and disappear as quickly. She wondered if he had a Penelope waiting for him. It was a shattering thought and one she didn't wish to dwell upon. Not, she thought, that it made any difference. He certainly had shown little interest in her as a woman. And who would want all the trouble that came with her? A ready-made family, a run-down ranch in the middle of a feud, and one disaster after another.

But she knew a need and want she'd never known before, a feeling of unfullfilment that was new, an aching that wouldn't go away.

The doctor arrived almost at dusk and was immediately claimed by Chad, who told of the latest calamity. Sullivan's face creased with concern.

"What are you going to do, Willow?"

"I don't know. I'll think of something."

"Are you sure it wasn't Newton?"

"Yes," she said slowly, "but I almost wish it had been. Brady won't forgive himself for this."

Sullivan sighed. "I thought he'd defeated his craving for alcohol."

"It's all this gunfighter business."

"And your white knight?" he teased, remembering that she had mentioned the mysterious benefactor in that fashion.

"He was burned pretty badly," Willow said, "but he didn't want any help."

His face grew serious. Burns were nothing to ignore. "Perhaps I'll look for him tomorrow. You have no idea where he came from or who he is?"

She shook her head.

Sullivan looked worried. "I've been asking around. No one else knows either. Perhaps tonight we'll hear something."

"I really don't know if I should go to the dance." She didn't want to go. She wanted, instead, to think about the stranger, about the new kind of emotions he stirred in her.

"Yes, you should," Sullivan said firmly. "You need to get away for a while."

"But Brady's not back, and I'm worried about him."

"If Brady and Jupiter aren't back by morning, I'll help you find them, and tonight we'll see about a barn raising."

Willow lifted her gaze to his eyes. "Do you really think . . . ?"

"We won't know until we find out," he said, but he hid his reservations. Alex wouldn't like anyone helping her, and people here still paid attention to Alex.

Without more argument, Willow fetched her shawl. It had been a long time since she'd been to a social gathering. Perhaps she should mix more with the townspeople, but there was always so much to do, and she had a tendency to become impatient with their warnings and censure.

Despite her reservations, however, there was something reassuring about the people, the music, the laughter when they walked into the hotel dining room that had been cleared for the occasion. Willow tried to ignore the sudden cessation of talk as she and Sullivan walked in and curious eyes turned her way, but almost immediately the chattering started up again.

Although Willow knew he would not be there, she couldn't stop her gaze from wandering around the room. All the faces were familiar, all but one.

The man stood alone, dressed entirely in black, including a black hat he hadn't bothered to remove. There was something about the casual arrogance of his stance and his watchful eyes that made her gaze linger. His hair was dark, and his eyes obsidian and cold.

Was this Lobo?

But then she saw Gar Morrow walk over to him and speak quietly, and both their faces turned toward her and Sullivan.

So this was Gar's man. So this was the look of a gunfighter. She thought briefly of the dime novels she'd often found in the hands of her students, and wondered whether this man had deliberately dressed to meet that image. Did Lobo also have that look of ruthlessness, of cold professionalism? She felt herself shiver slightly as Gar and the man approached them.

As if sensing her disquiet, Sullivan placed a hand under her arm, his fingers tightening against her skin with reassurance.

Gar declined his head politely. "Miss Taylor, this is Canton. He's at your service," he said. The man in black smiled, but the smile lacked any warmth.

"Miss Taylor," he acknowledged.

Willow met his gaze directly. "Mr. Canton," she replied. "I told Mr. Morrow, I don't need any help."

"Oh, but I think you do," he said smoothly. "If what I heard is true."

"And what have you heard?"

"That Lobo has been sent to run you out."

Sullivan's hand tightened on her elbow. "Do you know this man Lobo?"

"I do."

"What does he look like?"

"You couldn't miss him. His eyes . . . they're a peculiar shade of blue. But he would also announce his presence. He doesn't take much time with preliminaries." Canton smiled again, a remote, impersonal smile.

Blue. That didn't help much, Willow thought. Half the people in the world seemed to have blue eyes. She did. Her courageous stranger did. Well, blue-green anyway. But where Canton's dark eyes were cold and blank, her palladin's eyes had been angry and bewildered.

"You haven't seen him yet?" Canton persisted.

She shook her head.

Gar looked puzzled. "As far as I can tell, no one else has either, but one of Newton's men told one of mine that he's here. He's been camping out on the Newton's ranch."

"It's not like Lobo to waste time," Canton remarked, and there was professional admiration in his voice.

"I heard you had some trouble at the ranch," said another voice, and Willow turned around. Mayor August Stillwater had approached and was listening.

Canton's brows went up. "Trouble?"

"An accident. A lamp spilled over in the barn but we got the animals out, thank God."

"You know I would buy the ranch," Gar said quickly. He didn't have anything close to the money that Alex had, but he could scrape up a decent price.

"I would no more sell it to you than I would to Alex," Willow said softly but determinedly.

"You may not have any choice," he retorted. "Without a barn—"

"I'm trying to arrange a barn raising," Sullivan broke in smoothly, and Canton looked at him inquisitively.

Gar looked from man to man. There was a sudden tension in the room.

"I'll send my men," Gar offered.

"I don't think that's wise," Sullivan said. "It'll just make Alex angrier."

"All right, Sully. But remember, Willow, if there's anything I can do to help, contact me. Or Canton. He'll be nearby." He retreated.

Canton stood there for a moment, tipping his hat slightly. "Miss Taylor," he said with a smile that made her shiver before he turned and followed his employer. Everyone backed well out of his way.

Despite the merry sound of a fiddle starting in the background, Sullivan's face was grim as he turned back to her. "I have a feeling all hell's going to blow loose here."

"If only Alex and Gar . . ."

"I know," Sullivan said. He visibly tried to relax. "I wanted you to enjoy this evening. Will you dance with me?"

She smiled back and curtsied. "I would be honored, sir."

Sullivan was an adequate but not easy dancer, and Willow was grateful she had to pay attention. She didn't want to think about Canton or Gar Morrow or Alex Newton. She didn't want to think about the storm clouds forming over the valley. But just as her eyes kept casting around the room for a tall, blond cowboy, she caught Sullivan's eyes also searching—for, she suspected, the black-haired daughter of Alex Newton.

When the music ended, she excused herself to go talk with Betty MacIntyre, wife of the general store owner and mother of her prize pupil, Robert.

The news about the barn and the planned barn raising had already reached the woman, and she clasped Willow's hands. "Mr. MacIntyre will be there to help."

"I don't want him to get in trouble with Alex because of me."

"He'll be there," Betty insisted, though Willow knew her husband wouldn't be as enthusiastic, just as he wasn't that enthusiastic about seeing his son go to college halfway across the country.

Just then there was a commotion at the door, and all heads turned to watch Marisa Newton and the Newton ranch foreman make a grand entrance. Right behind them was a second man, a rough-looking individual Willow had never seen before.

Willow's gaze automatically went to Sullivan and watched as his gray eyes hungrily followed Marisa. Marisa was a lovely girl, slender and graceful with long dark hair and dark brown eyes. She wore a simple but obviously expensive blue dress that hugged her soft curves. There was an exciting quality about Marisa, a vitality that made everyone turn and look.

Willow saw the girl's glance find Sullivan, and something golden flared in those eyes before she turned away. Something had once happened between those two; Willow would wager on it if she were of the betting persuasion. But although she had always felt something urgent and alive between the two, Sullivan had said little.

At once, Marisa was surrounded by young men, and Willow returned to Sullivan's side. There was a quiet desperation in her friend's usually calm eyes, and she hurt for him, even more at that moment than in the past, for now she, too, had been touched by the magic of attraction, of infatuation.

Marisa was six years younger than she, and Willow had taught the girl one year, the first year Willow had been in Newton. Marisa had been seventeen then, very bright and fast, but with a hell-bent streak that resulted in constant mischief and misadventures. Her father doted on her, which, Willow thought, was part of the problem. Marisa was altogether too intelligent to do nothing, and that was all her father allowed her to do: nothing.

Willow smiled at the girl, who looked embarrassed and startled before cautiously smiling back. Willow realized suddenly that Marisa had not expected her to be there, particularly on the arm of Dr. Sullivan Barkley.

Marisa suddenly broke away from the crowd surrounding her and hurried over.

"I have to talk to you," she whispered to Willow, but her gaze fastened on Sullivan.

"Now?"

"Privately," she said as she motioned toward the foreman who had accompanied her. He was standing in a corner, drinking punch, but his eyes were trained on Marisa. "Four dances from now," she said. "Will you meet me outside? In back?"

Willow nodded, and Sullivan captured Marisa's attention. "May I have this dance?"

Marisa's usually merry eyes glittered brightly. She nodded, taking Sullivan's outstretched hand, her lips trembling slightly.

With interest Willow noted how Sullivan was a much better dancer with Marisa than with her. Or maybe it was just the instinctive understanding between the two. Willow wondered how it would feel to dance with her stranger, and she felt an aching emptiness as she watched Sullivan and Marisa together, their expressions rapt, their movements in total harmony.

Willow had frequently thought Sullivan foolish for not courting Marisa, despite what she suspected were his reasons. Sullivan had a chronic illness, and he had barely more than a livable income, while Marisa was one of the wealthiest young women in Colorado. Pride, Willow often thought, could sometimes be a terrible affliction.

And Marisa's father, who had once regarded Sullivan as a friend, now looked at him as an enemy. Anyone not wholly with him in his feud with Gar Morrow was against him. Sullivan was no longer welcome on the Newton ranch.

Willow knew Sullivan, knew his pride and stubbornness. She had recognized his embarrassment the first time she had seen him suffering a spell of malaria, alternately shivering with chills and burning with fever, and she knew he was determined Marisa would never have to endure it.

And yet, as she watched them, she thought no two people could be better for each other. Sullivan's quiet compassion and Marisa's spirit would complement each other.

The banker asked Willow for a dance, and then Mr. MacIntyre, mostly, she thought, due to his wife's urging. Canton stayed by Gar Morrow's side, but his gaze continued to rake the dancers and study each newcomer.

Some of the men became more voluble after trips outside, and Willow suspected a bottle was enhancing the rather bland punch. But such thoughts were fleeting because nothing stayed in her mind long other than "the man." She wished she could put a name to him, for it was awkward, even in her thoughts, to think of him as the man, or the stranger. He didn't seem like a stranger, not now.

"Ouch." Bob MacIntyre's yelp was loud enough to summon attention, and Willow's face turned red as she realized she'd stepped on his foot.

"Let's rest," she said, and smiled at his grateful face as he returned to his wife.

Frustrated with herself, Willow went outside, avoiding the small circles of men who were surreptitiously dumping liquor into their cups. She walked to the front of the building, surveying the dirt street that ran through the middle of town, and the buildings that faced it. They were rickety and poorly built for the most part, thrown up quickly to serve the growing number of ranches in the area as well as the wagon trains heading west. But this was home to her. Although she missed the great forests in the East, she loved the sunrises over these plains and the sunsets across the purple mountains to the west. There was challenge here, challenge and growth and opportunity.

"Willow?"

She turned and saw Marisa. "You look lovely tonight," Willow told the younger girl warmly.

Marisa didn't smile. Instead, her tongue nervously licked her lips. "Thank you, but I came to warn you."

Willow couldn't stop a smile. "You mean the gunfighter? Then you can join everyone else. I don't think there's a person in town who hasn't."

"But . . . I met him, and he's everything they say. I tried to convince him to go away and he wouldn't. Papa, well, he's . . . I don't know, but he's—"

"Obsessed," Willow supplied sadly. "Before all this started, I thought he was my friend."

"He's not any longer. Please sell the ranch."

"I can't, Marisa. You know that."

"But the man he hired, he's—"

"He's what?" Willow asked gently.

"Frightening. I think he really would . . . do something terrible."

"Do you think he'd hurt the children?"

"I don't know. I just know he took Papa's money and he won't leave."

"Thank you for telling me."

"I'm sorry, Willow. It's just that Papa hates Mr. Morrow so much."

"I know."

A tear appeared in one of Marisa's eyes. "Nothing is going right."

"You mean Sullivan?"

Marisa looked up at her with surprise.

"Miss Newton." The voice was harsh and Willow and Marisa turned to see the rough-looking trailhand, the man who had come in with Marisa and the foreman, watching them.

"Are you spying on me?" Marisa said angrily.

"I don't think your pa would think much of you out here with her."

Marisa started to retort angrily, then looked helplessly at Willow.

"Go on in," Willow said. "We'll talk another time."

Willow watched the girl go in. Marisa had grown up a lot in the past two years. Now if only she could climb out from under her father's bitterness.

Willow waited a few more moments, taking the time to search the skies for her favorite constellations—the scorpion, the lion, the hunter. All had special significance. Tonight the lion seemed to stand out the strongest.

She wondered if her stranger was also looking upward, and she remembered lines from *The Odyssey*. "Looks ever toward Orion and alone, dips not into the waters of the deep."

Odysseus, she mused. He was thought by many scholars to be a solitary, restless wanderer, endlessly driven by a lust for new experience, by others as a man not rigid in his adherence to the heroic code of conduct, a man who often lied, used poisoned arrows, and definitely not beyond deceit, as proven in the fable of the Trojan horse.

And what kind of man was her hero? Kind, certainly. Heroic, definitely. A wanderer, probably. The ache returned. The confusion. The undefined yearning.

She didn't know what interrupted the fanciful flow of thoughts . . . perhaps the sudden silence inside the hotel.

Afraid, she went inside and stopped at the doorway. Canton was holding Marisa's hand, as if they had been dancing. Newton's trailhand was facing Canton and Marisa, his fingers near his gun. Everyone else was backing away, the music had died. The silence was overwhelming.

Sullivan moved over to Marisa, drawing her away.

"She don't dance with dirt," the Newton cowboy said.

A smile played around Canton's mouth. "You like to elaborate on that?" His voice was soft, the words slightly drawled. There was death in them, in the restrained tone, in the look of his eye. It was, Willow thought, the look of a snake ready to strike, just that concentrated, that implacable.

Men were pushing their wives and daughters out the door, then returning, choosing locations out of the line of fire. Willow knew she should leave, but she couldn't. Her legs just wouldn't function. Neither apparently could Marisa's, despite Sullivan's attempts to make her leave.

"Yeah," the man said, sneering. "I heard of your reputation, and I don't see nothin' so special. And the boss wouldn't want carrion like you touching his little girl."

The Newton foreman was moving forward. "Yates, not here."

"Yeah, right here. Where everyone can see who's the best gun."

"Newton wouldn't want this."

"But I do," the man said. "What about you, Canton? Or are you a coward?"

The man in black just smiled.

Yates reached for his pistol, but before it cleared the holster, a shot rang out, and blood spurted, staining Yates's shirt as he sunk silently to the floor. Marisa turned her now-white face into Sullivan's chest, and Sullivan held her tightly against him.

Canton looked around. "He drew first."

A number of heads nodded as if it were a question rather than a statement.

"I'm sorry to interrupt your party. I didn't intend it," he added, and spun around, leaving a room stunned by sudden death.

The Newton foreman went over to Marisa. "I think we'd better get home." Sullivan relinquished his protective hold and went over to the fallen man, checking his pulse and shaking his head slowly. He looked up, his troubled look finding Willow. She could almost hear him across the room.

Now you know what you're up against.

She heard a man behind her. "It's starting, by God. Gun-fighters, range war. There's not one of us going to be safe."

Willow watched as two men picked up the dead man and dragged him out. Everyone else quietly left, each one avoiding her, even Bob MacIntyre.

Six

The drive back to Willow's ranch was quiet and tense.

Willow had never seen a man die violently before, although she had been with both her father and Jake when they had died.

But her father had been in pain, and death was a release, and Jake had been ready to go and join his beloved wife. He'd simply gone quietly to sleep.

Sullivan looked at her in the light of the full moon.

"Now do you see what you're facing?"

Willow took a deep breath. There had been so little reverence for life during those few seconds at the dance.

"But why did it happen?"

"I imagine Newton's man was disgruntled that his boss had sent for a gunfighter. He'd wanted to prove he was as good as any professional. He really didn't give Canton much choice."

"There's always a choice," she whispered, still seeing the blood on the dead man's shirt.

"Not for a man like Canton. And from what I heard, he's a preacher next to Lobo."

Willow's hands tightened together.

"It isn't worth it, Willow. Jake couldn't know it would go this far, that Newton and Morrow would send for men like these."

"But the ranch is mine," Willow protested. "I've never had anything that was really mine before . . . and the children love it."

"And if that man hadn't come along a few days ago, Sallie Sue might be dead, and Chad. You certainly can't depend on Brady. It's too much for you."

Willow thought of the house she had come to love, of the livestock that had become pets for the children. They had all flourished, particularly Chad. They loved the ranch as much as she did. Not only that, Jake left her the ranch to keep peace; she wouldn't deserve any money from its sale if she violated that act of faith.

"Perhaps I could hire someone. . . ." Her thoughts went to the sandy-haired stranger.

"With what, Willow?"

"Room and board. The boys can stay in the living room. And if it rains, I might have some money from the garden."

"It's dying, Willow. And what about Alex? He isn't going to give up."

But Willow wasn't listening. The seed of the idea she'd just mentioned was blooming. There had to be a reason their stranger kept showing up exactly when he was needed.

They reached the ranch and Sullivan was grateful to see it still standing after the events of the past few days. "You'll send for me if you need anything?"

"Of course," she said, "and thank you."

"You'll think about what I said."

"No," she said with a mischievous smile.

"Dammit, Willow."

"We'll be all right, really we will," she soothed him.

He read her mind. "You can't depend on a guardian angel all the time."

The smile left her lips. "I know. But somehow I know . . . I just know everything will be all right. Even Brady."

"I wish I shared that optimism, but after tonight . . ."

She reached over and touched one of his hands with affection, quickly changing the subject. "You know Marisa is in love with you."

He shook his head in denial.

"Now *you're* closing your eyes to facts."

His eyes clouded. "You're changing the subject."

"Yes, I am, but I'm also right. Good night," she added in a hurry, and quickly stepped down from the buggy. She didn't want to hear any more, not now. She wanted to think. Alone.

"Willow . . ."

But his protest didn't stop her. She got to the door and looked back, waving her hand, and disappeared inside the door, standing against it until she heard the buggy drive away.

The house was still, although an oil lamp sat on the kitchen table. Everyone was apparently asleep. She wondered if Brady had returned; she'd not looked at the corral to see whether Jupiter was there.

She opened the door again and went out to the corral. Jupiter was still missing.

"Oh, Brady," she whispered. "Be safe."

She walked back to the house, some of the lightness gone from her step. Her hand shook briefly on the doorknob. Was she right to stay? Or was she endangering everyone dear to her?

She thought of the dead man in the hotel, the gunfighter named Canton and the unseen yet menacing Lobo. And then that shadow was replaced by another, a man against the sun, a man with eyes like jewels.

Willow stiffened her back and went inside. She'd never given up before. She wouldn't now.

The old Apache woman's eyes were full of hate, her mouth twisted into a cruel smile as she tied the rope around the boy's neck. It was a rope Lobo wore for the next six years.

Jess Martin. That had once been his name. Funny how he'd almost forgotten it.

During the days after his capture by the U.S. army, officers had asked him his name but he'd never told them. He'd allowed his questioners to believe he had forgotten. Jesse, as his brother called him, had died years ago. Lobo had no wish to recreate him.

He was Lobo, Apache warrior, white outcast. A wolf with all the characteristics of a wolf, except one. He had no desire to mate for life. He didn't need anyone.

He had been grateful that day, years earlier, when Apache raiders had arrived at their village. His feet were torn and blistered, his legs aching, his throat parched, his stomach empty and cramping from lack of food.

He had been grateful until he was pushed into the old woman's wickiup and made to understand that he now belonged to her, grateful until she had fastened the rope around his neck and pulled, showing him how she could so easily choke him if he showed any signs of disobedience.

That night, still without food, he was bound and leashed like a dog to a stake outside her wickiup. And that was the name given him by his new masters: Dog Boy.

He was less than that. The woman's husband and son had been killed by white soldiers and she hated whites with all the tenacious strength in her old body.

The collar was cleverly fastened. It was a slipknot that could be tightened but not loosened. It was attached to a six-foot piece of rope, which was often in the old woman's hand during the day and tied to the stake at night. He toiled in the fields with the women and did other women's work: cleaning game, tanning hides, and any demeaning task the woman could find. He was fed only enough to keep him alive, never enough to stop the ache in his belly.

The most degrading thing, though, was the rope. After months they stopped tying his hands and feet at night, merely attaching the rope to the stake. They knew he could take it off and escape, but part of the humiliation was their knowing he would not. He had seen what had happened to another slave, a Mexican woman who did try to escape. It was the kind of death he'd witnessed several times over the following years, enough times that he learned not to get sick. He'd been only eight the first time, and he had not had the courage to try the impossible. It didn't take him long to discover it sometimes took more courage to stay alive.

The dreams wouldn't go away. Lobo finally gave up any attempt at sleep. His hands and arm hurt like hell. Perhaps the pain in them, pain he had once known so well, brought back memories he didn't want, images he'd thought he'd banished years before.

Lobo rose and walked to the river. He'd hated the Apache, yet he had become one of them. He'd become as fierce as any of them, and he'd almost died with them. He would have if a young army lieutenant hadn't seen his blond hair and light-colored eyes the morning the soldiers burned their village.

He had been lying on the ground, two bullets in him, his right shoulder useless, when three soldiers approached him and he heard the cock of a pistol. He stared helplessly but defiantly at his would-be executioner as he heard the screams and wails from women and children, the last guttural cries of defiance from warriors.

"Christ, he's white," one of the soldiers said.

"So what?" Those words came from the man aiming very carefully at Lobo's heart. "He's a savage now."

"You know orders. We're to rescue any captives."

"He don't look like no captive to me."

He'd understood the English words only with great concentration. In the past sixteen years he'd heard English spoken only by captives, and none of them lasted long. Still, enmity had a common language. He could feel hate radiating in the air.

"What's going on?" It had been a new voice, one of authority, and Lobo's gaze had moved to the newcomer. Behind the blue-clad officer, dawn was just reaching its first tentative rays of light over the Arizona mountains. Lobo could smell death everyplace, yet he saw life too, and he suddenly did not want to lose it. Still, he kept his eyes blank, his face impassive. He would not beg. He never had. He never would.

"A white man, sir," said the soldier who had stopped the other man from shooting.

"He was fighting with 'em, Lieutenant," argued the man with the cocked gun.

The officer looked down at Lobo. "Do you speak English?"

Lobo's gaze rose again to the sunrise. The part of him that was Apache didn't want to answer. Another part wanted to live.

He compromised. He nodded his head once, a barely perceptible movement.

The officer hesitated. Lobo knew what he was thinking. Wounded Indians had killed white soldiers before. And he, dressed in Apache clothes and with a face made hard and impassive by his life, must have seemed no different from other Apaches. Lobo was surprised when the officer spoke.

"Tie him securely and put him in one of the wagons."

And so Lobo came into a hostile white world just as years earlier he'd gone into a hostile red one. And he belonged to neither.

He'd never cared before. He didn't now, he told himself. Yet he couldn't forget those gentle hands on his burns, and for the first time he knew regret for the life he had chosen, for the life that had chosen him.

Lobo rode into Newton Monday. He passed by a small white building with a bell, and he knew that must be the school. His jaw clenched as he left it behind and found the general store.

He was wearing a brown shirt and well-worn denim pants. Without knowing exactly why, he had carefully unbuckled his gunbelt and placed it in his saddlebag.

His hands were still sore and bandaged. He had decided to visit the doctor and get some salve, and then purchase a pair of gloves and a new shirt. He needed the gloves if he was going to ride on.

He found the doctor's office, but no one answered when he knocked, so he went to the general store.

There were several men at a counter, and he quickly discovered through overheard snatches of conversation that they were buying ammunition.

"You should have been there. I ain't never seen anyone so fast. Yates never even got his gun free."

"You say his name was Canton?"

"Yep. Old Gar hired him. Never thought I'd see the day Gar hired guns."

"Well, Newton started it, sending for that renegade Indian."

"Damn both of them. This used to be a right nice town. Now I won't 'low Carrie to even come to town."

One of the men turned and noticed Lobo, and the others saw their friend's expression. One by one they turned and stared at the newcomer, eyes falling down to the man's waist. There was a collective sigh of relief when they saw he didn't wear a gunbelt. Hostile looks turned friendly, or at least neutral.

The storekeeper moved over toward him. "Anything I can do for you, Mister?"

"I was looking for the doctor."

"He's out delivering a baby," the man said. "No telling when he'll be back."

Lobo ignored the stares he was getting. "Do you have any salve for burns, then?"

Six pairs of eyes went to his hands.

"Say, you wouldn't be that fella that helped Willow Taylor, would ya?" one man said. News traveled fast in Newton. They all knew about the fire, all the details, in fact, and Dr. Barkley had been deviling them to help with a barn raising come next Saturday.

Christ, Lobo thought, wishing like hell he'd never come into town. "Burned them on a coffeepot," he lied. "Now, about that salve. And some gloves and a shirt."

Interest faded. The stranger, with the exception of the cold eyes, looked like any vagabond cowboy looking for a job. Didn't even wear a gun.

The transaction was quickly completed. Lobo handed over the coins carefully, just like a man with few of them. He picked up his purchases, took a few steps and stopped, turning back.

"Heard you mention a man named Canton. Marsh Canton?"

One of the men reassessed the stranger. "You know him?" he asked carefully.

"Heard of him. What's he doing here?"

"Killed a man Saturday night. I hear tell he's come to go against another gunfighter named Lobo. You know him?"

"Heard tell."

"Well, he better be good. Ain't never seen anything like Canton." The voice was full of awe. "Would be somethin' to see, awright. Them two."

"You staying around town, Mister?" another asked.

Lobo shrugged indifferently. "Where's Canton now?"

"Gar Morrow's place, I s'pose."

Lobo nodded and left.

"Don't say much, does he?" he heard a man behind him sputter.

"Wonder why he was interested in Canton. You don't think . . . ?"

"Hell, no. Didn't even wear a gun. B'sides, Lobo's part Indian, I heard tell. That one sure ain't got no Indian blood."

Lobo's lips twisted into a half-smile as he mounted. There was something to be said for rumors. But what in the hell was Canton doing here?

He had always considered the possibility they might meet someday. The thought had never particularly bothered him.

Until now. For some fool reason, it did now. And he didn't know why.

Excitement seemed to hum in the classroom. Ethan was almost uncontrollable as he dunked a pigtail in an inkwell and threw spitballs at Robert.

The tension was also evident all over town. Ever since the shooting Saturday night, everyone waited to see what would happen next. Damning eyes, curious eyes, speculative eyes, all focused on Willow, who seemed to be the center of the storm.

After school she walked over to see Sullivan while the twins were cleaning the blackboards, but he was gone. She stood in front of his office, feeling strangely bereft. She badly needed someone to talk to.

She had hoped her stranger would have appeared the previous day. She had waited, but only Sullivan came, bringing a harness for Willow's buckboard and horses. He had also gone in search of Brady and Jupiter, but both of them were still missing.

Willow had been filled with apprehension since she woke that morning. Her hand had trembled as she'd helped Estelle with breakfast, and she'd watched with unusual concern as Sallie Sue fed her small flock of chickens. Willow did not smile as she usually did when watching the child give special attention to the spoiled and ungrateful Brunhilde.

Everything seemed tranquil on the surface, but something ominous was brewing.

The feeling persisted throughout the school day, as if all hell, as Sullivan put it, was about to blow loose. Or maybe it was her intense disappointment that the stranger did not appear. She almost prayed for a catastrophe since that seemed the only time he materialized.

Some of the town's apprehension was evident in the fact that nearly one third of her pupils didn't appear for class. It had grown to nearly forty pupils, up from the fifteen when she'd first arrived. It had not been an easy battle to build that number.

In the first months she had vocally wondered why she had so many more boys than girls. It had been Betty MacIntyre who told her that most ranchers and farmers didn't think it necessary that girls learn anything their mothers couldn't teach them.

Willow had spent the next eight weekends riding a rented horse from ranch to ranch, convincing parents to send their daughters to school.

That was how she had met Jake.

She had ridden by his place on a Saturday morning, and he was watering Jupiter. She was hot and tired, and saddle sore.

When she explained her purpose, he'd eyed her with interest and asked her inside. He didn't have children, he said, but he wondered . . .

He'd stopped, but Willow had seen both the shame and

longing in his eye, and she knew what it meant. She had seen it before. It wasn't unusual for many adults to have never learned to read and write. Schools were few and far apart, and many families had just not seen a need for book learning.

Jake had been gruff, and even rude, but she'd known he was just feeling her out. When he'd asked her to come and visit again, she knew she had passed some kind of test. She'd made several more trips before he'd finally admitted his need, and she'd spent several evenings a week teaching him how to read and write.

It was for his wife, he'd said. She had often read to him from the Bible, the only book he had. She hadn't cared that he couldn't read, but now he wanted the comfort of the Good Book. It would bring him closer to her, and he felt that need now that he was approaching old age and death.

Willow remembered her burst of pride when he'd read his first complete sentence. It had been worth all the time she'd spent with him. But then he seemed to sicken and he talked more and more to her about his two friends, Alex and Gar, who now hated each other. He feared dying for what would happen to the two men, yet he wanted to join his wife.

But Willow could prevent it, he sometimes muttered. Willow could somehow breach that schism that he could not. He knew it.

Willow wasn't so sure. Yet, as he lay dying, she could no more deny him his last wish than she could resist teaching him. Like Jake, she felt there had to be a way to keep peace in the valley.

Now, after the dance, she wasn't so sure. Some of her confidence had drained from her the next day when nothing had gone right: when her stranger didn't appear, when Brady and Jupiter didn't come home, when it didn't rain and the garden grew more straggly.

And nothing improved on Monday, when the town seemed on the edge of eruption.

Was she doing more harm than good?

She no longer knew.

As she drove home with the twins, she scoured the hills,

wanting desperately to see the person whom she had come to believe was their salvation. He had to be someplace. She wouldn't allow herself to believe that he had been injured worse than she'd thought, or that he'd ridden away. There was a new empty feeling in her, and she knew that only he could fill it. So she looked at every hill and strained her eyes against the glare of the sun.

But she didn't see him. And she was alone.

As before, Lobo heard the horses long before they came into view.

He had returned from town and doctored his hands before buckling his gunbelt back on. He had forced himself not to delay along the road, not to watch for her. He was no lovesick school kid, and it was time for him to stop acting like one.

He practiced his draw, knowing it was important not to let his hands stiffen up. He tolerated the pain, even took satisfaction in it when his hand proved as quick as always.

Canton was here! The stakes were growing higher.

The last time he'd seen Canton was months before in Denver, where his fellow gunfighter also made his base. Unlike Lobo, Canton cultivated an image. He always wore black and kept his gun highly polished, the notches on its handle evident to all but the most casual of observers.

Although Canton didn't seek out challenges, neither did he try to avoid them. His presence was always highly visible, which invited trouble, and, once confronted, Canton made sure he finished whatever someone else started. Good for the reputation, he once told Lobo, and the deadlier the reputation the greater the money.

So was the danger. But Canton seemed to care little about that. He was a man who enjoyed living on the edge, who cared not a whit whether he died doing it.

Lobo felt differently. He never drew attention to himself, merely did the job. He dressed indifferently, casually—like any cowhand—for he did not fancy being challenged every time he entered a new town. His occupation was a business;

he saw no reason for giving away his rather unique skills for free.

He allowed the legends to grow because they benefited him. A man in fear was a man whose hand shook; terror was an ally in his business.

Because of his background as an Apache warrior, everyone seemed to think he would have dark skin and hair, and he did nothing to dispel those beliefs. Even when a man saw him at work, the legend surrounding him survived. He grew taller, darker, fiercer. It was only when a victim faced him, and saw the light turquoise eyes as cold as death, that he realized who and what he was facing. Some of them ran then, and never talked of it. The ones who hadn't were dead.

It was a singularly lonely and empty existence, but it had been enough. Since he'd never known any kind of personal warmth, he hadn't really believed it existed, not for him anyway. He didn't need anyone, didn't want anyone, a philosophy that had helped him survive. If he didn't believe in soft emotions, he couldn't miss them, couldn't be seduced by them. Freedom had been his one goal, the only thing that gave him satisfaction. Gunfighting gave him that freedom, as well as the highly desirable benefit of being left alone.

His thoughts were interrupted by two men riding up very cautiously.

"Mr. Newton wants to see you," one said.

Lobo eyed them coldly.

"I'll be along."

"He said now," the second man replied nervously.

"I said I'll be along," Lobo scowled, one hand resting on the gun he'd returned to the holster.

The two men looked at each other mutely, deciding their jobs weren't worth their lives. "Yes, sir, Mr. Lobo."

Lobo raised one sandy eyebrow at the strained courtesy, his lips curling in derision. He turned his back to them, as if in dismissal, and he heard the sound of departing hoofbeats. He'd let Newton stew awhile. He didn't like a man who went after women and children, and yet something indefinable kept him from leaving. He kept seeing the boy, Chad, and little Sallie Sue and the woman's dark blue eyes. There had to be a way of getting them off the land without violence, but that didn't seem possible, not with the way the woman was determined to stay and Newton was obsessed, would stop at nothing to have her land.

It was late afternoon before he condescended to approach the Newton ranch.

His new gloves covered his burned hands, his shirt the nasty red welts on his arm. His gun was strapped against his thigh, and his eyes were dangerously bright, like a fire burning deep in their depths.

Newton quickly noted the change. He'd feared the man before when the eyes were icy cold, but now they seemed the eyes of a devil. But, he reassured himself, Lobo was *his* devil.

Lobo watched the fear with quiet amusement. He saw the frustration in Newton's face that he, Lobo, hadn't come to heel.

"I expected results by now," Newton said.

"I told you I would do it my own way," Lobo said lazily. "If you want me to leave . . ."

"Can you do it?"

"My way, I can."

"Am I permitted to ask about your way?" Newton said sarcastically.

"No."

Newton's face grew red with fury, but he dared not say anything. Now that Gar Morrow had Canton, Newton needed Lobo more than ever. He had started something he was beginning to wonder whether he could finish.

"I'm hiring more men," Newton blustered.

Lobo shrugged with indifference.

"Morrow's hired Canton."

"So I heard."

"I want you to kill him."

Lobo's lips tightened. "That's not why I was hired."

"I'll give you another ten thousand. He insulted my daughter."

"That reason enough to kill a man?"

"Are you afraid?" Newton asked, instantly regretting the words.

"I don't like you, Newton," Lobo said after a long, menacing silence. "I'm not sure I want to kill a man for you. I agreed to a certain job, and I'll do that, but no more. Not for the likes of you."

Lobo turned and left the room, leaving Newton trembling with fear and fury.

Seven

Chad looked at the late afternoon sun, and then at his workmanship. He winced.

If Brady really did find Jupiter, the corral would never hold the old bull, not after embers from the barn fire had fallen on the top rails and burned halfway through them.

He had struggled with them all day, trying to replace them with pieces of lumber from the outer fence he had dragged behind a horse. But he couldn't fasten them securely, not without help, and Estelle had proved to be worse than useless.

Chad finally got the idea of hoisting the rails to the top of the fence with rope and then tying them before nailing them to the posts. He badly wanted it done by the time Willow got home. He wanted to prove himself now that Brady had disappeared.

Chad didn't want to leave the ranch. It was the only home he'd ever known, and Willow was the only family he'd ever had.

He would protect her with his very life.

Chad knew what was going on, although Willow was trying

to protect him and the others by keeping silent about it. However, word spread rapidly, and the other day the twins had come home, bursting with excitement about the gun-fighters gathering in Newton. It didn't take much to figure everything out.

He'd eavesdropped on Dr. Sullivan and Willow, and had heard enough to know how badly Alex Newton wanted the ranch. He knew, from his years in the saloon, that Newton usually got what he wanted.

Well, he wouldn't get this ranch. Not with Chad there.

He was sweating in the hot July sun. School would be out in another week to recess for several months while students helped with the harvest or with driving cattle up to Denver. Willow would tend the garden as she had last year—if there was anything surviving. The corn was shriveled, the beans dying on the vines.

Chad looked up at the ball of fire in the sky and ran his sleeve across his wet forehead. He could sure use some help. He wished again for the tall stranger, as he had for the past several days. Chad just couldn't believe he'd disappeared like that. He'd been an . . . omen. Like Willow talked about in her books.

Chad had never looked up to a man before. His pa had been a drunk, like Brady, and though Brady never hit him, knocking Chad around had been his father's favorite activity. Chad had hated him, had hated the ragged clothes he'd worn, had hated the one-room shack that was always dirty. He'd hated the saloon where his pa made him work instead of going to school like the other kids. He had been pushed, spit upon, slapped, and laughed at. Then his pa died, and the sheriff wanted to send him to an orphanage.

Chad had heard about such places, and he'd decided he would run away first. He was doing just that when Willow found him in her kitchen, stealing food for his escape. He'd thought she would be at school, but she had dismissed class early to take an ill child home.

Instead of being angry or hauling him off to the sheriff, she had sat him down and fixed him a hot meal. She hadn't threatened him, or he would have pushed her away and run.

She asked him where he planned to go, and how he would make his way with no education.

"I can be a cowboy. They don't need no book learning."

"Then how do they know if they're getting their right wages, or whether someone's cheating them, or whether they've lost some cattle or not?"

Chad thought about the questions. "I'm too old to go to school," he said finally. "And I won't go to no orphanage." Willow, whom he called Miss Willow then, studied him carefully. He was ten years old, small and thin for his age.

"Bet you can learn faster than any of them," she challenged him.

"I won't go to school," he insisted.

"If I teach you here, privately, would you try . . . would you try to outsmart all of them?"

It was the challenge that did it. He wanted to show those other snobs, those who had called him a dummy and laughed at his clothes and mocked his pa. So he had moved in with Miss Willow and she'd made him understand he was worthy of love and responsibility. He had worked terribly hard with the books as well as at the job she'd got for him at the stable. He loved horses and animals although he'd never had one of his own. The one time he had brought home a kitten, his pa had killed it, and he'd never dared to show interest in a critter again.

Not long after Miss Willow took him in, she also adopted Sallie Sue, then the twins. Her little house was bursting with people. Then she'd inherited the ranch, and they'd moved out there.

Chad had loved it from the first moment. Now he had four horses to help look after, along with Jupiter, and he was hoping that they could eventually build a herd. He had learned to read and write, and Willow said he was almost caught up with other boys his age. He would go to school next year.

But things had changed since then. The fire had been a disaster. The garden, upon which Willow depended so heavily, was dying, and old man Newton was bringing in gunmen to take their ranch away.

Chad tried to balance one of the rails and it started to fall. He grabbed for it, tripped, and the heavy wood smashed his hand, sending blood spurting over his clothes, the wood, and the ground.

Without thinking, he hollered, and the sound brought out Estelle and Sallie Sue, both of whom stopped at the sight of so much blood. Sallie Sue started wailing, while Estelle rushed over to Chad.

Holding his hand, Chad hopped around in agony. Pain sliced through him with a sharp edge as blood dripped steadily. Falling to his knees to the ground, he knew nothing but red-hot heat.

"It'll be all right, boy." The voice was deep and strong, the hand on his shoulder large. He hadn't heard hoofbeats, and he wondered briefly how the man had come to be there. Oddly some of the pain seemed to ease as the stranger's strength flowed into him.

Manfully, he struggled to stand up, then turned, his uninjured hand cradling the injured one. Two fingers looked unnatural, and he knew they were broken. The jagged rip in his skin was still bleeding.

The man knelt, taking his bandanna from around his neck with gloved hands and tearing it into several pieces. He wrapped the strips around the boy's fingers. "Hold it tight," he said, and he picked Chad up as easily as if he were a small puppy.

"Is your . . . is Miss Taylor here?"

Biting his lip in an effort to keep back tears of pain, Chad shook his head.

"I'll take you into town. That hand needs doctoring."

"I . . . I wanted to help," he explained as the man settled him on a horse that seemed to have appeared from nowhere.

The man's strange-colored eyes softened. "I know. It'll be all right."

"But the animals . . ."

"I'll see to the animals when we get back." He swung onto the saddle behind the boy.

Chad didn't protest any longer. He felt weak and funny,

but secure. He hurt but he knew he was safe. He nodded and allowed himself to relax against the man's muscular body.

The wagon was just outside the ramshackle gate that led to the house when Lobo spotted it. He pulled up his horse as the woman saw the boy.

"Chad," she exclaimed, surprise mixed with sudden fear at the sight of Chad's white face. Her gaze went from the boy to the face of the man holding him.

"He was trying to mend the corral," Lobo said laconically, his hand tightening slightly around the boy who was now swaying. He would lose consciousness soon; Lobo had seen the signs before. "I was taking him to town . . . for a doctor."

"He's not there," the woman said, her hands twisting with anxiety. "How bad—"

"I think two fingers are smashed, and there's a bad cut."

He watched her weigh alternatives. One thing he could say about her—she didn't go into hysterics easily, not like so many other women he'd known. She sat there on the buckboard seat, thinking, fully in control of herself just as she had been during the fire.

When she obviously reached a decision, she looked up at him with an expression both determined and pleading. "Could you . . . would you take him back to the house, and then ride into town and leave a note for Dr. Barkley?"

He stayed ramrod stiff, his eyes betraying nothing, his horse as still as he, though Willow could see the animal's muscles flex. She felt the energy of both master and beast, energy and tension barely held under control, ready to explode into speed and action. She thought, as she had before, of wild, untamed things, although the rider appeared only too human now with his arm protectively around the boy.

Chad looked pale, unsteady, his lips clenched tight. The blue cloth around his hand was turning red with blood. Willow felt her stomach lurch as she waited for the stranger to agree.

She knew it was only seconds, but she felt a lifetime pass

as their eyes met and held. A riveting sensation flowed between them, a silent, inexplicable comprehension of their impact on each other. She saw his jaw tighten as if to deny something they both understood and experienced.

He nodded curtly in answer to her question and turned the horse back to the house. She followed, her emotions in turmoil. She worried about Chad, yet her whole being whirled in confusion at seeing the stranger again, at the sight of the face that had been stamped indelibly on her mind. But no matter how often she had conjured him in her consciousness, the reality was much stronger, much more compelling. She had never known a presence that was so forceful, so powerful.

Both Estelle and Sallie Sue, whose face was stained with tears, were on the porch. The man dismounted, then brought the boy down, taking care not to jar him. Willow slipped off the wagon, leaving the twins to care for the horses.

Sallie ran up to her. "Chad still hurt?"

"He'll be all right, pumpkin," she said softly. Passing Estelle, she pressed the woman's stiff arm comfortingly.

Willow followed the stranger into the bedroom where he'd taken Brady several days earlier. Whereas he had dumped Brady unceremoniously, he was gentle with Chad, watching him for a moment after setting him down.

When he turned, his face was hard, his eyes cold. "How many more accidents do you need?"

Willow bit her lip, understanding only too well what he was saying. So he, too, believed she should leave. That hurt. She knew it shouldn't, but it did.

"Who are you?" she whispered.

Lobo knew right then and there he should tell her. He should scare the living daylights out of her, but he saw a certain desperation in her face, a tear hovering at the corner of one eye. Yet her back was straight, and he thought how much she was like her name, strong and supple, bending with the wind but not breaking. And he couldn't give his name. He couldn't.

"Jess," he said roughly, not knowing exactly where the answer came from. He hadn't called himself that in years; the name hadn't even surfaced in his consciousness until the other day. And yet now it came readily.

"Jess," she repeated softly, and he felt a churning in his stomach. It sounded right on her lips.

But he wouldn't stay to wallow in the impossible. "I'll go for the doctor, and then I'll be back to fix the fence."

Willow swallowed hard. He had done so much already, but she still knew so little about him, only a part of his name. "You . . . don't have to—"

"I told the boy I would," he interrupted. "Chrissakes, this place is a disaster."

Ignoring the expletive, she reached out and touched his wrist. Her fingers lingered there, feeling the warmth of his skin, until he jerked away as if seared. She had felt compelled to make contact, to prove to herself he really did exist and wasn't some absurd figment of her often too active imagination.

"Thank you," she said almost breathlessly. She, too, had felt burned by the touch, by the intimacy of the gesture that was suddenly more meaningful than she had intended. But then, everything about him was more than she expected and understood. She tried to smile. "It seems that's all I ever say to you."

"Leave here, lady, go someplace safe," he said, but some of the fierceness had left his eyes, and the current between them was almost overwhelming. He wanted to move toward her, to hold out his hand and see whether her skin was really as soft as it had felt during those few brief, fiery seconds, whether her eyes would continue to welcome him.

"I can't," she said in a soft voice.

"Why?" That was the question plaguing him. Why did she hold on to the godforsaken piece of earth and the scraggly garden?

"I've made promises."

"No promises are worth your life . . . and theirs." His eyes went to Chad.

"I can't," she said. Quiet desperation was back in her voice, and it made him want to reassure when it was his job to frighten.

"Why?"

"Stay for supper tonight, and I'll tell you," she said as she moved over to Chad, her gaze going to his hand. She gently unwound the bandage and frowned at the wound.

It was no longer bleeding freely, and she stroked Chad's arm in comfort. "Is the pain terribly bad?"

Chad shook his head bravely while she placed a pillow under the arm and bit her lip. "I hope Sullivan comes soon," she said.

"Sullivan?"

"The doctor."

Lobo felt some new emotion pound through him. Jealousy? Was jealousy that something dark and furious building inside him at the way she so easily mentioned the name of another man.

"I'll go for him," he said abruptly as if to wipe away disturbing feelings.

"And you'll stay for dinner?" She repeated the offer, her gaze holding his, demanding, in her own gentle, persistent way, an answer.

Lobo hesitated. Perhaps this was a chance to convince her of certain facts. He thought about sitting across the table from her, about having her cook a meal for him. No one had ever cooked a meal for him.

"Jess?" Her voice was tentative as she uttered the name. It took him a while to realize she was addressing him.

"How are your hands?" she asked when he didn't respond.

He looked down at them. The gloved fingers were clenched into fists. He shrugged, which was his usual reply to most questions.

"Would you tell me if they weren't better?"

"No," he replied. There was no humor in the answer, not the slightest trace of a smile on his lips. His gaze returned to her face, to those sky-blue eyes that threatened to drown him in their depths.

Chad groaned, and the sound broke the spell between the two adults.

"I'll go now," Lobo said, then hesitated. "Why don't you write a note in case he's gone. He might come faster if it's from someone he knows." He kept his face impassive as he felt a surge of humiliation. He couldn't tell her he didn't know how to read or write, nor did he wish to leave a message at the general store. He didn't want his presence to bring her criticism or embarrassment. And it could. He knew that only too well. Decent people didn't associate with the likes of him.

But she didn't seem to notice his deception and she disappeared shortly, leaving him with Chad and Sallie Sue, who was looking on from the doorway. Sallie inched up to him and pulled shyly on his hand.

He looked down to a small face, partly frightened, partly wistful, partly determined. "I like you," she said, ducking her head slightly, and Lobo remembered when she'd thanked him for saving Jupiter from the fire. There was an earnestness in the innocent and sweet face that made him hurt inside.

Lobo stooped down, sensing how big he must seem to the child. His hand went to her shoulder, then quickly withdrew, but his head cocked as if in question.

"You lithted me from the hole," she lisped. "I was thcared."

The side of his mouth quirked up. "So was I," he confided.

She looked at him with disbelief, then darted out of the room on chubby legs.

He looked up and saw Willow Taylor standing in the doorway, a bemused look on her face. "She's a little bashful," she said almost apologetically.

He shrugged and held out his hand for the paper she was holding. Even through the glove he felt an electric shock when her fingers made contact. In confusion, he turned back to Chad and gave him a brief nod before hurrying out.

The trip into Newton was endless. The note seemed to burn through his pocket. He had taken only a quick glance at it, noting how neatly written the unintelligible lines were. A black gloom settled over him as he realized how great a distance separated him from the people in the crumbling but love-filled house he'd just left. He couldn't even read, for chrissakes, couldn't do a simple thing like pen a note for a doctor.

If he were smart, he would leave the note and then head

north. Not to Denver, not to anyplace familiar, but to new sights and new mountains. He would ride and bury himself in the challenge of pure survival, of enjoying the solitude, the freedom he continued to crave.

You promised the boy you would come back, he reminded himself.

But you're only going to bring grief to them and yourself.

Why should I care about them?

Why?

Yet there was a pull he couldn't resist. He tried to tell himself it was the look in the boy's eyes, a look with which he identified, a look that said Chad had seen more than a boy his age ever should. He tried not to think it was the woman, for that idea was pure disaster, as sure as stirring a mother bear protecting its cub.

Jess. Why did he tell her that? Because, he admitted to himself, he didn't want to tell her his true name. He hadn't wanted to see fear and revulsion on her face.

The town was just ahead, the first lights starting to flicker as dusk enveloped the ugly buildings. He saw a light inside the doctor's office. His gut tightened. He didn't want to meet the man Willow Taylor referred to so easily, and yet he had to for the boy's sake.

Lobo dismounted and knocked at the door. The well-kept wooden structure apparently served as both office and home for the doctor.

The door opened quickly, and Lobo found himself facing a lean man dressed in broadcloth trousers and a white cotton shirt, the sleeves rolled up like his own. The doctor was tall, although not as tall as himself, and his face was weary and drawn. The eyes, however, were lively and curious, and they regarded him quizzically. "Yes?"

Lobo could only stare for a moment. Like Willow's, the gaze that held his now was compassionate; the smile, while questioning, was real; and the manner gentle. Lobo's turmoil deepened as he realized how suited these two people were. Wordlessly, he handed the doctor the note.

The man took it to a lighted oil lamp in the corner and

quickly read it. In seconds he had donned a coat and grabbed a bag. "Is it bad?"

"Bad enough," Lobo said as the doctor looked at him curiously.

"I'll take my horse instead of the buggy," Sullivan said aloud as he locked the door. "It'll be faster. Are you going back?"

Lobo wondered at the casual acceptance of a stranger until the doctor turned to him, his gaze moving from the gloved hands up to his eyes and settling there a second. "You're the one who has been helping them."

It was not a question but a statement, and Lobo saw no reason to answer. In fact, he saw no reason to linger. The street in front of the saloon was busy, and he didn't care to be seen and recognized. Lobo ignored the doctor's piercing look, spinning around and heading for his horse.

Night was falling, and it was too dark to fix the fence or anything else. Lobo did not want to go back to the Taylor ranch. He did not want to see the doctor—the sawbones, he thought derisively—and Willow Taylor together. He did not want to watch something he did not, could not, would never have.

He would fulfill his promise to Chad in the morning, when the doctor and Willow were gone. He thought of Willow's invitation to dinner, of the warmth in her eyes. And he wanted both; he wanted them badly.

Yet he suspected Dr. Sullivan Barkley would not be so easily satisfied about him, as Willow Taylor had been. The doctor would recognize the brand of death that he and others of his kind wore. Somehow he couldn't bear the thought of Willow Taylor knowing who he really was, and seeing her face turn white with fear and disgust . . . even if that had been his original purpose.

With a muttered curse he swung away from the road and headed toward his camp on Newton's ranch.

* * *

Willow waited and waited for the man named Jess. She even prepared the meal herself, not wanting to scare him away forever with Estelle's cooking.

Sullivan came and tended Chad's wound, sewing the wicked gash and fixing a splint to the fingers. He teased Chad briefly about throwing around posts and gave him a dose of laudanum. But minutes later, in the kitchen, his face was grim. "Those fingers may never heal normally," he said.

Willow swallowed. "Perhaps we should move back to town."

Sullivan grimaced. He wanted to agree, but he also knew how much Willow hated to back down from anything, and furthermore how much she had come to love her place.

Willow went to the window and looked out. "I don't think he's coming," Sullivan said gently.

"He said . . . he would fix the fence."

"It's a little dark for that."

Willow turned back to him. "It's so odd . . . the way he always appears when we need him. And then disappears."

Sullivan silently agreed. There was something about her visitor that disturbed him, but he couldn't exactly identify what. He knew damned little about him, only what Willow had told him, and Willow was anything but objective on the subject. He was worried about Willow's growing dependence, even obvious infatuation if her shining eyes were any indication, on the stranger.

Neither were the others objective. Chad certainly held the man in awe, and even Sallie Sue smiled at the mention of him. The twins couldn't stop talking about the way he'd rescued Jupiter, and Estelle, well, even Estelle didn't seem as frightened of him as she was of other men, although God knew she had reason to be afraid of anything that wore pants.

Sullivan didn't like it. The visits were too convenient, the insinuation into the lives of the family he'd adopted too strong. And the man's face was so hard, his eyes so unfathomable. He sure as hell didn't fit Sullivan's idea of a white knight. There was something wrong about the whole thing, but he didn't know what. He just damn well couldn't piece it together.

Jess. That was what Willow said his name was. At least it was a start. He would try to find out more about the mysterious stranger.

"The offer's still open," he said now as he carefully watched Willow's face. "I'll take the boys if you want to move back."

For the first time, Willow really considered the suggestion. There had been too many accidents, and she knew she had been lucky beyond normal expectations. They couldn't always depend on the stranger. But the animals? She would have to get rid of them. Of Jupiter, if he was found, Sallie Sue's chickens, the extra horses. She couldn't afford to keep all four in the livery stable. No one would want the old bull; he was more trouble than he was worth. And Estelle? She had gained some measure of happiness and security on the ranch. As Brady had.

"I'll talk to the others," she conceded.

Sullivan hesitated. He didn't like leaving her there alone. Brady was gone. Chad was incapacitated. He compromised with himself by saying he would return tomorrow to check on Chad.

He refused the offer of dinner. He'd been fed, he said, at his last stop, and he was tired. He put his hand on Willow's shoulder. "If you need anything—"

"I know," she finished for him. "I'll find you."

After he left, she ate dinner with the children, but her mind was elsewhere. She'd always believed that if she wanted something bad enough, she could have it. She had always believed that things worked out the way they should.

In the year and a half they had lived on the ranch, they'd survived very well. They'd had none of the accidents they'd had in the past few days.

And yet it seemed as if a higher being had waited with his bagful of mishaps until there was someone to look after them. Their own palladin, their own Odysseus. It was as if it were a sign to stay.

That night she read more of the adventures of Odysseus to the children. "Odysseus and his men," she recounted with drama, "landed on the shores of the Lotus-Eaters, and there they found the most enticing plant, the lotus.

"They ate of this plant, this lotus, and suddenly they forgot all about their homes and families. They forgot all thoughts of duty, and they wanted nothing more than to dwell in Lotus Land, and let the memory of all that had been fade from their minds.

"But Odysseus had avoided tasting of honey-sweet flowers, and tricked his men back on ship, chaining them there until they had left Lotus Land far behind," she concluded with a sigh.

How could she make Jess stay? What kind of lotus plant would attract him? The thought was ridiculously fanciful, but Willow couldn't let it go.

"And then what happened?" Jeremy's expectant voice broke into her whimsy.

"They sailed away to confront another danger—the Cyclops, a wild race of one-eyed giants," she said with a gleam in her eye.

The twins wanted her to continue, but she said no, they had to wait until tomorrow.

When everyone was finally abed, she went outside. Jess was someplace near. She knew it. Just as she knew he would be back the following day to fix the fence.

She would offer him a job. She knew she didn't have much to pay him with, but he didn't seem to have anything steady.

With a hopeful smile on her face, she finally went inside and changed into a cotton nightdress. She blew out the light but she couldn't sleep. She kept seeing turquoise-colored eyes and a mouth that twitched ever so slightly at the corners as if it were totally unfamiliar with smiling. She recalled that momentary gentleness as he looked at Chad, and the bright, flaming intensity as he had stared at her.

She'd never met anyone like him. She wanted to know everything there was to know about him, and yet she sensed he would fight bitterly to keep himself uninvolved.

Willow smiled. He didn't know how determined she could be.

Eight

He was at the ranch when she arrived the next afternoon. His shirt was off, and his bare chest glistened with sweat and seemed to glow with the sun as he wrestled with fence posts.

Chad was watching, sitting on one of the repaired rails, his hand lying protectively in his lap as Jess very efficiently set a rail in place and secured it with wire. Muscles rippled along the full length of his body as he moved, and Willow thought she had never seen anything quite as gloriously perfect. Like a Greek statue pictured in one of her books.

He was, she thought fancifully, nothing less than poetry in motion.

He had looked up when she had driven by, but then went back to his task, his face as impassive as always. The twins bounced down from the buckboard and ran over to watch, their mouths pursed full of questions. Even Estelle was on the porch, cautious but interested.

Willow watched as he finished with the last railing, and she neared. He wasn't wearing gloves, and his hands were still red and raw-looking. But she couldn't tell he was feeling any pain at all from the way he handled the tools.

He gave one last look at the fence, apparently satisfying himself that it was completed, and started for his horse as he fingered a pair of new gloves. Willow plotted a collision path with him, and he stopped just seconds before he would have crashed into her.

She took his hands, preventing him from hiding them within the gloves. She touched them lightly, turning each hand one way, then another, so she could see how they were healing.

Lobo had thought he'd be gone before she returned. And he intended to leave, but her touch was like a cool breeze against the skin of his hands, soothing the aching, burning rawness renewed by the physical effort. He was aware that several blisters had broken but had ignored the fact in his haste to finish the job and get the hell out of Newton. He had promised the boy, and there was no telling what the kid would do if the job wasn't completed. Lobo was supposed to be getting the lot of them out of there, not helping them to stay. But there was something about the damned kid and those trusting eyes. Lobo wasn't about ready to admit to himself there was also something about the woman.

"Please come inside," Willow said. "I want to talk to you."

He hesitated. All he wanted was to make a fast getaway.

Instead, much to his own amazement, he found himself nodding.

When they arrived in the kitchen, they found themselves followed by a trail of children. Willow grinned as she looked from one fascinated face to another, then chased them outside. "You too," she told Estelle, who was hovering in the background. When all the curious ears were gone, she looked at him, her face solemn, her eyes searching.

"I have a proposition for you," she started.

One eyebrow arched.

"I . . ." she said, hesitating.

The eyebrow went higher, but the eyes were as unreadable as always.

"I'd . . . better see about those hands," she continued awkwardly, not sure whether she could present the offer she'd intended. He looked so forbidding.

"No need."

"But—"

"I've had worse burns," he said.

"But not because of me," she countered.

"It wasn't you. I don't like to see animals wasted."

"And Brady . . ."

"If I'd known he started it, I would have left him there."

It was a condemnation, and she winced at the harshness of it. She suspected it wasn't true, but his look challenged her to believe it. He was willing her to accept it.

His face was a study in indifference. It seemed impregnable until she remembered the previous night, the way he had looked at Chad before he had caught himself. There had been compassion in that look, and understanding. And Willow knew she had not imagined it.

The memory gave her courage. "I . . . we . . . were wondering if you . . . possibly needed . . . a job."

He glared at her with disbelief.

She hurried on. "I can't pay much, and there's not even a barn now to stay in, but you could sleep in the room with the boys and there would be meals and . . ."

And we need you. The words were unsaid, but they hung in the air.

There was a flicker of amusement in his eyes, and then they went totally blank again as he frowned. "You mean you really plan to stay. Lady, don't you have any sense?"

She looked wounded by his words. "I told you yesterday I had to stay."

He grated his teeth in frustration before answering. "What about the kids? Don't you give a damn about them?"

"We took a vote last night. Everyone wants to stay."

"A vote?" Willow cringed at the disbelief in his voice. "Lady, you're as crazy as that damned bull of yours," he continued.

"Willow," she insisted. "My name is Willow."

He sighed heavily, as if he were in the presence of a madwoman.

"Why did you fix the fence if you didn't think we would stay?" she asked suddenly.

Damned if he knew, he had to admit to himself. The craziness must be contagious, like cholera, and every bit as deadly. "I promised the boy," he said shortly. "I didn't want him trying it again. But for chrissakes, I thought you'd have enough sense to give up after all that's happened."

"That's why we need you," she said with the sweetest, most trusting smile he'd ever seen. It struck right to the core of his gut.

"Why are you so set on staying?" he finally asked.

"I'll tell you while I put salve on those hands," she said.

He glowered at her, his eyes hard and frosty. Finally he nodded, but with such reluctance that she suspected it was far more difficult for him to accept help than to climb down into a well full of rattlesnakes or drag a reluctant bull from a flaming barn.

"Sit down, and I'll go get the salve," she ordered, her head indicating a seat at the large kitchen table.

He surprised himself by obeying. He looked around the kitchen when she disappeared. There was a big pot on the stove from which an odd aroma came. His nose twitched as he tried to identify the smell, but he could not.

The kitchen was cozy, with flowered curtains and a colorful woven rug. There were numerous pictures, obviously drawn by the children, on the wall, and pegs from which polished pans hung. The room was cluttered with books and clothes, not neat like his room in Denver, but it was scrubbed bright and smelled clean and fresh. There was warmth and comfort and . . . he felt an odd, blinding sense of coming home.

For a moment he allowed himself to wonder how it would feel to live in such a place, but he quickly dismissed the thought as being as crazy as the woman was. Even a hotel room soon became a prison to him after a few days; he could never stay long in one place. He needed only grass under him and a sky above. He needed space and freedom as he needed to breathe.

"Let me see them." Her voice jerked him back to the present and once again he surprised himself by lifting his hands, palm up, to her.

"They'll never get well if you keep using them like that,"

she scolded, and her fingers ran over them, spreading cool, soothing salve on the raw areas.

He felt a curious weakness, a warm sensation that was becoming all too familiar when he was with her. The heat in his belly was bad enough, but the growing longing in his mind was even worse. He had never known a touch could be so light, so gentle. He had never known a woman's look could curl his insides. He'd never known the kind of weakness that settled in his limbs, one that kept him from pushing away when he knew that was exactly what he should do.

She looked rapt as she accomplished her task, all her attention on his hands. She was wearing a blue dress, simple but appealing with its small touches of lace. It was nearly the same color as her eyes. A tendril of dark auburn hair escaped from a twist in the back of her head, falling against a lightly tanned face. She was all softness and warmth and beauty, and she scared the hell out of him.

"You were going to tell me why you want to stay," he said, more harshly than he intended.

She looked up, the blue eyes full of worry and determination, and even a plea for understanding.

"If I leave," she said slowly, "this town will erupt into warfare."

He looked at her in amazement. Didn't she understand what was going on? "It already has, lady," he said.

She shook her head. "Not like it will."

"And you're going to risk your life and those kids' lives to prove that?"

"Alex won't hurt me. Not really."

"That's not what I hear."

"He won't," she insisted again. "And Jake trusted me to keep peace."

"Then he was a damned fool."

"And," she added with a stubborn look, "it's our home."

"It's only wood and nails. Rotting wood and nails, at that," he said roughly.

She shook her head. "It's the only home I've ever really had, that's ever belonged to me."

He sighed with frustration. Reason obviously wasn't one of her strengths.

"You can't run this place on your own."

"That's why I need you," she said with a quick smile that tugged at him.

"I'm not available."

"Why?"

Her hands had stopped working. One of them was resting on his, and he felt a jolt of electricity run through him, dizzying, tingling streaks of red-hot fire. "You can't afford me," he finally managed to say.

She looked at him, and he felt the appraisal in her eyes. "How much would I need to afford you?"

He wondered for a moment whether he should tell her whom she was trying to hire, and what his usual fee was. It would be one way to jolt some sense into her. Yet he couldn't force himself to say the words. His work had never bothered him before.

"I don't plan to stay in town much longer," he said curtly, standing up to leave. He saw her gaze move along the length of his body, resting for only a split second at his hip, where the gunbelt rested, and then continue upward. His body seemed to turn to liquid heat, and he wondered how she would feel next to him. It took all his will not to grab her and find out.

"You've seen the worst of the ranch," she said quietly. "But it's really a fine place. We just . . . need some help."

"You need more than 'some,'" he replied. "You need an army."

"I think you'd do just fine."

"Don't you ever give up, lady?"

"Willow," she said.

One of his hands went to the back of his neck. "You don't know anything about me."

"I know enough," she shot back. "I know you like children, that you're capable around the ranch, that you're very kind."

"Kind?" The word was an expletive the way he said it. "Christ, lady, I thought—"

"Willow," she broke in. "Everyone calls me Willow."

"I'm not everyone, dammit."

"No," she agreed evenly with a smile lurking on her mouth. His eyes, usually so cold, were now blazing. That fire was, she thought, very attractive. And dangerous.

"You're a lunatic, inviting a stranger into your home."

"You're not a stranger."

"I sure as hell am."

"If you meant us harm, you wouldn't protest so much," she said tranquilly.

He glowered at her, frustrated at her undeniable logic.

"At least stay for dinner," she attacked gently. "Although I must tell you Estelle cooked today."

He furrowed his brow. Things were moving much too quickly. He had never thought himself half-witted before, but he was quickly reevaluating his ability to think and cope. "Estelle?" he said.

"She doesn't really cook well, but we'd never tell her that," Willow said.

"Why?"

The bluntness of the question made Willow smile again. He was obviously unused to sparing feelings or mincing words.

"Estelle has had a bad time," she said slowly, wanting him to understand. "She needs encouragement."

"And the boy?"

There it was again, Willow thought, that interest in Chad, although he tried to hide it.

"Him too," she said.

"And you?" He didn't know why he asked it. He certainly hadn't meant to. He wanted as little to do with her as possible. He wanted to know as little as possible.

She looked at him blankly for a moment, and his mouth tightened as he continued roughly. "What are you doing here? Trying to run a ranch on your own. You don't belong here."

Willow turned his own question on him. "Why?"

Because you're too soft, too innocent. . . .

"This is harsh country, Miss Taylor."

Now she was frustrated. But at least "Miss Taylor" was better than "lady."

"Jess," she said, and it took Lobo a moment to realize she was referring to him. The name had a certain softness on her lips, and softness had never been applied to him.

He swallowed. He damned well liked the way the name sounded.

"Will you think about the job?"

"No."

Her eyes were wide, not pleading, but expectant.

"I won't be here long enough," he repeated, not knowing why he was making excuses. He'd never made one before in his entire life.

"Will you at least have dinner with us? Chad would be so pleased."

Christ, dinner with the houseful of lunatics! Yet the idea was suddenly terribly compelling. Part of him longed to stay, but another part, the sensible part, warned him away. He already felt partially trapped. A few more moments and he might as well surrender entirely. And she knew it. There was a gleam in her eye that told him so. He had the sudden feeling that she was not altogether as innocent as he had first believed. There was a sneaky streak in her. And he was damned determined not to yield to it. Not to her. Not to the boy. He couldn't afford it.

He shook his head, pulled on his gloves, and rose.

"I have things to do," he said curtly, brushing past her as she also rose from the table. But before she could make one more objection, his long legs had propelled him out the door, off the porch, and into the saddle. Without a backward glance he spurred the pinto into a gallop, as if all the demons in hell were after him.

Lobo had killed his first man, the son of an Apache chief, at twelve, and he'd killed his first white man when he was sixteen. The soldier had been one of the few whites he'd seen up close since his capture eight years earlier. There had been several others, a few slaves who'd survived Apache initiation, and renegade traders who brought whiskey and guns to the camp. But most of them had been as much Apache as white.

Lobo had killed the white soldier for the simple reason the man had been trying to kill him. Lobo had felt no regret at the action, only a certain satisfaction that it was not him lying on the ground.

Other killings also came easily. He'd never formed attachments with anyone other than his brother. A human being, particularly one shooting at him, merited no more concern than a food animal, perhaps even less, for the animal was innocent.

The Apache were hard taskmasters and tolerated no weakness. It was a lesson he'd learned well. But they did have their own code of justice and honor, and because of that he still lived.

Lobo slowed his pinto. If only she knew. If only she knew some of the things he'd done.

Christ, she would run like hell and never look back.

He pulled off one of his gloves, the salve making it sticky and uncomfortable. Damn. He rubbed his hand against his leg, and then against the back of his neck. The woman and kids had no idea what they were involved in. Newton had said he was hiring more men. Marsh Canton was in town. The whole territory was ready to explode. He'd seen it before, and he could smell it coming now.

It was time to leave. He'd failed and he knew there was no way to frighten her and her family of misfits from the ranch. He also knew that he had lost the ability to terrorize them, although he was realistic enough to know that Willow Taylor, like every other decent woman, would be horrified when she actually learned who he was. She wouldn't want to touch him, then, not even to bandage a wound.

But he couldn't forget her plea or her words. Or those of the chubby little girl. "I like you."

His stomach clenched in agony. His head swam with uncertainty. Maybe . . .

But then he remembered the room full of books. He sure as hell didn't belong there. Books. A teacher. Things he'd never known.

Lobo thought of the humiliation of not being able to read, not even the telegrams that summoned him to do what he did best. The words had to be read to him by one of the few people he trusted in Denver. He could write his name but not much more. He could recognize denominations of bills, but he couldn't add. He relied on his reputation to keep men from cheating him, and he had devised clever ways to keep people from learning he couldn't read or write.

Lobo had wanted to learn, not only wanted, but craved the independence and power he believed came with it. But he'd always been afraid of being laughed at, at seeing fear change to ridicule in faces around him.

And he had never asked anyone for help.

Now he was getting weak-kneed about a woman who would despise a man of ignorance.

He swore every Apache curse and white oath he could remember. But none of it did any good.

Nine

Brady scowled at the bull. It had taken him three days to find the beast.

Not exactly three, he admitted. He had taken two to recover from the barn burning. Even then he hadn't recovered from self-disgust.

He had not gotten far the first day before he had to stop. His stomach wouldn't hold anything, and his head pounded like a hammer striking an anvil. He'd reached town, located a worn saddle for which he'd paid five dollars, and suffered the looks of contempt he'd seen often enough. He'd also bought some food, but as soon as he tried to eat, it came back up again.

He was tempted to take his gun and blow out his brains. But first he had to return the bull. And then he had to find out more about the cowhand who'd rescued him. He had to pay back. Dear God in heaven, he had so much to pay back.

Something about the cowboy had tugged at his consciousness during the past several days, but he'd been in too much pain to focus on it. Gradually, his mind and body had cleared of the poison he'd managed to consume the night the barn burned, and the nagging became even louder.

Although the image of the cowboy remained blurred, Brady had the eerie impression of recognition. And it wasn't a favorable impression. Not that he could do anything if the stranger did intend some kind of harm.

Brady's hand went to the gun in his holster. He tugged out the weapon and held it. His hand shook even worse than it had several days before. He remembered how the weapon used to feel, almost like part of his hand. He had been fast and good. He had proved how good when he chased down the Lassiter brothers. One by one he had taken them out. The last man, Dale Lassiter, he had chased for six months. And he had watched him die with the pleasure of a man damned.

Brady looked at Jupiter. The animal had been easy to follow, once Brady's body was cleaned out. Tracking was a skill he hadn't forgotten, and Brady had been one of the best in his time. He had scouted long ago for the army and knew every trick, Indian or outlaw, there was.

But he had needed none of that with Jupiter. The bull had left a trail a mile wide, and seemingly happy to see him, it emitted a long, lonely complaint as if asking why he hadn't arrived earlier. It stood meekly as Brady roped his neck. Brady judged he was about twenty miles from the Taylor ranch, and already it was dusk. There were clouds in the sky, which meant the night would be dark, and he had no desire to drag the bull over rough country, risking its legs and those of his own horse.

He also didn't much fancy staying on Newton's land, where he was at the moment.

Brady unsaddled his horse and decided on a dry camp: no fire, no smoke. He tied Jupiter to a hefty cottonwood and searched in his saddlebags for some jerky. It was all he could keep down.

The problem of Jupiter solved, he turned his thoughts to Willow and the trouble she was in. He could help build a new barn, of course, but he couldn't do it alone, and almost everyone in these parts was scared of Alex. Truth be told, he would be, too, if he gave a damn about living. But he didn't. Not since Nancy and his boy, little Brady, died.

He closed his eyes, as he always did when he thought of them. They had dropped by his office to bring him lunch and were crossing the street when the Lassiters emerged from the bank with stolen money, their guns blazing at anything that moved. He'd heard the gunfire in his office just seconds after his wife and son had left, and he dashed out in time to see one of the outlaws' faces. He quickly identified the scarred visage from a poster.

Nancy lay in the street, her body over the boy, obviously trying to protect him. Both she and the boy were dead, and it had taken Brady weeks to accept, if not understand, the loss. His beautiful wife died because she brought him lunch.

He quit his job as sheriff a week later, when his posse had been unable to find the criminals. His jurisdiction went only as far as the territorial line. And that's where he heard the Lassiters had headed.

Now he was afraid that something similar might happen to people he cared about. And he was terrified that he would be just as helpless to prevent a second tragedy.

Compounding that worry now was Willow's stranger, the man who came from nowhere, who apparently claimed no name. Brady didn't like it. He didn't like it at all.

But what could he do?

Stay sober for one thing, an inner voice whispered.

But could he go back? Could he look at the scorched land where a barn had once stood? Could he face Chad's disappointment? Or would the calm acceptance in Willow's eyes be even worse?

He remained awake nearly the entire night, his system crying out for drink, every bone in his body aching, his skin covered with a cold sweat. He listened for every noise, each one sounding a little too loud.

It was early morning before his eyes closed.

* * *

Even after Jess's abrupt departure, Willow refused to be disappointed. He might have turned her down that day, but there was always the next.

The stew was dispensed equally, everyone taking a cautious look before venturing to taste. Much to Willow's surprise, the meal was unexpectedly good, and food went to mouths with more haste than usual.

Estelle smiled shyly at the actions that said more than words.

When she smiled, she was almost pretty, Willow thought, even with the glass eye that Sullivan had substituted for the one that had been almost gouged out. Estelle no longer ran like a frightened rabbit when a stranger approached, though she remained wary and shy.

Estelle had been with Willow nearly two years. She was a thin woman who had been beaten nearly to death by a customer of the saloon where she'd worked. She had gone upstairs with him, and had stumbled down nearly unrecognizable an hour later. The customer had disappeared.

When she had finally recovered from most of her wounds, she had no place to go and no job. She was terrified of any man other than Sullivan and Brady, and even with them she didn't seem at ease. Although she had lovely pale blond hair and fine features, she went out of her way to appear unattractive, tying the hair straight back from her face and wearing plain, bulky dresses.

Willow discovered that Estelle had been abandoned at thirteen by her mother, and that she'd worked in saloons ever since out of desperate need. There was a lost and hurt look about the girl that had touched Willow, and she'd had offered to take Estelle in until the girl could get on her feet. Estelle never left.

She loved the young ones, particularly Sallie Sue, but she had no confidence in herself, and Willow always worried about leaving Sallie Sue with Estelle. Quite simply, Estelle panicked, but lately she had seemed to grow stronger. The fact that she had helped Chad when Sallie Sue fell into the well and didn't hide when Jess entered the house were two major accomplishments for her.

And now she glowed with pleasure as the food she cooked was being eaten with relish. Again Willow wondered what would happen to Estelle if she had to leave the ranch, the one and only place of safety and security she'd ever known.

"Good," Sallie Sue said, licking her lips.

Chad scraped the stew from his plate and looked at Estelle speculatively.

The twins eyed empty plates longingly until they were refilled.

Willow glanced over at Estelle, who was beaming.

"I . . . thought we might have . . . company," Estelle said hesitantly. "I added some spices." She ducked her head. "I just sorta guessed."

So Jess had worked some more magic of his own, Willow thought, and had to smile. Somehow she knew he wouldn't be exactly pleased at the knowledge.

But Estelle, apparently, had seen something in the stranger that made her trust him, a rare thing, particularly since it had apparently inspired her to do something other than drop meat in a pot.

There was even dessert. Cookies. Burnt cookies. But Willow thought they tasted fine. It was the first time Estelle had tried something on her own; in the past she had only copied Willow, afraid to stray from the most basic instructions, and even then somehow doing something wrong.

Everyone helped clean up after the meal, and then Willow and the children sat down for another episode of Odysseus. The legend was meaning more and more to each of them each day. They all in their own minds saw the stranger as their own particular Greek hero.

Tonight was the tale of the Cyclops, the one-eyed giants who took Odysseus and his men captive.

As Willow told the story, she reminded herself they were coming to the end of Odysseus's adventures. He had left his wife, Penelope, twenty years earlier to take part in a great expedition against Troy, and after many years and more adventures he was trying to get back home to his Penelope.

But Willow didn't want the story to end.

* * *

The barn raising was planned for Saturday. By Thursday, Sullivan knew he would be lucky to have a handful of volunteers. Alex Newton had heard, and he had issued an edict. Any person who helped Willow Taylor would incur his displeasure.

No one in town could miss the increasing number of hard-eyed men with pistols strapped to their thighs wandering about town, visiting the saloon at night. The legend named Lobo, according to common gossip, was already at the Newton ranch. Pressed for details, one drunken cowhand said the gunfighter was seven feet tall, and as dark as the devil. Although no one quite believed him, the fear and rumors grew. No one, certainly none of the peace-loving townspeople, wished to arouse Alex's enmity, and therefore that of Lobo, or any other of his breed. Everyone was walking on eggs.

But Willow, as usual, had faith. If only a few people came, they could at least get the barn started, and then, well, the rest would follow. Maybe Jess would reconsider. Perhaps Brady would come back, and he and Sullivan and Chad . . .

Maybe, maybe, maybe. Something would work. Willow knew it. Brady would return with Jupiter, and everything would be as it once was. She was beginning to doubt the existence of the man called Lobo. There had been rumors of his presence for a week, but she certainly had seen nothing of such a man.

As she drove out of town after school, she ignored the hard-eyed men standing outside the saloon, many of whom stared at her with everything from lasciviousness to open admiration.

"Like seeing whiskey from a jailhouse window," one man said, sparking a loud and obscene comment from another, followed by coarse laughter. Willow's face flamed and she shivered slightly.

The twins moved closer to her on the seat, and Willow urged the horses to a faster pace. Something was happening to this town, something evil, and she seemed helpless to do anything about it.

Where was Jess?

And where was the man named Lobo?

She wondered if the waiting wasn't meant to intimidate and frighten.

Willow was terribly afraid the gunfighter was succeeding. For the first time she was beginning to know real fear.

Halfway back to the ranch with Jupiter trailing behind, Brady suddenly knew where he had seen the stranger before. The half-blurred vision had haunted him day and night, and then realization struck like lightning.

Lobo! The man who had been helping Willow and her family was the gunfighter who called himself Lobo.

The old bull bellowed in surprise as one of Brady's hands unconsciously tugged hard at the rope.

Brady remembered now. Damn, he remembered it all so clearly. He had seen the gunman once in Fort Worth. Brady had been delivering a prisoner, and the sheriff had pointed out Lobo as one of the hired guns involved in a range war.

Brady had been particularly interested because the man, except for his cold eyes, did not look like the usual gunman. He dressed like any cowhand, was cautious toward the sheriff but not arrogant, and displayed none of the cockiness Brady associated with his breed.

Brady had asked the sheriff why the man was roaming the streets so easily, and the sheriff scowled. "He ain't done nothin' yet to break the law. But he will. His kind always does, and I'll be watching."

Lobo was one of Newton's men, and Newton had only one objective: to obtain the ranch at any cost. So why was the gunfighter helping Willow?

To worm himself into her life? Why would that be necessary? There was little question that Willow would have quit the ranch if he and Jupiter had died in the fire. All Lobo had to do was stand by and watch.

One of the twins had called the man Willow's knight in shining armor.

A gunfighter! And not just any gunfighter. Lobo. The wolf. And from everything Brady had heard of the man, he was aptly named.

Brady had always hated gunfighters. He'd never allowed them in his town, whether they were wanted or not. He would find some reason to lock them up until they left willingly. He'd never been able to understand men who killed for money, or simply out of plain meanness.

He'd never understood it until he went after the Lassiters, and he'd discovered the dark side of himself. That discovery, however, had made him hate gunfighters more than ever, for he hated himself.

He felt his stomach tighten again, but he couldn't blame it on whiskey.

Brady had left Willow and the children alone with Lobo.

He didn't know what the gunfighter was up to, but it couldn't be any good.

He pushed his horse forward at a faster pace, ignoring Jupiter's unhappy pawing at the ground and balking.

Several hours later he reached the ranch. Wispy smoke, apparently from the old iron stove, curled lazily above the ranch house. It looked peaceful and serene. Brady turned his gaze toward the corral, searching for strange horses, and was surprised to see the fence newly repaired. He stared at it with apprehension.

His attention was suddenly diverted as Estelle and Sallie Sue came out on the porch, and then Chad. Chad's hand was heavily bandaged, and the look on his face was wary until he saw Jupiter. A smile broke out then.

Chad walked over to the corral and opened the gate. Brady led the bull inside and through a second gate, which would separate Jupiter from the horses. When Brady finished, he dismounted and joined Chad.

He unsaddled his horse, setting it across the top rail of the corral.

"Who fixed the corral?" he asked.

"Jess."

"Who's Jess?"

"The stranger. I was trying to fix it myself, but . . ." Chad looked down at his hand sheepishly.

"But?" Brady urged.

"But I dropped one of the posts on my hand, just when Jess came by. He went to fetch Dr. Sullivan, and then yesterday he fixed the corral." Hero worship was written all over the boy's face, and Brady felt sick. Hero worship for a gunslinger whose days were numbered! Well, he himself had certainly proved no example. Chad had had enough drunks in his life, and now the boy's expression was wary as he steadily returned Brady's gaze.

"Willow will be real pleased you found Jupiter," he said.

"Where is this . . . Jess, Chad?"

"I don't know. He just sorta comes and goes."

"He didn't say anything about who he is or where he's working?"

"I told you his name is Jess," Chad replied impatiently.

Brady wondered if he should tell the boy the truth. But Chad would never believe him or, if he did, he might want to be exactly like the gunfighter.

Maybe he was wrong. Maybe the whiskey had eaten into his brain. Maybe the man just reminded him of Lobo. God knew he was in no shape Saturday to make any kind of judgment.

He would wait and bide his time. He would make sure he was here next time "Jess" stopped by and find out exactly who and what the man was. His hand went to his gun, and he was ashamed to realize his fingers trembled. He saw Chad's eyes follow the movements, and the shame deepened.

How could he face a gunfighter with a hand that shook?

But he must. He knew he must. Or he would lose the last vestige of humanity he had.

Willow searched the hills all the way from town for the tall figure on a pinto horse. But all she saw was parched land and a sun too bright. With a numbing sense of disappointment Willow drove the buckboard through what was left of the gate; most of it had been destroyed to repair the corral. She immediately saw Jupiter and Brady's horse, and felt a sudden surge of relief.

She climbed down from the buckboard, leaving the twins to take care of the horses as they usually did. That particular task was something they enjoyed, filling them with a sense of pride and responsibility.

Brady was inside, looking like death warmed over, eating some bread and butter. His eyes were bloodshot, his face flushed. He was wearing the same clothes he'd worn at the time of the fire, since all of his other ones had been destroyed in the barn. They were filthy and torn, and still smelled of smoke as well as three days on the trail.

"Thank you for bringing Jupiter back," she said.

He forced tortured eyes to look directly into her own. "It was the least I could do. If you want me to leave . . . ?"

"Oh, no," she said. "You've helped us so much."

He groaned at that. He knew he should leave, but he couldn't, not now, when he suspected that their Jess could be Lobo. If she had asked him to leave, he would have stayed on the outskirts of the ranch and confronted the gunman there. He wouldn't blame Willow one iota if she wanted him gone.

"I'm sorry about the barn, Willow. So damned sorry."

Willow went over to him and put a hand on his shoulder. "It's done, Brady. It's over. There's nothing we can do but rebuild it. There's going to be a barn raising Saturday . . . if anyone comes. Alex apparently is warning everyone away. But Sullivan will be here, and Mr. MacIntyre and some others. We can use your help then."

"And this Jess?"

Willow stiffened at the hostility in Brady's voice.

"Chad told you he fixed the corral?"

Brady nodded.

"I—I offered him a job."

"And . . ."

"He turned it down, said he wouldn't be here very long, but I'm hoping . . ."

Don't hope, he wanted to tell her. But at the moment he

had no more right being there than her Jess did. Even if Jess was indeed Lobo, he hadn't done the damage that he, Brady, had inflicted on the ranch.

Yet.

"But don't think he would replace you," Willow hurried on, afraid he would misunderstand. "You're part of the family."

Brady thought of Estelle and himself. With the two of them, Willow sure didn't need any more family, especially a renegade white man who'd lived with Indians and was now a notorious gunman. What in the hell did he want anyway? What game was he playing?

"I would like to meet this Jess," he said cautiously. "Do you know where he might be?"

She shook her head.

"Or when he might return?"

"No," she said softly. "But I think he will."

Brady said nothing more. He would say nothing until he was sure of the man's identity and intentions.

Even if the knowledge killed him.

Ten

Marisa defiantly dressed in her riding skirts and ran down the steps. She heard her father call her name, but she didn't stop, although it hurt to hear the frustration in his voice. She continued out the door and to the barn.

They'd had the same argument all week, ever since she returned from the dance Saturday night, and the ranch foreman, Herb Edwards, told her father about the gunfight.

She was forbidden to go into town.

It was, she said, his own fault that the town was now dangerous. He was the one who started it all with his useless feud with Gar Morrow. And how could she respect him when he hired a gunslinger to run out a woman and children.

"She has no right to the place. I helped Jake keep it."

"She has every right. Jake willed it to her."

"He wasn't in his right mind."

Marisa sighed. "I visited him just before he died, and he was in as sound a mind as you . . . were." She emphasized the last word, and saw the anger gathering in his eyes.

"Papa," she whispered, "don't do this. Don't bloody this valley."

"You would let your mother's murderer go free and use land I helped settle."

"Your quarrel is with Mr. Morrow, not Willow," Marisa countered.

"And with anyone who gives him aid and comfort, and that includes that doctor you've been making eyes at. Well, don't you think I'll allow that either, young lady."

Marisa glared at him. She only wished there was something between Sullivan and herself, but that, she feared, would never happen. He had never asked her out, had never spoken more than friendly words. She had longed for more for a long time now. There was a quiet strength in him that she admired immensely, and she respected the fact that he was one of the few men who didn't kowtow to her father.

"You may not have anything to say about it," she returned angrily, letting him think there was more afoot than there was.

"He's helping that woman," Alex bellowed in rage.

"And I'm going to help her too," Marisa said. "She was the best teacher I've ever had, and she's always been kind to me, and I'm going to do anything I can to help her. I even asked that . . . gunman of yours to go away."

Alex stared at her in disbelief. "You did what?"

Marisa stuck her chin up. "I asked him to go away."

"You rode out alone and met him?"

"Yes, and he was very rude."

Alex swore, something he'd never done in front of his daughter before. "He didn't . . . ?"

"Ruin me?" Marisa's voice was a taunt. "And if he had? You brought him here."

"If he touched you . . ." The words ended in a choke as he tried to rise from the wheelchair.

"No, Papa," she replied quickly, suddenly frightened for him. "He didn't touch me. He just wouldn't listen."

Alex settled back in his chair. "Stay away from him."

"Stay away from him. Stay away from Willow. Stay away from Dr. Barkley. Stay away from town. You can't keep me a prisoner because of your own hatred." She spun around and ran upstairs, leaving Alex staring at the spot where she'd been standing.

She'd done what he had asked for the next few days, hoping she could change his mind. But each empty day deepened her loneliness, and each day she'd felt more and more that he was wrong, that hate and sorrow had twisted him from the man he once was into a stranger she didn't know and didn't like.

Marisa had never known why her father blamed Morrow for the death of her mother. She did know that her mother died on her way back from Morrow's ranch, killed by some renegade Indians. But it had always been Morrow whom her father blamed, not the Indians. She also knew her father was in a wheelchair because he forced a fight with Morrow not long after her mother's death. But she had never known why, and when she'd asked her father, he tightened his lips and turned away from her.

Now she was ready to outwardly disobey him for the first time in her life. He had always been indulgent with her, and denied her few things, and this new rigid attitude caused both rebellion and sadness in her. He had always been bigger than life to her, even in the wheelchair, and she had always coveted his approval. He had loved her, and she loved him very much. She barely remembered her mother; there were only soft images, and she no longer knew which were real and which were created out of need and longing. Her father had been her only parent most of her life, and he'd always been there with affection and love.

But now he was wrong and she'd spent many restless nights trying to reconcile the father she loved with the avenging man who would hire a gunman to chase a woman and children from the only home they knew.

Marisa had found in Willow Taylor a woman to admire, a woman she would like to emulate. Marisa had been half wild at seventeen when Willow Taylor came to town. School had been a sporadic thing, what with the coming and going of teachers, and Marisa had not been overly enthusiastic about the new one. But almost immediately there had been something compelling about the new teacher who'd treated her as a person of value, not a spoiled brat, which, Marisa had to admit, she'd often been. Miss Taylor lured her pupils into wanting to learn, to know more, to explore the adventures of knowledge. For the first time, history became exciting, numbers fascinating, geography important, the classics captivating. Willow had a habit of ending each day with a story that would continue the next, and the next, until the pupils would no more think of missing an episode than missing a special holiday.

For Marisa, Willow Taylor became all that she imagined her mother would have been. She'd come to admire the teacher even more when she flouted town opinion to take in Chad, and then Estelle. She'd wished she had that much conviction about something.

And now she did. Marisa was determined to be as strong as Willow Taylor.

She hurried to the barn and asked one of the hands to saddle her horse, telling him only that she was going for a ride on the ranch. But she was really going into town to talk to Sullivan. She wanted to find out if he knew more about her father's hatred toward Gar Morrow than she did, if there was anything either of them could do to stop the quarrel before it consumed everyone in Newton. And she wanted his calm, soothing presence. She wanted even more, but she doubted whether she could ever have it. Every time she looked into those gray eyes, she felt her legs grow weak, although Sullivan usually treated her more as a child than a woman—until the dance. His eyes had met hers when they danced, and there was warmth and longing in them. When he held her after the killing, she felt so safe and secure. She felt as though she belonged in his arms.

Her father was on the porch as she rode out, his hand gesturing to her to return, but she merely waved at him.

The main topic in town, she soon learned, was the barn raising at Miss Willow's ranch. After the second "tell your pa we won't be there," Marisa's blood started boiling.

"But I will," she told them sweetly, sending even more reverberations up and down the usually sedate town. "I hope to see you there."

She made her way down the street—to the dressmaker's, the lumber store, the gun shop—telling them all the same thing. She would look for them at the barn raising.

Behind her, tongues wagged in confusion, and little groups of people knotted on the streets, trying to decide what the latest development meant. While Marisa had some devil in her, she had always supported and defended her father. Did this mean that Alex had changed his mind?

When she finally reached the doctor's office, two townsmen, including Mayor August Stillwater, were already there, evidently consulting with Sullivan on the latest news. Their faces flushed when they saw her, and she said, "I'll see you tomorrow at the barn raising."

The mayor tipped his hat politely and nodded in a noncommittal way and escaped. So did his companion.

Sullivan leaned against his desk and grinned at her. "Starting a little trouble, Marisa?"

She raised innocent eyes to him. "I just want to help."

"Your 'help' is throwing the town into turmoil." He chuckled. "And I suspect you know that."

"Another town meeting?" She giggled. Although she hadn't attended any of the previous ones, she'd heard plenty, particularly how Dr. Sullivan Barkley had defied the entire town.

"Possibly," he allowed, his eyes crinkling with amusement.

Marisa thought how he had one of the nicest faces she'd ever seen. It wasn't anything like the gunfighter's face, which was too hard. Sullivan's gray eyes were smoky and at times even mysterious, but they also twinkled with wry humor. His mouth was wide and smiled easily, and though she knew the lines in his face were probably caused by his malaria, they looked more like laugh lines. There was so much character in that face, so much integrity, and yet there was also a small-boy's mischief. No one ever accused Sullivan of stuffiness, although they cursed his stubbornness.

She met his steady gaze, and she felt a flush climbing up her neck and spreading over her face. She longed to touch him, or have him touch her, but he seemed rooted where he was, one of his fists clenched in a tight ball.

"And what can I do for you, Marisa?" he finally said.

A great deal. A kiss would be a nice start. But she suppressed the words. "I want to help Willow," she blurted out.

Surprised, Sullivan studied her more carefully. He had always been attracted to Marisa, although she was much younger than he was. She had so much spirit, so much liveliness. A room brightened when she entered it. But he was thirty-six, nearly twice her age, and he had seen more death and destruction than anyone should. He had also caught malaria in Louisiana, and he was determined he'd never inflict the results of that disease on a wife. But now, as he looked at her, part of him wavered, the part where his heart resided.

He had not realized how much she had grown up. Her expressive brown eyes glowed as she returned his gaze. Her dark brown hair, almost black, was tied back with a blue ribbon that matched the color of her silk shirt. A dark brown riding skirt rode over slightly rounded hips, and slender ankles were encased in fine leather boots. Alex Newton never stinted when it came to his daughter, and Sullivan knew it must be difficult for her to go against her father.

"Are you sure you want to oppose your father in this? He may never forgive you."

"He's wrong," she said simply. "And I'm afraid for Willow. But if the whole town supports her, he'll have to leave her alone."

"I don't think so," Sullivan said. "It's gone too far now. He'll just hire more men."

"I've met one of them," she said, and Sullivan noted the slightest shaking of her shoulders, as if she were trying to shed fear.

"Who?" he replied sharply.

"The man they call Lobo."

Sullivan's face tightened. "Tell me about him."

"He's frightening and mean. He has the coldest eyes I've ever seen. I asked him to leave and he . . . sneered at me." Marisa shivered. Any illusions she'd had about gunslingers were destroyed Saturday night when one had so coldly killed her father's man.

Sullivan saw her eyes cloud and knew she was remember-ing the killing at the dance. He couldn't restrain himself any longer. He held out his arms, and Marisa went into them, her body still trembling with memories.

He held her tightly, his hand soothing the hair that smelled like flowers. The trembling stopped, and then she turned her eyes up to him, a tear hovering in one corner. He knew he shouldn't, but he couldn't resist catching the tear with his lips. Then his mouth moved downward, nuzzling soft white skin until their lips met.

There was an instant conflagration, and the kiss erupted into blue-hot splendor. First gentle, his lips caressed and explored, but then grew more demanding as she responded, her body inching closer to his. He had wanted this for so long, and now he knew she wanted it too. Denial had only served to build the pressure and need until he felt like a bottle ready to explode.

She opened her mouth instinctively, invitingly, and his tongue entered, probing sensitive nerves until her trembling started again from an altogether different cause. Sullivan's arms went tighter around her, wanting, needing, craving the warmth she offered. It had been a long time since he'd felt this kind of belonging, this kind of gentle yet fierce heat.

But Marisa deserved more than a man who never knew when the malaria would strike next, who needed to be cared for like a child during those sieges, who may not live a full life. She deserved much more.

With a groan of agony he moved away from her, his gaze finding her passion-flecked eyes and wonder-filled face. Fear slowly replaced the wonder as she saw the sudden denial in his eyes, in his face.

"Sullivan," she whispered. "Don't go away from me."

"It won't work, Marisa," Sullivan said slowly. "I have noth-ing to offer you."

"I don't want anything but you."

"I'm damaged, Marisa. I have an illness that won't ever go away. I won't inflict that on you."

"It doesn't matter," she replied desperately.

"But it does. To me it does. I don't ever want you to see me that way."

"But . . . I . . ." She wanted to say she loved him, but her pride prevented it.

He took her chin and cupped it. "I'm a great deal older than you are, Marisa, and I've seen things that no man ever should." He paused for a moment, then continued. "Your father would never approve, and no matter how you feel now, you would regret the loss of him."

"Must you always be so noble," she said, suddenly furious with him. None of his reasons meant anything now, not after that heart-shattering kiss, not after the expression in his face that made her believe that he possibly loved her too.

Sullivan tried to smile, but he feared it was more a grimace. "I thought it was reason, not nobility."

"It's not reason at all," she retorted. "It's excuses. You're just hiding behind them."

Sullivan was silent, wondering whether she was right. Perhaps he had been hiding ever since his family and fiancée were killed during the war. But it was a self-imposed exile he wasn't sure he could break.

"Then there's all the more reason for you to stay away from me, Marisa. You need someone who can give you a whole heart."

There was a finality in his words that frightened her.

"I don't give up easily," she said.

He smiled for the first time since the kiss. "I know you don't."

She hesitated a moment, then decided it best to leave and concoct a new plan of attack. "You'll be at the barn raising?"

He nodded.

"Me too." She grinned. "I'm even going to make some chicken."

His eyebrows rose in surprise.

"I'm quite a good cook," she added, the light of combat in her eyes.

"I imagine you're good at a great many things," he said.

"You'll find out just how many," she said impishly, and then rushed out the door before he could say anything more.

It wasn't until she was halfway back to the ranch that she remembered she'd meant to ask him more about the feud between her father and Gar Morrow.

There was, as Marisa guessed, indeed a gathering of the good folks of Newton that evening. It wasn't exactly a town meeting, for the organizers did not want certain people to attend.

It was, instead, a poker game in Bob MacIntyre's general store.

Mayor Stillwater was there, along with the Reverend Massey, banker Amos Folley, Sheriff Carrol Posey, Bob MacIntyre, Dr. Sullivan Barkley, and the gunsmith, Al Lewis.

Al Lewis was all for leaving things alone. His business had increased tenfold in the past two weeks.

His opinion was ignored by all but the reverend, who sent him a glare that promised heavenly retribution someday. And then the good man focused his attention back on the two pairs in his hand.

"We have to make some kind of decision," the mayor said as he asked for two cards. "Are we or are we not going to help Miss Willow?"

"Three dollars to stay in," the banker said, and the money was promptly produced by four of the seven players. Sullivan, Al Lewis, and the mayor dropped out with moans of disgust.

"Raise you another dollar," the reverend said, adding, "It's the Christian thing to do."

"But is it the wise thing to do?" Folley chimed in. "Mr. Newton, after all, is the biggest man in the territory."

"Newton's own daughter is coming," Sullivan interjected.

"That's what I heard. Raise you again," MacIntyre stated. "Wonder what old Alex thinks about that."

"Girl always was independent."

"Gotta give it to her, takes spunk to stand up to Alex," the gunsmith said. "Wish more of this town had some."

"So you could sell more guns and ammunition," Stillwater charged. "You'd be happy if we had a gunfight every day."

"Be mighty interestin', bring more people here," Lewis retorted mildly. "More business for us all."

"I raise another dollar and call," the reverend said as he cast another baleful look at the gunsmith. "Most people just want our peaceful little town back."

"Full house," MacIntyre said.

A disgusted reverend threw his cards in.

"Your deal, Sully," the mayor reminded Sullivan.

"We still haven't decided what to do."

"I promised my wife I'd go. Miss Willow's done a lot for my boy," MacIntyre said bravely. "I sure as hell won't let Alex scare me out of doing what's right."

Silence greeted that line of thought.

"What about you, Sully?"

"You know the way I feel about it," Sullivan said. "It's our town, not Alex's or Gar Morrow's, dammit. Now, who's got the guts to go, to do what's right?"

"Give me three cards," Lewis said. "I gotta keep my shop open Saturday, lots of business. So I can't come."

August Stillwater grumped. Al Lewis had run for mayor against him, had almost beaten him. If Lewis wasn't going, well, he'd show the town Mayor Stillwater had some backbone.

"Count me in," August said.

"Good for you," Sullivan said. "Sheriff?"

"Well . . . mebbe I should just kinda keep an eye on things here. . . ."

"Reverend?"

"Well, if Miss Newton's going, I suppose her pa can't be too unhappy. He's a big contributor to the church, you know."

"Cecil, don't temporize. The Lord won't like it." Sullivan chuckled as the reverend looked offended.

"I said I would go," he sputtered.

"Amos?"

"Can't take sides. Hurt the bank, and that would hurt the town," the banker said self-righteously.

"What should we tell the other folks should they ask?" This came from a still-nervous August.

"Follow their conscience," the reverend said reverently.

"Cockfeathers," MacIntyre muttered.

"I call," Sullivan said.

"Call what?"

"The hand, you idiot," MacIntyre told the sheriff.

"Well, I can't figure out iffen we're talking about the game or Miss Willow."

"Three kings," Sullivan crowed.

"Got me beat."

"Me too."

"So we're all agreed."

"On what?"

"That we'll all follow our conscience."

"Hell, that's no agreement."

"Well, it's the best we can do," August said. "And I'm cleaned out. Mrs. Stillwater will be madder than a wet hen."

"Tell her it's your mayoral duty."

"I tried that before."

"So MacIntyre, the reverend, August, and myself will go to the barn raising," Sullivan said, trying to bring the important issue back into the disjointed conversation.

"Yep," MacIntyre said disdainfully. "The others can hide from old Alex."

"And his hired gun. Don't forget him," Al Lewis interjected, and the conversation quieted somewhat.

"Anyone seen him yet?"

"Naw. Maybe old Alex's just talking."

Sullivan kept his mouth quiet. Better they think that. Better for the barn raising in the morning.

On that note the divided group of town fathers gathered their winnings, mourned their losses, and departed.

Eleven

On Saturday Lobo watched as the wagons wended their way to the Taylor ranch from the hill overlooking the trail.

There weren't enough, he thought. Not nearly enough to do the job. But there were more than he had anticipated.

He'd made another venture into town the day before and had bought bacon, coffee, and flour. He'd ignored the questions directed at him.

Lobo had heard all the news in those few minutes at the mercantile. Everyone in town was wondering who would cross Alex Newton and go to the barn raising. He'd even heard the wriggling tongues say Newton's daughter was going to openly defy him. That was surprising news.

She had even more gumption than he'd thought. He'd been sure only morbid curiosity had brought her to him that day last week, but apparently she really did care about Willow Taylor. A number of people cared enough to risk their lives about Willow Taylor.

Only briefly did he wonder how it would feel to be liked enough that people would risk their lives and livelihoods for you. But he quickly dismissed the thought as both stupid and indulgent. It was far better, he knew, not to have to depend on others for anything, better to be completely self-reliant, to live free of obligations or responsibilities.

He bit off a curse and turned toward his camp. His hands were almost fit again. He didn't know exactly why he continued to stay. He had failed, and now he could never convince the woman to leave, especially with a new barn going up.

He knew Newton was hiring additional guns. He had seen them on the ranch and in town. There was no mistaking the breed, not if you were one of them.

And the Taylor brood was sitting there like a bunch of lambs surrounded by wolves. Damn him, but he had apparently discovered a secret but powerful partiality to lambs.

Lobo didn't particularly understand his sudden protective instincts, and he liked them even less. But they were undeniable and compelling as well as damned confusing.

He watched the last of the wagons pass, noticing the doctor at the rear, and he felt a mean jealousy constricting his insides. He had heard the doctor had taken Willow Taylor to the dance. The desperate pain he'd felt at the knowledge was new to him, and he didn't like it either.

Hell, if he had any sense, he would leave now. He sat in the saddle, watching the last of the dust settle, and he made his decision. He would visit Alex Newton that afternoon, make sure the rancher understood that nothing had better happen to the woman or her kids, or he, Lobo, would return and make Alex pay. He would then ride out in the morning, put this place and all his confusing unwanted emotions behind him for good.

By noon the laborers had produced a skeleton of a barn. Willow had made an enormous bucket of lemonade and dispensed it generously as she watched, in amazement, the speed of the work.

Willow was surprised that so many men had showed, twenty at least, in light of Newton's threats. Marisa had also come with a basket of chicken, which she added to the pile of food brought by other women. She had then pitched in to carry nails, hand hammers to men on ladders, take out water or lemonade and anything else that was required.

Sullivan walked over to Willow, and as his eyes followed Marisa's swishing form, he said he didn't think they would finish today, but another Saturday and they would have a fine barn, perhaps not as large as before, but large enough for Willow's current needs.

Willow smiled, but her eyes were searching the horizon. A hollowness echoed inside her when she didn't see a tall figure on a pinto. For some reason she had expected him to be there.

Perhaps it had just been wishful thinking.

Willow saw Brady scanning the surrounding fields and hills also. He'd been very quiet since he'd returned. He'd declined to sleep in the boys' room but slept outside, and Willow hadn't missed the fact that his gun stayed strapped on his waist for the first time since he'd come to stay with them.

Even Estelle had seemed anxious. She frequently glanced out the window as she busied herself in the kitchen, her eyes searching the gate. Willow knew that she, too, was looking for their stranger.

But try as she might, Willow couldn't tempt Estelle outside. "It wouldn't be right," Estelle said. "They're good folk."

"You're as good as any of them," Willow retorted, but Estelle only shrunk back and shook her head, and Willow knew she would cause more pain if she pushed the subject.

Chad, too, kept looking. More than once he approached Willow. "You think he'll come?"

"I don't know," she replied, again looking toward the horizon.

Even Sallie Sue joined the chorus. "Where'th Jeth?"

Brady came over for a drink of water, overheard the exchange, and scowled deeply. But before Willow could ask him why, he turned abruptly and returned to work, handing lumber up to a man on a ladder. He had tried hammering, but his hands weren't steady enough.

Willow looked at him thoughtfully and wondered why he seemed so wary. Every time she mentioned the stranger, his eyes became cold and his face aloof. Willow wondered whether he felt slighted or hurt, or even embarrassed because he hadn't been there when help had been needed. Whatever it was, Brady had become more wary and taciturn than usual, and it worried her.

By dusk the barn was framed and roofed, and they all promised to return the next Saturday to complete the interior and loft and doors. It was much more than Willow had expected, and even though her stranger hadn't appeared, she felt a quiet contentment and joy that so many people had helped.

Willow asked Marisa and Sullivan to stay for dinner. They had more than enough food left over, and she didn't want it to go to waste, she said.

Sullivan looked at Marisa. There was a new and tender expression in his face, Willow thought.

"Will you?" he asked Marisa.

Marisa looked directly into his eyes. "Yes," she said simply.

"What about your father?" Sullivan asked.

Marisa bit her lip. "I helped the cook make the chicken for dinner last night, and added a few pieces for a 'picnic' today. Then I left the house before dawn." She smiled, but it was a small, nervous smile. "I left a note telling Papa where I would be, and invited him to help. I didn't think he would send for me, not with so many people here. He knows I'd would refuse to go, and he'd be embarrassed."

"And when you get home?"

"There will be a grand fight." Despite the light manner with which she said the words, there was a current of sorrow in them.

"I'll take you," Sullivan said.

"No, that would just make it worse." She bit her lip. "He's wrong this time, and I have to make him see that."

"I don't know if anyone can do that."

"I can try," she said.

"And this gunfighter?"

"I haven't seen him for several days, but I know Papa's fuming about him."

"Why?"

She shrugged.

"But you haven't seen him anymore?"

"No, he's like a shadow. You know he's there, but every time you turn to look he's gone."

Sullivan looked at Willow, who was listening. "Just like Willow's stranger."

Marisa looked puzzled.

"It seems Willow has a mysterious guardian angel, and when anything goes wrong, he just seems to appear. Then he disappears."

Marisa turned to Willow with a gleeful look. "A beau?"

Willow flushed right down to her toes. "He's apparently a drifter. He . . . just happened along. . . ."

"And saved Sallie Sue from the well, and Chad from a bull, and Brady from the barn fire," Sullivan said with a grin.

"Tell me more," said Marisa, enraptured.

"He can make a horse do anything," Chad contributed.

"I like him," Sallie Sue chirped.

"His name is Jess," Willow said. "That's about all I know about him. Except he's been very kind."

Marisa cocked her head. "What does he look like? Maybe he works for Papa."

"I doubt that," Sullivan said. "All your father's men know exactly how he feels about this ranch."

Estelle appeared then, turning her head slightly so her bad eye didn't show to Marisa. "Supper's ready," she said.

Only one extra place had been added to the big round table, and Willow looked at Estelle questioningly.

"Oh, I'm not hungry," Estelle said, ready to flee the room.

Willow and Sullivan exchanged glances. It was Marisa, not lack of appetite that bothered Estelle, who still felt more than a little unworthy of the "good folk."

Marisa found herself looking from one to another, and comprehension slowly dawned. "It's because I'm a Newton," she said. "You don't want to sit with the daughter of the man who's causing so much trouble."

"Oh, no, Miss," Estelle said, horrified. "You . . . you're . . . more than welcome. I just didn't think . . . you . . . I —I mean I . . ."

Sullivan wanted to kiss Marisa just then. There was nothing she could have said that would have disarmed Estelle so quickly. She knew what an outcast was.

"Then you'll join us?" Marisa said gently.

"I . . . well . . . there's no room."

Chad rose from his chair gallantly. "You can have my chair. I'll go out and eat with Brady."

Only then did everyone else realize that Brady was not with them. Willow went to the door and saw Brady sawing timber. Willow wanted to call him, but she knew how bad he felt about the barn. This was his way of trying to compensate.

Supper was a rather subdued affair. The mysterious stranger was not mentioned again, as Sullivan and Marisa found each other of much greater interest and Estelle continually fluttered up and down in confused helpfulness. The twins carried much of the conversation, competing with each other over who had been the most valuable during the day. Sallie Sue took several bites of food, then her chin sleepily sunk down to her chest, giving Estelle an excuse to leave.

Marisa watched as the former saloon girl gently picked up the child, whispering softly to her as she took her into the bedroom.

"She seems so good with Sallie Sue."

"She is," Sullivan said, his hand finding hers under the table. "You're quite surprising yourself."

Marisa turned big inquisitive eyes his way. "You must have had a very sorry opinion of me."

"No," he said. "I just—"

"Thought I was young and spoiled," she finished for him. "And I am. I usually get what I want." There was a very definite implication in her tone, but then she grinned impishly. "And I think Estelle is very nice."

"Do you?" Sullivan said.

"Think Estelle is nice or get what I want?"

"Get what you want."

"I'll tell you very soon," she said. "And now I think I'd better go, or the whole Newton army will be over here."

"I'll see you to the gate of your ranch, at least," Sullivan said.

"In your buggy? What about my mare?"

"I'll tie her to the back."

She looked at him, and he looked at her, and Willow knew she could be a million miles away for all that she was noticed.

"That sounds like a wonderful idea, Doctor. But I'll help Willow clean up first."

Willow shook her head. "No, I think I'd rather not have your army over here. Estelle and I will take care of it. You two go."

Marisa looked at Sullivan in question, and he nodded, rising.

"Thank you," Willow said. "Thank you both."

She watched as the two left. Sullivan tied Marisa's horse to the buggy, and there was something very gentle in the way he handed her up. Again Willow felt the yearning that had haunted her lately. Something inside hurt and longed and wanted in ways she'd never felt before. She tried to smile as they waved to her, but her smile wobbled precariously on her lips. She wondered if anyone would ever touch her like that.

She wondered if Jess would ever touch her like that.

Where was he?

"You want me to do what?" It seemed to Lobo he kept repeating the same words in Alex Newton's presence.

"Burn that goddamn barn down."

"Hell, no."

"If you don't, then someone else will."

"If you touch that place . . ."

Lobo let the implied threat linger unsaid in the room. He didn't need to spell it out.

"I heard you were tough. That damned woman's gotten to you."

"I don't make war on women and children. I told you that in the beginning."

"You said you could get them off."

"I was wrong. She's not going to budge an inch off that ranch, and you know it. You lied to me from the beginning.

Told me just my presence would scare her off. Well, it didn't."
The last was said a little smugly.

"I didn't ask you to be their guardian."

Lobo and Newton glared at each other.

"I'm warning you, Newton, leave them alone."

"That barn's going to burn."

"Even your daughter was there," Lobo taunted. "What are you going to do to her?"

Newton's face went white. He had indeed thought about sending his foreman and others to fetch Marisa, but he knew she wouldn't come easily and he would be the laughingstock of the territory. Better to treat it as a young one's lark, and accomplish his task another way. But all the same, Marisa's action only hardened his resolve. She would learn not to back him into a corner. "That's none of your business, Lobo. You're through here now. Get the hell out."

"Not yet," Lobo growled.

"What do you mean?"

"Like I said, I don't want anything happening to that woman and those kids." As he said it, he realized he'd just ventured into unknown terrain. The moment Alex had said he would burn Willow out, Lobo knew he couldn't leave no matter what he'd decided earlier.

"Turning gallant? I've heard talk of her 'mysterious do-gooder.'" Alex laughed, the harsh, bitter laugh of a man who seldom truly smiled. "The lobo? The wolf? Does she know who you are?"

Lobo's fingers tightened into fists behind his back, but his eyes didn't change. "I don't want anything happening to them," he repeated in a tone full of menace.

Alex suddenly regretted his bravado. Hell, now he had to get rid of Lobo. When Willow Taylor found out who he was, she'd send him on his way. Alex just had to make sure she found out quickly. Then his newly hired guns would do what should have been done in the beginning—burn the Taylor woman out.

Lobo watched the change in Newton's eyes, the rage turn to cunning. He threw Alex's two thousand dollars down on a nearby table. If he'd decided to ride off, he would have taken it, but now he was changing sides, and his particular code dictated the return of money.

"If you come after her, you'll find me, Newton."

"You think she's going to want you when she finds out who you are?"

Lobo shrugged. "Makes no difference. It'll be between you and me."

"Even you can't stand up to twenty-five guns."

"Maybe not, but they'll have to go through me first. Want to choose the first one who'll face me, or are you going to let them pick lots?" Lobo grinned again, and Alex realized exactly what he'd unleashed.

"Get out of here," he demanded. "And off my land."

"Yes, sir," Lobo said mockingly, and turned. He heard the sound of a drawer opening, a sound so slight that most men wouldn't have heard, and he whirled around, his Colt Peacemaker in his hand.

"You wouldn't happen to have a gun in there, would you?" he said gently.

Alex's face turned pasty, and sweat gathered around his brow as his gaze darted down to the drawer.

Lobo strode over and looked into the drawer, where a pistol lay. He looked at it curiously, as if it were a child's unusual toy. "That wasn't very smart, Mr. Newton."

He picked up the gun and strode over to the table where he reached for the two thousand dollars. "That little move is going to cost you."

Without another word he walked out of the room, leaving Alex grateful that this particular misjudgment had cost him only money.

Lobo decided to stay where he'd been camping that night. He'd move into town in the morning; let Alex Newton know he was still around. He didn't think Newton would try anything that night, not the way his eyes looked when Lobo held the gun on him.

And then? He didn't know what then. The next move was Alex's, and Willow's.

He knew she had turned down Gar Morrow's offer of Canton. Would she also turn down his help? When she knew who and what he really was?

Like that girl in Prescott, Arizona, when she'd found out he'd been with the Apaches . . .

He'd been at Fort Verde, carried there bound hand and foot, for four weeks while his wounds were tended. The sound of English gradually brought back the language to him, and though he offered little information to questioning officers, he'd finally been released once they were satisfied he would not return to the Apaches.

Lobo had been uncertain about who and what he was then. It was 1867, and it was already clear to him that the Apache's way of life was doomed; there were too many soldiers, too many whites pouring into the area. He felt no emotion about that one way or another. He had been their prisoner and in order to survive had become one of them, and now in order to survive he would have to become a white man again. Survival—that was all that counted.

Once released by the army, he explored his new world. His long hair was cut, and he forced himself into heavy whiteman's clothing. He was offered a job as scout for the army, but he'd turned it down. While he held little affection for his former captors, neither did he wish to help destroy them. The army had given him a small sum of money, but he had no experience with paper money, and was soon cheated by a gunsmith. A helpful soldier who was fascinated by the White Apache explained to Lobo that he had paid twice the price. Lobo made a second visit to the store, and very carefully offered several options to the gunsmith. His money was returned, and the gunsmith told him to keep the gun, free of charge.

Lobo had learned then what the Apache had always believed. Whites cheated. The Apache had a brutal but honest code of conduct; whites did not. It was a lesson Lobo never forgot. As a result, he usually explained options prior to a transaction. It saved a great deal of trouble later.

He was in his mid-twenties when he left the Apache, and he'd had little experience with women. He had used women slaves as other warriors had, but he avoided Apache women and a permanent Apache union, though he couldn't explain why. So he was unused to the niceties of courtship when he left Fort Verde to strike out on his own.

In Prescott he'd found a job as horse wrangler for a stable owner who bought wild horses. He'd quickly been attracted to the daughter of his employer, a lovely young girl with dark brown hair and brown eyes. Her name was Laura, which he thought very pretty, and her eyes had filled with admiration as she watched him break the wild ponies.

They took walks at first, and then short rides, both with her father's approval. He was invited to dinner; he'd learned acceptable manners from his time at Fort Verde. He hid the fact he could neither read nor write, studying for hours a signature of the name John Smith until he could copy it perfectly. It was the handle he used then, and still used, when the name Lobo wasn't convenient.

But then a discharged soldier came into Prescott, saw him and told the stable owner that John Smith was really the White Apache, that he had lived with the Apache, had burned and killed with them.

Lobo had watched the girl's eyes fill with horror and then loathing. The Apaches were well hated in the area. He had been fired that day and told he'd be shot on sight if he showed up again.

He'd thought about killing the stable owner and the soldier, but he'd seen similar loathing and terror in the eyes of others within hearing range. He couldn't kill everyone. But he'd learned another lesson that day. He was neither white nor Apache, and would never belong in either world. His was a world alone, and from then on the only rules he would observe would be his own.

But then he'd come to Newton, and in a matter of days he'd glimpsed a different kind of world, a different kind of life, and part of him yearned to taste it. But always a wary voice in the back of his mind warned that this time would be no different than Prescott. *She'll despise you when she discovers who you are.* She and the boy and the little girl. White Indian. White Apache. To many, there was no worse curse.

The tension in his body was communicated to his pinto, and the horse responded with nervous steps. Lobo leaned over and whispered in its ears, and the horse lengthened its stride until they were both racing from the past.

Sullivan and Marisa saw the horse and rider gallop through the gates of the Newton ranch, and both exclaimed almost at the same moment.

"What in the hell is *he* doing here?"

"What's Papa up to this time?"

They both stared at each other.

"You know him?" Sullivan asked, incredulous.

"Do you?" Marisa returned.

"That's Jess. Willow's stranger."

Marisa paled in the moonlight.

"That's also Lobo," she said slowly, "the man Papa hired to drive Willow off the ranch."

Twelve

Lobo saw the buggy and cursed when he recognized both the doctor and Newton's daughter.

He wanted to be the one to tell Willow Taylor who he was. Painful as it might be, he owed that much to her. And he had to judge her reaction for himself. It was, he knew, the only way he would ever be able to get her out of his mind and soul.

Her horror should accomplish that fast enough.

Lobo turned his horse toward the Taylor ranch. The house was some four miles distant. He slowed the pinto to a trot and moved cautiously but steadily across the rolling plain. He saw other riders, cowpokes coming in from a day's work, checking on the various herds grazing on the rich Colorado grass. There were no fences in the area, not yet, although there was talk of such.

Usually cattle of several ranchers mixed together, recognizable only by the brand and separated in the spring and fall at branding and roundup time. But because of the bad feelings between Newton and Morrow, the two ranchers kept their stock separated, a never-ending task, requiring nearly twice as many hands as usually required. Newton killed Morrow cattle on Newton land, and as a result Morrow killed Newton cattle found on his range.

Lobo considered the feud stupid and unproductive, but it was such arguments that kept him employed.

He was virtually ignored by the Newton hands, who knew a number of gun hands had been recently hired. Some of the old hands were, in fact, thinking about leaving. They didn't want to be caught in a crossfire. It wasn't their battle.

The day had passed into velvet darkness lit by a moon that was nearly full. The evening was cool, unlike the day, which had been blistering hot, and Lobo tried to enjoy the night, as he usually did. The night had always been his escape, a time that wore easiest on him. But it didn't now.

He kept seeing her face. And he imagined her disappointment and disgust when he'd tell her exactly who and what he was. But he no longer had a choice.

Yes, you do, argued a persistent voice from deep within. *You can just ride away . . . as you should have done in the beginning.*

But he kept seeing Newton's face and knew the rancher would stop at little now to get his way.

He saw the house, dark except for one brightly lit window, and then the barn. He was surprised at how much had been accomplished that day, and he wanted to kill Newton for suggesting the barn be burned. There was so much hope in that building.

As he approached the corral, a man appeared from within the new structure, a hammer in his fist.

Brady Thomas! So he had returned. Lobo's gaze went to the corral and he saw the bull there. Perhaps Thomas wasn't as useless as he appeared.

The man walked toward him as Lobo slowed his horse to a walk.

"You're Lobo," the man said. It was not a question but a statement.

Lobo said nothing, just looked at him. The silence was answer enough.

"What do you want here?"

"That's none of your business."

"But it is."

"Protectin' them now? After burnin' down their barn?"

Even in the soft glow of moonlight Lobo saw the man flush as he moved the hammer to his other hand and rested his right hand on his gun. Lobo could see it tremble.

"I asked you before, what do you want?"

Lobo slid down from his horse, not even bothering to keep his eyes on the ex-sheriff. The insult was deliberate and obvious.

"Damn you," Brady Thomas said.

Lobo continued to ignore him and walked his horse to a hitching post, where he tied the reins.

"Lobo!"

Lobo didn't turn around but continued toward the porch.

"Stop, or so help me I'll shoot you in the back!"

Lobo turned around then, and the two men were face-to-face, inches apart.

"I don't think you will," Lobo said in a soft drawl. "You don't have the guts anymore." His eyes raked over Brady with contempt. "Go climb back in that bottle."

Brady's right hand clenched and unclenched near his gun. "What do you want with her?"

"That's between her and me."

The ex-sheriff straightened his shoulders, and determination flitted across his face. But the image was ruined by the hand which, though not trembling as badly as a moment earlier, was still shaking.

A moment of unfamiliar pity struck Lobo. This had once been a strong man. Chrissakes, what happened to him?

"Why do you think I'm Lobo?"

"Fort Worth. I saw you there six years ago."

Lobo raised an eyebrow in surprise. "Six years?" He was surprised the man remembered.

"You were pointed out to me."

"Was I?" Lobo said in an amused tone. "Should I be flattered?"

"No," Brady said flatly. "All the mad dogs were."

Lobo grinned, but it was more like a wolf's baring of teeth.

"You thinkin' to get yourself one now?" His gaze was contemptuous as it went down to Brady's gun.

"Why are you here?" Brady said, trying to make his voice authoritative, but knowing he failed miserably.

Lobo waited several seconds, just long enough to show how little the question meant to him.

"Damn you," Brady Thomas whispered, and once again Lobo felt a certain sympathy. Whatever else Brady Thomas was now, it wasn't a coward.

"Have you told her who I am?" Lobo said abruptly.

"No," Brady said.

"Why?"

"I wasn't sure until you rode up."

"And now you are?"

"I remember that pinto and your eyes."

"And you're ready to face me with a shaky hand?"

Brady flinched. "At least she'd know who and what you are, *Jess.*" The statement was a devastating blow. Lobo wondered if the ex-lawman knew how powerful the strike was.

"That's why I'm here," he said easily, his eyes revealing nothing. "To tell her."

"Why?"

"Why?" Lobo shrugged. "Because it's time."

"God damn you. I'm tired of your riddles."

Lobo turned his back on Brady and started up the stairs just as the door opened. Willow was silhouetted in the doorway. "I heard voices," she started to say to Brady, and then saw Lobo standing in the shadows. "Jess!"

There was a silence. Lobo challenged his opponent with that silence, and Brady knew it. Yet Brady couldn't say anything, not when he heard the sudden delight in Willow's voice. He'd never heard it before, and the sound stilled him.

"I knew you would be back," Willow said, so unabashedly happy that neither man could speak.

Even Lobo was unsure of himself. She wore a light blue night robe, and her hair hung freely down her back. Her eyes shone in the moonlight, almost as bright as the stars overhead. His throat constricted. The next few moments would be the worse torture he'd ever suffered.

"I have to talk to you," Lobo said quietly, ignoring the man next to him.

"Of course," she said.

Brady growled in his ear, "If you hurt her . . ."

Lobo ignored him and started up the steps, leaving Brady frustrated and uncertain when Lobo closed the door in his face.

There was something about the gunman that surprised Brady, though he couldn't say exactly what. But for some reason he didn't feel that Willow was in danger at that particular moment. He satisfied himself by sitting on the porch steps within hearing distance of any outcry.

Once inside, Lobo looked around. "The kids?"

"All in bed. It was a busy day." Her smile was even grander, like a sunrise, Lobo thought. Full of hope and innocence.

His tight lips didn't relax. "I noticed."

"I didn't think so many would come," she said, suddenly very nervous. He'd always looked hard and unyielding, but never as much as now. His eyes were incredibly brilliant, but they said so little.

"You aren't going to leave here, are you, no matter what anyone threatens or does?"

Willow didn't care for the frightening intensity in his voice. "Jess—"

Now was the time, Lobo thought. Now. "That's one of my names, Miss Taylor."

"One . . . of . . . ?"

"The other is Lobo." He knew nothing outward showed the tension that made his insides rigid with expectation. He knew he must look relaxed with his legs spread apart and his hands at ease at his sides.

"Lobo?" she repeated, dazed.

"I was hired to drive you away from here," he said evenly, expecting an explosion of tears and outrage. And some fear anyway. There was always fear.

A moment's silence passed as he watched her digest his announcement. Then, unexpectedly, the corners of her mouth turned up. "Are you usually better at your work than you've been here?" Despite the twitching lips, the question was posed quite seriously, as if she were really curious.

Much to his consternation, Lobo felt the sides of his own mouth quirking up. "Usually," he said just as seriously, though a touch of humor warmed his eyes.

They both stood there, once more caught up in a whirlpool of something neither understood, carried along by the swirling, compelling currents that battered all reason, that pulled them together until nothing existed but the irresistible attraction between them.

Willow felt the touch of his hand against her neck, the fingers almost reverent against her skin, and the sensation was warm and tender beyond anything she'd ever imagined.

Her breath was gone, caught someplace between her heart and her throat, as she looked up into the incredible turquoise of his eyes. They weren't cold and empty now, but raging with confusion and want and need, emotions she knew were mirrored in her own face.

Tentatively, almost fearfully, she lifted her hand, tracing the mouth that was so severe, so joyless, and moved up to his eyes, tracking the lines that spread outward. Pain lines. Not laugh lines. She almost cried as she sensed the hurt he had endured.

Her gaze met his, and she trembled with the knowledge that she was knocking at a room full of secrets and hidden dangers.

But she didn't care. The warmth from his hand drifted down to her insides, causing small tremors and explosions in the strangest of places. She lifted her face in invitation, and his mouth touched hers.

His lips were smooth and strong, yet so gentle to belong to such a strong man. His kiss was tentative, almost as if he were kissing the wind, an illusion that would disappear.

That disbelieving wonderment stretched between them, arousing so many new, frightening, demanding feelings that neither dared to explore.

For the moment the kiss was enough. It bound them together more completely than any rope, any chain. His fingers moved from her neck up to her cheek, each touch posing a question that she answered with her eyes, as if words might shatter the incredible fragility surrounding them.

She felt the restrained passion and power and strength in his deliberate, gentle touches and in the rigidity of his body, and something intuitive in her told her not to rush him, although she wanted more than anything to feel the full force of his arms around her, the completeness of an embrace.

Willow was afraid to say anything, even his name, although it took every ounce of self-control not to do so. She watched his eyes close, as if in pain, and open again as his lips became harder on hers.

She trembled and opened her mouth. His lips moved hungrily against hers, as if seeking something. . . .

Just as her very senses spiraled out of control, she heard him groan. Suddenly his mouth was gone from hers, and he was gazing down at her with such intensity that she felt she would catch on fire.

His hand caught a curl and touched it, reveling in its feel before he dropped it.

"I didn't mean that to happen," he said in a harsh voice, his face marked with anger. "Chrissakes, you don't know what you're doing," he spat out. "I don't know what *I'm* doing."

He stepped back, shaking his head at his own folly, and paced back and forth across the room like a caged animal. "Didn't you hear what I said? I'm Lobo. I'm your enemy, lady. Don't you understand that?"

Willow felt the return of the giant lump in her throat. They were back to "lady" again. Her hand reached out, wanting desperately to touch him again, to share again that moment of belonging and . . . enchantment. But it fell to her side when he made no effort to approach her again. Instead, some unintelligible, guttural sound came from his mouth. She could only imagine its meaning.

She waited until he stopped pacing and turned back to her. The perplexity on his face made him look vulnerable, exposed, and angry. She could feel his anger radiating throughout the room.

"Then," she replied in as common-sense a tone as she could manage, "why did you help us so many times?"

"Have you thought it just might be to gain your trust?"

"Like the . . . Trojan horse?"

"The what?" Exasperation deepened his voice into something like a growl.

"The Trojan horse," she said. "It's an old myth. A Greek army laid siege to a city with defenses so strong it couldn't be taken by force. So the Greeks offered a gift, a giant wooden horse, which was accepted and pulled into the city. But the givers had filled the wooden horse with armed men, and at night, when the city was sleeping, they emerged from the wooden horse and attacked, taking the city. There's a saying, 'Beware of Greeks bearing gifts.' "

The corner of his mouth moved slightly. "Yeah," he said finally. "Something like that."

"But the Greeks didn't warn their victims." He scowled at her irrefutable logic, and Willow couldn't stop the small victorious smile that curved her lips.

Just then they heard the sound of a buggy outside, followed by a pounding on the door.

She looked at Jess.

"The sawbones," he guessed aloud.

Willow looked perplexed as she went to the door and opened it to Sullivan. He looked at her as if to assure himself she was all right, and then his gaze went to the man standing relaxed in the kitchen.

"Lobo?"

He leaned lazily against a wall and nodded.

Sullivan's gaze went back to Willow. "Are you all right?"

"Of course," she said, as if entertaining a notorious gunslinger who had been hired to get rid of her was an everyday occurrence.

"Do you know who he is?"

She nodded, her eyes going from one man to the other. They were both bristling like dogs protecting their territory.

Sullivan stared at her in frustration, and then turned again to Lobo. "What are you doing here?"

"That's none of your business," Lobo said coolly.

"It's very much my business. Willow is my friend."

Lobo raised an eyebrow. "Friend? You do get around. Was that another friend you just took home?"

Sullivan bristled. "I asked what you were doing here?"

"I'm visitin'," Lobo replied with a drawl. "And you?"

"You came from Newton's." It was an accusation rather than a question.

"For a sawbones, you have good eyes."

"What do you want here, dammit?"

"That's between the lady and me." Lobo wasn't used to questions, and he damned well wasn't going to take them from this man.

Willow looked at the two men in stunned amazement. Then she noticed that Brady now stood in the doorway, obviously ready to add his bit. The room was full of tension, needing only a spark to explode.

As if on cue, Chad, clad only in long underwear, appeared from his room, one hand rubbing his eyes. "Wha's the matter?" His eyes sparkled when he saw Lobo. "You came back," he said with undisguised delight. Sullivan and Brady scowled, and something like embarrassment crossed Lobo's face at the open hero-worship.

"Go back to bed, Chad," Willow said evenly.

"But I want to stay. . . ."

"Please."

Chad looked at Lobo. "Will I see you tomorrow?"

Unable to resist taunting Willow and the two men, Lobo nodded, the slightest smile curling one side of his lips.

"You won't go away again?" Chad asked.

"Not for a while," Lobo replied, his tone softening a fraction, Willow noticed.

"Go to bed now, Chad," she insisted in her most authoritative voice.

"All right," Chad said reluctantly. Turning to Lobo, he added, "If . . . you promise to stay."

Lobo nodded, and Chad retreated, glancing quickly at the others. "G'night."

As soon as he was gone, Sullivan turned to Willow. "He's not staying!"

Since Jess's statement came as much as a surprise to her as it did to the two men, she could only look back at him. She realized that even though she now knew the stranger was the man called Lobo, she could think of him only as Jess. Her Jess. Their Jess.

She turned the full power of her blue eyes on him now. "Are you going to stay?"

"Is that offer of a job still open?"

"Yes." Nothing had changed as far as she was concerned. Jess or Lobo, he had helped them repeatedly at the risk of his own life. She would trust him with her own life now.

Lobo nodded almost imperceptibly as a gleam flashed in his eye, an open challenge to the other men in the room.

"Willow!" Sullivan protested.

"It's crazy," Brady declared.

"It's done," she told them. There was the smallest hint of victory on Lobo's lips, and Willow wondered whether he'd taken the job to provoke the other two.

But she didn't care. Her heart had started pounding faster when he'd answered Chad, and now she could barely breathe. Her gaze met his, and electricity flashed between them like lightning on a summer night.

"I'll bed down in the barn," he said, sauntering arrogantly through the door and out of sight.

"Willow, do you know what you're doing?" Sullivan's face was creased with worry. "He just left Newton's. They probably hatched some scheme together."

"I think he was about ready to tell me before you two came in," she said.

Brady looked down at the ground, his face a mask of humiliation and helplessness, and Willow felt a jab of regret. "He won't take your place, Brady. You're family."

But Brady didn't say anything. He just stared at her for several moments, then followed Lobo out the door, leaving Willow alone with Sullivan.

"Willow, he's a very dangerous man."

"He's more than that," Willow said. "He's much more than that."

"You can't keep taking in every lost soul you see, especially a predator like that."

"You didn't see him with Chad," she said.

"I know about wild animals. You never know when they'll strike."

"Sullivan . . ."

"Not this time, Willow. I won't support you this time. Not with him."

Willow bit her lip.

"You turned down Gar Morrow's offer of a gunslinger. Why not now?"

"Because . . . Jess is . . . he's . . . well, he's a friend."

"Goddammit, Willow, you might as well have a rattlesnake as a friend. They're both just as predictable."

Willow had never heard Sullivan swear before, and she knew it was a measure of his concern. But she also knew she was right about Jess. "Even Estelle isn't afraid of him," she tried again. "And you know yourself she doesn't trust easily or without good reason."

He sighed. "Everyone else in the world is, and *with* good reason."

"He wouldn't hurt Chad or the twins or Sallie Sue."

"And you?"

"I can take care of myself."

"The hell you can. Look at what's been happening."

"Nothing's happened. Because of Jess."

"Lobo, dammit. His name is Lobo, and the name suits him."

"I don't think so," she said stubbornly.

"Tell him to leave."

"No."

"Listen, Willow. You know the way the town felt about Estelle, and even Chad. If Lobo stays here—"

"He's no different from any other hand."

"He is, Willow, and you know it, and the town knows it."

Willow felt herself shaking. He was right. She might lose her job now. Only with Sullivan's help had she been able to keep it. Still . . .

"I won't ask him to leave," Willow said stubbornly.

"Then I will."

"No!" The word sounded like a pistol shot, and even Willow was taken aback by her vehemence.

Sullivan's face whitened. He stepped closer to her, aware suddenly of something new in her face. She had always been pretty, but now she appeared radiant, her eyes full of fire. "There's nothing between you and him?"

Willow felt herself blush, and she turned around. "Can I make you some coffee?"

"Don't change the subject."

"I'm not. I just thought we both needed some coffee."

"You didn't answer me."

Willow spun around. "No. The answer is no. He's just been very good to us, and there's something about him that makes me think he's so very alone."

"He made it that way himself, Willow. Gunfighters don't have friends."

"Well, he does now. Ever since he saved Sallie Sue."

Sullivan gave up temporarily. At least Brady and Chad were there. That was something. "No coffee. I have to go." He saw the relief on her face. "But I'll be back tomorrow evening."

"There's no need, really."

"There's every need in the world."

Now it was Willow's turn to surrender. She knew he wouldn't change his mind. "All right."

"You'll send Chad for me if you need anything."

She nodded.

He hesitated as if hating to leave. "You're sure?"

She grinned at him. "I'm very sure."

"Dammit, I hate to leave you with him."

"I'm not alone, you know."

"You might as well be," he said with frustration.

"He's been here half a dozen times now, and he's never so much as—"

Sullivan's eyes narrowed. "As what?"

"Said anything or done anything that gives any cause for alarm."

"Just being who he is gives cause for alarm."

"Oh, Sullivan, you worry too much. And how was Marisa when you took her home?"

"You're changing the subject again."

"Because I think you and Marisa look grand together."

He smiled then. "You're hopeless."

"Good night."

"Good night, Willow." And as he closed the door, he prayed to God it would be.

Lobo threw his blanket down in the corner of the barn. It smelled like newly cut lumber, which was not unpleasant. Still, he would rather have been outside, especially when Brady Thomas took a place alongside the opposite wall.

But if Newton made a move, it would be the barn, and he also wanted to make sure Thomas didn't do something stupid again.

Neither of them had a lantern. Neither of them wanted to return to the house to fetch one. So they felt their way, and when Lobo finally lay still, he missed the stars and the moon above, and the fresh, sighing breeze that cooled the evening.

He wondered what in the hell he'd just done, why he had agreed to stay on the ranch when he'd intended to stay in town. It had been partially the doctor, partially the kiss, partially the boy. And all three reasons were stupid, the kiss most of all.

He thought about that kiss. It had been unlike any he'd ever known. Gentleness had never been an attribute of his, and yet he had been consumed with it when he'd looked into those sky-blue eyes.

What was he expected to do anyway, for chrissakes? He had been so damned sure she'd be disgusted when she found out who he was. But he should have known better. After all, she'd taken in a one-eyed saloon girl and a drunk ex-sheriff who burned down barns. Hell, he was practically a choirboy in this company. The thought almost made him chuckle.

Almost.

Thirteen

Willow couldn't sleep. She kept remembering the taste of his lips on hers.

Jess. Lobo.

She knew she'd been falling in love with the former. She had dreaded the latter. How strange that they'd turned out to be same person.

And who, really, was he?

Like Odysseus, he seemed to be many men, to have many contradictions.

The following day was Sunday. Perhaps she would have time then to discover something more about him. It was a delicious thought, delicious and irresistible and frightening.

She had accustomed herself to the idea of being a maiden lady, although she'd never truly thought of herself that way. But she knew others did. She was twenty-five, and she'd never experienced the wonder and awe of being in love, and she'd never been willing to accept anything less.

She had almost come to believe that man-woman love was something to be found only in books, an emotion reserved for the gods, that ordinary people merely settled for companionship or security or the joy of having children.

But her heart pounded frantically when she thought of Jess just yards away. Her hands ached to touch him, and she felt a deep yearning hunger inside. She finally understood why the gods and goddesses suffered so many torments for love.

She'd known this odd hunger from the first time she'd seen him. He'd stood scowling, his body covered with soot after risking his life for Brady and Jupiter. She'd felt struck by a thunderbolt, mesmerized by the magnetism that had bound them together so completely for several seconds.

A gunfighter. A man who killed for a living.

An involuntary shudder went through her as she remembered her revulsion at Gil Morrow's suggestion that she be protected by a man who made his living by the gun. She thought of Canton, of how coldly he had killed a man at the dance.

She couldn't possibly think of Jess that way, not the man who'd climbed down a well to rescue a child, who'd wrestled a bull to save a boy and braved a burning barn to pull out an obstinate bull. No matter what others saw when they looked at him, she saw only those things.

But, dear God, he was still a wanderer, a man who probably would die violently any day.

She rose and went to the window and looked down at the barn, and something in her warmed just knowing he was there. Gunfighter or not, she felt irrevocably linked to him, and she wasn't going to go through the rest of her life without reaching toward him, without exploring these wonderful, tingling, wanting feelings. No matter the cost. She'd always gone after what she wanted. She couldn't stop now.

Willow thought of his eyes, those glittering turquoise eyes that were so good at barricading his emotions. If she hadn't seen that brief naked compassion for Chad, she might think they were merely empty.

She had always been very good at unraveling layers of protective barriers from people, ever since she was a young girl and had mothered some of her father's young pupils. She had heard and seen more than he'd ever suspected, and despite the fact that she had a hopeful nature, she also realized that terrible things happened to people and often shaped what they were. That thought kept her from hating Alex; she knew something truly heartbreaking had changed and twisted him.

What had happened to Jess?

A gunfighter.

She tried to imagine him as a character in one of those dime novels her students read. In her mind's eye she saw him standing at one end of the street while another man approached. She saw them both go for their guns. She saw him fall. . . .

No! her mind screamed. No!

Then her mind moved to another scene. Jess in her kitchen, his hand rubbing the back of his neck as if troubled, his eyes lit with a very brief glint of humor. She saw him holding Chad and looking down at him. She saw him rush into a burning barn for a bull.

And her stomach flip-flopped.

A gunfighter!

A teacher!

For chrissakes, a teacher. A pillar of the community.

Lobo didn't know what time he finally gave up trying to sleep. He rose and left the barn, automatically strapping on his gun as he moved silently to the fence and sat on the top rail.

He looked up at the sky. Two more days and it would be full moon. He'd always heard strange things happened at full moon, but nothing could be stranger than the events of the past ten days.

What kind of fool was he? Hungering, like some wolf cub whose mother was killed. Hungering for something that didn't exist.

Why was his body so tied up in knots, so consumed by an ache that spread to the empty places within him like a prairie

grass fire? He had never been aware of such emptiness before, but now he felt it with a vengeance. He'd let himself feel
the warmth in that ranch house, the affection that so
abounded between its occupants, and now it pierced him like
a knife in the gut, turning and twisting until he was aflame
with quiet, desperate agony.

He swallowed, telling himself he was as crazy as an Apache
with locoweed. He was imagining the whole thing, making
something out of nothing. His gaze went to the house. He
saw a shadow at the window and the very slight movement of
the curtains. It gave him little pleasure to know that Willow,
too, couldn't sleep.

As if burned, he turned away, looking toward the mountains. The last refuge for a wounded wolf. He should go there
and heal himself, as he had in the past, fill those empty
places with the smell of the forest and the icy touch of cold,
unfettered wind. He'd done it before when he'd been
wounded in a gunfight, when he'd found himself a complete
outcast in two societies that had laid claim to him and then
despised him.

Why didn't she despise him?

Because she didn't know enough to. She didn't yet completely understand. And when she did, she'd be like everyone
else.

He was so consumed in bitter thoughts that his usually
sharp ears didn't hear the soft tread of slippers or the softer
swish of a skirt. And when his consciousness detected another presence, he jumped down and went for the gun. The
weapon was in his hand when he whirled around and saw
her standing there, her eyes wide with surprise as her gaze
fixed on the gun.

"Chrissakes, lady," he said roughly to conceal his fear. He
could have killed her. "Didn't anyone ever tell you about
sneaking up on a man?"

"I didn't think I was sneaking," she said with a tremor in
her voice.

"What in the hell are you doing out here?"

There was no warmth in his voice, Willow thought, only
irritation. She wondered if she'd made a mistake. But he'd

looked so alone, and something had compelled her to hurriedly pull on a blouse and skirt and go to him.

Somehow she knew that explanation would not be welcomed. "It's a beautiful night," she said instead.

He allowed himself to look at her then, really look at her. He purposely made his perusal rude and insulting, his gaze lingering on her breasts as if mentally undressing her. In the light of the moon he saw a flush creep up from her neck to her face.

"Are you going to put the gun away?" This time there was no quiver in her voice, and Lobo was stunned by her lack of outrage. There was only an understanding of what he was trying to do: send her running and screaming back to the house.

He slowly holstered his Peacemaker and turned away. "Go back inside," he said. "You don't belong out here. Not with me."

"Why?"

"Haven't you heard?" he said in a taunting voice. "I'm the White Apache. No woman is safe with me."

"Then why do I feel perfectly safe?"

"Because you're a damn fool."

"People keep telling me that," she admitted.

"Do you ever listen?" he asked. There was a note of curiosity in his voice.

"Not if I think I'm right."

"Are you always right?"

"No." It was a reluctant admission.

He turned to her, and his eyes seem to bore into her soul. His lips were as firm and unmoving as ever, and all she could think of was the way they'd felt on hers.

"Go inside, lady."

"Willow."

He shook his head, and his lips softened for the slightest fraction of a second. "Go inside, Willow."

"I can't sleep," she argued. "You obviously can't sleep either."

"I like the night," he whispered. "I couldn't sleep inside."

"Jess . . ."

"Lobo." He corrected her just as she had corrected him with her name. She sensed that he was willing her to accept the name and all that went with it.

"Where did Jess come from?"

He was silent for a very long time, as if he were weighing whether he should tell her.

"He died a long time ago," he said finally.

"How old was he?" Willow knew he was talking about himself, about the Jess that once was, that still was. Only he wouldn't admit it.

He rubbed the back of his neck and shrugged. " 'Round seven. I'm not sure." Lobo didn't know why he told her that. He hadn't intended to. He didn't want to tell her anything. He didn't want to give any of himself away to anyone.

But she didn't pry any further, and he was surprised. She turned away, lifting her gaze to the sky. "Orion, the hunter," she said.

His eyes followed hers, but he didn't know what she was talking about.

She sensed his confusion. "Patterns," she said. "The stars make up constellations, pictures in the sky," she added when she saw his look of bewilderment.

Hell, they just looked like stars to him. His eyes went back to her. She was even prettier in the moonlight. The auburn hair was darker and her eyes were a deeper shade of blue, so deep and glowing that he ached all over again.

"See," she said, pointing. "That group up there looks like a dipper."

He looked, but he didn't see. It still appeared like a bunch of stars to him. Besides, he couldn't concentrate on anything but the sweet smell of her hair, the gentle curve of her lips as she spoke.

"Yeah," he replied because an answer seemed expected.

She smiled suddenly at the lack of conviction in his voice. He was obviously not a dreamer.

Willow looked up at him, at the strong profile, the lips that seldom smiled. But they had for a moment, when he'd kissed her very, very gently. She wanted to ask him so much, but she was afraid that questions might push him away, might make him bolt as he had many other times.

She chose the one she hoped was the least likely to send him running. "Why did you decide to stay?"

He was silent for so long, she was sure he wasn't going to answer. He was still looking up, and she wanted to kick him to bring his attention back to her.

"I don't like people telling me what to do," he said finally.

He must mean Sullivan, she thought. Sullivan wouldn't be happy to know he was responsible, if, indeed, he was, and Jess wasn't just using him as an excuse.

"Did you really work for Mr. Newton?"

He shifted against the fence. "Yeah."

"And now?"

"I don't like people who lie to me."

Willow bit her lip. She decided that milking a wild range cow would be easier than getting Jess to talk. Anything would be easier. "And Alex Newton lied?"

"He didn't mention certain important details."

"Such as?" she prompted him.

"I don't fight kids," he said flatly. "Newton didn't bring up anything about kids when he sent for me." There was a long pause, as if he were considering his words. "Something like that can hurt a man's reputation," he added a bit defensively.

"And that matters so much."

"Lady, when you're in my business, it matters a hell of a lot." He was deliberately rude, but Willow wasn't easily driven away.

"Alex won't like it," she told him.

"He'll get over it."

Willow hesitated before asking, "Is it over, then?"

He turned and glared at her. "Lady, it's just beginning. Newton's hiring every gun hand he can find. You're going to have a range war, and if you care about those kids, you'll get out of here."

She looked away from his intense study. "This is the only home they've ever had."

"Nothing will convince you?"

"Can you assure me there won't be a range war if I leave?"

Lobo snorted. "With Canton here! Hell, no. The pot's boiling and no one seems much interested in dousing the fire. But you don't have to be in the middle of it."

"Do you know . . . Mr. Canton?"

"Yeah, we know each other."

"He killed someone the other night."

"So?" The short word was nothing less than a challenge. His implication that gunfighters killed hung unsaid in the night air.

Willow swallowed the sudden lump in her throat. He was trying to frighten her off, and the more he tried, the more she wondered why. "Why do they call you Lobo?"

He shrugged. "The Apache gave me the name. It seemed as good as any."

"As good as Jess?"

He scowled. "I told you he died."

Willow didn't say anything, but the silence was heavy with her doubt.

He turned away from her. "Lobo fits, lady. Believe me."

"The wolf is a social animal," Willow said as if reading out of a book. "He mates for life."

Lobo turned and stared at her icily. "Unless he's an outcast, chased from the pack, and then he turns on his own kind." There was no self-pity in the observation, only the cold recital of fact.

"Is that what happened?"

Lobo felt his gut wrench. He'd never meant to say what he had, had not even consciously thought it before. A cold dread seeped through him as he realized how much control of himself he was losing.

"Lady, I've done things that would make you puke. So why don't you go back to your nice little house and leave me alone."

Willow hesitated. She sensed the turmoil in him, and it echoed her own churning emotions.

"I don't care about the past," she finally said.

He laughed roughly. "I don't scare you at all?"

She knew he wanted her to say yes. She knew she should

say yes. She should be fearful of someone with his reputation, his life. But she wasn't.

"No," she answered.

"You don't know me, lady."

"Willow."

He shook his head. "And the last thing you should do is be out here with me."

"Sullivan would agree." The woman inside her couldn't resist the retort. If he didn't like people telling him what to do, perhaps Sullivan's warning would make him stay.

That snapped his head around. "He got any call on you?" His eyes were like green-blue fire.

"Only that of a friend," she said.

"He was making cow eyes at Newton's girl."

"Good," Willow said with satisfaction.

He looked at her suspiciously. He didn't understand her. He didn't understand anything about her. Any other woman he knew would be spitting mad not to be the center of attention.

"Were you with the Apache long?" she asked softly.

It was a sneaky question, and he stiffened. "Long enough."

She sensed his withdrawal, if it was possible that he could distance himself any farther than he already had. The kiss might never had happened, except it was so vivid in her mind.

Her hand went out to his, which was wrapped around the post. "Thank you for staying."

His hand seemed to tremble, and she wondered if she imagined it.

"You may not be grateful long," he replied shortly.

"You will stay, then?"

"A few days," he replied. "But the town won't like it. I'm usually not welcome."

"If Alex can hire you, I can," she answered defiantly.

"But Newton has money, and you . . . ?"

Again the implication was clear, and she knew she was flushing a bright red. She hoped the moonlight didn't reveal it, but she saw the glint in his eye and knew her hope was in vain.

Her thoughts turned to what had been nagging her, to the violent death that had occurred a week earlier. "Mr. Canton . . ."

"Marsh Canton," Lobo supplied.

"You won't have to fight him if you stay?" Her hand shook slightly as she posed the haunting question.

The glint was still in his eye. "A lot of folks been waiting for that."

"I don't want you to stay if—"

"I think, lady, that Marsh Canton and I are probably on the same side now."

"I've never seen anyone so . . . fast," she whispered.

His right hand went to his neck. "He's good. Aren't you going to ask me if I'm just as good?"

She didn't want to think of him that way. She preferred thinking of him hauling poor Jupiter from the barn. "No," she whispered.

"That's what I do, you know," he persisted almost angrily. "I'm no hero like you want to believe. I'm a killer just like Canton. You want to know how many people I've killed?"

Her gaze was glued to his eyes, to the swirling, dangerous currents in them. She heard the raw self-contempt in his voice, but what he was saying didn't matter to her, not to the way she felt about him, not to the way she wanted to . . . touch and hold and . . .

"I was twelve when I first killed," he continued in the same voice. "Twelve. About Chad's age, I guess. I found I was real good at it."

His eyes, filled with tormented memories and even rage, blazed directly at her. And she felt her need for him deepen, felt her heart pound with the compulsion to disprove his reason for self-derision.

But she couldn't move, and she had no words that wouldn't anger or hurt or sound naive and silly. That, she sensed, was what he was waiting for so he could have a reason to leave. The currents running between them were stronger than ever, and Lobo was willing her to say or do something to destroy it, but she was just as determined not to. Silence stretched between them but something else too, something so strong that neither could back away.

If she'd offered compassion or sympathy, Lobo could have broken through her hold on him. But she gave neither. Instead, he was warmed by the unfamiliar glow of understanding, of unquestioning acceptance. He basked in it, feeling whole for the first time that he could remember. All of a sudden he realized this was what he'd been searching for, not freedom but something so elusive he'd never been able to put a name to it.

And it was too late. His insides churned and twisted with pure agony as he realized that one indisputable fact. He carried too much trouble with him. His reputation, which he had so carefully nurtured, was a noose around his neck. The older he got, the more the rope tightened. He could live with that, but he couldn't live with the fact that it was also a noose around the neck of anyone foolish enough to care for him.

He forced himself to take a step back, to fight his way out of the moment's intimacy, one deeper than any he'd ever shared with a person, deeper than when he plunged his manhood into a woman. Christ!

"Lady, you should run like hell!" His voice was harsh, grating. "You and those kids don't need the kind of grief I bring."

She worried her lips as she sought for something to say, to somehow express her belief in him, but before she found the words, he spoke again.

"And I sure as hell don't need *you.*" He emphasized the last word as if trying to convince himself, and once again he stepped back.

"Jess . . ."

His mouth seemed to soften for a moment, and he hesitated. But then his mouth firmed again, and his eyes turned hard. He bowed slightly, mockingly. "If I'm going to be of any use to you, ma'am, I'd better turn in."

He strolled lazily back to the barn and disappeared within, leaving Willow feeling desolate and alone.

Fourteen

When Willow rose the next morning after a restless sleep, she went to the window, moved the curtains, and looked toward the barn. She didn't want to. In fact, she tried to keep herself from doing so.

But she might as well have tried not to breathe.

Her eyes searched for him, though she knew he probably still slept. It had been very late when she'd returned to her room, and the sun was just now touching the earth. She heard noises downstairs; Estelle must already be up.

It was Sunday. No school.

She usually took the children into town for church services, although Chad always declined as Estelle did, and she understood. Both felt uncomfortable in crowds. To force the issue would only worsen matters.

But all thoughts of church, of leaving the ranch even for a few hours, fled when Jess came into view. He and Brady were hauling lumber into the new barn. Brady's movements were stiff, but Jess's were smooth and graceful, seemingly effortless.

He was not wearing a shirt, and his skin was bronze and

glistening in the early morning sun. His sand-colored hair was streaked, thick and tousled as if he'd run his fingers through it. Daylight did nothing to diminish the aura of danger and strength that was so much a part of him; neither did it soften the harsh planes of his face.

Willow swallowed hard, wondering how she could be attracted to Jess though he was a paid killer. For that attraction was still there, that fierce, compelling need, that budding excitement in the pit of her stomach whenever she saw him. But now there was also fear.

A gunfighter, she thought again. He was everything she should detest. He was not, as she'd thought, a paladin, or knight or crusader. But he had become their protector. For some reason he had chosen to become that.

But that didn't change what he was.

She shook her head as she concentrated on the man. Even from this distance she could feel his pull on her, and she wondered whether he was also feeling that attraction. Or was it all her imagination, that of a lovestruck old maid?

She went to her closet and frowned at her dresses. All of them, except for the one she'd worn to the dance, were eminently practical and respectable; Willow had little extra money for luxuries.

Calling herself all sorts of foolish woman, she finally decided on a dark blue dress, which, though a little faded, gave depth to her eyes and luster to her lightly tanned skin. It was also cool, with little puffed sleeves.

She donned it, knowing that doing so meant she was not going to go to church. The dress, though modest enough, was not appropriate for attending service.

Feeling a little like a student skipping school, she brushed her hair until it shone and debated at length over whether to leave it loose or shape it into the usual convenient knot. She compromised with herself, braiding it into one thick plait that fell halfway down her back. Despite ominous whispers in the back of her mind, she felt reckless and ridiculously happy when she opened the door and walked into the kitchen.

The twins were setting the table, and Sallie Sue was gazing

out the window, holding tightly to her favorite rag doll. Estelle was at the stove, stirring the contents of a pot. The smell of something baking floated up from inside the old stove.

Willow wrinkled her nose. There was also the slightest odor of scorched food.

Estelle was humming. The tone was sweet and clear, and Willow realized suddenly that she'd never heard Estelle hum before. When Estelle realized Willow was there, she turned and smiled shyly. "I told Jeremy to add another plate. Is that all right?"

Willow didn't have to ask why. She merely nodded and asked curiously. "You like him, don't you?"

Estelle ducked her head slightly. "He don't look at me funny . . . like I was a freak or something." Shame was heavy in her voice, and Willow wondered whether it would ever go away. It was caused not only by the eye, but also by Estelle's past. She had been made to feel worthless and unclean for so long, she'd come to believe it. Willow blessed Jess for not judging Estelle, and she wondered briefly if he didn't do it because he himself had been judged so many times.

The scorching smell became a little more pronounced, and Willow thought she'd better do something. "Where's Chad?"

"Outside," Estelle said.

"Jeremy, why don't you go call him and Brady and Jess."

Jeremy obeyed eagerly, happy to have Jimmy finish their mundane chore.

"D'you think he likes oatmeal?" Estelle asked worriedly. "We don't have any bacon."

"I think oatmeal and biscuits will be just fine," Willow said, wishing they had something more substantial. But the drought and the imminent demise of her garden had made her very careful with money. They did have coffee, milk, and fresh butter, and the jelly given to them by Mrs. MacIntyre.

The door slammed open, and Jeremy flew through. "They're coming," he said, and Willow breathed a sigh of relief. She had questioned whether Jess would eat with them or not. Estelle and the children would have been terribly disappointed if he had chosen not to mention herself.

He came in last, buttoning a shirt, his face damp from a quick washing. He looked awkward in the kitchen, as if unused to being in a gathering, but he sat easily enough where Chad indicated, between him and Sallie Sue. Chad's eyes shone and his gaze seldom left the man next to him.

Brady took his usual seat, his face flushed, and Willow wondered whether it was from anger or work or both. His eyes filled with suspicions and dislike whenever he looked across the table at Jess, and Jess's were no more friendly when drawn to Brady. The air was tense with their mutual dislike, and Willow swallowed, wondering whether an explosion was imminent.

Estelle ladled out the lumpy oatmeal and, sure enough, the bottom of the pot was brown and burnt. When Estelle returned to the stove, Willow saw Jess raise one eyebrow. Then he shrugged and started eating. She smiled to herself, once more warming to his consideration.

The others, who had been awaiting his reaction to the food, sighed with relief, all except Brady, who continued to glare.

The biscuits came and, to Willow's surprise, they were golden and light. Jess's eyes filled with approval, and shy, retiring Estelle nearly swelled with pride.

Sallie Sue held out a biscuit to him. "Pleathe put jelly on mine."

Everyone turned and looked at him, and he nearly smiled as he looked down at the small girl's serious face. He took the biscuit solemnly and very carefully spread it with butter and jelly, receiving a broad, happy smile in return. Even Brady's sour look softened slightly, and they ate in almost agreeable silence.

"I looked at the garden," Lobo said suddenly. "Why don't you dig a trench from the river?"

Willow felt hope begin to tug at her. "I've . . . thought about it . . . but I don't know how."

"I've seen it done," Lobo said. "I think with all of us we can do it. Do you have a plow?"

"I . . . we . . . did. It was in the old barn."

A chair scraped across the floor, and Brady rose. He

stalked out of the kitchen without a word, and Willow wondered whether she should go after him. He was hurting. It was in his every movement.

Lobo shrugged. "Can you get one?"

"I can try."

He nodded, finished his coffee, and stood. Almost as an afterthought, he looked at Estelle. "Your cooking sure beats mine." It was, Willow thought, probably as close to a thank-you as he could manage, but Estelle understood and smiled.

Willow was almost jealous as he jerked open the door and disappeared outside.

"I asked you before, how long you planning to stay?" Brady's anger was throbbing as they worked together on a stall for Jupiter.

"When your hand stops shaking enough to give them some protection," Lobo said.

"I don't get it. What in the hell do you want?"

Lobo stopped hammering, and he looked almost puzzled. "Damn if I know."

Some of the antagonism slipped from Brady's voice. "Did you really quit Newton?"

"Hell no. I'm just doing this 'cause I like sweating." He paused. "Look, I know you don't like me. I damn sure don't like you any better. But I wouldn't harm them, and I won't let anyone else harm them. That's the first and last time I'm sayin' it."

Brady placed a new board in place while Lobo hammered it. Brady wanted to say the gunslinger was hurting Willow just by being there. Brady wasn't so far gone he didn't recognize the look on Willow's face, and it chilled him straight to the bone. He'd never met an old gunslinger. They died either by the bullet or the rope, never old age.

But Brady didn't say anything. Because Lobo was right. He couldn't protect Willow, and perhaps this man beside him was the only one who could. But at what price?

"I haven't lost my nerve," Brady growled.

"No," Lobo agreed. "You've just let the bottle get you."

Brady's hands tightened around the board, though it no longer needed support. "I'll beat it."

"Like you did the other night?"

"You won't let me forget that, will you?"

Lobo shrugged in what was becoming a very familiar gesture to Brady. "Can *you?*"

"No." The voice was devoid of emotion.

"Why?"

"Why did it happen? Partially because of you. What you represent." Brady's voice was defeated. "Maybe you're right. Maybe they would be better off without me."

"Is that what you think?" Lobo asked with detachment. "Give me another board."

Brady handed it to him as he tried to figure him out. He'd known dozens of gunfighters; they'd come through his towns swaggering and boasting and killing. But Lobo was different. There was no swagger in him, only deadly purpose, and for some reason he'd turned it against the man who'd hired him. Brady knew he ought to be grateful, but he wasn't. He feared for Willow, feared for her even more now than when Lobo was on the other side.

By midday Brady was ready to drop, but Lobo seemed affected neither by the heat nor the work, and Brady couldn't make himself quit before Lobo did. He felt the sweat rolling down his face and trickling down the back of his shirt as he lifted and carried lumber to the barn. Although he'd taken care of chores in the past months, it had been a very long time since he'd worked this steadily and this hard, especially after a binge. His heart pounded with fatigue, and he felt sick to his stomach, but still he kept pace.

Brady knew that Lobo was not much younger than he, but Brady felt a hundred years older and knew he looked it. And yet as he worked, a certain satisfaction that he wasn't quitting settled over him. He didn't even need a drink, and that fact surprised him more than anything. Perhaps he was just too exhausted to care about anything but getting through the day without disgracing himself, without proving himself inferior to Lobo.

It was midafternoon when Willow appeared with a basket

containing sandwiches, coffee, and cups. She had sent for them around noon to come inside for lunch, but Lobo had declined and Brady followed suit. Now Brady welcomed the break, thanked Willow, and took a cup and sandwich outside to a tree. As much as he hated to leave Willow and Lobo alone, he needed some rest and he needed it away from Lobo's damning, probing eyes. He'd hesitated for a moment at the barn door, but he knew little could happen so close to the house with the children running in and out.

After Brady left, Lobo stared at Willow and her offerings. He'd tried his best to avoid her, purposely avoiding the midday meal. The intimacy of breakfast, the faces that had turned so trustingly toward him, had made him uncomfortable and confused. He didn't deserve such trust. He didn't want it.

So he'd turned all his energy to the barn, and it had quietly amused him that Brady Thomas felt obliged to try to keep up. Lobo had purposely kept his pace fast, knowing he was challenging, even taunting, the other man. But it was time someone did that. Lobo had neither sympathy nor pity for Thomas's obvious distress; he'd brought it on himself.

But the pace had also partially been for himself. The activity kept his mind from the ranch house, from the woman who lived there. It had been all he could do the night before not to touch her, to pull her into his arms and see whether she felt as good as he remembered. This morning at breakfast hadn't been much better. She'd looked so damn fresh, so pretty, so untouched and innocent.

He had considered lighting out more than once during the early morning hours. But he'd given his word, and he never went back on his word. At least that was what he'd been telling himself.

As he looked at her standing in the light streaming through the open barn door, he knew he'd been lying to himself just as he had since he first saw her. Warmth started prickling again at the pit of his stomach, and his heart seemed to swell and quicken.

He wanted to dismiss these odd reactions as foolishness or the result of too much work, but he knew that wasn't true.

His hands ached to touch her; his lips wanted to wander down her face; his eyes wanted to feast on her. And there was a certain pain, a certain constriction in his throat as he realized no one had ever gone to trouble for him before. Not voluntarily. Not because they wanted to.

The sudden ache the realization brought made him frown. "You needn't have done that. I don't need much."

She tipped her head up, her eyes sliding over his body as he'd done to her the previous night, and he moved uncomfortably under her scrutiny.

"You're too thin," she pronounced with a slight smile.

His eyes turned cloudy as he fought back a retort, and suddenly he realized she was teasing him. Mischief showed all over her face.

He narrowed his eyes in a way that usually made people cower. "Whites eat too much," he growled.

"Is that what you learned from the Apache?" The question was posed quite naturally as she held out freshly baked bread.

"Along with other things," he said, not reaching out to take it.

His voice was a warning, as if he were daring her to ask more. She accepted the challenge. "What other things?"

"How to use a knife. How to scalp." The last was dropped like a cannon shell. He only partially expected her to pale, perhaps to leave; he'd already learned she had more grit than most women, or even men.

"I didn't think Apaches scalped," she said, apparently not at all concerned.

He stared at her. That was the last thing he'd expected her to say.

"They don't, usually," he answered, wondering where she'd picked up that piece of information. Most whites lumped all Indians together and believed they all practiced scalping. "But after a big victory they sometimes take one for a religious ceremony. It's sort of an obligation to the most high for giving them victory. Whites," he added balefully, "took a helluva lot more scalps than Apaches."

An interested look came to her eyes, not condemning or horror-stricken.

"There was a bounty on Apache scalps, but scalp hunters seldom cared if they were Apaches or a tribe friendly to whites, or even Mexicans." Christ, but he was saying more than he'd ever said before, particularly about his years with the Apache.

She had dropped her hand with the bread in it. "How long were you with them?" she asked.

He didn't say anything for several minutes. Instead, he leaned against the newly built stall and seemed to study his hands. "A long time," he said finally, reluctantly.

"Your family?" She couldn't let it go, not now when he was giving her answers.

His eyes darkened, and she could see his mental retreat from her. "I'll take some of that coffee," he said, ignoring the question and taking the cup in his fingers.

His hands were gloveless, and still red, but not as raw as they had been. She reached out and took one, turning it palm up. It was hard and callused, but the fingers were long and tapered. She thought of what he had just said about scalping, and she could visualize the knife in his strong, capable hands. What she didn't understand is why the vision didn't repel her as it should have. Perhaps because he'd intended it to.

She held out the basket again, and the bread, and this time he accepted, probably, she thought, because he didn't want to answer any more questions.

He didn't sit, but ate standing up, chewing each piece carefully and slowly. Once more she wondered about the years he'd lived with the Apache, those years that had indelibly left their mark on him, separating him from others but not extracting the core of him. It had been that core, she thought, that had spurred him to help Sallie Sue and Chad and now her. She only wished she knew how to peel away all the protective layers covering what he obviously considered weaknesses.

He finished eating, and his eyes turned to her. "How did a lady like you come out here?"

She basked in his interest. "My father died. He taught at a school in Boston and I did too, but when he died—"

She stopped for a moment, but interest glinted in his eyes, and she continued. "The headmaster . . . didn't think it was proper for an unmarried female to live alone, and I was dismissed."

"And?"

"I'd always read about the West, and there was an advertisement in the paper."

"So you decided to come to the Wild West," he said dryly. "Soldiers and Indians and gunfighters."

"And farmers and ranchers and storekeepers," she added, her gaze on his face, trying to understand the cynicism in the rough voice.

"Why don't you go back where you belong?"

"Where is that?"

"Not here," he said abruptly.

Willow's temper flared. "I'm tired of everyone telling me that."

"Everyone's right."

"Everyone's not right," she said.

The glint came back into his eyes.

"You're the stubbornest woman I've ever met."

"I've been told that too," she replied defiantly.

"And does it ever get you in trouble? Other than now," he quickly amended.

"Frequently." She grinned suddenly. "But something always comes along to make it right. Like you."

"It'll take more than me to solve this one."

"I have Brady."

He nearly choked.

"And Sullivan."

"A sawbones," he jeered.

"And Chad," she continued blithely, knowing she was irritating him. At least he was talking to her, even if his face did say he thought she was a raving lunatic.

But he just shook his head and turned away. "I got to get back to work, so we'll have a nice new barn for Newton to burn," he said wryly.

"You don't really think—"

"Lady, he offered me the job. Said if I didn't, someone else would."

For some reason, she'd never thought Alex would go that far. Try to frighten her yes, but use actual violence?

"Is that why you came here?"

He turned back to face her.

His eyes were turbulent, but she still couldn't read them. She didn't know whether they reflected anger or frustration or another emotion.

But the very intensity of the gaze fired the attraction that was always there. She felt like a lightning rod, catching and absorbing currents of energy that streaked between them in waves, the focus of bright flashing brilliance that made every nerve in her body tingle until she wondered how she was still standing. He stepped toward her, and she toward him, two irresistibly drawn lodestones with no will of their own.

Willow saw his face lower, felt the warmth of his nearness, and closed her eyes to better savor all the soft, humming sensations assaulting her body. His lips nuzzled hers for the briefest of times, and she felt bereft when they pulled away, but then she felt the whisper of his breath against her hair, her eyes, and his hand traced lines along her neck in possessive tenderness.

Without warning, the gentleness turned demanding as his hand tightened around her, and his mouth found hers once more. She felt the hungry need of his lips, and she answered with the same urgency. Almost immediately, his kiss deepened, and she sensed contained rage in him that should have frightened her but didn't. Instead, the sensations in her body seemed to spin out of control, each exploration on his part sending them careening like a child's whirling top.

She felt completely wanton, something she'd never believed possible, never even imagined, as her hands went around his neck and buried themselves in his thick hair. Nothing mattered but him, nothing mattered except the tender violence of his mouth, the restrained power of his arms; nothing mattered but the continued voyage into a world of feelings and sensations and emotions she'd never known existed.

Her head tipped back as his hand wrapped around the braid, and his mouth opened slightly, giving her a taste of him. She'd never experienced anything so intimate, like this exchanging of the essence of each other, and she exalted when his tongue tentatively entered her mouth, cautiously probing, sending shivers of heat through her. She could think of nothing else to describe it, nor did she want to think long. She wanted only to experience.

His tongue went deeper, and she found her own tongue imitating at first and then inventing its own movements, reaching out to capture more of this elusive man who made her feel as no other had.

She heard a small growl in his throat, a sound that changed into a groan as his hands moved along her neck and then her back, as though wanting to claim as much as possible, and she relished the hungry search, even though a part of her urged caution. But it was hushed in the need to feel, to learn, to give, to take.

To love.

A gunslinger. A man with no reverence for life. A loner who wandered from one fight to another.

Yet it was there—love. It was fierce and sure and right, and it scared her more than anything else in her life.

The knowledge so surprised her that her lips suddenly tightened, and she took a step back. He immediately withdrew, his hands like vises on her arms, his eyes glittering like gems displayed in sunlight. "Christ, lady," he said, his voice a harsh rasp.

He looked dazed. She knew she did too. And neither could move as they studied and memorized each other, as if there may never be another time.

Both of them heard the heavy footsteps at the same time, and whatever she'd glimpsed in Jess's eyes disappeared as Brady appeared, his gaze going from one to the other.

Willow kept looking at Jess. "You'll come to supper with us tonight?"

Lobo, fighting all kinds of demons inside him, would have

agreed to almost anything to halt the overwhelming desire that made him forget the most basic of his rules.

He nodded and walked back to the stall on which he had been working.

And Willow, indulging in a rare sense of triumph, left to prepare a meal he wouldn't forget.

Fifteen

True to his word, Lobo appeared for supper. He'd debated the issue over and over, and he felt more than ever like a wolf being drawn into a trap. But he'd committed himself.

In a few days he would be gone, and these few days would fade from both their minds. He would go on to do what he did best. And that wasn't, he knew, being any part of a family.

But he'd changed to his clean shirt, and he'd washed and shaved, feeling about as foolish as a green kid on his first roundup.

When he arrived, everyone was already seated at the table. They all looked at him, anxiously awaiting his appearance. The expectancy did both good and bad things to him. There was a feeling of warmth, a rush of unexpected pleasure that was rare. At the same time, there was a throb of warning deep in his gut.

He silently took several slices from a platter of ham, and then potatoes and green beans. The food smelled good, as good as any he could remember. But then, he'd never cared that much about food.

The twins chattered excitedly about the barn. They'd

wanted to put Jupiter in it, but Brady had pointed out to
them earlier in the day that the barn wasn't quite finished.
There was also a second reason, but that one was kept silently between Brady and Lobo.

The two men had decided to keep watch by the gate and
had tossed a coin to determine the first watch, which included suppertime. Brady had lost, although Lobo thought
that he himself was probably the real loser. It would have
given him a good excuse to skip the agony of supper with
Willow.

And agony it was as he looked across at Willow, often finding her own gaze on him, wide, wistful, and wanting.

Tomorrow, he vowed silently. Tomorrow he'd make it clear
that he was nothing more than hired help and would, from
then on, take his meals by himself. As soon as he felt the
ranch was safe, he would make tracks. He'd go a very long
way from there. Maybe Canada, or even Alaska, where civilization hadn't started yet, where it was cold enough to cool
this burning deep inside him, where there would be no one to
bother him. Yeah, Alaska.

Thus decided, he listened absently to the rapid conversation floating around him, mostly between the children. Estelle was quiet, answering only when spoken to, and Willow
almost as quiet, her gaze intent on him as if she realized the
decision he'd made.

"Thtory tonight?" Sallie Sue asked just as Lobo and the
others heard the sound of approaching hoofbeats.

"Riders coming," Lobo heard Brady yell, and he rose from
the chair, turning quickly to Willow. "Keep everyone inside
unless I say differently."

He didn't wait for an answer. He'd loosened the leather
cord that held his Peacemaker next to his thigh when he sat
down to eat; now he quickly tightened it, and his hand went
to the grip, his fingers almost caressing the walnut as he
always did before trouble.

"Jess."

He turned toward Willow. She was standing, her face tense
and worried.

"Be careful," she whispered. "There's nothing's worth your life."

He smiled, but the expression had no humor in it, and its very coldness seemed to freeze her. "I thought this ranch was," he said abruptly. He went outside to the porch, where he watched Brady hurry his still-saddled horse into the corral and stride over to join him on the porch.

The riders were coming through the gate.

"I count around fifteen," Brady said.

Lobo nodded. "Can you use that gun?"

Brady returned his steady gaze. "I don't know."

"I guess we both might find out." Lobo slowly went down the three steps of the porch and stood silently, his hands at his sides, his eyes wary as they sized up the riders. Brady moved with him and stood at his side.

It was dusk, the moon already riding high in the gathering darkness. Lobo stood patiently as if to greet guests.

He recognized one of the men, a Newton hand he'd seen on the ranch. Some were obviously recently recruited gun hands; others were probably Newton hands trying to curry favor with the boss. The Newton foreman was absent.

"Kinda late to come visitin'," he remarked to the man who seemed to be the leader.

"I have a message for the lady," the man said, and spit contemptuously on the ground. He looked back among his men, and Lobo could see handmade torches ready to be lit.

"Do you," he said. "Well, I'm taking the lady's messages at the moment."

Lobo heard murmurs from the back of the pack. One of the riders nudged his horse up to the man in front and quietly uttered two words. The man's arrogant pose faltered. "You ain't Lobo," he said.

"That a question or a statement?" Lobo said.

"Lobo works for the boss," the man whispered.

"Not anymore." Lobo smiled. "I quit yesterday. I work for Miss Taylor now." His hand went up and relaxed on the grip of his gun. "You said you had a message?"

The man hesitated, considering his options and not much liking the fact he was the one in front. He was fast, but he was no match for someone like Lobo, and he knew it. Newton hadn't said anything about Lobo changing sides; he'd been told only to burn the new barn.

He didn't like backing down, not in front of the others, but the offered bonus wasn't worth mixing horns with the likes of Lobo. He tried to keep his fear from his face.

"Yeah," he said finally. "Mr. Newton says to tell Miss Taylor he'll give her anything she wants."

"That all?" Lobo said, his smile stretching wider. It was the most frightening smile the Newton man had ever seen. "Sure took a bunch of you to deliver it."

"Mr. Newton wants her to know he's serious," the leader said harshly, his voice made that way by the sudden dryness in his throat.

"Wouldn't like to pitch in and help us finish that barn, would you?" Lobo said, a small taunt in his voice.

Already, some of the riders were backing away, and the man in front was quickly realizing it. He knew he'd just lost face with the others, and he hated Lobo for it. "Just give her the message," he said.

"I'll do that," Lobo said. "And I'd be careful of those things you're carrying. Someone might get the wrong idea."

The man jerked his horse's head around.

"Who should I say came calling?" The mocking voice stopped the Newton man, and he turned back. Lobo was standing there, still seemingly relaxed, but his stance had widened as if to gain balance, and his hand had lifted ever so slightly, enough to give him a clear path to the gun.

"Keller," the man said.

"Then you can give Newton a message from me, Keller, since you're so good at that. I've been working on that barn all day. I'd take it real poorly if something were to happen to it. Or," he added in a lazy drawl, "if anything were to happen to Miss Taylor, or anyone who lives on this ranch. You understand?"

The man nodded.

"Make sure Newton does too. Tell him I'm here to stay."

"You can't fight all of us."

Lobo looked at the retreating cowboys. "No?" The question was an open taunt.

Keller's hand went to his pistol, but before his fingers even reached the holster, Lobo's Peacemaker was in his hand and he had spun to an almost kneeling position, his legs bent, one hand under the gun to balance it. Very slowly, Keller took his hand away from his gun and rested both hands on the neck of his horse, his palms up.

He turned his horse slowly, as if not to provoke his antagonist any further, and the horses and men moved toward the road.

When they were almost out of sight, Chad flew out the door, his eyes shining. "Galloping galoshes. I ain't never seen anything so fast. Will you teach me?"

Willow followed him. "I've never," she corrected Chad automatically, but she looked stunned.

"Will ya?" Chad persisted.

Brady turned away without a word and started toward the barn.

"We'll talk about it tomorrow," Lobo said to Chad. "Now you go inside."

"But—"

"Go inside, Chad." Lobo purposely made his voice cold.

Chad stared at him as if betrayed, but he turned around as told, his shoulders slumping.

There was suddenly just Willow and Lobo standing there, as still as statues.

"Now you know what I do," Lobo said. "I frighten people."

"You don't frighten me," she said, but that wasn't altogether true, and she knew he heard the tremor in her voice.

His hand went up to his neck. "Not as much as I should," he agreed in an exasperated voice, his bright eyes clouding.

Willow swallowed. She'd seen every deadly movement he'd made, and she tried to dismiss their meaning from her mind. "He's really not going to quit, is he?"

For the first time he heard doubt in her voice, and he was angered at how much he cared that doubt existed. He should be pleased. But he'd discovered he liked her strength, that unwavering belief that everything was going to turn out just the way she wanted. And he was fascinated with the way she always seemed to find the best in people, even in himself, chrissakes.

Seemingly of their own volition, his hands went to her shoulders and rested there. Her body relaxed slightly, and he felt her trust, even after what she'd seen of him. It felt so damned good. Warmth flowed through him like a healing river, and he felt incredibly alive, more alive than he'd ever been in his life. His hands tingled with the pleasant sensation of merely touching her, and he felt cleansed as his gaze met hers and he saw his worth in her eyes. Not because he was a gunslinger, not because he had saved the barn, but because she trusted and liked and cared about him as no one else ever had.

His hands trembled slightly, knowing the moment wouldn't last. She had seen only what she'd wanted to see of him. When she discovered all the other parts, that light in her eyes would fade. How could it not be so?

She was a teacher. He couldn't read or write.

She was a person who loved. He was a person who had never loved.

She was a person who cared, who saved broken lives. He was a person who took them.

She embraced life. He ran from it.

The last conclusion startled him even though he knew it was true. He'd certainly never considered himself a coward; he wasn't afraid of death or pain or discomfort. But he suddenly realized he was terrified of caring for someone. He looked at his hands. He had never known them to tremble like that, to shake like Brady's.

He wanted to run. Christ, he wanted to run just like Brady was running from his devils into a bottle. Lobo knew he was not a whit better, not even a mite stronger. If anything, Brady had it all over him in courage. He'd come back to the ranch after the fire. Knowing what he'd done, he come back and tried to make things right.

All Lobo wanted to do was saddle his horse and run while he still could.

"Did you mean what you said?" Her soft voice broke into his thoughts.

His gaze met hers. Her eyes were so blue. So pure. So irresistible. "Did I mean what?"

"That you're here to stay?"

His mouth tightened in the scowl that was becoming hauntingly familiar to her. "Do you really want that?"

"Yes." The reply was so damned honest and soft and—

"You're a fool, then. I only bring trouble."

"So far you've prevented it."

"That won't last . . . Willow. The good people of Newton won't much take to my bein' here."

She smiled, her lips inviting. "I've outraged them before."

He thought of Estelle and Brady, and a corner of his lips twitched as his eyebrow arched warningly. "I think I'm a different matter. You want to know how many towns I've been asked to leave?"

"I don't think so," she replied, a bewitching, impish grin on her face.

"And I'll be asked to leave this one."

She touched his right hand, which still rested on her shoulder, then leaned her cheek down on it. "I don't care," she whispered.

He stood there, slightly awed that he could feel so much from such a simple gesture.

"I'll stay until there's no more danger," he said abruptly, taking his hand away although it was hard to do.

"And then?" she asked softly.

"And then there'll be another job," he replied hoarsely, and he spun around and left her staring after him.

From her upstairs room Marisa watched the riders return. Dread lodged in her throat as she wondered whether they had been successful.

Earlier she'd heard her father give the orders to burn the Taylor barn, and she'd run to the stable to get her horse and ride ahead to warn Willow. But Cady, one of her father's oldest hands, stood at the door and refused her admittance.

"Mr. Newton's orders," he said regretfully. "You're not to leave."

"Cady," she pleaded.

"I'm sorry, Miss Marisa."

Marisa noticed the foreman, Herb Edwards, coming their way. If she'd thought to cajole Cady, she knew it wouldn't work now.

Herb tipped his hat slightly. "Miss Newton. Your father has left orders that you're not to leave here unescorted anymore. There's too many strangers in the area."

Marisa glared at him. "In other words, you and my father are holding me prisoner."

Herb sighed, which told her he didn't like what was going on any better than she. "Talk to your father about it."

"I will," she said, and spun on her heel to confront her father.

But he was in a meeting with some rough-looking men, and when she entered his study, he told her coldly he would see her later. His voice was harder than she'd remembered, and she didn't like the looks of the men in the room.

Minutes later she heard the sound of hoofbeats, and when she looked up she saw the riders. There was something about them, something ominous and dangerous that sent shivers racing up and down her spine. But when she ran downstairs to see her father, he would say nothing, only that it was now too dangerous to ride alone and repeated Herb's words.

She wondered briefly why the gunfighter hadn't been among the hard-eyed men in her father's study. But then, everything she had seen of him had yelled "loner" at her. Whatever he did, he apparently did it alone.

Marisa wandered restlessly throughout the house. Questions battered at her. Why did her father hate Gar Morrow so much? Where was the man named Lobo? What was happening at Willow's place?

She needed Sullivan. She wanted his confidence and the quiet integrity that made her feel warm and protected. But she needed him for other reasons too. Just being near him sent her senses reeling. Just his touch as he helped her up and down from his buggy sent delicious shivers through her. She had dreamed of him from afar for years, but the flesh and blood person was so much more than she'd imagined. He made her smile and laugh and care. He made the sun brighter, the moon larger, and the stars benevolent guardians. His slight dry smile could lighten her heart, and his chuckle delight it.

She had not known until recently he'd felt something of what she felt. And then she'd found his gaze on her, deep and probing, but most of all caring. She'd felt a glow spread through her, and in his own dazed look knew it was reciprocated.

But she didn't understand why he did nothing about it, why he affected an aloofness and held her at arm's length when she saw the sudden blaze in his eyes.

The house, a large two-story structure that somehow had always seemed out of place to her in this raw country, echoed with an emptiness that was becoming more and more real to her every day.

She finally went up to her room and leaned against the window, her eyes searching in the distance for movement. She didn't know how much time had gone by when she heard the riders return. She looked out in the direction of Willow Taylor's ranch, and saw only darkness. She relaxed slightly. At least there was no red glow of fire.

The men rode in at a hard gallop. The leader threw his reins to another man and quickly mounted the stairs to the porch. Marisa heard the quick knock at the door, and then the sound of it opening. She waited several minutes and then slipped downstairs.

The housekeeper had gone to bed, and the door to her father's study was closed. She slipped off her shoes and silently moved closer to it.

"Dammit," she heard her father say. "Can't anyone do anything right?"

"You didn't hire me to go against Lobo."

"Lobo?" Her father's voice was almost a roar of rage.

"He said he's changed sides. He said he's there to stay."

"One man," her father said. "One man, and twenty of you turned tail and ran?"

"I'd rather face twenty men than that one," the answer came.

"Find a way to get rid of him, or you can pack and get out now."

There was a long silence, and then the rough voice came again. "There might be a way. There's a hill overlooking the road from the woman's ranch into town—"

"Don't tell me about it," her father said. "Just do it. I don't want to know the details."

"It may . . . take a while."

"I don't care how long. No one double-crosses me, goddammit. I brought him here."

Marisa heard footsteps nearing the door and she flew up the stairs. She reached the safety of her room and considered what she'd just heard.

Lobo had changed sides. She couldn't believe it. Had he succumbed to Willow as the town had?

And was he to be ambushed?

Marisa watched her father's visitor leave the house and walk to the bunkhouse. And she knew she had to warn Willow.

Somehow, she would get away tomorrow. She would visit Willow. And then?

She suddenly realized that this whole mess had started because of Gar Morrow. Perhaps she would go to Morrow's ranch herself and ask him why the bitter feud.

He could only order her away.

But first she would have to slip by her guardians. And she knew exactly how.

Sixteen

Monday morning broke clear and still, a golden haze spreading over the horizon. Willow looked out the window for the first sign of a cloud, but there was none. The sky was a light gray-blue, relieved only by a pale yellow sun, which would soon turn egg-yolk dark, hot and fiery.

Yet she felt strangely content, and she knew exactly why. He'd said he would stay.

Willow didn't know why he made her feel so safe, particularly after the night before. She supposed she should have the same fear so many others did of him; she'd never seen one man drive off so many . . . and with only words and a gesture, ominous as it had been.

Not even the man at the dance had been that fast at drawing his gun.

Jess was all danger and vitality and strength and grace. And complexity.

He so wanted her to think badly of him: Lobo—outlaw gunslinger, White Apache. An uncaring, unfeeling killer.

Although part of her realized some of that was true, she could see the other Jess shining through the fragile armor like a nugget of gold long hidden beneath the surface. She'd learned to spot it long ago, when she'd nurtured young boys at her father's school, many of them frightened, many of them belligerent because of that fear.

She knew her childhood had been a strange one, and that it had made her see things differently than other people. Her mother, who had desperately wanted a boy so she could name him George for Willow's father, had died when Willow was born. Willow had grown up without the nurturing of a mother, and she'd grown up quickly. She'd also become play-mate to the boys who boarded at the school, and then big sister and finally a substitute mother. She'd played with them, reasoned with them, and taught them, and she'd learned a great deal about people.

She'd learned that giving trust to a boy considered "bad" usually brought rewards. She'd learned that fighting often hid loneliness. She'd learned that nearly everyone wanted love, even when they protested against it. Perhaps those who did were the ones who wanted, and needed, it most of all. And she had, in those years, learned how to breach most defenses.

Time. Patience. Love. They'd worked with Chad, who had trusted no one for years, and Estelle, who had known noth-ing but abuse, and even Brady.

Jess had had more time to strengthen his defenses, but they were beginning to crumble, one at a time. She thought something quite magnificent would emerge.

Or was it too late? A little voice pierced her optimism. She still knew so little about him. She still didn't know why he had taken up the gun, or how he felt when he—

But she wouldn't think about that, not just then.

She scolded herself for daydreaming. One more week, and school would be out for a month for the harvest. She would have time then to spend with Jess, to learn more about him.

Willow took one last look out the window, and her gaze was caught by movement at the corral. She watched as the object of her thoughts vaulted atop his saddleless horse and left the corral, out of her sight. She flung on a nightrobe and nearly ran to the front door, flinging it open just in time to see man and horse become a fast blur. Jess was leaning forward over the horse's neck, his legs hugging the sides of the horse. They were so together, so in harmony, and they were beautiful to watch. There was an untamed wildness about both of them, an aura of complete freedom as if they were at one with the wind. She felt an ache rise within her. She could never capture the wind, never hold it within her grasp.

He might settle for a day or two, but then freedom would call again.

The fresh early morning air brushed Lobo's face, drying the water from his quick wash. The first touch of the sun felt good and cleansing. He relished the feel of the horse under him, of the understanding that flowed between them. They were two creatures who respected each other and knew each other and responded to each other. He tried to wipe everything else from his mind.

After Newton's men had left the previous night, Lobo had taken watch on the hill overlooking the ranch until Brady spelled him during the early morning hours. They would do the same that night.

The decision further committed Lobo to the ranch, and again he felt the wrench of his stomach that told him he was getting in far too deep. Yet he didn't know how to extricate himself, not without leaving everyone on the ranch exposed to the rage of a thoroughly unpredictable Alex Newton.

But he dismissed that for now, his body and mind absorbing the earthy pleasures of a new day, the smell and sound and feel of natural things, uncomplicated, satisfying things.

He raced the pinto until he knew it was tiring, and then he slowed, enjoying the familiar feeling riding without leather separating him from the horse. He almost always used a saddle now because it allowed him to carry necessities.

When he was with the Apache . . .

There had been few good days then, and those few had been like this one, when he could steal a few hours of freedom, when he could escape suspicious eyes. They had never trusted him, because he had never taken an Apache wife or joined in their ceremonies. But he had proved himself a warrior when at twelve it was kill or be burned.

The old woman had died, the woman who'd owned him. He'd been both glad and sorry. Glad because he hated her. Sorry because he knew what her death meant to him. He was old enough now to be trouble; the work to be extracted from him was no longer worth the trouble of constant guarding. And it had been a long time since this family of Apaches had taken a live captive.

So Dog Boy had done the only thing he'd known to do, challenge the son of the chief. Life was the prize.

The Apaches had laughed. Sano, the son of the chief, was thirteen and a head taller than the boy slave. He'd also already had years of training as a warrior; an Apache boy was instructed in the ways of the warpath almost since infancy.

But Sano accepted. It would be good sport, he said.

His arrogance had been his weakness, and Dog Boy had learned to detect weaknesses. He had also learned how to use a knife, having prepared countless numbers of hides. And he had stark desperation on his side.

The fight was long. A rope was tied around one wrist of each boy, and both were given knives. Dog Boy was quick; he'd learned to dodge feet and hands, and despite long years of hunger, the wiry body was deceptively strong from hard work.

His disadvantage was size. He knew he couldn't allow Sano to land a blow or get on top of him. So he dodged in and out, as much as the rope binding them allowed, nicking and cutting his opponent. Sano became careless in rage, lunging and leaving himself open. And then Dog Boy's knife went into his heart.

There had been silence, a sudden pall, when seconds earlier there had been taunting cries. The chief stared down at his only son, his hand reaching for his own knife, and Dog Boy thought he would die. But then the hand fell and the Apache turned away.

He had become the property of the chief, and his status had changed. No longer did he do women's work. He helped with the horses, was even trained in using the bow and arrow, though he was never allowed near the few rifles they owned. But he was always watched, guarded, mistrusted, until years later when some soldiers attacked the camp and he killed several of them. He did it only to save his own life, not because they were the Apache's enemies, but from then on he climbed another plateau. The Apache band needed every warrior, and now he was trained as one. While still watched and not wholly trusted, he was no longer guarded day and night. He'd killed whites and, by doing that he'd become Apache.

There had been times he could have escaped, but he had no place to go. There was no family. He had no more in common with the soldiers or white settlers than he did with the Apache. Part of him, perhaps, even came to think of himself as Apache. He raided with the others, taking Mexican captives and selling them, and although he never raped a woman, he tested his manhood on a woman captive who seemed to have no objections. She lay quietly under him, and though he felt physical relief, he also knew self-disgust and a terrible emptiness. He never used a captive again.

The fact that he didn't rape captives or take an Apache for wife set him even further apart from the others. If he hadn't been so cunning and deadly a fighter, Lobo knew he would have been killed. As it was, he had been challenged to fights to the death by other Apaches. He fought for his pinto, a colt he'd stolen from a ranch, and a woman who'd preferred Lobo over another even though Lobo had no personal interest. Then came that last raid by soldiers. The numbers were overwhelming, the surprise complete.

Lobo was introduced to yet another kind of life, one in which he was again looked upon with distrust and derision and often stark hatred. But he learned not to care about anything or anyone except, perhaps, his pinto.

And he hadn't. He'd never given so much as a damn about anyone since his brother was left to die alongside an Apache trail. He'd never taken responsibility for anyone. And now he suddenly had. Through some absurd series of events he found himself responsible not only for one other person, but for a passel of children and misfits, not to mention a woman with the bluest eyes he'd ever seen.

He stopped by the river and allowed the pinto to drink. She would be gone from the ranch now, gone to teach school. The thought brought back the old yearning, the hunger to learn, but he could never ask her. That would be the greatest humiliation of all.

Damn. He wanted her more than he'd ever wanted anything, and she might as well be the sun, she was so far out of reach.

Word traveled quickly in the little town of Newton.

"Did you know . . ."

"I heard . . ."

"A gunfighter? At Miss Willow's?"

"Now she's gone too far . . ."

"I can't believe . . ."

"But I have it on the best authority."

"Jest don't seem right, her being the schoolmarm and all."

"Naw . . . it's jest another rumor."

"One of Newton's men told me hisself."

"Is she crazy? I heard tell he lived with Apaches."

"More Indian than white's what I heard."

"Took on a whole mess of Newton's men, I hear tell."

"Why, now, do you s'pose he did that? Miss Willow ain't got the money to pay *his* kind."

"Yeah, why?"

"Hmmm."

A town meeting was called for that night.

Willow didn't linger after school. Rushes of anticipation assaulted her as the day wore on, and grew more intense toward dismissal time.

When the last child, except the twins, had left, she hurriedly closed the door and started for the buckboard as she cast a hasty, anxious glance toward Sullivan's office.

He'd said he was coming the previous night, and he hadn't,

which meant he had some kind of emergency. But she knew he wasn't going to give up. And she didn't particularly want to argue about Jess in front of the whole town of Newton.

Not, she had assumed quickly enough, that they didn't already know about her new ranch hand.

Surreptitious glances kept coming her way—at recess, and when parents came to pick up their children. They were there now on the faces of some of the loiterers on the street.

There would, she suspected, be another town meeting.

But at the moment she didn't care. She'd weathered many of them before, and nothing mattered except the safety of her family and . . . Jess.

Before she could mount the wagon, a grim-faced Sullivan strode over to her. "Are you all right?"

"Of course," she replied.

"Mrs. Corbett had a baby yesterday."

"I suspected as much." Willow smiled. "Boy or girl?"

He looked at her suspiciously. "A girl."

"Both of them fine?"

"Yes. But I want to talk to you about—"

"I know," Willow said, "and I'm not changing my mind."

"You know the whole town is talking about it."

"Since when do you care what the whole town talks about?" she said, a bit more snap in her voice than she intended.

"When I agree with it," he replied stiffly.

"Sullivan," Willow started carefully, "Jess helped Brady all day yesterday, and some of Newton's men came last night, obviously intending to burn the barn. He stopped them."

"Jess?" Sullivan said, his voice rising toward the end of the name. "Jess? His name is Lobo, Willow. *Lobo.*"

"Jess is his real name."

"Jess?" he said again in disbelief.

"Before he was captured by the Apache."

Sullivan lifted one eyebrow in surprise. "Did he say any more? His last name?"

She shook her head.

"Jess? Well, I'll be damned."

Willow couldn't help the smile of satisfaction on her face. She'd finally disconcerted him.

"Did he say anything else? Like how many men he'd killed?" Sullivan asked in an acid tone.

"He asked me if I wanted to know."

"And do you?"

"No. I don't care what he did before."

Sullivan glared at her. "Don't you?"

"If you'd been stolen from your family and raised by Apaches, maybe you'd have done some of the same things he's had to do to survive," Willow said.

"That doesn't make them right, Willow, nor does it justify what he does now."

Willow looked at him steadily. "You usually don't judge people."

"I care about you. I care about those kids."

"And two of them might be dead if he hadn't saved them."

He sighed. "I can't even begin to guess at his motives, Willow, but men like him don't change. Nor do they live long."

Willow felt herself stiffening, and she felt again that fear that had been hovering around her since Jess's revelation about his true identity. She knew Sullivan's last observation was right, but she defended herself with anger of her own. "And you, Sullivan, are you really living?"

His gray eyes turned dark. "What do you mean?"

"I mean Marisa."

A muscle twitched in his jaw. "What about Marisa?"

"It's obvious the way you two feel about each other, but you won't do anything about it."

"I won't saddle her with an invalid."

"I've never seen anyone less an invalid."

He stilled. "You've seen me when I've had attacks of malaria."

"You believe Marisa is too shallow and too selfish to love you then?"

His eyes grew even darker. "Marisa is a lot stronger than people believe."

"She's just selfish, then?"

"How can you say—" He stopped, finally realizing what Willow was doing. "I won't expose her to it," he said.

"And you call me stubborn," Willow said in disgust.

"You're changing the subject, as always," he retorted. "We were talking about you."

"*You* were," she pointed out. "*I* want to talk about Marisa."

He grinned suddenly. "I might listen to you if you listen to me."

Willow glanced at him suspiciously. It sounded to her like a very bad bargain. Sullivan would get the best of it. But perhaps he would start thinking seriously about Marisa.

"I might *consider* it, if you will," she said. "And in the meantime I have to get home."

Sullivan frowned. "You will be careful?"

"I'll be very careful. And you'll be at the meeting tonight?"

"You know about the meeting?"

"I guessed."

"One thing about you, Willow, you've certainly increased the number of town meetings since you arrived."

She grinned. "You'll defend me as usual?"

He shook his head. "This time . . ."

"Thank you, Sullivan," she said as she climbed onto the buggy seat, obviously ignoring his reservations. "You're a good friend."

He stared at her with frustration. "I don't know . . ."

But he was speaking to empty air with a mouthful of dust, and he hoped like hell he was wrong about the heartbreak he thought she was courting.

Marisa bided her time nearly all day Monday. It seemed as if she was never left unguarded. Cady was her only chance for escape, and she could never find him alone.

She fumed and worried and paced nervously.

Everything was changing for the worse. A whole new breed of men was taking over Newton. The gunfighter Saturday night at the dance. Lobo. Keller. Men with hard eyes and cold voices. And her father was responsible for bringing them there.

She had to find out why.

Again she thought of Lobo. An ambush. She really shouldn't care. He was one of them. But for some reason she did. Perhaps because of Willow. He had, after all, apparently taken up Willow's cause. Though why, she couldn't figure. He hadn't seemed interested when she had talked to him when he'd first come to Newton. He had scared her as much as Canton had at the dance.

But an ambush. The thought of her father being involved in one hurt to the core. Whatever else he'd been—hard, often ruthless—he'd always been honorable.

And if she told Lobo or Willow about a planned ambush, would the man named Lobo come after her father in retaliation? Could she ever live with that if he did?

Sullivan. He would know what to do.

She tried several times to go to the corral, but each time she ran into Keller or one of the other new hands she was afraid she couldn't manage. She didn't like the speculative way they stared at her. Even Lobo hadn't leered at her in that knowing, waiting way.

It wasn't until late afternoon that she found her way open. Willow would have left the schoolhouse for her ranch, but Sullivan would be in town unless he was away on a call. Please, she prayed to God. Please let him be there.

Fixing her most innocent expression in place, she wandered down to the barn. Cady was there, mucking out the stalls.

"Miss Marisa," he said, his hand touching the brim of his hat in respect.

"Good afternoon, Cady. Isn't it a lovely day. Just perfect for riding."

"Now, Miss Marisa, you know your father's orders."

"Of course," she said, "but I'd hoped you could go with me. Just for a little while," she wheedled.

He'd never been able to resist her, and he couldn't then. Marisa felt only a twinge of guilt as Cady saddled her horse and helped her up into the saddle.

"Where to, Miss Marisa?"

"Toward town," she said.

He looked doubtful for a moment, then shrugged as she gave him her most pleading smile.

The day was bright. The sky was a clear blue, and the land shimmered under the sun. She knew she should hope for rain; they all needed it, particularly those who didn't have access to the river. All the streams had dried up, and the few farms in the area were suffering. Still, since she could do nothing about creating rain, she would enjoy these minutes of freedom. She didn't know whether she'd get out again after the day's adventure.

Nearly halfway to town Cady started protesting. But she flashed him a smile. "I need to see Dr. Barkley."

His mouth instantly pursed into concern. "Somethin' wrong?"

She gave him a reassuring smile. "Just a headache. I thought he might have a powder."

"But your father . . ."

Marisa merely spurred her horse ahead, setting a pace that made talking nearly impossible. She continued it until they reached Sullivan's office. She didn't wait for Cady to help her dismount. She slid down on her own.

"I'll meet you in ten minutes," she said, and hurried toward Sullivan's office, opening the door without knocking, and closing it before Cady could enter.

Sullivan looked up from a chair, where he was sitting, reading a book, and his face looked both concerned and delighted when he saw her. "Anything wrong?"

"Everything," she said, moving toward him, her gaze on his face. She reached out a hand to him, and he took it, holding tight.

"Tell me."

Doubt suddenly assailed her. Was she betraying her father? Or would she be betraying others if she didn't warn Willow?

"It'll be all right," Sullivan said in the deep voice that was at once assuring and strong. "Whatever it is . . ."

And then she was in his arms, feeling as if she belonged there. He was holding her tightly, his strength radiating into her. She remained still for several minutes, wanting the comfort, the instant, sure knowledge that Sullivan could work everything out.

His hand soothed her hair, and then moved to her chin, bringing it upward until her gaze once more met his. "What is it?" he repeated.

"Is it true . . . that . . . that the man named Lobo has gone over to Willow?"

"Yes," he replied grimly.

"Why?"

He tensed. "I don't know," he said. "I wish I did."

"I keep remembering the time I met him. He was rude and . . . even nasty, but he didn't . . . make me cold like some of the others."

"He's a strange man," Sullivan said. "Chad practically worships him, and even Estelle tolerates him." He was quiet for a moment. "God knows I don't understand him or why he helped Willow when he was supposed to be working for your father. And I don't know why Willow trusts him as much as she does."

"And you don't?" Marisa asked softly.

"Can't say that I do. No matter what's he done for Willow, he's trouble, Marisa. Pure and simple. And I don't think Willow has any idea how much."

Marisa bit the corner of her lip. "Father's men are going to ambush him. I heard them talking."

Sullivan groaned. "Willow said your father's men tried to burn down her barn last night. It's starting, Marisa, and I don't know how to stop it."

"I know," Marisa said. "I heard them talking, and I tried to leave to warn Willow, but . . . my father won't let me ride alone anymore."

Sullivan's mouth became even grimmer. "How did you get here?"

"Cady," she said. "He's outside now, probably having fits."

He nodded slowly. He'd treated Cady's back problems.

"I didn't think Papa would go this far," Marisa said in a sad, soft voice.

Sullivan's arms went around her and tightened, and her

head settled against his heart. She took comfort in the quiet, steady beat, in the whisper of his warm breath across her cheek. She looked up, and their eyes locked, his steady gray ones worried but also filled with protectiveness.

"I wish I knew why," she continued. "Then maybe I could do something."

"I don't know if anyone can do anything now," Sullivan said slowly.

"But do *you* know why?" she insisted. "I know it has something to do with my mother, but that's all."

Sullivan tightened his grip. "All I know is he blames Gar for your mother's death."

"What should we do about Willow and . . . that man? The ambush?"

Sullivan hesitated. "We have to warn them."

"Do you . . . think he might go after Father?"

"I won't tell him who's behind it. Just that I heard some men talking about killing a famous gunfighter. God knows, that's an occupational hazard for someone like him. From what I've heard of the man, it'll be enough information."

There was a knocking on the door. "Miss Marisa!" Cady's voice was loud and insistent.

Sullivan raised an eyebrow.

"I'd better go," Marisa said, her voice wistful.

Sullivan held her tight, looking down into misting brown eyes.

"Miss Marisa!"

"I have to go," she whispered again. "But I'm going to try to talk to Gar Morrow. Maybe there's some way we can stop this."

"Not if the drought continues and Gar uses Willow's land," Sullivan said bleakly. "I don't know if anything could stop it then."

"Sullivan . . . ?" There was a soft, pleading note in her voice, and it was all he could do not to lean down and kiss away the worry on her face. But he feared starting something he couldn't stop. And then he recalled his earlier conversation with Willow. Was she right?

He couldn't resist any longer. He lowered his head, and his

LAWLESS • 203

lips touched hers lightly. Feeling her response, he deepened his kiss, and he tasted the exotic blend of hunger and innocence. Her mouth, her lips, her body, felt so good against his. Soft and yielding. He felt things he hadn't felt for years, excitement and desire and wondering delight. There was a deep ache in his loins, a stirring of something more than desire, of the need to have and protect and cherish and love. He had been alone for a long time and, because of the malaria, had long ago abandoned once-cherished thoughts of a wife and children. Now fierce and raging in their strength, they flooded his consciousness, drowning everything else, every reservation he had. There was only sweetness, such incredible sweetness, and his need for her.

"Miss Marisa!"

The pounding on the door was even louder, more insistent, and Sullivan knew in a moment the door would fly open. He reluctantly took his lips from Marisa's mouth and stepped back. "You'd better go," he said.

Her eyes were shining, her lips pursed seductively, red and swollen from his kiss. She looked so lovely, and there was a certain awe in her face, all directed toward him. "We'll talk later," he said softly.

She nodded and stepped away as the door opened and Cady stood there, his face red as he glanced from Sullivan to Marisa. She saw understanding dawn on Cady's face, then sympathy.

"We better go, Miss Marisa," he said slowly. "Your father will be as mad as a pricked wild hog."

Marisa nodded slowly as her gaze met Sullivan's. There was something different about his eyes. There was promise there. Despite everything, she felt a glow inside, a happiness that countered all the worry and fear and apprehension of the past several days.

"Everything will be all right," Sullivan said. "I promise."

And Marisa knew that it would. She looked up at the gentle eyes and strong face, a face lined with pain that made it only more dear to her, and she felt safe and wanted. She felt she could do anything, be anything for him.

She nodded, her eyes saying more than words could. She, too, was making promises.

He smiled, and she thought the whole world was shining.

Then Cady's hand tugged hers, and they left. Only then did her eyes survey the street, the strange faces, the increasing number of men. Only then did she see their measuring looks, and was jolted back to reality.

Seventeen

Estelle watched the two men from the ranch-house porch.

Both Brady and the newcomer were working on the barn doors. The building appeared almost complete now.

Strange how comforting the newcomer's presence was. She had been frightened the first time she saw him, the day he had rescued Sallie Sue. But later, though he was silent to the point of rudeness, there was something about him that she trusted.

He was an outsider, too. She had recognized that right away. He looked on others with wariness. And she recognized something else, a friendlessness that was so much a part of her until Willow came into her life.

It was odd that she could feel sympathy for a man, for an outlaw, for that's what she understood he was. Well, she had walked outside the law, too, not from choice, but from necessity, and she wondered if he also had had no choice.

Estelle felt her insides bunch up as she recalled scenes that kept invading her life.

Her mother, drunk, entertaining men in the same room

where Estelle slept. Estelle didn't even know the name of her father; she doubted whether her mother knew either.

She huddled on a cot while her mother sold herself in one cheap hotel after another. When Estelle was old enough, her mother's friends started casting eyes her way. And then one day her mother disappeared. She said she had somethin' to do and for Estelle to wait in the room. Estelle, who'd known her mother's slaps well, waited. Night came, dawn came, and then night again. Hungry and scared, she left the room and started asking about her ma, finally discovering she had left the day before on a stagecoach.

Estelle was thirteen. She had no money, not so much as a dollar, and she was thrown out of the room. A man spotted her huddling in an alley in Omaha. He had been kind, had fed her, and told her he would help her find work. He did, first in a dance hall, where she wore skimpy skirts, and then in bed. Estelle was too lonely and frightened to protest. He was the only one who seemed to care whether she lived or died.

She traveled with him as he played poker, and she plied her trade, often entertaining his friends for free. She had tried to leave once, and he'd beaten her, saying he would do worse next time. In Newton he'd cheated once too often and was killed. She was eighteen then, and knew only one way to survive. She became the town's soiled dove, an outcast among the decent women. And then one night a man came to her room and nearly killed her.

Estelle remembered that night, every terrible second. He had done the most awful things to her, stuffing a gag in her mouth so she couldn't scream. And then he'd started hitting her so hard that she lost consciousness. She woke to horrible pain.

Dr. Barkley had been kind, although it had taken all her strength not to scream when he touched her. And Miss Willow had been an angel. No one wanted to take her in, except Willow, and even then Estelle trembled with shame and fear. She'd seen the schoolmarm from a distance, but she had never attended school, and she knew Miss Willow was a world apart. And yet no one had ever been so kind, so patient, so accepting. She had never made Estelle feel dirty as the others did.

Estelle had been with Willow two years now. It had taken Estelle a year to call her friend by her given name, but by then Willow Taylor was like the family she'd always wanted and never had. Estelle knew she'd caused Willow trouble; she'd heard about the town meetings and the gossip, and once she'd even tried to leave. But Willow had stopped her, said she needed Estelle to take care of the young ones. It was the first time Estelle had ever felt needed, much less wanted, and she'd stayed.

But she couldn't get over her fear of men. She invariably viewed them as attackers, as enemies who would use her and beat her, except for Dr. Barkley and Brady.

Estelle liked Brady. She sometimes wondered whether it was for the same reason she liked the stranger. Brady, too, was an outsider, an outcast. She didn't, however, like the way he drank. Many of her former customers came to her drunk, including the one that terrible night. She didn't trust a man who drank.

Brady usually did his drinking away from the ranch. When he was there he was kind to her, even thoughtful. He didn't look down on her as most lawmen would.

It made her sad when she saw him standing alone, a lost, despairing look on his face. But as he respected her privacy, she respected his. And she tried not to think badly of him when he fell back on his drinking; at least she didn't until the night the barn burned. Then she found it hard to understand. He knew how much was at stake. This was the only home Estelle had ever known. She loved it. This was her sanctuary, a word Willow had taught her.

And she had a terrible fear that this life would be taken from her.

Until the stranger came.

Like Willow's stories, like the legends, he was the knight who appeared to make things right.

And Willow was his lady. Estelle knew it deep in her bones

when she saw them together. He made Willow's eyes sparkle, and anyone who made Willow happy was Estelle's friend.

He had done something to Brady, too. Brady stood taller today. His hand had been steadier at breakfast. He frequently glared at the stranger, but there was also growing respect in his frequent glances. Best of all, Estelle knew Brady hadn't been drinking again.

Estelle also realized that the stranger had done something for her. His brief observation about the breakfast biscuits had filled her with pleasure and new confidence. She knew her cooking was usually not very good, and she knew Willow and the children often lied about it, but she had been slowly improving, and his comment had the ring of sincerity about it.

He was a dangerous man, Estelle knew that. She'd seen him draw. She'd seen the fear in the other men's faces. But she also knew deep in her heart that she was very glad he was there.

Brady looked over at his nemesis. Lobo was the very devil. Brady became more and more convinced of that by the minute. The man was purposely tormenting him, taunting him, challenging him.

Brady didn't want to be challenged. He didn't want to think. He didn't want to put a gun back in his hand.

Whenever he closed his eyes, he saw the last man he'd killed. Dammit, he didn't want to kill again.

Yet whenever he looked up at Lobo, the man's eyes were judging and condemning him.

Why in the hell did he care?

He'd always hated gunfighters. They were all alike, this man as much as any. He had the same cold eyes, the same arrogant mouth, the same response to trouble.

And if Brady wanted to look into his own soul, which he didn't much care to do, he resented Lobo, resented the trust Willow gave him, the hero worship in Chad's eyes, especially the pleasure in Estelle's face. That knowledge didn't say much for him, but there it was. Ugly and real.

"Goddammit," he swore aloud, and was even further annoyed at the amused look in his fellow worker's eyes, just as if Lobo knew exactly what was going through Brady's mind. It was disconcerting. Brady hit a nail through the wood with such force, the plank split, and he looked at it with disgust.

"Ready to quit?" Lobo taunted him.

Hell yes, he was. "Hell no," he said.

Lobo was surprised at how satisfying it was to build something.

As a boy and young man he'd lived in wickiups and never had more than he could carry on horseback. As a white man he didn't have many more possessions: a bare room in Denver with several changes of clothes, a saddle, a rifle, a pistol, a saddle roll, and a horse.

The sum total of his life.

But now he felt pride in what he was helping to build. He and Brady had finished the entrance to the barn, the stalls, and the hayloft. Little was left now except completing the doors for the wide opening off the hayloft, and the painting.

Lobo had pricked Brady Thomas all day. If there was one thing Lobo knew, it was men; and he sensed that Thomas's pride, as beaten as it was, responded to challenge. There was something left in the man: a spark that possibly could be fanned into something worthwhile again.

Lobo didn't care a whit about Brady Thomas himself. He didn't like lawmen. He didn't have any use for drunks, or for weak men. He seldom liked anyone. He never stayed anywhere long enough to strike up anything but the most casual acquaintance, and his reputation had kept most people away. If Thomas had been alone, Lobo would have handed him a whiskey jug and ridden away without a second thought.

Now Lobo was committed to the people who lived on the ranch. But he could not stay. Somehow he had to make sure that Brady Thomas would pull himself together enough to protect Willow and the kids when he left. The sooner the better.

He smiled grimly as he considered his task. Lobo, the savior of men's souls. What a joke, on himself most of all.

Nonetheless, he continued to push Thomas, watching as his red face became redder with exertion and anger. Yet he didn't quit, and that said something about him.

Lobo's own body tensed as the day wore on into afternoon. Willow would be returning soon. He had tried to forget her kiss, the boiling, searching passion he had felt in her. It had surprised him, for she was a lady, and for some reason he'd thought ladies didn't feel such things. Not that he'd had any experience with ladies; they'd always seemed so cold and aloof, sweeping their skirts aside when he passed as if he were dirt.

He hadn't cared, for he hadn't thought any better of them. But now he did care, and it was more troublesome than he wanted to admit. He wanted Willow. He wanted her in a way he'd never wanted a woman. He knew she wasn't a woman who gave herself outside marriage and that marriage was not a hand he'd ever hold. He had nothing to offer but trouble. And no woman was worth his freedom.

He was shaking slightly as he looked out toward the gate, wanting to see the wagon, dreading it at the same time. He didn't like the way his knees went weak. He didn't like the curling warmth that disabled him, or the worry that might slow his gun hand a fraction of a second. He didn't like being responsible for someone else, and he didn't like the trust in their eyes, for it bonded him to them as strongly as chains.

Hell, he didn't like any of this. So why didn't he get out? He looked at his reluctant companion. Thomas wasn't ready to stand alone. Perhaps he'd never be ready.

A few days. What were a few days?

Everything, part of his mind warned him. Get out while you can, while you're still alive and whole.

He heard the wagon, its old springs creaking, and he looked toward the ranch gate. She'd tamed her hair into a bun in back, and some strands had worked loose, curling around her face. Her back, as always, was straight and proud, and he saw her face turn toward the barn and her gaze rest there on him.

He couldn't see her eyes, but he could see the change in posture, the way her body moved suddenly, and he knew that she was experiencing the same excitement that was running up and down his spine. He deliberately turned away and spoke to Thomas. "I'll take the first watch tonight."

Thomas nodded grimly. He hadn't missed the brief exchange, and he knew Lobo wanted to avoid dinner, to avoid being near Willow. And he agreed. He was surprised that he agreed with anything Lobo said. But he didn't want Lobo any closer to Willow than the man himself apparently wanted to be.

By the time Lobo and Brady had finished hanging the loft door, Willow had climbed down from the wagon and was watching them intently. The blue of her eyes was even purer and deeper than he recalled, and her expression was hopeful.

"Jess," she said. "It looks wonderful."

"Lobo," he corrected her.

Chad appeared. He'd been with Lobo and Brady most of the day, handing them nails and boards and doing whatever he could, considering his injured hand. He had disappeared shortly before Willow returned home, and Lobo had been grateful. He was uncomfortable with Chad's admiring gaze and hopeful glances. The boy was waiting, Lobo knew, to learn some horse tricks, but that took time, and Lobo knew he wouldn't be there that long, so he'd kept putting the boy off.

But now he was grateful for the distraction.

He brushed his hands against his pants, forcing his eyes from Willow's face, from the anticipation in it, from the hope in it. He had no right to accept what she was offering.

"You'll join us for supper, won't you?" she said, and he saw her right hand nervously play with the material of her dress. The gesture surprised him and moved him. She usually seemed so sure of herself.

He shook his head. "I'm taking first watch tonight."

"But . . . you have to eat."

"I have some hardtack. It's all I need."

Her eyes clouded in a way he hadn't seen before. He wanted to change his mind, but that was the worst thing he could do for either of them.

"Can you finish up?" he said to Thomas, who nodded curtly.

Lobo rubbed the back of his neck, forcing himself to move away.

"Where . . . where . . . are you going?" The words were hesitant, as if she knew he needed to leave.

"The small rise north of here."

"I'll bring you something later."

He shook his head. "No," he said flatly.

"I'll take something when I relieve him," Brady said helpfully, receiving Lobo's inquisitive gaze and Willow's frustrated one.

She started to say something, but Lobo didn't give her a chance. He moved quickly to the corral, where he saddled his pinto, his movements all business and concentration. He checked his rifle, then swung up into the saddle and without a glance backward rode toward the gate.

Willow, disappointed but not surprised, stared after him.

Patience, she cautioned herself. Patience.

Hell, Lobo cursed as he settled on the rise, his pinto staked yards away out of sight of the trail.

He kept getting in deeper and deeper.

He knew exactly how deep as he gazed up at the sky and found the dipper. And the lion. Pictures in the sky. Hell. He'd been happier when they were just damned stars.

Nonsense, all of it. Especially the feeling of emptiness. He'd never recognized it as such before, and he didn't much like identifying it now. He had done well enough, hadn't he? He was alive. He was even rich. That was a hell of a lot more than he could say for most of the people he'd met.

He pulled out a blade of grass and stuck it in his mouth. Something to do besides think about things not worth thinking 'bout.

The town meeting started promptly. As usual, it began with a prayer before the room broke out into chaos.

"Miss Willow hired a gunfighter?" It was an exclamation full of doubt.

"That can't be right. Miss Willow wouldn't hurt a fly on a pie." Sullivan identified the speaker as Bob MacIntyre.

"Heard it right from someone who wuz there."

"Don't care what anyone says. I don't believe it."

"Whole town gone plumb crazy. Wouldn't doubt nothin' anymore."

"My wife can't walk the streets anymore."

"But Miss Willow and a gunfighter?"

"Ain't right."

"Damn sure well it ain't right, beggin' yer pardon, ladies. A schoolmarm associatin' with the likes of that killer. Shameful. That's what it is."

"Well, Miss Willow weren't never an ordinary schoolmarm."

"That's for true."

"But what should we do?"

"We could tell her he ain't welcome in this town."

"That never done any good in the past. Lookit Estelle."

"We could fire her."

"Then whatta we goin' do? Remember how much trouble we had getting a teacher. And say what you will 'bout Miss Willow's peculiarities, she's a fine teacher."

"But what kind of example . . ."

"Now, you know Miss Willow's a lady."

"But it don't look good. Her and that gunfighter."

"But there's chaperons."

"Hell, a soiled dove and a drunk. What kinds of chaperons are those?"

"We'll be the laughingstock of the territory."

"Well, I don't wanta go through trying afind a teacher again. 'Member Abner? Took our money and ran off to the gold fields."

"And that Sam Morgan. My six-year-old was smarter than he was."

"Ain't no one saying nothing about her teaching. It's the company she keeps."

Sullivan leaned back against a wall and listened. Willow, he was afraid, was in over her head this time. He could calm

the qualms of these people temporarily, but he wondered whether he should. Perhaps their indignation would do what he couldn't.

He was deeply worried about Willow. He'd seen the expression on her face when she'd said the name Jess. He hadn't ever seen another like it. Willow, he feared, was falling in love, and he couldn't imagine it happening with a worse person than Lobo. That gunslinger will break her heart, Sullivan mused.

But Sullivan seldom interfered in personal lives. He didn't want any interference in his own, and he tried to respect others in the same way. Yet Willow still had a quality of innocence about her, despite her years in the West. She apparently believed that Lobo had a streak of decency someplace, but he was still a killer. And that took a particular type of hardness.

Sullivan's thoughts were interrupted as the voices grew even more heated. "We oughta to tell her—the gunfighter or her job."

"You know what she'd say," the storekeeper said. "And I for one don't want to lose her."

"Besides," said another, "she'd still have the ranch."

"But she couldn't keep it without—"

Mayor August Stillwater interrupted. "I think we're all jumping the gun here. We don't even know it's true. Why don't we send a delegation to find out. And see what she says."

"But we ought to be prepared. Just in case . . ."

The mayor looked at the speaker. "You forget how she took care of your Jonathon when your wife was sick." He turned to another one of the critics. "Or you. Your Ethan was headed straight for trouble till she straightened him out." He turned to Sullivan. "Doc, you know anything about this?"

Sullivan shrugged. "Just that Lobo's the stranger who's been helping her out. She didn't know who he was, though, until Saturday night."

"Why d'ya suppose he's doing it?" The question came from the back of the room.

Sullivan narrowed his eyes in thought. "You all know Willow. She has a way about her."

A few heads nodded, then more.

"You think he might try to hurt her?" The question came from Mrs. MacIntyre.

No. Not the way they meant anyway. Sullivan hesitated. It was strange how sure he was of that. He finally shook his head slowly.

"Then why . . . ?"

He looked at them, at each individual face. "Why did you go out to help with the barn, knowing Alex would be angry?"

"But we're not gunfighters."

"You're human beings," he said as he shrugged. "I can only guess that he's one, too."

"But he lived with Apaches. Indians ain't got no feelings. It must be a trick."

All of a sudden Sullivan found himself defending Lobo. "He's no different from anyone else. Willow said he was stolen as a child. He wasn't Apache by choice."

"That ain't what I heard."

"I think we've all heard a lot of things. Do you believe everything people say?"

"Wellllll . . . maybe not, but it still ain't proper. A man like him at Willow's place."

"Any of you want to volunteer instead?" Sullivan's voice was challenging. Sheepish faces looked up at him, though he still heard a few disgruntled mumbles.

"I'll talk to her," Sullivan said finally, "and express your concerns. And I'll keep an eye on the place."

Mayor Stillwater nodded eagerly. He hated dissension in his town, and now the whole valley was filled with distrust and rumors. Any small relief was welcome.

"Won't do no good," came a mutter from the back.

But everyone else was nodding their heads.

And Sullivan was wondering why in the hell he'd just done what he had.

An hour later he was still wondering. As he rode through the gates of Willow's ranch, his gaze went to the silent barn, to the house still filled with light.

The door opened quickly when he knocked.

Willow stood there, some of the eagerness in her face fading slightly as she recognized her visitor. But a welcoming smile was almost immediately in its place.

"How did the meeting go?" she asked with humor in her eyes.

He shrugged. "They don't like Lobo staying here."

"His name is Jess."

"Whatever the name is, they don't think it's right for a gunfighter to be staying with the schoolmarm."

"But they didn't fire me?" she guessed.

"I told them I would express their concerns."

She giggled slightly at the solemn way he delivered the message, and he, too, had smiled. She was incorrigibly optimistic. "Consider them expressed."

The smile almost immediately faded from his face. "It's serious this time, Willow. They're worried, not only about appearances but about the town."

"I know," she said. "I am, too."

"He doesn't help things, you know."

"He's been very kind. I won't ask him to leave."

Sullivan sighed. "I expected as much. Where is he anyway?"

"Out on the rise above the trail. He and Brady are taking turns, just in case Alex sends his men back."

Sullivan nodded. "You're all right?"

She nodded.

"Good night, then."

"You won't stay for coffee?"

"No," he said. "I just wanted . . ."

". . . to express concerns." Her mouth twitched. "Thank you."

He shook his head slightly, and left. He had one more thing to do.

Lobo had watched with something akin to pain as the sawbones passed him by on the trail. It was obvious the man did not see him, and Lobo did nothing to attract attention.

Instead, he knew a pain that moved from his gut to his heart to his mind. The doctor was everything Willow should have. Educated. Apparently a gentleman. A man who cared about others, everything he wasn't.

It didn't matter, he told himself. He would be gone before long.

He shifted, rolling over slightly from his position overlooking the trail, the same place he'd first seen Willow. He saw her now, as she had been that day, her laughter floating in the wind.

Damn Newton. It was Newton keeping him there when he should leave. There was no telling when he might make another move. Lobo was only sure that he would.

Lobo heard the noise of hoofbeats long before he spied the rider. The sawbones hadn't stayed long. Lobo was surprised at how pleased he was at the knowledge. He expected to see the rider continue on, but he didn't. Instead, the horse and rider turned toward his direction and Lobo stood slowly and lazily as he understood the man was seeking him out.

Sullivan sat in the saddle and looked down on the gunfighter. He was tempted to stay astride, for although Sullivan was taller than most men, Lobo was taller still. But in the moonlight he could already see the cold amusement in the gunfighter's eyes, and he knew that Lobo was aware of the brief feeling. He dismounted, holding the reins of his horse, and matched Lobo stare for stare.

"Need somethin'?" Lobo asked.

"You really think Newton will storm this place?"

"Sooner or later."

"And you're going to stay until he does?"

"Does that bother you?" Lobo's question was lazy, without real interest.

Sullivan matched the cold stare. "Maybe it does."

"Is that why you're here?"

"No. I came to warn you."

Sullivan received some reaction then: a lift of the chin, brow furrowed.

"Warn me? From who?"

"Something I heard in town. An ambush is being planned. I thought you should know."

"Who?"

"I don't know."

"Don't know or won't tell?"

"Does it make any difference?"

"I guess not," Lobo said, his mouth relaxing slightly. "I don't suppose you can tell me more."

Sullivan shook his head. He turned to mount again. He'd done what he'd come to do. He doubted he would accomplish anything more.

"You didn't come to tell me to leave?"

The question came as a surprise to Sullivan, and he turned around. "Wouldn't do any good, would it?"

"No."

Sullivan met the icy blue-green eyes. "I won't say I like you staying here. You're causing Willow one hell of a lot of trouble."

"There'd be more if I left."

"I wonder," Sullivan retorted.

Lobo shifted slightly, his stance tensing. "What do you mean?"

"Willow doesn't see things like other people do. When she looks at you, she doesn't see a gunfighter. She sees the man who saved Sallie Sue, a hero. Which are you, Lobo?"

Something like anguish flashed briefly in Lobo's eyes. Then he turned away. "Thanks, Doc, for the warning."

Sullivan knew he was dismissed. He mounted, wondering exactly which warning Lobo was referring to.

Eighteen

Jess was already working early the next morning. Willow wondered when he ever slept, if he ever tired.

She also wondered whether she would get used to going to the window and not seeing Jess there.

He appeared to be reenforcing the corral now, his movements quick and purposeful. She'd never seen anyone quite so capable at everything, nor one with whom she felt safer.

Her eyes feasted on him. He was standing in the sun, his hair reflecting gold and his skin bronze. He was all grace as he moved, the muscles in his shoulders bunching under the light cotton shirt. As usual, the sleeves of his shirt were rolled up and his hands were covered with leather gloves. Somehow the combination made him appear irresistibly masculine and appealing.

Willow's face heated, knowing her thoughts were unbecoming to someone in her position. She had even wondered how someone like him, someone so incredibly vital, could be attracted, in even the smallest way, to an old-maid schoolteacher. Yet the attraction between them was obviously mutual, the sparks as much on his side as hers, and she had felt the need and want in his kiss. She didn't know why he'd hesitated in taking it further; she should be glad that he did, but she wasn't.

She had thought about him constantly since the first time she'd met him. She'd thought about what she was risking. Nothing less than her heart. Other things—her place in the community, her beloved job as a teacher—no longer mattered as much. She'd never known man-woman love, and she was too much the romantic to pass it by now.

In her own quiet, determined way, Willow had always grabbed life. She'd done it at the Boston school, almost forcing the headmaster to give her a position; she'd done it when she came west, and again when she'd decided to take on the ranch. She knew people considered her naive and often foolish, but she'd always known exactly what she was doing, and the risks involved. She thought that if you wanted something badly enough, and worked hard enough for it, you got it. It suited her that people thought her more flighty than she was, because then they allowed her more tolerance. She used that flightiness shamelessly because she was a woman, and she needed every weapon she could get.

It wasn't that she never felt uncertainty. She did, all the time. Uncertainty and fear. But she'd learned to cover it up, to push it into a corner of her mind, as she did now. As she pushed away the knowledge that her Odysseus was really a paid gunslinger.

But she could not entirely dismiss that fact or another one. By either name—Jess or Lobo—he was as elusive as the wolf he called himself. She realized she could never hold a man like him, nor could anyone, just as Penelope could never hold her Odysseus, but like Penelope she would take what she could and treasure it, making memories to cherish in years to come.

She dressed quickly, determined to find some way to spend time with him alone. The examinations would be Friday, and she would dismiss class early this day to give her students time to study. And then she would find a way.

Willow wasn't surprised that he didn't join them for breakfast. Chad, who went out to call him, returned crestfallen, saying that Jess just wanted some bread and butter and that he'd eat in the barn. To Willow's surprise, Estelle volunteered to take it. Brady kept his eyes on his plate, but Willow saw the muscles in his jaw tighten, and she wondered why.

Willow would have liked to take it herself, but she was too startled and pleased at Estelle's offer. Two weeks earlier Estelle would never have made such an offer, would have, instead, hidden in her room at the thought. She looked at Estelle more carefully, noticing other changes. The fine blond hair had been brushed carefully, and some of the tight, pinched look was gone from her face.

Willow saw the startled look in Brady's eyes and knew he'd noticed something different too. There was something else about him, a protectiveness she hadn't noticed before. "I'll go with you," he said suddenly, and Estelle smiled shyly and nodded.

Well, well, well, Willow thought. Somehow Jess's presence was making more than a few changes around there. She wondered if he had any idea how he was affecting the whole household. As far as she could tell, Brady had not had another drink since the day he left to find Jupiter. He already looked healthier, and his steps had more spring. Estelle looked almost pretty, and her cooking had certainly improved. Chad, who had also been wary of most strangers, was full of eagerness for each new day; even his studies had improved. Sallie Sue openly adored the new arrival, and the twins, well, the twins were probably the least affected. They had always been enough for each other, chortling over their own secrets and staying within their own charmed circle. But even they had shown new willingness to do chores when the stranger was around. They, too, it seemed, wanted his approval. The barest nod seemed to please all her brood except Brady.

She knew Jess had no idea what he had done in a matter of days, and that was incredibly sad to her.

Willow was startled when, after she and the twins climbed aboard the buckboard, Jess rode up on his pinto. "I'm going along with you," he announced stiffly. "There's some things I need in town."

Willow's gaze met his. They were as startling a turquoise as ever, and as indecipherable. She nodded, too surprised to speak.

"I'll ride on ahead," he continued, "and meet you on the other side of the rise."

There was nothing ominous in his voice, yet she felt a shiver of fear run up her spine. She thought about Sullivan's visit, and the way he had asked where Lobo was. The question had surprised her, for she knew he didn't approve of the gunman, and especially of him staying there. She had half feared he'd tried to convince Jess to leave. Now she wondered. She knew her eyes reflected the question, but she received no answer, only a steady stare, before he turned the pinto away and left a trail of dust in his wake.

On the way she saw him on and off in the distance, moving quickly as if looking for something. She wondered what he needed in town and whether he had any money or should she have offered some of the little they had. He'd obviously given up a lucrative offer from Alex, and she'd always heard that men in his profession never kept money for long. He certainly didn't appear to have much; she'd never seen more than two shirts, although he'd kept them scrupulously clean. The only things of value he seemed to have was the horse, pistol, and rifle, the rifle obviously fine and well maintained, the wood glowing when the sun hit the stock.

She owed him some wages, but she had the feeling his pride would be wounded if she offered them.

He'd disappeared as they approached town, and she knew he didn't want her to be seen with him. She ached inside with that knowledge, that he felt he would hurt her by being seen with her. Then she smiled as she thought how proud she'd be to sit next to him, to be at his side. No matter what he thought of himself, she'd never met more of a man.

She didn't see him again in town. As she'd planned, she released school early. All the children from outlying ranches had their own horses, and she knew they'd have no problem getting home.

The sun was still high in the sky when she reached the ranch. She noticed Jess and Brady digging holes outside the

fence that surrounded the house and garden, and she wondered what they were doing. She'd find out soon enough. She
saw Jess look up at the sound of the wagon, his glance fixed
on her for several seconds before returning to what he was
doing.

Her curiosity piqued, she dismounted from the wagon as
the twins started to unhitch the horse, and she made her
way over to Brady and Jess. Her glance quickly took in the
package next to a hole.

Jess's eyes seemed to measure her. "None of the kids are to
go outside this fence," he said curtly.

"What . . . ?"

"Dynamite," he said, watching her face carefully, his eyes
still cold.

"Dynamite?"

"Either Brady, Chad, or I will be here to keep the younger
kids away," he said. He pointed to a piece of red cloth on the
ground about ten feet away. "Everyplace there's a piece of
red cloth, there's dynamite just a little dust underneath.

"But—"

"You want to stay? There's only one way to do it. Fight
back. You ready for that?"

She looked at Brady, whose grim expression didn't waver.
"He's right, Willow. Alex's men will be back, and this time
they'll be prepared."

Willow felt sick. She'd never thought it would go this far.
Did she want men to die for a piece of land? Even this piece
of land? Even her home?

"If everything goes according to plan, no one should get
hurt, but the explosions will scare the hell out of them,"
Brady said with reluctant admiration. "The dynamite can be
detonated by"—Brady hesitated a moment before turning toward his companion—"By . . . his rifle. That's why the red
pieces of cloth are there."

"But if they come at night?"

Jess shrugged. "I placed each bundle of dynamite at the
same angle from a fence post. I'll be able to estimate in the
moonlight, though it might take me an extra shot or two."

Willow looked at his face. There was no pride in the statement, no arrogance. It was said as a matter of fact, although
she couldn't imagine it being possible. She looked over at
Brady and watched his expression, surprised to see the belief there.

"If anyone walks . . ."

Lobo shook his head. "It would take more than that. A
gunshot or something very heavy, like a wagon. Even then I
doubt it would ignite. It needs a direct hit. All the same, I
want the kids to stay away."

She nodded. "Are you almost through?"

"Two more," he said. "Then I'll take a look at the garden,
see if we can plow a ditch from the river. It's a long shot, and
the crop's almost dead, but it's worth a try.

Once again Willow could barely believe everything Jess
had accomplished. The barn was finished, the corral
strengthened, the dynamite purchased and planted. Now the
garden. Did he ever stop? And what about food? An idea
started forming in her mind.

"I'll go with you to the river," she said quickly. "I know
exactly the place to run a ditch."

He looked at her dubiously. So did Brady.

"I'll be only a few minutes. Brady, can you saddle the
horse?"

He eyed her suspiciously. "I can go."

"No, I need to get away for a little while." She gave him her
most pleading smile.

She *did* need to get away. Brady knew that. Between the
school and the ranch and her adopted family, she never had
any time to herself. He'd complained of that frequently. He
could hardly refuse now. Yet he couldn't help feeling he
shouldn't leave those two alone, not when he felt the raw,
vibrant attraction between them, not when he noticed the
way their eyes met and didn't waver. His only comfort was
the look of dismay on Lobo's face.

Willow didn't wait for an answer, or approval, or consent.
She dashed to the house and up the stairs to change into the
dress with the fullest skirt and her boots. She didn't have a
sidesaddle, and she barely knew how to ride. Brady had tried

to teach her, but she hadn't been a very good pupil. She would probably disgrace herself. But she didn't care. A few moments alone with Jess, perhaps even longer. That was worth almost anything.

She quickly twisted her hair into one long braid, then stopped at the kitchen to carefully place some fresh bread and cheese and a canteen of water into a sack.

When she arrived back at the corral, Jess was standing impatiently, a scowl on his face. But Willow's one riding horse was saddled and waiting, and, after only a brief pause, Jess strode over to her, offering his cupped hands to help her mount.

Willow put her hand on his shoulder, feeling the muscles underneath the shirt, the heat of his skin reaching through the cloth, and she was unable to move for several seconds, reluctant to lose the intimate contact with him. But then she put her left foot in his hands and let him boost her up into the saddle so easily, she might have been a feather.

She was pleased that Betsy, named by old Jake, was elderly and easygoing, yet even then she felt at a terrible disadvantage. She'd never seen anyone ride as well as Jess. But Willow stiffened her back, and with one hand on the reins and the other clutching the saddle horn as well as the bundle that Jess eyed curiously, she kicked Betsy into an awkward trot toward the well-worn path to the river.

It had been a cattle trail when Jake used to have a herd, and it was the path Gar used when his creek went dry. The river was only a quarter of a mile away, and there was a shady patch of cottonwoods nearby where on Sundays she would sometimes take the children for a picnic.

They rode in silence, Jess obviously concentrating on controlling the pinto, which danced skittishly, wanting, she supposed, to chase the wind as she had seen them do several days earlier. She was glad he purposely kept his eyes turned from her, for she felt awkward and ungainly. She knew the calves of her legs were showing and that her skirt was bunched awkwardly around her thighs. Yet nothing could dim the pleasure of being with him, of riding next to him, even when he was glowering, as he was then.

When they reached the river, she turned north and showed him where Gar watered his cattle. Jess would have to build his ditch farther away, or it could quickly be trampled and destroyed. They moved slowly up the river to the stand of trees.

Jess stopped and studied the terrain. It went slightly downhill toward the Taylor ranch. "Ever have any floods?" he said.

"Not as long as I've been here," she replied. "But I heard there was a bad one about eight years ago."

"The river flows south," he said. "If we try to plow a ditch, we'll have to dam just below here to send water toward your garden.

"That would cut off Alex," she said.

His lips moved in a mirthless grin. "Exactly."

"What are you thinking?" she asked.

"Perhaps we can solve two problems."

She looked at him. His eyes were suddenly alive with an idea, and his countenance was not as cold, not as forbidding as usual. "I . . . don't think I understand."

"This is your land. You can do what you want with it?"

"I—I suppose so."

"If we build a dam, then we can get water to your crop—and have a bargaining tool."

Willow didn't miss the "we," and she felt a rush of pleasure. "Alex will be furious."

Jess shrugged. "He already is."

"But can just the few of us do it?"

"I don't know," he answered thoughtfully as he eyed the river. It was low now, its bed wide. "We'd have to cut down some of your trees so they would fall over the riverbed and then stuff the cracks with mud and grass. We can use some of the dynamite we have left to dig the ditch to your garden."

The dynamite. Willow's attention changed direction. "Where did you get it?"

"The general store," he said. "I suppose they supply the mines west of here."

"But the money—"

His mouth tightened. "I didn't ask you for any, did I?"

"But—"

His mouth crooked in as close to a smile as she'd seen. "Thank Newton. Expenses he paid me."

"But—"

"Look," he said, cutting off the expected protest. "He lied to me. No one lies to me. I told him that, right at the beginning. He owed me. For that matter, he owes you for all the trouble he's causing."

Willow stared at him, at the lean, bronze face that was almost like a sculpture in its implacable harshness. His eyes, which showed traces of excitement moments earlier, were still now, watchful and waiting. Shivers ran up and down her spine as he regarded her levelly, almost as if he were testing her.

She nodded slowly. She could be starting something difficult to finish, but Jess was right. Alex was already a dangerous enemy. Perhaps a dam would make him see reason and understand how they all had to share water.

Now that the decision was made, her mind turned to something else. "I want to show you something," she said. Before he could decline and suggest returning, she urged Betsy forward, through the cottonwoods, until she reached one that towered over all the others, its roots partially above ground and knurled with a natural artistry that had always awed her. The huge branches reached partially over the river, and shaded a good portion of ground. Without waiting or turning to him, Willow slipped down from Betsy and walked over to where one of the roots made a perfect bench. Only then did she dare a look in Jess's direction.

He was still sitting on the horse, his expression bemused, his hands resting over the mane of his horse. Leisurely, he moved his right leg over the saddle horn and slid down from the pinto. His gaze, now hot and intense, met hers with challenge. He walked toward her with the grace of a stalking cougar, and she wondered whether she was fully prepared for the consequences of her own trap.

She could not move, did not want to move. Warmth suffused her body and she felt herself trembling. She dropped the sack she was holding, and she hid her hands behind her back so he wouldn't see how much they were shaking. Not with fear. She didn't think she would ever really fear *him*. But she did fear the strength of her emotions and feelings for him. She also relished them, for never had she felt so alive and vibrant, even wild and . . . wanton.

Her cheeks were flushed. She felt the heat in them, and she knew her eyes were saying things that her mouth couldn't. She didn't know how to say them to him. And she didn't have to. From the beginning they'd had a special communication, an intimate knowledge of each other, of the feeling that ran so rampant between them. He wanted her. She wanted him. Their bodies strained toward each other as heat radiated around them.

He finally spoke in a hoarse voice. "Do you know what you're doing?"

"Yes," she said simply.

"I won't be staying."

"I know."

"Do you, lady? Do you really?"

She reached out for one of his hands, seductively pulling off the leather glove, her fingers playfully brushing his skin. His hand quivered as she drew circles on the palm. There were still traces of the burn—a lingering redness and broken blister. She lifted the hand to her mouth, and held it against her cheek as she looked up at him. "Yes," she said.

"You're loco," he said, the words almost lost as his lips reached for hers, then burned their imprint on her consciousness. The kiss was hungry, no, more than hungry, ravenous.

Any reservations Willow had disappeared as the kiss deepened and the yearning between them exploded. His tongue entered her mouth and she welcomed it with her own, exploring and seeking and delighting in the discoveries. The warm rush she'd felt earlier was nothing compared to the volcanic heat now flooding her, sweeping into every pore, galvanizing every nerve. An uncontrollable tingling started in the core of her being and swelled to encompass all of her, demanding something she didn't entirely understand. Her legs turned weak, and she felt his arms steady her, cherish her, possess her.

She looked up and was consumed by eyes that now burned with fire. Her heart raced as new sensations galloped through her. Soft, longing ones; fiery, passionate, demanding ones.

His arms tightened around her, and she felt his body tighten under his clothes, smelled the warm scent of earth around him. When she shivered, his hands rubbed her back, his fingers touching and kneading and exciting. His lips left hers, and she suddenly felt bereft, but then they started traveling along her neck, leaving trails of heat until she felt herself glowing with it.

He mumbled something she didn't understand, and she wanted to say something, to call him Jess, but she was afraid she might break the bonds that were still fragile and tenuous. She bit her lip until it bled, holding back the word, holding back anything that might bring back that wariness, that intense fear of involvement.

Lobo had never touched with gentleness before. He hadn't known he was capable of it. But from the moment she had taken his hand, had given him softness and tenderness, he knew sensations and feelings that he'd kept tightly locked away nearly all his life. For the first time he could remember, he wanted to give, to share, to belong, and, strangely, he was discovering he knew how. He wanted her to feel everything he was feeling, every touch of newborn wonder, of exciting discovery, of emotions wild but sweet. Even as he wanted to mock himself for feelings he'd always scorned, he knew they were more real than pain, or fear, or triumph.

Her touch inflamed and healed at the same time, and he desperately wanted to do the same to her. He'd always taken in lovemaking, and always with women with experience. Willow, he was sure, had no such experience, and he had none with women who didn't. He didn't know what to do, and he was frightened of hurting her.

And yet he could not stop. His heart and soul and body longed for her with a compelling fierceness that brooked no denial. And when his eyes searched her face, he saw the same need in her.

Lobo felt her hands in his hair, her fingers making patterns along his neck, caressing and teasing, and her warm breath tickled the skin of his cheek. Her eyes, the summer-blue eyes, were dazzling in their clarity; no doubt at all lay hidden there.

His hand reached up to her face, tracing her lips, delighting in the softness of her skin, the soft, becoming blush from the passion streaking between them.

He knew he shouldn't continue. It would be like snatching a bite of a feast that would be jerked abruptly away from him. For his sake, for hers, he knew he should stop.

But no one had ever looked at him like that, no one had ever touched him like that. He was like a thirst-ravaged man who was offered a drink of water, and he could no more refuse it than he could stop breathing.

He felt the heat curl inside his loins, but more than that he felt a warmth in the upper region of his body, in the area of his heart. It was more seductive even than the physical, the pleasure more perfect, the satisfaction more complete.

Lobo guided her down to the ground, and he pulled her body against his, rejoicing at how readily it moved with his, how completely they fitted together, despite the difference in size. He felt his manhood swell and heat and ache, and it was different from the other times he'd felt a man's need. He wanted more than quick relief; he wanted to bury himself in her and make her totally his in a way no other woman had been. The feeling was so intense, so unexpected, it scared the hell out of him.

But nothing could stop his hands, which suddenly knew exactly what to do, how to seduce, how to caress, how to cradle, things he'd never considered before. He looked down at a face beautiful in the shaded light, the eyes full of stars and a mouth swollen with his kisses, and he knew he'd never seen anything quite as awe-inspiring as before. Not a sunrise over the mountains or a desert sunset. The look was for him. Lobo, White Apache. Gunslinger. Even killer. Yet at the moment he felt the sum of all the heroes who'd ever existed.

He bent his head and kissed her slowly, tenderly. His hands moved over her with the same wonder, resting but briefly on her still-clothed breasts before moving on, exploring, feeling the shivers of her body as she reacted.

And then her hands were doing the same to him, and he felt jolts of sensation run through his body until he thought he would explode. His body shook with the effort to keep his hands gentle, to avoid frightening her, to keep touching when any minute he knew she would realize her mistake and jerk away from him. He didn't know what he would do then, so he kept his touch light though it was more painful than anything he'd experienced in a life grown accustomed to pain.

He felt her hand at his neck, her fingers running through his hair, and then along his jaw, and he thought nothing had ever been, could ever be, so loving. He hurt at the agony of it, at the need inside him, at the fierce fire that consumed while it soothed. His kiss deepened, his tongue sliding over her lips, and she opened them and her tongue met his, feeling each other, exploring secret places with a joint rhythm and yearning that drew their bodies even closer together until he could feel her breasts pressed against his heart, and he knew his manhood was straining against her with demanding heat.

She'll go now. She'll gasp or scream and run. But her body leaned only farther into his, until he felt every nerve end screaming. His kiss suddenly became violent, violent and ragged and full of need. But still she responded, his schoolteacher so full of unexpected fire that he suddenly knew neither could stop what they had begun.

"Jess," she whispered.

He pulled his mouth from hers and searched her face again, delighting in the emotions running across it. She was so open, so open and fresh and clean and pure. He knew he had no right, until he saw the right in her eyes, and his lips caressed her temple, then her cheeks, tasting the clean sweetness of them. His mouth moved down to her neck, his tongue fondling and stroking until he felt her entire body quiver and her hands tighten almost desperately around his neck.

One of his hands covered a breast, and he heard a slight noise, almost like a moan, and then he heard a similar sound from his own throat. His other hand found the buttons in front of her dress, tiny little buttons, and his hands, usually so efficient, faltered and fumbled. But then her hands were unaccountably helping, and he could only stare as the cloth moved and he saw the creamy white skin beneath, the swell of soft mounds until they disappeared under the cotton of her chemise.

His hand found its way under the material, his fingers cupping the soft, rounded flesh that swelled in his hands. One finger played with a rosy red tip, and he felt it growing taut with excitement, and heard her quick gasps of breath.

Lobo felt his own blood quicken, his own breath change its pattern. Everything was new. He felt touched by the sun, basking in some kind of light that pried into the closed, shaded parts of his life. His hands were no longer tools of death, but now instruments that gave pleasure and wonder.

He closed his eyes, capturing the moment, the feelings that he was sure he'd never know again.

"Jess." The name again was like a song in his mind, and he swallowed hard before looking at her. Invitation was in her eyes. There was fear too, but mostly invitation, and longing.

"Are you sure?" His question was tentative.

"I've never been so sure of anything," she whispered and, despite the murmurings of a conscience she was holding at bay, she *was* sure. There was something very right about the feelings between them, the wholeness of them. She'd been waiting for this for years, and she knew with all her being that there would never be another Jess. Even if he left tomorrow, she knew it was right. Right for her. She hoped right for him.

"I can't stay," he warned her again.

"I know."

And Lobo knew she did, that she wasn't lying. She was willing to accept whatever he gave her, for however long he chose to do it. And that knowledge made him humble and unworthy. Until she lifted her hand to his mouth and held it there, her fingers quieting any additional words, and then all rare good intentions went to the devil.

He finished undressing her, and he sat and looked with incredulity at the slender, lovely body. He watched her eyes, hesitant and shy, watch his for reaction, and his fingers touched the auburn hair, unbraiding it and letting it settle around her shoulders like a cloud. Her blue eyes were bluer than ever, wide and searching, and he saw sunlight dapple her skin through the leaves of the tree, turning ivory into gold and silver.

"Christ, but you're beautiful," he said in a hoarse, emotion-filled voice.

"So are you," she said simply.

He shook his head, but a small smile touched his lips. "I think you're the first to ever think that."

"Hmmm," she said. "I noticed it from the beginning, from the day I saw you on horseback framed by the sun."

He raised an eyebrow in question.

"The hill overlooking the trail."

He shook his head. He was definitely slipping.

But for the moment that didn't matter, only the face that looked at him with such yearning did. His fingers slightly trembling, he began to undo his shirt buttons, and she helped him.

He shook off the shirt and watched her eyes as they widened when they saw his chest, and he felt a momentary surge of pleasure. Then his hands went to his trousers, and this time his fingers were sure. Yet part of him quaked inside. What if he frightened her? Despite her openness, he was sure she was inexperienced, a virgin. The shyness in her eyes, the way she held her body, told him as much. There was no brazenness, no open disregard for nakedness that he'd seen in loose women, only a certain wonder at her own responses.

His hands stroked her skin, and he leaned down to kiss her breasts before he pulled off his trousers. He felt her body

234 •   *PATRICIA POTTER*

tense just as her mouth softened. Her hand went to his nipples, and played with them until he felt jabbing jolts of electricity strike him.

"I knew you were beautiful," she said, her hand moving to the scar on his shoulder and then downward, following an arrow of golden hair that disappeared beneath his trousers. Her hand rested there, and she swallowed as she saw the bulge grow larger. Then she looked up at him. "I need you," she added simply.

No other words could have inflamed him more. No one had ever needed him, had ever wanted him. And now she was offering him the moon and the sunrise. Her mouth parted and he leaned down and touched his lips to hers with haunting gentleness. His hands slipped his trousers down. Carefully, he settled his body on top of hers to allow her to know it slowly.

Hesitantly, his mouth moved from her lips to her breasts, licking them, sucking on them, letting them brush his cheek. Then his tongue trailed downward to her stomach and he felt her whole body quiver, just as his was.

Willow felt like a very precious object. She had been surprised at first by his gentleness but now she wondered why she ever thought he would be otherwise. She'd seen him tenderly handling Chad, and putting jelly on a biscuit for Sallie Sue, glimpses of a side he'd hidden so well.

She loved him so much. Loved those turquoise eyes that sometimes flared with a fire he tried to contain, that tense body trying so hard to hold back when he was crying out for her, just as she was for him. She loved that scar on his shoulder because it was part of him, and she loved the strength in him and the grace.

Her hand went to his cheek and guided it up until once more their lips met. This time there were no reservations between them, only an all-consuming need to become one, to give to each other in a way they'd never given before.

She felt his manhood at the entrance of the most secret, private part of her, and she relished the hot, pulsating skin that moved against her. A deep, intense craving gnawed at the deepest core of her, making her move shamelessly against him and savor the contrast of her soft body against his hard one.

The very tentativeness of his movements when she could see the need etched on his face and in his taut muscles made her throb with love for him. She ached with compassion for this man who was so afraid of caring, yet had so much caring within him.

Then everything dissolved as he probed deeper, and she felt a sudden sharp pain, so unexpected that she cried out. He stilled, but his manhood continued to quiver against the inner confines of her body. The pain receded, and the need in her overcame the surprise, the need to wipe away the self-disgust that flitted across his face.

"No," she whispered. "Don't go away. Please don't go away." And her body said more than her words did as it arched against him and her arms pulled him down. She heard his long, raw cry and felt his heated lips back on hers.

He was all fierceness now, but still his mouth treasured her. The fullness in her, the strangeness of it, changed into something so sensuous and beautiful that instinctively she started moving with him, reaching for some unknown destination. Heat flooded her as his rhythm increased, as he ventured deeper and deeper. Pleasure rolled through her like rumbles of thunder, each wave more powerful than the one before as the momentum mounted and she was lost in one great storm of flashing lightning and bursts of splendor.

She cried out, and his lips captured hers as he thrust once more, igniting one final explosion that left her entire body feeling wonderfully sated and warm.

She looked up at him and saw the disbelief in his eyes, the wonder, the passion that made the blue-green color even more brilliant. He made no move to disengage himself from her, and she treasured the feel of his body so intimately connected to hers. His mouth touched the corner of one of her eyes, and lingered there, catching a tear that had gathered.

"I'm sorry," he whispered.

"No," she said. "That's not regret. It's gratitude." She was rewarded with a smile both unexpectedly boyish and uniquely sweet.

They lay there together, still linked in the most intimate of ways, both reluctant to break the enchantment and closeness of the moment, both afraid to say anything that might shatter their peace and contentment. His hand took hers and simply held it. She suspected that was the first time he'd ever done such a thing, and her fingers tightened around his.

"I never knew," he said finally. "I—"

Her throat went tight at the emotion and awe in his voice.

He moved slightly, and she felt the sudden loss of his warmth. She rested her head against his chest and heard his heartbeat. There was a light film of moisture on him, and she licked it, feeling him react in the most basic of ways.

"Be careful, lady," he said roughly, but there was also a note of tenderness, almost a caress, in the sound. She felt a rush of love for him, overwhelming everything she was or knew or cared about.

She knew he saw it in her eyes, for he suddenly moved away, his eyes filling with despair, his hands reaching for his clothes.

"Jess?"

"Lobo," he answered, his voice low and angry. "Lobo."

And clutching his clothes, he stalked off into the trees.

Nineteen

Willow dressed slowly. Her body still tingled and quivered. Each sensation remained wondrous to her.

She should have been bereft at his abrupt departure, but she wasn't. She knew how much he'd tried to keep his distance, to keep from being involved, and how much his abysmal failure must have bothered him.

And it was, from his viewpoint, an abysmal failure indeed. For he had done much more than mate with her. He had given her part of himself. In his tender touches and gentle gestures he had reached deep inside himself, into parts even he didn't know existed, and opened himself up.

He was probably regretting every lovely minute now.

But like Pandora's box, once released, those feelings and emotions would be impossible to confine again. He might try. In fact, she knew he would.

He would fail.

She wanted to go after him, but her instincts told her that would not be wise. He had to work out things on his own. He had to come back on his own. And he would for a while. And then . . .

Willow didn't want to think about "then." She was willing to take this time, as much of it as she could have.

She rose slowly and went over to the riverbank. The water was very low, not much more than a foot deep in some places, and she thought about Jess's plan. It was both dangerous and ingenious, and she wondered again at how very good he was at whatever he did, whether it was working with horses, or raising the barn, or building the defenses around the ranch house.

She also knew from the other night he was equally good with a gun!

But she simply couldn't think of him as a cold-hearted gunfighter. It wouldn't be the first time a man's reputation had been twisted and embellished. Perhaps that was it; perhaps everything about him had been exaggerated until there was no distinguishing between truth and myth.

Nothing she'd been told of him fit what she had seen of Jess, what she knew of him.

Exaggeration? Lies? She swallowed deep as she thought of them. Vicious, he'd been called. Vicious and merciless.

Not her Jess. Not the man who had pulled Sallie Sue from the well, or saved Chad from a rampaging bull, or pulled a lawman from a burning barn. Not the man who had touched her so gently.

And then she sensed his return, sensed more than heard. She turned slowly and looked at him.

His lips were taut, his eyes veiled. Everything about him radiated tension. "I'm sorry," he said stiffly, and Willow knew that he'd probably never said those words before. They sounded unfamiliar on his lips, rough, almost disbelieving.

Willow moved over to him, her hand reaching for his. "Come sit down with me for a while."

"There's a lot of work to do." Yet he didn't pull away, and the back of his hand went up to her cheek and moved along it. "We should go."

"Please," she said, and his head bent slightly in surrender. He allowed her to lead him to the bank, where she sat, her movement forcing him down, too, and then she leaned her body against his chest. "Don't ever be sorry," she said. "That was the most wonderful experience in my life."

She looked up and saw a muscle flex in his cheek and his lips clench together. He was fighting something, her probably. Certainly himself.

"I can't give you anything but trouble," he said finally.

"You've already given me at least three lives," she replied. "And a barn. Estelle, who's ready to live again, and Brady, who looks better than he has in a long time." She suddenly flushed. "And today. You've given me today. And nothing can ever take that away."

He stared at her. She'd misjudged everything. He hadn't meant to do any of what she'd just said. If he'd had time to think about it, he would have done none of them. He was no good.

Lobo tried to think of the worst thing he could say to her, the one thing that might repel her. And he knew what it was. He tried to force the words, but the secret was the one he'd hidden the deepest, had protected the most. And now was the time to tell her.

He didn't know how. How could he tell her he couldn't read or write? Someone like her, whose life was books and learning?

The words finally came because they had to. But they came hard and ragged. "I can't . . . even read."

He was startled at the puzzlement in her eyes.

And she *was* puzzled. She was surprised that he couldn't read, mainly because he was so competent at everything. But then she thought back to his past, and it made sense. But she didn't understand why he felt the shame he obviously did. This was obviously something very important to him, and she felt again that vulnerability in him that was so appealing, that separated him from the man everyone else apparently saw.

"That's easily remedied," she said softly. "Learning to read is one of the reasons Jake left me the ranch. Jake wanted to learn, and I taught him on weekends. And Chad . . . I teach him at night. His father wouldn't send him to school."

"Jake?"

"When I came here, he wanted more than anything to read the Bible. He was . . . shy . . . about it, and I used to come over on Sundays and teach him to read. I think he was prouder to write his wife's name in his Bible than anything he'd ever done."

Lobo remembered Newton's insinuations about Willow and Jake, and he wanted to kill the man even as he wondered over Willow's ready acceptance of what he considered a major flaw in himself. But then, he was amazed at her acceptance of so many things. It wouldn't last. He knew that. She would soon see him for what he was, not the man she fancied he was. And he didn't know if he could bear that.

Yet he had brought this all on himself.

She leaned back against him and looked up, her eyes full of love and pride, and her words momentarily eased his doubts, reduced to rubble the shame he'd always felt about his lack of education. "You know so much. You look at a problem and you know immediately how to solve it. That's so much more important than someone who knows books and nothing else." Her hand played with his. "There's so much strength in you," she added.

Waves of unexpected pleasure surged through him. He suddenly wanted to be everything she thought he was, but then despair settled in. He wasn't; he never would be. There was too much behind him. But for this moment he would enjoy it. His hands wound through her hair, separating the strands until it fell free around her face. It was so silky and irresistible. He leaned his head down and breathed the fresh, flowery scent while a breeze brushed both of them and scattered rays of sun played against their skin. He had never known such quiet contentment. For the first time in his life he felt peace and joy and love, and he reveled in it, knowing this moment was fleeting and would soon be only a memory. His body ached pleasurably with the recent joining, and he swallowed from the mystery of it, the mystery and glory that he never knew existed between man and woman.

"You are so beautiful," he said again.

Willow heard the haunting sadness in his voice, and she wanted to assure him and comfort him and love him. The stark loneliness was back, and so was a hint of helplessness. And helplessness did not fit this man of hers.

This man of hers.

And then she said words she hadn't meant to say, because she didn't think he would welcome them. But feelings overwhelmed her, and she couldn't hold them back. "I love you," she said.

He didn't say anything. He didn't jerk back as she had thought he would. Instead, he sat as still as a statue, and his eyes reflected the deepest sadness she'd seen in a human being.

His hands moved over her as if memorizing every curve. Her gaze didn't move from his face, and she saw a muscle twitch in his jaw. She ran a finger along the muscle's length, and it seemed to jump under her ministrations. He closed his eyes, and she knew he did so to close out the powerful emotions streaking between them. Passion, yes, but so much more than that, things she knew he didn't want to recognize or acknowledge.

"That's the worst thing you can do," he said finally.

"I think it's the best," she said as she leaned up and kissed his lips. When she pulled back, he tried to speak but she put her fingertips to his mouth.

"I'm not asking for anything," she said. "Not that you stay, although I want that, not for any promises. Just to be with you awhile."

"That's not enough," he said, his words catching in his throat and sounding uncertain to him.

"It is for me."

"It shouldn't be."

As an answer she merely moved closer to him, soaking up his presence, his scent, his warmth.

They stayed like that for a long while. Lobo knew he would measure the rest of his life by this hour, this afternoon. Of all the minutes of his life, these were the ones that made everything else worthwhile, that justified all the rest.

Willow finally broke the silence. She didn't want to, but she had to know more about him, know how to surmount all those barriers he erected.

"Do you ever miss the Apaches?"

"No." As so many of his answers, it was short and did not invite additional questions.

"Tell me about them?"

He looked down at her, at the calm, accepting interest that wasn't the lurid curiosity he saw in the eyes of others who had asked the same question.

He shrugged. "They're hard, but their life is hard. It always has been."

"Did . . . did you ever have a family among them?"

Lobo knew she meant a wife. "No," he said.

"Why did you finally leave?"

He thought she wanted to hear something heroic. Everyone did. But she had to know exactly what he was.

"I was captured again," he said coolly. "Soldiers this time. They surprised the band I was with. An ambush. They went among the Apache, killing those who survived the attack."

He heard her horrified gasp. "Yes," he added dryly, "soldiers kill too. Women and children as well as the warriors. I was wounded and they would have killed me, too, but they saw my hair, and there were rewards for white captives. Instead of shooting me in the head, they tied me up and took me to the fort. I was the only one who survived."

She looked at him with disbelief and horror.

He smiled slightly, but there was no emotion in it. "The Apache would have killed them, probably in more creative ways, if it had been the other way around."

"Would *you*. . . ?" She was immediately sorry she'd asked that question. She knew the answer from his face. You learned what you were taught, what you saw, what you experienced. She knew that. He'd obviously never been exposed to or experienced love or compassion or forgiveness, and yet he had saved Sallie Sue, and Chad and Brady, each time risking his life.

"Yes," he said again.

Willow was quiet, thinking about his past. She had been so lucky. Even though her mother had died, her father had been a loving though absentminded parent. And at the school she had been surrounded by friends, by safety and a place of belonging, of comfort. She knew he'd never had any of that.

"Was it . . . hard, when the Apaches first took you?"

He'd never said anything to another person about those years, had never felt the need to justify his time with the Apache. He simply hadn't cared what anyone thought. Now he did. He cursed himself for feeling that way, but he did. He swallowed and he closed his eyes as he remembered that raid on the wagon train: the fire, the screams, the shots, the curses, and finally the silence, except from the terrified whimpering of the few children who lived. For a short while.

"They took my brother and me . . . and five others," he said finally. "I was the only one who survived."

"Your brother . . ."

"He couldn't keep up. They left him in the desert to die." The words were cold statement of fact, but Willow felt his body tense again, and she knew much more lay behind the words.

"And then?"

"I was given to an old woman as a slave." This time there *was* emotion. Hard, bitter rage. Her hand curled around his as she felt the confusion and pain of a young boy torn from everything he knew and dragged into a completely hostile and unfamiliar world.

"But you . . ."

". . . became one of them," he finished for her. "Oh, yes, I became one of them. It was that or a painful death, and I didn't want to give them any more satisfaction than I already had." Each word was pronounced distinctly in a harsh voice that almost cracked with strain.

Her fingers tightened around his hand, and she drew it up to her mouth, touching the back of the hand with her mouth and holding it next to her cheek. She had to know the rest, and it was the rest that was so ugly.

"I killed the son of the chief when I was no more than a boy," he continued. "And I kept on killing, because that's how Apaches survive. They raid. They steal. From the Mexicans, from the whites. That's been their way of life since their storytellers can recall."

She started to say something, but he took his hand from hers and placed it against her mouth, silencing her. "No," he said. "You have to know everything."

Willow felt her heart thump wildly. He had tried to tell her bits and pieces before, but now he was forcing her to see everything. He was laying his soul open and she was both fascinated and frightened.

"The Apache didn't trust me, but they discovered I had a skill they could use. Killing. I've killed more than my share of soldiers, Willow. I've killed Mexicans on raids. I've even killed white settlers once when I was being 'tested' by the Apache. Chrissakes, they were fools, taking land in the midst of Apache territory. I couldn't feel sorry for them." He looked her straight in the eye as he said the words, expecting disgust and condemnation.

But her eyes remained the same bright blue, a slight mist reflecting in them, like a morning fog over a deep mountain lake. He was lying partly. He had killed soldiers, but as far as he knew, he'd never killed a settler. It didn't matter; he had been along on such raids and was as responsible as the Apaches who actually did the killing. He knew he was trying to frighten her away, to save her from pain later, and that was very important to him.

"That," he added slowly, "is how I got my name. Lobo. Predator."

"You're much more than that," Willow said, unable to bear his bitter self-examination anymore.

He shook his head. "Even the army recognized it. They wanted me to scout for them, to turn on my own kind—if anyone is my own kind. I guess the Apache was as much as any." His laugh was mirthless.

"And then . . ." she said softly.

He shrugged. "I wouldn't scout for them, but I quickly learned you needed money in the white man's world. I wasn't any damn good at begging for jobs no one would give a man who'd lived with Apaches, and nearly everyplace I went someone knew, or soon heard. Information like that travels. So I started to do what I do most naturally."

"But you're so good at a lot of things," Willow observed. Her hand moved over his arm, feeling the hard muscles, feeling its strength, its comfort and safety.

"You just keep wanting to see the best, don't you, lady?" he said. "Haven't you heard anything I've said?"

"I've heard everything," she said softly, "and I don't think I've ever respected anyone more. I don't understand how you even survived, and yet you still care . . . about people, about Chad, Sallie Sue."

"They're children," he growled dismissively. "Besides, I never meant—"

"To help them? It was just instinctive," she said with a glow of victory on her face. "What about Brady?"

"What about him?" Lobo growled again.

"You could have left him in the barn."

"Should have."

"But you didn't."

"Thought some damn fool woman or kid would go after him, then I'd have to go back anyway."

Willow suddenly grinned at the unexpected explanation, and his harsh face broke for a moment, his expression first sheepish and then, for the first time ever, amused as he realized how lame the excuse sounded.

"I love you," she whispered again. "And you have the most wonderful smile in the world."

It instantly disappeared into a scowl.

She leaned up and kissed the scowl away. His face softened again, and she thought how absolutely handsome he was.

"That's the last thing in the world you should do," he finally replied.

"Probably," she admitted.

"I'm fiddle-footed," he said. "Restless. I'm always moving."

"I know."

"And men come after me thinkin' they might be just a little bit faster."

"I know."

"Anyone around me can get in the crossfire."

"I suppose so," she said.

"What about the kids? I'm a god-awful example."

"You're a wonderful example."

"Chrissakes!" It was said in a low, almost baffled tone.

"Even when you swear."

"Hell."

"And they all adore you."

"Godammit, they can't! They need someone like . . . the doc." It nearly killed him to say so, but it was the truth.

He looked so frustrated that she had to smile, then grin, and he knew he'd been baited. Teasingly, lovingly, but nonetheless baited. He knew he should be angry, but she looked so fetching that he couldn't do anything but return her kiss, feeling himself tighten up all over again.

Her hands went up around his neck, and he was wrapped in her magic, in the sweet yet challenging love that did the damnedest things to him. He felt his maleness swell again, the heat pulsing once more through his body as his lips firmed on hers, and the kiss became a contest, a contest over who could seduce the other the quickest. Soft and sweet, then wild and hot, until every one of his objections drowned in the heat of the moment. He didn't bother to curse this time. He was lost before he knew it. Their hands were now familiar with each other's clothing, and soon they were naked again and their bodies were melting one into the other, this time with a knowledge that spurred their movements.

He felt like the richest man on earth, and the luckiest. His body, worshipping her as his words could not, moved slowly, reverently, within her until they were both spiraling out of control. He heard her small gasp as he reached deeper and deeper into the core of her, matching his movements to her response, and he wondered how he had gone through half his life without knowing that such exquisite pleasure existed. He could feel her body growing more and more fevered until she cried out with need, and he went as deep as he could, moving with ever-quickening rhythm as her body's pace met his and raced it.

And then there was a shattering climax, one that sent floods, then ripples, of pleasure racing through them, satiating them, exhausting them into a happy, relaxed peace. He lifted his mouth from her neck where he'd been nibbling, and watched her. Her mouth was shaped into a contented smile, her eyes glittered like the brightest stars, and her cheeks flushed like roses.

He didn't want to leave this time. He felt too good. His body felt too good. He didn't have the energy to fight off a grasshopper, much less good intentions, so he pushed them away from his mind, absorbing only the immediacy, the smell of her hair, the touch of her body, the tingling of their skin as they savored the exquisite oneness they shared. Her hand went up and down his arm, ruffling the blond hairs she found there, and when she looked up at him he was one of her storybook gods.

The first coupling had been good, but there had been hesitancy on the part of both, fear on the part of both, guilt on the part of both. But now there was none of that, only the knowledge that something quite wonderful had happened, and a humming sound, like the blissful purr of a kitten that knew it had finally found a home, came from her throat. Lobo tried to tell himself this had been a mistake, a terrible blunder, but he couldn't. If he lived a hundred years, this would be the one moment he'd never regret. He could only hope that neither would she.

The sun sunk lower, spreading a rosy haze across the place where they lay. His hands moved over every part of her body, fondling, loving, remembering. And then he moved slowly away from her, his intent gaze never leaving her face. There was so much he wanted to say, so much he needed to say, but he couldn't. He wanted to pledge love, but nothing had changed. He was still Lobo, hired killer, wanderer, a man decent folks despised.

He wondered if she understood as she said she did. He wondered if she really knew he would leave. He wondered if she would eventually hate him for this afternoon.

"We'd better go," he said, but not as roughly as before. There was a tenderness in his voice that made Willow want to sing, a sadness in his eyes that made her want to cry, a determination that made her want to scream.

She did none of them but merely stood and allowed him to

refasten her buttons. He helped her up on the horse, and stood there for a moment, looking up at her.

"You go ahead," he said finally. "I'll follow in a few moments."

"You will come back?" Willow couldn't keep the sudden worry from her voice.

He stood silent, and when he spoke he sounded defeated. "I'll come back," he said before turning away from her and staring at the river.

She watched him for several seconds. Despite the obvious despair in his voice a few moments earlier, his back was straight, the head proud as she'd always seen it, and her heart thundered. He looked both very strong yet unguarded, a combination that was irresistible.

Willow turned her horse and went in the direction of the ranch, forcing herself not to look back. Her body felt complete, but her mind worried, wondering what was in his head. Despite his assurance, she suspected that he was thinking of leaving.

Even if he didn't leave that day, he would leave soon.

But not too soon, God, she bargained, not too soon.

Twenty

When Willow arrived at the house, there were three strange horses there, and Chad was waiting for her at the corral.

"Mr. Morrow's here," he said, "and that gunfighter I heard you talking about."

Willow's heart stopped momentarily. It had been going at an accelerated pace, and now the beat stilled for several seconds. She remembered what she'd heard: Everyone wanted to see a fight between this man and Lobo.

But the man Jess called Marsh Canton was there with Gar Morrow, and that probably meant bad news of a different kind. Gar's stream was no doubt finally dry, and he needed to drive his cattle over Willow's land to the river.

She'd hoped to have more time, perhaps even time to build the dam. But she had promised Gar the water when he needed it, and that would hurry an open confrontation with Alex Newton.

"Where are they?"

"In the kitchen with Brady. Estelle saw them ride up and went to the bedroom. She doesn't like Mr. Morrow."

Willow knew why. Morrow was a widower and had often

frequented Estelle's bed. Willow didn't think he'd been cruel to her, but Estelle flinched whenever she encountered anyone from that time.

Willow looked back to the direction from which she'd come. She hoped Jess would take his time coming back, and she just as fervently hoped she could end this business shortly. Fear replaced the pleasurable tingles down her back, and she didn't much care for the change. What if he and this Canton met? What if there were a fight?

There shouldn't be, she knew that. Not now when Jess no longer worked for Alex. But she also remembered how quickly Canton reacted at the dance, how quick-trigger angry he'd become and how fast he'd drawn his gun.

Willow also admitted briefly to another kind of fear: She didn't want to be reminded that Jess, like Canton, was a gunfighter.

She went through the door to the kitchen, and saw Brady standing against the stove as he talked to Gar, Marsh Canton, and a third man who was a stranger. She was thankful that he didn't look dangerous.

Willow looked at Canton, whose gaze had turned appreciatively toward her. Her hair was still down, she thought absently, and her dress was probably full of leaves and dirt. She suddenly felt terribly exposed and awkward in front of what seemed like knowing eyes.

But she tried not to betray anything. "Can I help you gentlemen?"

Gar took off his hat and so did Canton, followed slowly by the third man, as if he were not quite sure what was expected.

Gar Morrow flushed slightly and his tone was apologetic. "I know I'm bringing trouble on you, Miss Willow, but my stream's gone dry and my cattle will be dying soon."

Willow nodded. She had promised, and she could no more sit still and watch cattle die than she could sell the ranch to Alex. "Can you wait a few days?"

"How long?"

"A week."

"Perhaps. No more."

She nodded.

He turned to the man in black beside him. "You've met Marsh Canton." It was a statement, and he had the grace to redden slightly as they both remembered the disastrous scene at the dance.

Her eyes were cold as her gaze turned in that direction. She nodded stiffly.

"He'll stay here if you like," Gar said awkwardly. "Alex will know we need your water."

Canton turned the full force of his charm on her, and she knew he was a ladies' man. There was both confidence and arrogance in the glance, and he had a breathtaking smile, but Willow saw the hollowness beyond it.

Willow would take Jess's frown over that smile anytime. At least it showed an honest emotion. She wondered whether this man had any at all.

"We're fine, Mr. Morrow. I thank you, but I think we can handle everything ourselves."

Gar looked around, first at Brady, then at Chad, and finally the twins, who were gaping at the man in black. "Think about it, Miss Willow."

"*We* have Jess!" Chad spoke up proudly.

The three visitors looked at Willow. Gar Morrow had heard that Alex Newton's gunfighter had gone over to Willow, but he hadn't credited it. Willow had nothing to offer; Gar knew she didn't have any money.

"Jess?" It was Canton who asked the soft question.

But no one hurried to answer him, not even Brady, who'd stiffened.

Canton spoke again. He'd not heard of a man named Jess, but he had heard that maybe Lobo had changed sides. Now he wondered aloud. "I'd heard that Lobo left Newton . . ."

"He has." The answer came from the doorway. Lobo stood there, seemingly at ease as he leaned against the doorjamb and surveyed the crowded room with glittering eyes that revealed little.

Willow felt her stomach turn over as she watched Jess and Canton eye each other speculatively. She'd never seen so much tension build so quickly in a room, so much wariness between two men, not even at the dance. Then it was a sudden squall, fast and dangerous, but over quickly. This . . . this was more like the lightning that precedes a long and violent storm.

Canton smiled again coldly. "Lobo," he acknowledged with the barest nod of his head.

"Marsh," Lobo replied with equal composure. His posture was still relaxed, but one hand was taking the glove from his right one, his gun hand.

"I'd heard you changed sides. Didn't believe it. You come high."

Lobo's eyes had not moved from Canton, nor had they blinked. Willow wondered how that was possible. "Call it a whim," he said.

"I never considered you a whimsical man," Canton countered, but the wariness of his stance didn't relax, nor did the coldness of his smile change.

Lobo shrugged, visibly conveying that he didn't care what Canton thought.

Willow was suddenly afraid that Canton would take offense, but only amusement showed in his eyes. The energy in the room, the menace, deepened, and she felt fear run up and down her spine, a coldness replacing the warmth in her heart. She was watching Lobo now, not Jess. It was almost as if he'd become another person. Like a chameleon, he was changing in front of her eyes from a tender lover to a cold killer.

Canton, his eyes every bit as watchful as Lobo's, hesitated a moment before speaking again. "We're on the same side, then?"

Lobo shrugged again. "I'm working for Miss Taylor. You're working for *him*."

Marsh Canton's speculative gaze shifted to Willow, as if he were wondering what she had to offer a man like Lobo. Lobo didn't miss the glance, and he stiffened, the fingers of his gun hand flexing. Canton saw the movement and lifted his hands, as if in peacekeeping.

The already high tension in the room increased tenfold.

Gar Morrow stepped back; Chad edged toward Lobo; Brady's fist tightened against the stove.

Willow had thought Marsh Canton's eyes were hard, but they were nothing like the ice now in Jess's. She suddenly understood how he got the name of Lobo. She'd never seen a more dangerous-looking animal. She shivered slightly. It was difficult to reconcile this predator with the man who had been a part of her, who had reached so deeply into her.

"We have no quarrel, Lobo," Canton said carefully, although there was no apology or fear in his tone. "Mr. Morrow is here asking to water his stock, and I came along to offer protection."

Lobo relaxed slightly, but his eyes didn't change, nor did they move from Canton as he addressed Willow. "Miss Taylor?"

The voice was icy, and Willow felt shivers run through her. "I told them we don't need any more help." Her voice faltered slightly.

Lobo's jaw tightened, but his eyes never blinked, never turned toward her. "That's your answer, Marsh."

Marsh Canton shrugged. "If you need—"

"We won't." Lobo's reply was like a gunshot, as sharp and short and emphatic.

Marsh ignored him and turned to Willow. "—me," he continued, his eyes bright with new interest, "I'll be at Morrow's ranch."

Everyone in the room turned toward Lobo at Marsh's defiance. Expectancy vibrated.

Lobo's hand touched his trouser leg, obviously fighting a need to react. Marsh's hand moved similarly.

Willow, her knees shaking, moved between them.

Lobo's hand dropped. His jaw clenched as he forced his eyes from her white face.

He turned to Marsh. "You have your answer," he said.

Canton nodded. He'd made his offer, and there was nothing more to accomplish there, no reason to bait Lobo any further. He knew it had been dangerous, but he'd been hired to protect the woman, and he'd wanted to know Lobo's interest. Now he did, and he was somewhat amused by it. Lobo

was the last person in the world he'd ever accuse of senti-
mentality, but there was no mistaking the protectiveness of
the man, or that brief agonized look before his usual implacable mask covered it.

Canton turned to Morrow, who looked embarrassed and
awkward. His employer put his hat back on and tugged at
the front of it in respect. "Miss Willow, we'll go, then. I'll let
you know about the cattle."

She nodded, unable to say anything, unable to take her
eyes from the man that was all Lobo and none of Jess. She
knew her eyes must show her confusion, and when he
turned toward her, his face was comprehending and suddenly weary. His lips tightened.

After the three men had left, the remaining occupants of
the room continued to stand. Brady's gaze went from Lobo to
Willow, and Lobo's eyes clouded slightly as he searched Willow's face. "Now you know exactly what I am," he said bitterly. "Marsh and I are two sides of the same coin."

"No," she disagreed, but there was a new uncertainty in
her voice that struck like a knife in the gut.

"You're too smart not to see it," he said grimly. "I was fool
enough to forget it." He went out and slammed the door behind him.

Willow started after him, but Brady stopped her. "Leave
him alone for a while." His eyes were unexpectedly kind as
his hand touched her shoulder.

"But . . ."

"He needs to be alone," he said.

"He thinks . . ."

"He's right," Brady broke in softly. "I saw your face, too.
You've set him on too high a horse, my girl. You've never let
yourself see the whole man."

"I love the whole man," she protested.

"Do you, Willow? Did you love him here in the kitchen or
did he scare you?"

"Of course he scared me," Willow said in a more temperate
voice. "He . . . surprised me, but that doesn't mean . . ."

"He's a gunfighter, Willow. He's been one for years. There's
not too many gentle ones of that breed alive."

"He's different," she said.

Brady was silent a moment. "I won't argue he's surprised me some, but that doesn't change the fact that he's a hard man, one who's survived in a business that doesn't allow human emotions or weaknesses."

Willow swallowed. She had seen him mostly as a heroic figure, a mythical one. In her own mind she'd transformed him into her own Odysseus: strong, compassionate, a warrior for right. Even as he was telling her about his youth, she saw him as a David fighting against overwhelming odds.

She suddenly realized Brady was right. So was Lobo, when he'd seen her face. By continuing to call him Jess, she had steadfastly denied the other part of him, pretended it didn't exist. But it did exist. And she'd just seen that part. Cold. Dangerous. Deadly. Ready to kill.

"If you try to change him, you'll end up killing him," Brady continued in a low voice.

"Would you care?"

"Strangely enough, I think I would," he replied wryly. "Damned if I know why."

Willow stared at him. He had been bitterly opposed to Lobo since he'd discovered who the stranger really was.

Brady shrugged, a gesture that reminded Willow so much of Lobo. Chad was also doing it.

"I have chores," he said.

"Brady . . ."

He turned to her.

"Do you think he'll leave?"

"Not until he finishes what he started," Brady replied.

"And then?"

"Yes."

Willow felt tears in the back of her eyes, and she turned away, not wanting Brady to see them. She knew that in some way she'd disappointed Jess—no, Lobo—that she'd badly let him down, and she hurt at the thought. She'd kept demanding that he be Jess. Perhaps he was. But he was also Lobo.

She didn't know if she could ever accept that part of him.

* * *

256 •   PATRICIA POTTER

Lobo stood on top of the hill. He'd done foolish things in his life, but never any quite as crazy as that afternoon. Ever since he sighted the ranch, all his rules, all his precautions, had flown away with the wind. He didn't know who he was anymore.

He'd half believed himself Willow's Jess that afternoon. During those few moments after she'd left the woods, he'd even imagined that perhaps . . .

What in the hell had he imagined? Lobo and the schoolteacher? Lobo as a farmer, a rancher? As a husband, a father?

It all was ludicrous now after the encounter in the kitchen. His life was full of such encounters. It hadn't meant more to him than just as another one, until he'd seen Willow's face and the dawning realization in it. And then he'd wanted Canton to draw. He'd wanted it very badly, because the pain in him was so strong. Willow had looked at him like a stranger, like an animal to be feared, and that was what he was.

He'd almost believed Willow's fairy tale. As if a few accidental deeds wiped away the rot in him. Well, she'd seen him for what he was. And she hadn't liked it.

The warmth that had settled inside him, the odd feeling of peace and belonging, was swallowed by a yawning hole, one made even deeper by those few moments of pleasure.

When would Newton strike? Soon, since Morrow planned to run his cattle this way. They had a day, perhaps a few, but no more. He wasn't sure he had time to build the dam, but right now hard work was mighty appealing. And they would need three watches. Chad could take days. For some reason Lobo didn't think Newton would strike in daylight. A coyote usually hid behind darkness.

He wanted it over. He wanted distance between him and this goddamned ranch. He wanted to forget eyes the color of a summer day, and hair that felt like silk. He wanted to forget Chad's admiring eyes and Sallie Sue's small, lisping voice.

Minutes later he was back at the ranch, giving orders to an unusually cooperative Brady and a grateful Chad. Lobo was ready to ride out if Willow appeared.

"I can really keep watch?" Chad asked so hopefully that

the words nearly broke through the new armor Lobo had pieced around his heart.

"Really," he said curtly, but Chad didn't seem to take offense. Everyone, it seemed, was walking gingerly after the confrontation in the ranch house.

As Chad took Willow's old riding horse out to the hill, Lobo and Brady found two axes and carefully fastened them to their saddles. They had two hours of daylight left, enough to get started on the dam.

When they arrived at the place Willow had pointed out earlier, Lobo picked a tree, and they took turns wielding their axes. It became a test of endurance, a competition. On his side, Lobo had rage and frustration that gave him almost superhuman strength, but Brady also had incentive. He was driven to prove himself.

In no time a large cottonwood fell across the stream, and then a smaller tree, then brush. They worked as dusk came, and then as the moon lit the sky. They worked until Brady thought he would drop from exhaustion. Still, Lobo continued, his strokes steady although Brady knew he must have the same bleeding blisters as he himself did. But no pain showed on Lobo's face, no exhaustion.

An hour later Lobo turned to him. "You best go spell Chad."

"Come back with me," Brady said, surprising himself, and getting a startled look from Lobo.

"No," the gunfighter said.

Brady gave him a level stare for several moments. It would be useless to try to convince him. Lobo was wrestling his own devils, and Brady knew from experience no one could help.

"All right," he said finally. "I'll see you in the morning." As he mounted and rode away, he could still hear the ring of the ax hitting wood.

He stopped at the now-dark house and fetched the box with the medical supplies. Lobo would need it when he relieved Brady a few hours later, and Brady knew damned well Lobo wouldn't ask Willow for it. He assured himself the only reason he cared was they all needed Lobo's gun hand.

*　*　*

Marisa found her chance to escape. She had been waiting for days, but after her ride into town, she had been watched. Her keepers were all polite enough but firm. Her father was worried about her safety.

She had not given up on the idea of talking to Gar Morrow. If she could discover the reason for the hatred between her father and his onetime friend, perhaps she could do something to dissolve it. She didn't know what exactly, but anything was worth a try.

All day men had been riding out. Even the new gunslingers who had been recruited. All the streams in the area were going dry, and the cattle had to be brought in to the river. Cady, who took care of the horses, had been working harder than usual until his back, bad since a fall on roundup, gave out. He'd sent a message to her for some tonic, and she'd spiked it with a little of the laudanum they kept around the ranch.

After she was sure he was sleeping, she saddled her own horse and rode out. The range was dry, and even the river which she rode alongside was low.

The horse felt good under her. She knew an exhilarating sense of freedom. On the way back she would stop and see Sullivan. Sullivan. Even the name was enticing to her.

She turned at the road that snaked by Gar Morrow's ranch, occasionally glimpsing other riders, all of them unfamiliar. Despite the heat of the day, she shivered slightly. Every stranger now was ominous, not like it used to be. Since the Indians had been driven from this area a few years back, it had been safe, and she'd never felt troubled riding alone. But now . . .

It was late afternoon when she drew up at the fenced entrance to the Morrow house. The building was much like her father's—a plantation-type structure from the South. Only Jake, whose wife had been ill, had chosen a one-story home.

There were several horses tied to the posts in front of the house, and at her arrival a man leaning against one of the columns of the front porch disappeared inside. Before she could dismount, Gar Morrow was coming out the door, and behind him was the gunfighter she'd seen at the dance.

"Miss Newton," Gar Morrow said, his face showing surprise. "This is—"

"Unexpected?"

"Unexpected," he agreed. "Is this a social call?"

"I would like to talk to you," Marisa said. "Alone."

Gar's brow furrowed. Marisa had once seen a photograph of him and her father and Jake. It had been in the attic, in one of the trunks containing her mother's clothes. All three had been handsome young men, even in the stiff, self-conscious pose. Gar had probably been the most striking of the three with a devil-may-care smile framed by a roguish mustache. Even the poor black-and-white picture could not hide the twinkle in his eye.

But now his face was worn with time. It held the same kind of bitterness as her father's, the same disappointment in life. Only pride remained, a fierce, indomitable defiance.

For a moment she thought he would refuse, and then he nodded his head and went to her side, helping her down. "Wait for me out here," he told the man in black.

Once inside the comfortable main room of the house, he offered her some sherry, and she accepted it. She watched as he took his time, obviously trying to understand her presence and the reason behind it. When he turned back to her, he was holding two glasses, and after handing her one, he took a deep gulp of the other.

"Miss Marisa, you have my attention."

"I—I was hoping you could tell me why . . . why you and my father are enemies?"

"He didn't tell you anything?"

She shook her head.

"Ask him."

"I have," she said hopelessly. "He won't talk about it."

His glance softened. "You look very much like your mother."

"Did she have anything to do with it?"

He sighed. "It's not right you being in the middle. But you'll have to ask your father."

"You were once good friends," she tried again, a desperate note in her voice.

He turned away and looked at the wall so she couldn't see his face. "Good friends trust each other," he said harshly. "Unfortunately, your father didn't trust me. And that's all I have to say."

There was pain in his speech. Marisa could feel it rush between them.

"There's nothing I can do?"

"Not now," he said roughly. "It's gone too far."

"But other people are being hurt."

He turned back to her, and his face was set. "I need that water for my cattle, and nothing is going to stop me from getting it."

"Perhaps . . . if I knew I could do something."

"No one can do anything now," he said.

"You're wrong. You have to be."

He started to hold out his hand to her, then stopped. "You're so much like her. Always the peacemaker." His lips tightened. "But he wants a fight, and I'll be damned if I'll let him run me out."

"Mr. Morrow . . ."

"I'm sorry, Marisa." He hesitated, looking suddenly weary and vulnerable. "I tried, Marisa, God knows I've tried. Over and over again, I've tried to convince him that nothing—"

He stopped, stubborn pride etched all over his face, and Marisa, with a sick feeling deep inside, knew he wasn't going to say any more.

She hesitated a moment. "Thank you for seeing me."

"My fight's not with you. God knows I didn't want one with Alex. But neither am I going to back down. He's wrong, goddammit."

The fierceness in his voice made Marisa feel cold once more. The chill stayed with her as she rose and went out the door. The gunfighter was at her side, helping her mount, his arm strong, but his gaze like that of a wolverine.

Marisa kicked her horse into a gallop. She wanted Sullivan.

She wanted warmth.

Twenty-one

God only knew what time it was when Lobo realized he was simply striking back at the deity—if there was one—and accomplishing damned little. There was enough underbrush and trees in the river to construct two or three dams.

He threw the ax to the ground and flexed his hands, realizing he'd been a muttonhead once again. His fingers were already stiffening, and he needed the full power of his gun hand for what might be coming.

Yet he relished the pain. He needed the pain to take his thoughts away from Willow Taylor.

For moments that afternoon he'd felt like a boy again, a boy with his life before him, a boy who looked at the horizon and dreamed. When had the dreams stopped? It was so long ago, he didn't remember. But before he'd met up with Canton, he'd been in a dream again, one so real he felt it deep to the core of him.

And then there was Canton, and the dream shattered. He had looked at Canton, and it was as if he were looking into a mirror. Willow deserved more.

Lobo stared at the pile of tree trunks and branches lying

across the river. Already the water was building up slightly on his side. It wouldn't take Newton long to realize something was wrong with his section of the river.

Lobo painfully pulled on his gloves, and he mounted the pinto. Time to relieve Brady. The ex-lawman was holding out far better than Lobo had expected, but Brady Thomas's body was no longer in the shape it once had been. Lobo was used to little sleep. Thomas would need rest far more than he.

As he rode to the hill, his eyes moved to the ranch house. There was a light in the window, and he wondered if Willow was still awake, if she regretted those hours that afternoon, especially after his meeting with Canton. He had seen that quick, startled realization, even momentary fear, in her eyes, and it had struck him like an arrow through the gut.

He'd half expected Thomas to be asleep when he reached the hill, but the man wasn't. The ex-lawman was stretched out along the ground, his head propped on one of his hands, his eyes steady on the trail just beyond. He didn't look up until Lobo stood beside him, but all the same Lobo knew Thomas was aware of his approach. The ex-lawman's body had tensed and then relaxed.

"Build another dam?" Thomas asked laconically.

"Not quite," Lobo replied in a soft, drawling voice. "No visitors?"

"Not even Doc Sullivan, and I half expected him."

There was a pause. "He come by often?"

Brady caught the note of what could be jealousy. "He and Willow are friends."

Lobo grimaced and sat down, his legs crossed Indian-fashion. "They seem—suited."

"Not the way you mean," Brady said, partially disturbed, partially bemused. This was the first time Lobo had spoken more than orders or insults to him.

"What do you mean?"

Even in the dim moonlight, Brady could see the intense interest in eyes usually so well guarded. Brady hesitated. "Doc Sullivan has eyes only for Miss Marisa, Alex Newton's daughter. Has for years, but he won't do anything about it."

"Why?" Lobo didn't know why in the hell he was asking such stupid questions.

"Same reason I 'spect you're so damned on edge. Pride. He's got as much as you do. And he's sick sometimes. Malaria. So he doesn't think he'll make a good husband."

"I'm not sick."

Brady raised one of his bushy eyebrows, but he said nothing. Instead, he picked up Willow's box of medical supplies. "Brought this for you. You keep abusin' those hands, you'll have to find a new profession."

"That would make you feel real bad," Lobo mocked.

"I don't care what you do after this is over," Brady said, and though it hurt to admit the next truth, he added, "But now Willow needs you."

Lobo gave him a sharp look, then turned his gaze toward the box. Thomas was right. He took off his gloves and looked at his hands, flexing them and feeling the pain. He took a tin of salve and rubbed the ointment into the broken blisters. He thought of the tender way Willow had done it, and he rubbed even harder. Could he never get her out of his mind?

When he finished, he passed the tin back to Thomas, noticing that the man's hands were more steady than he'd seen them. He was also wearing a gun.

"Let me see you draw," he said suddenly, and Brady flinched. He didn't want the gunslinger to see his hand shake.

"Thomas," Lobo said again in a low commanding voice. "I've got to know."

It was a reasonable request, Brady realized. They had to learn if he had the guts to draw anymore, or whether he could even hold the gun steady. He would soon find out. He stood, and so did Lobo, the two men no more than four feet away from each other, their legs slightly apart, balanced.

Lobo's hand was hovering near his gun. "Now," he said suddenly.

Brady's right hand went to the gun and drew it in one quick motion. It didn't catch on the holster as it had when he'd practiced the past few days, and his hand wasn't shaking. Lobo's gun was also out, had been out several seconds before his own, but Brady knew he hadn't done badly.

His gaze went to Lobo's face, and there was the slightest smile on the gunslinger's lips.

Brady knew he was smiling, too, as he slid the gun back into the holster.

"You didn't lose your nerve, did you," Lobo said. It wasn't a question.

"More like my taste for it," Brady answered curtly, not particularly liking the conversation but knowing it was important. They might face trouble together, and Lobo had the right to know what to expect.

"Want to tell me why?"

"I killed an unarmed man."

Lobo stared at him. "Knowing your reputation, I expect you had reason."

"Yep, thought I did, but that day I learned I wasn't any better than him. There wasn't any difference between him and me. Not anymore."

Lobo rubbed the back of his neck, wincing slightly when he felt some of the salve from his hand settle there. "Some snakes just need killing."

"A lawman can't think that way."

"Most of the ones I know do. They don't care if a man's bad. Just that he's wanted, or even might be wanted." There was a deep note of bitterness in his voice.

Brady turned away from him. "I didn't operate that way."

"I heard you were good."

"I heard you were fast."

"And not so good?" There was wry amusement in the question.

Brady turned back to him and faced Lobo. "I'd have run you out of town faster than a chicken runs from the dinner pot."

"You would have tried."

Brady chuckled humorlessly. "Yep, I would have tried."

"And now?"

Brady hesitated, then said honestly, "I'm damned glad you're here."

"It galls the hell out of you to say that, doesn't it?"

Brady let a few seconds go by. Lobo had been honest with him; he could be no less. "A day ago, maybe."

"I haven't changed, Thomas."

"Maybe I have."

"What if someone offers you a bottle?"

"You don't pull punches, do you?"

Lobo shifted his weight slightly. "You have to depend on me. I might have to depend on you."

"All right. I don't know what I'd do if someone offered me a drink. Good enough for you?"

"Yeah." Lobo sounded satisfied, and that irked Brady. He didn't know why.

"I'm getting some rest. You may be some damn Indian who doesn't need any, but I do."

Lobo let the word pass. He'd purposefully baited Brady. "Be ready to start again at dawn."

Brady walked away, his head shaking, and Lobo was glad to be at peace with the night. It was the only thing he understood.

Sullivan was not at his office when Marisa arrived. Instead, there was a note on the door. *Gone to Appleton ranch. Don't know when I'll be back.*

She tried the door. Perhaps she could wait awhile. It was not yet dark, and her father was going to be furious anyway. A few more minutes wouldn't matter.

The door was open, and she went inside. The office was plainly furnished, and she wondered about the rest of the rooms. She knew she shouldn't pry, but her eyes kept going to the door that led into what she knew were his living quarters. She had never been inside them.

Her hand went to the doorknob of the room, even as she told herself she shouldn't, and her fingers turned the knob, even as her conscience scolded her. She could smell the scent of spice and soap as she looked around a room as plain as the outer office.

It was uncommonly neat, but then, there wasn't much to clutter it except a wall lined with books. There was a bed, and a table next to it. An oil lamp sat next to a neat stack of books. In the middle of the room there was a table and two chairs, and there were more books. She went to the table beside the bed, reached for one of the volumes, and looked at its title. Poems by Walt Whitman. She opened it up to a place marked by a piece of paper and studied the title above the words, "O Captain! My Captain."

She read the mournful words and felt a terrible sadness.

"He was a nurse during the Civil War." The words came from the doorway, and Marisa dropped the book. She knew her face was red with embarrassment for snooping, yet she was so glad to see him, even more pleased to see the tender amusement in his eyes, as if he understood her need to know more about him.

"Who?" she asked, trying to absorb his words.

"Walt Whitman."

"Were . . . you in the war?"

"Yes."

"A doctor?"

He nodded.

"Was it terrible?"

"Worse than any hell a man can imagine."

"Is that . . . how you got malaria?"

"No. I caught it in Louisiana. That's where I was raised."

Marisa suddenly realized how little she knew about him. He had come to Newton not long after the war, and he'd never talked much about himself. The townspeople were too pleased about having a real doctor to ask too many questions.

"You were with the South?" Most people in Colorado had favored the North.

He nodded.

Her eyes went back to the book. "Willow used to read that poem in class. It's about Abraham Lincoln."

"Yes," he said softly.

"But . . ."

"There were good men on both sides, Marisa."

"Most of the men I know who fought in the war hate Rebs."

"I'm afraid so."

"Is that why . . . ?"

"I don't talk about the war because I don't like thinking about it. My father was killed at Shiloh, and my mother, sister, and . . . fiancée were killed on a boat shelled by Union troops. After the war, when I returned, I found that the land my family owned for generations had been taken for taxes. I probably should have cared more than I did, but with everyone I loved gone, it just didn't matter anymore. I'd had enough of hatred and killing, and I knew the Colorado weather was a helluva lot better for my health. And now you know everything, my curious little Marisa."

She did, and she wished she didn't.

"Fiancée?" she said.

He nodded. "That was a long time ago, Marisa."

"What was her name?"

"Julie," he answered softly.

Marisa felt all her insides hurt. "Is that why . . . you never married?"

"No," he said, and then hesitated a moment before continuing. "We were . . . engaged before I contracted malaria, just before I went to medical school. The attacks became worse during the war. I was thinking about canceling the engagement, but before I could get leave, she—was killed."

"Did you love her?"

It was a foolish question, Marisa knew, and she wished instantly she could take it back.

But Sullivan merely regarded her thoughtfully. "Yes. We grew up together. We were very much alike."

Marisa felt a crushing blow to her chest. She needed no one to explain that she and Sullivan did not have a great deal in common, only the intensity of attraction. But more than for herself, she felt a great sadness for him. He had lost everything.

"Don't look at me like that, Marisa," he said, as if probing her thoughts. "I have a very satisfying life now."

"You didn't say happy."

"A very happy life, then."

"You're lying."

His eyebrows drew together in mock consternation. "Am I now, Miss Marisa? And what do you think would make me happy?"

"Me." There. It was said. And she was glad.

The amusement left his eyes, replaced by something much more intense. "And how could an old man like me make you happy?"

"You're not old."

"Old enough to be your father."

"Only if you were a very precocious boy."

He chuckled. "Like you're a very precocious young lady?" But there was no sting to the words, only amazed appreciation.

"I know what I want."

"Do you, Marisa? Or is it just the challenge?"

"I don't think so," she said honestly.

He leaned back and laughed. "You are a remarkable young lady, Marisa."

"Remarkable enough to kiss?"

"Oh, yes, I think so." He was still chuckling when he leaned down his head to kiss her.

He had thought to make the kiss light, to erase the memory of the other one, but it was a foolish hope. One taste of her, and his resolve disappeared. Her touch made him feel young again, young and excited and full of hope.

His lips hardened against hers and he felt her arms go around him. He was thirty-six, and he'd lived like a monk more years than he wanted to remember. And now his body was reacting with an enthusiasm he hadn't realized he had. For years now he had buried himself in his practice, in books, and denied himself this kind of pleasure. He had long since decided not to marry, not to make any woman suffer over the illness that came and went without warning. And he'd decided not to make that decision more painful by letting himself fall in love.

But now he knew he had always been in love with Marisa

Newton, ever since she was an imp of a child always in mischief but never the malicious kind. She was so full of life, so full of light and laughter and gaiety. He had watched her grow, and when she had become a lovely young woman, he had admitted somewhere deep inside a silent, unfulfilled love. In agony he had watched her growing interest in him, the way she gravitated to him at parties, the way she lingered to talk in the street, the way her eyes warmed when she saw him.

He had tried to convince himself that Marisa wanted only to add him to the list of eligible men who courted her favors, but he grudgingly had to admit that she was too honest for that game.

Still, he thought no good could come from an entanglement with her. He would never be whole, never be what Marisa deserved. He didn't think he could bear to see her face when he was sick, when she might have to do everything for him, the most intimate type of care. He often became violent during those episodes, wrapped in the blind black fury of the past. One time, when Willow was caring for him, he'd returned to consciousness and saw the bruises on her. He'd never forgiven himself for that.

But as his mouth met Marisa's, he could think of nothing but the sweetness of the moment, how strong and wanted and needed he felt, not as a doctor, but as a man. The kiss deepened, and he knew a craving hunger, assuaged only partially by the warm glow that spread from every point of contact.

She opened her mouth slightly, and his tongue played along her lips, then inside her mouth. She moved closer, and he could feel her body trembling, just as his own tensed and grew rigid in response.

His arms went around her, holding her tightly, as if afraid she'd disappear. But then years of control took over. He stiffened, and his hands fell from her back as he moved away, but one hand went up and touched her mouth, now frowning in puzzlement and dismay.

"Don't go away from me," she said.

"I don't want to," he said honestly. "But if I don't, we might do something we'll both regret."

"You love me," she accused.

"Perhaps I do."

"I love you."

"Perhaps."

"Then why—"

"You may think you love me now, pretty Marisa. But what if you had to care for me like a mother cares for a baby?"

"I would love you more."

"Because you'd pity me." She'd never heard bitterness in Sullivan before, and she flinched.

"No," she denied. "No one could ever pity you."

Her answer would have pleased him if he'd believed it. Perhaps she herself believed it, but he couldn't. "Pretty Marisa," he said again. "You think you could be a doctor's wife?"

"I can be anything I want to be."

"No big ranch? No stable full of horses?" He knew she loved to ride.

He was gently mocking her, and she felt the birth of anger inside. "You don't think much of me, do you?"

The mockery instantly disappeared. "I think a great deal of you, Marisa. If I didn't, I'd marry you today."

She grinned at the admission. "Would you?"

He nodded.

"Well, then I'll just have to do something to destroy that good opinion of me." She gave him an impish grin and spun around.

"Marisa!"

"Good-bye, Sullivan."

Sullivan watched the door close, wondering what in the hell she would do this time. He felt like kicking himself for saying some of the things he had, for admitting to feelings that were foolish. But they had been bottled up inside for a long time and had simply exploded.

He walked over to the window and watched her ride away, part of his heart going with her.

Marisa rode home slowly. She knew all hell would break

loose when she arrived, and she wasn't particularly eager to encounter it, not in the mood she was in.

More than anything, she needed to talk to someone. About her father. About Sullivan. She had been trying to catch Sullivan's attention for years. Even as a girl she'd been fascinated by the tall, quiet, handsome doctor who always seemed so in control yet always alone. Her heart caught when she saw the gray eyes, solemn yet so caring, rest on children, or anyone in need. And then, when she was older, the fascination had turned into something more, something that made her ache inside.

The road went past Willow's place, and she decided to stop by. Even if her father learned of it, Marisa didn't think she cared. She loved her father, no matter what he did, and she knew he needed her. But she couldn't support him in this obsession for vengeance.

It was past dusk, and the lights in Willow's ranch house were like a beacon. Marisa had hardly reached the hitching post when the door flew open, and Willow stood there, her face eager. Marisa watched some of the expectancy fade away, but a smile remained. "Marisa, I'm glad to see you."

Marisa dismounted and joined Willow. "Can we go for a walk and talk?" she asked.

Willow needed that as much as her guest apparently did. "Of course," she said, closing the door.

They strode in silence to the barn, and Marisa looked at it with amazement. So much had been done since the barn raising days earlier.

"Lobo," Willow explained. "Lobo and Brady together." She'd decided that evening, after Lobo left, that the only way she could bring him back was to make him understand that she accepted him and all he was.

She'd thought and thought about him, wondering if she *did* love all of him? Or did she love only Jess, who had ridden into her life, silhouetted against the sky and blazing sun like a golden knight?

Could she love a tarnished one? A man who represented everything she'd been taught to fight. Violence. Death.

Then she'd felt that warmth he created in her, the sense of

belonging, the gentleness she knew was rare. But could she accept the other part?

Was her fascination superficial, the need to bind wounds as she was wont to do? Was it merely the need of a woman to save a lost soul?

But she'd loved him before she knew the dark side. And when she discovered that other part of him, she still loved him.

But that was before she had seen him with Canton, had seen deadly things she hadn't known before.

So many buts. The internal conversation had continued all afternoon and into the evening. She'd seen him ride back for Brady, and leave again. And she'd been unable to do anything but watch because she didn't know how she felt.

Finally, she made a bargain with herself. She had to accept him as Lobo. She would try. Anything else would be a grievous wrong against him.

"What's Lobo really like?" Marisa said curiously, her own problems momentarily laid aside.

Willow smiled softly. "He's like the wind with all its moods. Gentle one moment, stormy and unpredictable the next."

"Gentle?" Marisa questioned. She would never forget the harsh face and cold eyes, the cynical look that had raked her body that morning on her father's land.

Willow grinned. Everyone seemed to see Lobo in a different way. "Yep," she said with exaggerated humor.

"I don't believe it." But another look at Willow's face, and Marisa did.

"Do you think he'll stay?"

"No," Willow said softly, "but I'll take what I can right now."

Marisa looked closer. Willow in love? With a gunslinger? Nothing seemed more unlikely.

"Do you love Lobo?"

Did she love Lobo as well as Jess? And the answer came swiftly. "Yes."

"Even though . . . ?"

"Even though," Willow confirmed. Suddenly despite her afternoon's debate, she knew she did, reservations and all.

Thoroughly fascinated, Marisa put all her surprise into one startled exclamation. "But he's a hired gun!"

"He's a lot more than that, Marisa. I've never seen anyone so good with horses, and the children . . . they worship him. Even Brady's a different man since he came."

"But he's a killer."

Willow had no immediate answer for that. Despite her brave words, she didn't know much about that side of him, just what people said, just what she'd seen that afternoon. The potential. The ease. But she hadn't seen the killing. She wondered whether she still really believed it. She only knew about the man she'd seen and been with, and the man she loved.

"What are you going to do?"

"Love him until he goes," Willow said. "If he'll let me," she added, not knowing whether he would, after her reaction that afternoon.

"And then?"

Willow looked at Marisa helplessly. "Keep loving him, I suppose."

Marisa couldn't stop herself from sighing. "And I came to you for help."

Willow immediately turned to Marisa, all concern. "What's wrong?"

"Sullivan."

Willow shook her head. "Stubborn as always?"

"I just threw myself at him."

"And what happened?"

"He said I was too nice to marry."

Willow smiled. "I doubt if he meant it that way. What exactly did he say?"

"That he thought a lot of me, and if he didn't, he would go ahead and marry me."

"Idiot," Willow observed.

"He is not," Marisa said, indignant.

"No, he is not. He's just stubborn like another man I know. It must be a masculine trait."

"You're pretty stubborn yourself," Marisa said, giggling.

They looked at each other and started laughing.

"What should I do now?" Marisa asked after their mirth subsided.

"Be patient. I've seen Sullivan look at you. I think unconsciously he's been waiting for you to grow up and know exactly what you want."

"I know what I want."

The smile on Willow's face faded slightly as she studied Marisa. "Are you sure, absolutely sure? Being a doctor's wife isn't easy."

Marisa stopped walking. "Neither is being the daughter of Alex Newton. I hate this town now. I hate these . . . new gun hands. I hate what's happening to my father and to this whole territory."

Willow winced at the force of the words. "Do you want to come stay with me? There's not much room, and it could be dangerous, but . . ."

Marisa put her hand on Willow's arm. "Thank you, but I'm afraid that would just make things worse for you."

"I don't think it can be any worse," Willow replied.

"Besides, I can try to reason with my father."

"But you just said—"

"I don't think anyone can now, Willow. It's like he's gone mad. Nothing matters except getting this ranch and ruining Mr. Morrow. But I'm the only one who can try."

Willow took her hand. "You've been a good friend, Marisa."

"No more so than you. I'll try to warn you if my father makes a move. I won't let him hurt you or the children."

"We have Lobo now."

"Have you thought he might be the spark that ignites this thing?"

"He won't start anything, Marisa. He's just here to protect the young ones. He . . . seems to be very protective of them."

"And you," Marisa said.

Willow didn't answer, but her face went red, even in the soft glow of the moon.

"I'd better get back," Marisa said. "Thank you for listening."

"Sullivan will come around."

"And your Lobo?"

Willow shook her head slowly. Perhaps for a day, even several, but no more. "No. I don't think so."

"Well, I'll pray for both of us," Marisa said unexpectedly. "Be careful."

Marisa gave her a quick hug, realizing she'd never done that with a woman before. She'd never had a close friend, not until Willow. "I will," she said, and left before Willow saw her trembling mouth.

Twenty-two

Chad appeared on the hill just as the sun was breaking over the eastern horizon. The boy's eyes were still sleepy, but he wore an eager-to-please smile on his lips.

"Brady asked me to take over the watch."

Brady, Lobo thought, was suddenly taking much on himself, but still he knew the ex-lawman was right. Lobo was dog-tired, body and mind, and that wouldn't do anyone any good.

Lobo regarded Chad's face, and again remembered his brother. He wished he didn't, yet the flashes came more regularly now, as if some barrier had been broken. "Can't think of anyone I'd trust more," he said gruffly, and was rewarded with a blinding smile.

Disgusted with himself for the momentary weakness, Lobo swung up into his saddle. A few hours sleep, that was all he needed.

He didn't want to go back to the ranch but that was probably the only place to go. And then he thought about the woods where he and Willow had made love. It didn't matter where he slept, outdoors or in the barn, as long as he was close enough to hear any shots.

Lobo turned his horse toward the river. Willow would soon be gone from the ranch, on her way to school, and then he would return, pick up Brady and something to eat, and they would finish the dam and start the irrigation ditches.

When he reached the woods, he looked around for a place to sleep and found the spot where he and Willow had made love. The grass was still bent where they'd lain, and the sight of it hurt.

A showdown was near—he could feel it with every instinct he had—and then he would go.

"Damn," he whispered, knowing how hard leaving would be. But he had no choice. His name and reputation would only draw more of his ilk; Willow and the children would never be safe. Not that she would want him to stay, not after yesterday. He closed his eyes and swore a more profane curse.

He dismounted, taking the brimmed hat he kept tied to the saddle in case of rain but seldom used otherwise. Hats were a garment, a convenience, of the whites, one he'd never grown used to. But now he placed it over his eyes, his hands brushing stubbled cheeks as he did so. He was asleep in seconds.

Brady waited for Lobo at the barn until past sunrise, and then decided to work on the dam on his own. He saw Lobo by the trail, and smiling at the prone form, he passed him and went to the dam.

He could hardly believe how much Lobo had done after he'd left the previous night. Only a trickle was going through. In another day Newton would have damned little water and there would be hell to pay. Brady went to work, using mud to fill in the remaining holes. When he was through, he cleaned himself in the river and went to wake up Lobo.

Brady knew about men and guns. He particularly knew you woke someone like Lobo very carefully. So he approached on foot, leading his horse, hoping to make enough noise to wake Lobo. As he expected, Lobo was sitting up, his gun out of the holster and probably lying under the hat sitting innocently in the man's lap.

"Feeling better?" Brady said.

Lobo grunted.

"I finished the dam. What now?"

"Try to get some water to that garden."

"How?"

"Plow a ditch from the garden to here, then blast the embankment and hope the force of the water will carry it to the garden."

"It'll be a damned long ditch."

"Yeah."

"Who's going to do the plowing?"

Lobo raised one of his eyebrows. "Heard you been doing some of that. Pretty good too.

"Heard you like learning new things."

Lobo smiled suddenly, and Brady was surprised. Brady was beginning to understand Willow's attraction to Lobo, and that was downright frightening.

"Tell you what," Lobo said with a gleam in his eye. "I'll match you shots for it."

"You know you're a hell of a lot faster—"

"Not speed. Accuracy. I heard you used to be damned good."

"Used to be is right," Brady said bitterly.

"Afraid to try?" Lobo taunted.

Brady shrugged. "Why not?" he answered, and those few words cost him a lot more than he indicated. He wasn't at all sure he wouldn't totally disgrace himself.

"You pick the target."

Brady looked around. There was a soft pine that would absorb the bullets without ricochet. He went to the bank of the river, grabbed some mud, and drew two lines across, three inches apart. The pine itself was no more than four inches in width.

Lobo nodded his approval, and Brady remembered the challenge the night before. He wondered briefly if this was another one of Lobo's tests. He felt a surge of anger, resentment and determination all at once.

Lobo stood easily, his legs slightly apart in a stance all too familiar to Brady. Lobo's jaw was rough with bristle, and he looked more of an outlaw than before, yet Brady no longer felt the menace he once did.

"You first," Lobo said.

It was a command, and Brady stiffened. He wasn't sure whether it was from his own uncertainty or annoyance, but whatever the reaction, it strengthened his resolve. His hand fell to his gun and tightened around the handle, and he slowly pulled it from the holster. He felt cold and jerky, but his hand wasn't shaking. Thank God it wasn't shaking. He lifted the gun and pointed it at the target on the tree. His trigger finger trembled slightly, and he hesitated, feeling the wary, watching presence of Lobo behind him, yet he didn't sense impatience.

Brady swallowed, then took careful aim, and his finger pressed against the trigger, slowly but with a confidence that was slowly returning. The gun discharged and he saw the bullet hit the pine between the two lines. He lowered the gun to his side, feeling a burst of quiet, bittersweet victory.

"Not bad," Lobo said, and Brady thought he heard some satisfaction in that voice, though he wasn't sure. It was too damned difficult to tell anything about Lobo. Whenever Brady thought he had him pegged, Lobo did something that made him feel one hundred percent wrong.

Brady stepped back, holstering the pistol, while Lobo went to the pine. "Nearly dead center," the gunman said. He looked at Brady, his lips twisting in a wry smile, and once again Brady wondered about him, and what he was feeling. Brady tried to remember the scraps of information Willow had told him about Lobo, but they had been few. Nothing seemed to fit this man, nothing he'd learned in his years of law-keeping, nothing he'd learned of men. Lobo defied every conception, every expectation. Even now Brady didn't know if he was merely being baited or made to face his own demons, though the latter seemed unlikely.

"Your turn," Brady said finally.

Lobo brought up his pistol with a smooth draw, and without seeming to aim, fired. Splinters flew from the spot between the two lines drawn by mud.

Both men advanced to study the bullet holes. The indentations in the pine were side by side, not more than a quarter of an inch apart.

"A draw," Lobo ruled, and Brady nodded.

Lobo shrugged. "Guess I'll learn a new thing at that."

Brady couldn't stop grinning at Lobo's use of Brady's earlier challenge. Neither could he stop the grudging respect that was growing inside. Despite the scowl on Lobo's face, there was a gleam in the man's eyes, as if he'd scored a victory, not sentenced himself to a day of plowing.

"Someone told me I was pretty good at plowing," Brady responded, his lips twitching.

Brady thought Lobo was going to smile as a flash of understanding passed between them. But then the moment passed, and Lobo retreated into the ultimate loner, needing no one, wanting no one. Brady knew a sudden loss, which stunned him. He turned around. "Let's get going. Willow will be long gone now."

The two men mounted and rode back to the house in silence.

The day was never going to end.

Willow sat behind the desk and watched her students struggle with their examinations. She had spent the morning with the young ones, listening to them read and do their sums orally. Then she passed out papers and asked them to write about the person they admired most.

The older children had more complex examinations, and they were bent over their desks, most of their faces furrowed in concentration, even Ethan, which gave her a thrill of satisfaction.

The twins glanced at each other and grimaced, but Willow's attention had wandered and she didn't notice it. Nor did she notice the strange looks she was receiving from some of the other students.

Although she was looking straight at the children, she wasn't seeing them. She was seeing Lobo as he was the previous afternoon, standing by the tree, looking young and happy and expectant. Then his features slowly dissolved into the expression she'd seen in the evening: cold, hard, bitter. His soft words turned into clipped, deadly ones.

She had waited for him to return. After Marisa had left, she'd waited and waited, even knowing deep inside that he wasn't coming. Still, she'd hoped. She had wanted to touch him, to tell him she loved Lobo as well as Jess. And she did.

Her body ached today in needing him again. She needed the feel of him moving inside her; needed his most intimate caress; needed his touch, restless and loving, fierce and tender. Now that she'd tasted the splendor of his love, how could she live knowing she would never again have that radiance? That ecstasy and excitement, that tender trembling?

Others had lived without it. She tried to think of those sailors' wives, of whalers' wives who had to wait for their men for years. She thought of Penelope and how she'd waited for nineteen years for her Odysseus to return. Willow had once thought that romantic. No longer. It would be the worst kind of Hades.

But she'd promised herself, and had sworn to him, she needed no more from him than the present.

"Miss Willow, I'm finished." A small voice disrupted her thoughts.

Willow went over and collected the paper, smiling at Hiram, her youngest and most enthusiastic pupil next to Robert, who was still bent over his desk and writing intently. Although she would miss all of them during the next weeks, she relished the thought of spending more time with Lobo. She wanted every precious second she could get.

As she looked over her students, she felt more than the usual affection for them. She felt naked greed for a child of her own, something she had never felt so strongly before. She'd always loved children but had been satisfied with taking care of those who belonged to others. Now she wanted a little towheaded boy with turquoise-colored eyes, one to whom she could give everything Lobo had never had.

After the children left, Willow quickly gathered her things. She'd never wanted to get home so quickly. Despite the specter of Alex Newton, the next days seemed to stretch blissfully before her.

Willow and the twins were almost home when she noticed a rider following her. She felt fear as she recognized the horseman from the night Newton's men came to burn the barn. There were two other men to the right of him, and they seemed terribly sinister.

Willow slapped the reins against the withers of the horses, spurring them on to a fast gait. She wanted to get home; she wanted the safety of Lobo.

"Hold on," she told the boys, who climbed in the back and grabbed the sides. The wagon rocked and bounced until she felt she would be thrown off, but she knew if she stopped or slowed, something terrible would happen. She felt it in her soul.

There was a gunshot, and then the horses bolted and she no longer had any control. The reins were useless in her hands; so was the brake she tried to use. At any moment the vehicle would overturn, crushing her and the boys.

The landscape was flying by, passing in a whirl of colors. Terror flooded her. She didn't want to die yet, not when she'd just discovered the richness of life, the joy of love. She tried to take control again, pulling on the reins, but the horses had the bits in their teeth and she didn't have the strength to hold them back.

Willow heard more gunshots, and sensed a rider nearby. She wished she had a whip or gun or some sort of weapon, but she didn't. Glancing around, she saw the horseman riding next to the wagon, his body low over the neck of a pinto.

Her heart was already thundering harder than the horses' hooves, and now it twisted spasmodically as she saw him prepare to jump. He half rose on the bare back of the horse, then leapt to the seat of the shaking wagon. He grabbed the reins from her and pulled back on them. As frightened as she was, she noticed the strain of his muscles against his shirt, the strength in his arms and his legs as his low, magnetic voice soothed the horses. Slowly their pace grew less frantic.

Willow remembered how Chad had described the "stranger" jumping from his horse onto Jupiter's back. She hadn't believed it, and even now she couldn't credit her eyes. She'd never seen such skill. Her heart had stopped in those few seconds when he seemed to hang in air.

Another horseman came up beside the wagon, and Willow saw it was Brady.

"You all right, Willow?" Brady asked as Lobo continued to give all his attention to the horses.

"How did you know there was trouble?" Her lips were still trembling and she stuttered slightly.

"Lobo seems to have a sixth sense where you're concerned," Brady said wryly. "We were plowing a trench and all of a sudden he said we ought to come looking for you."

"Where did the other riders go?"

"They left when we came. Toward Newton's ranch."

"Sullivan warned us there might be an ambush, but for Lobo," she said softly. He turned with a surprised jerk when he heard her say the name. The horses were walking now, their skins glistening with sweat and their mouths dripping with foam.

Her gaze met his and held it. His eyes darkened to a bright green-blue, and she was mesmerized by them. There was nothing cold about them now, nothing aloof. They glittered with fire, with raw, scorching need, and she felt all her nerves sizzle in response. She put her hand on his arm. He flinched but didn't move away.

"No more riding by yourself," he ordered.

"She's not by herself," one of the twins broke in.

Willow saw Lobo weigh his answer instead of laughing, as most men would have. "No," he finally said, "and she's very lucky to have such brave companions, but I think she also needs someone like Brady, who can shoot."

With those few words he elevated Brady considerably in the twins' eyes and Willow saw the ex-lawman's gaze settle on Lobo a moment and then move away. Her heart twisted as she realized what Lobo was doing: preparing the way for his own departure. And in doing so, he'd given Brady the greatest possible gift—respect.

The twins dominated the rest of the trip, talking about the men with guns, the wild ride.

"I wasn't scared," Jeremy said.

"Yes, you were. I heard you yelling."

"You yelled louder."

"No, I didn't."

"Yes, you did."

Willow looked apologetically at Lobo, who shrugged.

"Thank you," she said. "I keep saying that."

"I wish you wouldn't."

"How did you know I needed help?"

He was silent. He didn't know how he knew. He and Brady had been taking turns plowing a deep trench when he'd felt an intense fear. He'd not known anything like it since he was a boy, and all of a sudden he'd realized why it was so intense. It was fear for someone else.

Without saying a word he'd run to the corral, not taking the time to saddle the horse but sprinting to its bare back. He knew Brady would be behind him in minutes; he'd sense what Lobo had not said. They were working that way now, with an unspoken communication between them though there was still wariness.

Lobo had not gone far before he heard shots and saw the wagon jolting down the road, followed by two men firing pistols. They'd turned quickly when they saw him, and he wished he'd been able to go after them, but he had to stop the wagon.

He remembered the horse, however. He remembered it well. It belonged to the man named Keller who had come to burn the ranch. The man with him was also working for Newton. Lobo didn't forget men he might meet again. And now he marked these two well. Especially Keller.

Lobo didn't think Newton had ordered this attack. Scaring Willow, burning her barn, yes, but the cold-blooded assault on a woman and children didn't seem to fit, even considering the man's rage. And murder could easily have been the result if he hadn't come along.

Maybe Keller got tired of waiting for him and decided to ambush an easier target. Maybe the man thought Newton would be grateful, would even pay the high fee everyone thought Lobo had been offered.

Guilt ran through him like the sizzling heat of a brand, and he wondered whether the doc was right, whether he was causing more harm than good, whether he was a lightning rod rather than protection. If Willow had been hurt or killed . . .

His shoulders tensed and his hands tightened on the reins. The nearness of Willow was agonizing. He smelled her light scent, the intoxicating blend of soap and flowers, and each time their skin brushed, he felt touched with fire. He ached to put an arm around her, to comfort her after the terror she'd been through, but he kept his arms stiffly by his side. If he gave in to his need again, he could never stop, not when everything in him yearned for her.

He had to be clearheaded, not drugged with sensations that had no place in the life he'd chosen, if they were to survive the next few hours, the next few days. He had to be clearheaded in order to go when he must go.

He sat rigidly on the bench seat of the wagon, his lips drawn tightly together, his eyes hiding worry and need. His shirt hid the bunched muscles in his back, and his gloves hid the wretched condition of his hands. He was hiding from everything, fleeing from feelings that were so dangerous.

As they reached the hill, Chad stood up and waved at them, and they continued on, Lobo's pinto following behind without urging. The house, the yard, looked peaceful enough; even the chicken house was unusually calm.

Lobo heard Willow's exclamation as she saw the trench running from the garden toward the river. She turned to Lobo. "How is it coming?"

"I think it's deep enough. The water's already built up behind the dam. We're going to blast the bank this afternoon. The force of the explosion should carry the water to your field."

"Dynamite?"

He nodded.

She hesitated. She'd worried when he and Brady had buried it along the fence line, but at least that was underground and could be detonated only by a direct shot. This was different. "Won't it be very dangerous?"

"Not if you know what you're doing," he said curtly.

She didn't ask more. The reply told her he did know what he was doing, and though she wondered how he learned, she was certain he didn't want to tell her.

"May I watch?"

He shrugged, and his next words were spoken with a raspy voice, as if they were hard to force from his throat. "I can't stop you."

When the wagon stopped, the twins scampered out and took the horses in tow.

"Walk them for a while, then rub them down carefully," Lobo told them. The twins nodded their heads in unison, their faces saying they would agree to anything Lobo asked. Willow saw an all-too-brief unguarded look on his face before he turned away and slipped down from the wagon, holding out his hands to help her dismount.

His arms around her waist were possessive but gentle as they lingered a fraction of a second before letting go. One of his hands went up and brushed a wisp of hair away from her face.

The touch was so light, she scarcely felt it, only the heat radiating from it. She looked up and her gaze met his, so intense, so sensual that she felt every nerve responding to him. But she remained emotionless, unable to move, unable to talk. He was speaking to her in ways that only her heart understood.

And wept at the understanding.

There was love and denial in his eyes, passion and restraint in the set of his mouth, tension and want in the taut but graceful body. His hand hesitated a moment longer, then dropped and he turned toward his pinto. She felt lost and bereft as he walked away, leading the animal into the corral for water.

Brady tied his horse to the hitching post and watched Lobo. Willow noticed that the antagonism was gone from his eyes, and that he was standing taller, his shoulders no longer slumped. He was wearing his gun again. She wondered if one of the shots she'd heard on the trail came from him.

When he saw her gaze, he grinned guiltily, as if he shared some secret. She smiled back, but she knew it was only the shadow of a smile.

Lobo's horse had finished drinking, and he saddled it, then checked his rifle before replacing it in its scabbard. He disappeared into the barn, returning with a shovel, and went to one of the areas along the fence where he'd buried the sticks of dynamite.

Estelle had come out on the porch, her gaze moving from Lobo to Brady and lingering on the older man. There was a small smile on her vulnerable face. Willow thought how pretty she looked. Her blond hair was recently brushed, and her slender frame was straight, not bent as it sometimes was. There was a softness in her expression that made one dismiss the blank stare of the left eye.

Brady turned and met her gaze, and his own eyes widened slightly, filling with something like admiration.

If Willow had not known them both so well, she might never have seen the silent communication. She felt pleasure at the exchange; warmth curled inside at the budding regard between two people who'd seen so much trouble and pain. Hope started spiraling in the pit of her stomach. If Brady and Estelle . . . ?

Lobo finished digging and lifted two sticks of dynamite. There were still several in the ground. He nodded to Brady, who quickly mounted his horse.

Willow went to Lobo. "Can I ride with you?"

Her body pressed next to his was the last thing in the world he needed. Christ, he was already exploding inside. But one look at those pleading blue eyes and there wasn't a damn way he could deny her. He silently handed the dynamite to Brady and swung up on his horse, then held one hand to her.

She was incredibly light and graceful as she moved up behind him in the saddle, her arms going around his waist in complete trust. He felt her legs against his, her body cradling his back, her head resting on his shoulders, and he'd never felt quite as strong. She felt so good, as if she were part of him. It was a terribly dangerous feeling, and to banish it he tightened his legs against the pinto, commanding it to gallop.

But instead of helping, the faster gait merely pushed the two bodies closer together. Although her skirt bunched up between them, he could still feel her circling his hips, and it brought back every magical moment when he'd felt buried inside her and they'd been in complete harmony. He wondered if these feelings continued into marriage, and then he thought how stupid that idea was. He would never find out. Hopelessness suffused him, and a feeling of emptiness.

Willow noticed they were following the ditch. It was about two and a half feet deep, and ran more than one-third of a mile. She wondered how he and Brady had been able to accomplish so much. She turned around and saw Brady riding carefully behind, dynamite cradled in his arms.

After Lobo helped her down, she went to the river, noticing how much higher it was.

"The dam's effective," Lobo said curtly. "That means Newton's running very low on water. We can expect a visit soon, I think."

"What are you going to do now?"

"See whether this works or not." His tight lips softened slightly.

He knew what the garden meant to her, to the children. If they could harvest enough food for the winter and next spring, then part of Willow's small salary might buy them a cow, perhaps even a calf, the beginning of a herd. The beginning of some security. He wanted them to have that. He wanted it very badly.

"If you know any prayers," he said, "you can start using them now."

She watched as Lobo and Brady dug, Lobo giving instructions but listening as Brady made a suggestion of his own. The ditch was extended to within several feet of the water, and then Lobo buried several sticks of dynamite in the bank. "Get back," he told both her and Brady. "Beyond the trees."

"But you . . . ?"

"I'll have plenty of time if I don't have to worry about you two," Lobo replied. Brady nodded and guided Willow away.

Her heart came to a stop as she watched Lobo light a fuse and jump the bank, not running but moving quickly with a long, easy lope until he was next to her.

Several seconds went by, then a few more, and she felt Lobo's restlessness. He started to move, ready to go forward, when an explosion shattered the air, sending dirt and rock every direction.

Twenty-three

The three watched as the earth parted and water started to rush down the ditch.

Willow turned to Lobo and saw a slow smile cross his face as they walked over to the ditch. He had been afraid the dry ground would instantly absorb the water, but a steady stream was snaking its way toward the ranch.

"You did it," Willow said, her eyes lighting up like a sun-glinted sky.

Lobo looked over at Brady. "We did it," he corrected her.

Willow's gaze followed Lobo's. "Thank you," she said to Brady, whose brown eyes were alive with satisfaction. "Thank you both."

Filled with exhilaration, she grabbed Lobo's hand. He swung it behind her back, drawing her close, and he kissed her.

The kiss was wonderfully hard and passionate, and she returned it, his excitement and triumph irresistible. She forgot everything as she reveled in it, forgot even Brady's presence.

She closed her eyes, wanting only to feel. Her body cleaved

to his, now familiar yet still magically compelling. She felt her whole being melt and meld with his until she couldn't tell anymore who was who. Feelings mingled and meshed until she felt tears behind her eyes. Willow finally looked up at him, at the glowing green-blue eyes, at his mouth eased into an unfamiliar smile. The beauty of it, the rarity that made the smile so infinitely precious, was all-consuming, and Willow was unable to remove her gaze. She swallowed under the strength of his magnetism, the vibrancy of his body, and she knew she was staring at him with undisguised longing.

There was a clearing of a throat behind them, and she felt Lobo stiffen as they both remembered Brady. They broke off the kiss and turned toward him.

Brady, while not exactly disapproving, was nonetheless grim. "I think we ought to prepare for Alex. Some of his hands, at least, would have heard the blast."

The light in Lobo's eyes faded, and Willow felt as if the sun had just gone into eclipse. He nodded. "They'll find the dam fast enough, especially since they probably don't have much water this morning. You take Willow back. I'll stay with the dam, make sure no one disturbs it, at least until the water reaches the garden for several hours. If you have unwelcome visitors, fire two shots close together. I'll do the same."

Brady nodded.

Lobo still clutched Willow's hand, and now he let go. "You leave with Brady."

"But . . ."

"No, Willow. We do this my way."

Icy determination was back in his eyes, the implacable look back in the set of his face, the grimness in his lips. She lifted her hand to his cheek for just a moment, unwilling to relinquish the closeness they'd just shared.

"You'll be careful?"

"I'm always careful, lady," he answered, but this time the address caressed her, and now she treasured the word she'd hated.

Brady rode up behind her, and she joined him in the saddle, but she turned her head to look back at Lobo.

He stood watching, the lean, graceful body relaxing against

292 • PATRICIA POTTER

a tree, the easy stance belied by the intensity of his eyes, by the fierce blue-green that was so bright she could see it even yards away. Fear struck her then, fear that she might never see him again, and it seemed to send waves of doubt to him, for he suddenly stood straight and smiled, a rare, brilliant smile of reassurance.

She watched until a tree blocked the sight of him, and her hands tightened around Brady's waist.

"He'll be all right," she heard Brady say. There was a strange note in his voice, and she tried to identify it. He must know after that kiss how much there was between her and the man Brady had despised.

Willow knew she should feel ashamed. She'd never believed she would give herself, give her body, except in marriage. Yet nothing had seemed so right as the union with Lobo.

She'd questioned that rightness later, and perhaps she would again, but now she didn't, not after he'd saved her again, not when he'd smiled so brilliantly with personal triumph.

"You don't approve?" she asked.

They were riding beside the ditch, and the water was gurgling along. "I think it's going to reach the garden," Brady said, changing the subject.

But Willow wasn't ready to let go of her question. "You don't, do you?"

He turned and looked at her. "It's not up to me to approve or disapprove. I have no right to do either."

"You're my friend. You have every right."

"Don't ask me impossible questions, Willow."

"You've changed your opinion of him, haven't you." It wasn't a question but a statement.

"Maybe."

"Brady!" she said with exasperation.

Brady was silent. He didn't know what to say. He *had* changed his opinion of Lobo, but the man was still trouble, would always be trouble. He could see no way Lobo would, or could, stay, and he was desperately afraid Willow's heart would break. He knew only too well the pain of losing some-one, and Lobo was so obviously a loner, and his past, no matter the reasons behind it, precluded much of a future. Nothing could change that.

He felt a grief that surprised him, grief not only for Willow but for the gunfighter. Brady had seen that brief, unguarded look when Lobo had taken Willow in his arms. He had little doubt that the gunfighter loved Willow.

Damn him. Damn Lobo for being what he was, and thank God for it. But he was still poison for Willow.

Brady was relieved when they reached the house. He helped Willow down, and she looked at him with that soft, pleading yet stubborn expression he'd seen so often.

She would need someone after Lobo left, if they survived the next few days. The sense of regained purpose seeped through him, and he wondered whether it had been the kill-ing that had weakened him, or the death of his family . . . the loss of everything that made his life meaningful.

Well, now he had a new reason to live. Willow. Chad. The twins. Sallie Sue. Estelle. Pretty Estelle, who was finally healing. And Lobo. He even cared about what happened to Lobo! That was the most surprising discovery of all.

Willow was still looking at him. He wanted to lie and say he did approve, that she had changed Lobo and he had changed her, and they would all live happily ever after. But he didn't see how that was possible, and he couldn't lie, not to her. He knew that Lobo, the wolf, couldn't survive in the civilized world of Willow George Taylor.

He thought about his wife, and the love they'd shared. Would he be better off never to have known it, than to have known, and then lost it?

No, he answered himself with an aching awareness. He wouldn't have surrendered a moment of that time, even knowing . . .

Brady dismounted and met Willow's gaze. "Take it," he said unexpectedly. "Take every moment and value it."

* * *

Herb Edwards, foreman of the Newton spread, was informing his boss about the low level of the river when Keller knocked on the study door and was called inside.

Herb didn't like Keller. In fact, he didn't like anything about what was going on these days. Herb Edwards was a good cowman. He wasn't a gun hand, and he didn't like killing. Most of all, he didn't like the men his boss was hiring. They did what they wanted, and disappeared when they should have been riding the range, bringing in the weaker animals for water.

The newcomers were dangerous and arrogant. He'd been relieved when the man named Lobo disappeared from Newton's ranch, but his place had been quickly taken by five more, five he wouldn't have spit on.

Keller was the worst of the lot, and apparently the leader, even after he'd lost face at Willow Taylor's place. Herb hadn't been there, but he'd heard from some of his men who'd gone along to curry favor with the boss. Herb sensed Keller was not going to let matters rest, that he felt his honor was at stake, even if he wasn't quite brave enough yet to take on Lobo man to man. But it was obvious he was building up to it.

Alex looked at Keller impatiently. "What is it?"

"One of my men heard an explosion over toward the Taylor land," Keller said. "I was just wonderin' if it didn't have something to do with the way the river's going dry."

"Go find out," Alex said.

Keller touched the brim of his hat. "You said not to go on the woman's land without your permission."

Alex half lifted himself from his chair, the muscles on his arms straining. "You have it."

"Mr. Newton . . ." Herb started.

"Don't tell me to wait, Herb. That damn river's never gone dry before." Newton turned to Keller. "No violence. Not until I say so."

"What if we're shot at?"

"In that case, in *only* that case, shoot back."

Herb's fist clenched into a tight ball. He realized those

words gave Keller all the permission he needed. "Mr. Newton, I'll go too."

"I didn't think you wanted any part of this business."

He didn't, but he was afraid of what would happen.

Alex searched the faces of both men. Keller was standing arrogantly, his hand on his gun. Herb was tense, looking stubborn. Herb had been with him more than ten years. He trusted him, and he knew how bitterly Herb resented Keller and Lobo. He finally nodded, giving his approval to Herb.

The two men walked out. Alex clutched the sides of his wheelchair, hating his helplessness, feeling impotent just as he had every day since his wife had died, since he'd come home unexpectedly one brilliant fall afternoon to find his Mary missing, since the housekeeper had told him where she was.

Alex had been exuberant that day. He, Jake, and Gar had combined their herds; and he and Jake, along with hands from all three ranches, had just completed delivering a joint herd of cattle up near Denver to the gold and silver mines. They were about thirty miles from Newton on the return trip when he'd decided to ride on ahead. He was lonely for Mary and their three-year-old daughter, Marisa. He had been gone four weeks. After their separation of nearly two years—he'd left them in Texas with his sister while he made their future —he hated to be gone the few weeks that were necessary.

He was fifteen miles from town when he smelled smoke. He'd turned his horse toward the odor and found the ashes of what had been a small farm home. Three bodies were visible, a man and woman and young boy, all killed with arrows.

There had been renegade attacks in the past, but the new crossroads of Newton had been spared. When he and Jake and Gar had come to Colorado, first to mine, then to raise cattle, they'd taken pains to live in peace with the remnants of Indian tribes in the area.

There was nothing he could do at the burnt-out farm, so he spurred his horse on, fear beginning to gnaw at him. There were few hands left at his ranch; he had taken most of them with him on the Denver drive. Gar, who was originally going to go with them, had decided to stay and look after their three ranches, but he was miles from Alex's place.

Alex wasn't able to block his apprehension as he rode fast for his ranch. When he'd seen the large house standing tall on the rise that overlooked the river, he felt a flood of relief. He'd spurred his tired mount toward the porch.

Alex had almost jumped from his horse in eagerness, despite aching bones, and he'd strode quickly into the living area, calling for Mary. But only Therese, the hired help, answered.

"Where's Mary?" he said, and something inside him lurched when he saw Therese's apprehensive expression.

"She's not here, *señor.*" Therese said sorrowfully.

"Where is she?"

"She . . . she's gone over to *Señor* . . . Morrow's, I think."

The reply surprised Alex. He knew Mary liked both Gar and Jake, that she had even been courted by Gar before she had chosen Alex, but he'd never known her to visit him. He suddenly thought of the Indians again. "Did anyone go with her?"

"No, *señor*. No one ever does."

It took a moment for her words to register. "Ever?"

Therese clapped her hand over her mouth as if she'd said something she shouldn't, and she started to back away.

"Therese!"

"*Señor?*"

"What do you mean, ever? How many times has she gone?"

"Not so many, *señor.*"

Alex felt his guts bunch up inside. "How do you know that's where she went?"

"I heard them talking, *señor*, when he came over here."

Alex's heart was pounding now. Mary and Gar. He could understand Gar coming over to see whether everything was all right, but why would Mary go to Gar's home? He was a bachelor, always had been. Whenever Alex prompted him to find a wife, he'd always said no, that there was only one Mary in the world and Alex had her.

"Why, Therese? Did you hear why?"

Her face turned red, as if she knew something, and Alex felt himself tense all over. Gar and Mary had always liked each other. They had always bantered in a way that was foreign to Alex, but he'd enjoyed sitting back and listening. Now he wondered. Why had Gar decided not to come to Denver? Why had Mary gone to the ranch?

"Why, Therese, Why?"

"I don't know, *señor,*" she said. "I just heard . . ."

"Heard what?"

"The *señora* said she'd been waiting, that now you were gone . . ."

"Now I was gone . . . ?"

"This was their chance."

The pounding in his heart had climbed to his head. He felt a hammering in it. Mary and Gar. Mary and Gar. No, he screamed inside. Not his best friend and his wife. Not Mary.

He whirled around, unable to stand the strong suspicions. He would go after her, confront them. Perhaps Therese had misunderstood.

His horse, drooping wearily at the hitching post, lifted its head at his return. He knew he should find another mount, but he didn't have the patience. He had to discover the truth. He rode like the winds of hell.

He was halfway to Gar's house when he spotted the carriage he'd bought for his wife. It was sitting alone on the golden hills just off the trail, the white carriage horse gone. He slowed his pace, anger being replaced by a fear he'd never known before.

She was lying across the seat, her dark hair flowing across the fine leather, blood winding its way from her mouth. He dismounted and slowly walked to her. He knew from the angle of her body that she was dead.

An arrow had pierced through one of the breasts he'd loved and caressed. Another had pinned her arm to the carriage seat. His hand moved over the silkiness of her hair, the smooth ivory texture of her skin, and finally to the fine dark brown eyes. He closed them slowly.

Alex stood there, his life, so recently rich and full and good, in tatters. He didn't have the solace of memories now. They had been ripped from him moments ago in his own home.

Gar. He had been the cause of this. The loss and grief were so strong, Alex needed something to take its place so he could survive. Gar, his friend. Gar, whom he'd trusted with his life and his wife, had now stolen both of them. She wouldn't be dead if he hadn't tempted her, if she hadn't driven alone to his ranch.

Nearly mad with grief and fury, he'd ridden to Gar's ranch, and called him out. Gar came out, a smile on his face, until he saw Alex's expression. Without warning Alex took out his gun and shot, hitting Gar in the side as a cowhand came running up, throwing his employer a gun. As Alex aimed again, Gar's gun went off, and Alex knew an agonizing stab of pain before light became dark and he felt himself fall- ing. . . .

Sixteen years since then. Sixteen years of loneliness, of knowing betrayal by two of the people he loved best. Sixteen years of constant pain from Morrow's bullet. Gar Morrow had taken his wife, and then the use of his legs.

Alex swallowed down the bile. He had waited all these years, had waited because of Jake, the one man he'd trusted after Morrow's betrayal. Even then he would have moved against Gar Morrow had not Jake once saved his life and had called in the marker.

Both Gar and Jake had come to him, had denied Gar's guilt, but nothing changed the fact that Mary had died. Alex knew that Gar had wanted Mary; Mary had died returning alone from Gar Morrow's ranch. Alex couldn't listen to any of Gar Morrow's explanations. He knew, in succeeding years as he grew rich, that he could easily order Gar's death, but that would be too easy. He wanted Gar destroyed. He wanted Gar to see everything he'd worked for destroyed just as every- thing Alex had worked for had been destroyed that cold fall day.

*   *   *

Lobo was ready when Keller and six others came.

He knew they would follow the river, and his repeating rifle was resting in his hands when they appeared at the dam.

Lobo was in the shadow of the trees, nearly invisible, but he could see each one of them. Keller led the party, and Lobo could hear his curses as the man spied the dam.

He also heard Keller give orders to three of the men to break the dam up. He waited until they had taken off their guns to keep them from getting wet and had waded into the water.

Lobo stepped out from the shadow. "I wouldn't do that if I were you," he said, pointing the rifle straight at Keller's heart.

Keller stared, his face paling. "Lobo!"

"Unbuckle your gun belt and throw both it and your rifle to the ground. One at a time."

"Did you do this?" Keller nodded toward the dam, and Lobo knew the man was playing for time. What reputation remained to Keller would be shattered at being so easily unarmed by one man. His face was going from white to an angry red.

Lobo gave him a wolfish smile as he nodded toward the dam. "Not bad, is it? Now do as I say or I'll make sure you never hold a gun again."

Keller's eyes went dark with fury, but he did as directed.

Lobo turned to the man next to Keller. "Now you. Be very, very careful." After that man was disarmed, Lobo gave the same order to the third man. The three men in the river were standing absolutely still.

Lobo looked toward one of them, his rifle still aimed at Keller. "You. Get out and pick up those guns by the barrel, and throw them in the river."

Keller sputtered. "You can't do that . . . it'll ruin them."

"You're trespassing, Keller. Be grateful I'm taking only the guns."

"You can't dam the river—"

"This gun says I can do anything I want," Lobo said coldly. His rifle moved slightly to cover the man he'd just ordered to soak the guns. "Move!"

The man needed no more urging. He waded from the river, and one by one dropped the guns in the water.

When he was finished, Lobo gestured him and the others to remount. "Next time I find you on Taylor land, you'll lose your horses too," he said. "Maybe something even more important. Now get the hell out of here."

Keller's face suffused with rage. "This isn't the end of it, Lobo. You can't dam a river."

"Tell Newton he doesn't own the river. If he wants water, he's going to have to bargain for it."

"What do you want?" The question came quietly from another man, one who looked altogether different from Keller. Lobo turned his attention to him.

"It's not what I *want.* It's what I'm going to have," Lobo said. "Miss Taylor can do as she wants with her portion of the river. She wants to share it with everyone who needs it. *Everyone.* Tell your boss that. Tell him in exactly those words. No water for Morrow, no water for Newton. It's that simple."

"He's not going to let you get away with this." The bluster came from Keller.

Lobo laughed contemptuously. "You want to try to stop me? Now? I'm ready to oblige."

"I don't have a gun, damn you."

"Aw . . . no, I guess you don't," Lobo replied with a cold smile. "We'll just have to wait until next time. Gives me something to anticipate. Now get out of here before I decide to confiscate your horses as well. Oh, and tell Newton there's lots of places to ambush in these woods. Anyone tries to touch that dam gets a bullet for their trouble."

"Who's going to stop us . . . just you, Lobo?" Keller sneered.

Lobo studied Keller for a moment. "Just keep thinking that." He watched the reaction to his words flit across Keller's face. They carried a strong implication that Lobo was no longer alone.

Keller's face went even redder. "I'll see you dead, Lobo."

"The ground's full of them who've tried," Lobo said, his stance relaxing, as if he considered the six men no threat at all. His rifle lowered, but there wasn't a man watching him who considered trying to run him down or making any other hostile move. They'd all seen his speed the other night.

Keller turned his horse around, and Lobo saw his hand clutching the empty holster in frustration. Lobo suddenly pointed the rifle up in the air and fired, spooking the horses. One of the horses reared, almost spilling his rider to the ground. The others took off, all except Keller.

"I'm going to kill you," he said.

Lobo turned his back, as if Keller were no more than a fly, a contemptuous action that served only to infuriate Keller even more. Lobo wished Keller would make a move. He wished it with all his might as he thought how the man had tried to kill Willow and the twins earlier.

But there was no rushing noise behind him, and finally he turned. Keller was still there, his face full of indecision.

"One more thing, Keller," Lobo said tightly. "If you ever try to spook Miss Taylor's horses again, if you ever try to harm her or any of the kids, I won't wait for you to draw. I'll come hunting you." His voice was like dripping ice, each word freezing and hanging in the air.

Keller felt his face drain of color. He turned his horse, and spurred it into a gallop toward Newton's ranch.

Twenty-four

Willow and Brady heard the shot from the river and waited several seconds for a second one. When it didn't come, Willow looked anxiously at Brady.

Brady shook his head. "He said two shots."

"But . . ."

"Do you trust him or not?"

"Yes."

"Do you trust me?" There was a pleading look in his eyes.

"Yes." The answer came quick and sure.

"Then wait."

They moved out to the porch, where the twins, Estelle, and Sallie Sue joined them. Chad was on watch at the road. The next minutes were the most difficult Willow had ever spent. She pictured Lobo, lying bleeding, alone; and nothing was important anymore, not the ranch, not Jake, not the garden.

Willow's heart slowed, almost stopped, and her breath came just as slowly, passing raggedly beneath a lump in her throat. Brady's hand was on the handle of his gun. Estelle's face was white, and Sallie Sue was hiding her face in Estelle's blue dress. The twins, for once, were standing apart, their eyes riveted, like the others, toward a distant clump of trees.

Willow finally saw a figure move slowly toward them. Her heart relaxed as she recognized the pinto and the tall, proud, arrogant figure astride the horse. Her hand reached out, and Brady took it, squeezing comfortably, and she felt his own relief.

She didn't know how she could contain the joy she felt. She had to fight herself to keep from running to him, to not betray that she had envisioned him wounded and dying.

Yet she knew some of those emotions were on her face, for she'd never been able to hide her feelings. His gaze, as he neared, was fixed on her, and she saw the rare, slow smile with which he reassured her.

She was surprised by the number of weapons tied to his saddle and by the fact that his trousers were wet.

Lobo reached the small waiting group and dismounted. He cut loose the rope holding the pistols and rifles and they fell to the ground.

"You've been busy," Brady observed dryly.

Lobo nodded, then looked toward the twins. "Can you take these to the barn? Brady and I will clean them later." Willow noted the amazement on Brady's face at Lobo's use of his first name; it was the first time Lobo hadn't called him Thomas, and it obviously connoted some change in the relationship.

If Lobo had asked the twins to fly, both of them would have tried their darnedest. Their faces glowed with pride.

Lobo turned to Willow. "I've taken the ammunition from them." He hadn't needed to say it. She knew he wouldn't do anything to endanger the children.

"Where did you get them, Jess?" Jeremy asked.

"Some fellows were careless enough to drop them in the river," Lobo confided conspiratorially.

"Galloping goosefeathers," Jeremy said, using Chad's favorite oath. "All of them? There must be a dozen guns."

"Pretty near," Lobo confirmed. "It'll take you a while, so you better get started."

Jeremy, then Jimmy, nodded as they carefully gathered up

several pistols and rifles and disappeared with them into the barn.

"I could use something to eat," Lobo continued, looking meaningfully at Estelle and Sallie Sue. Sallie Sue beamed happily, sensing that all was well after those few tense moments of waiting, and Estelle, smiling shyly and taking Sallie Sue's hand, hurried into the house.

Brady suddenly grinned at him. "Anyone ever tell you you have a way with kids?"

Lobo looked disconcerted and then aghast.

Willow smiled at Lobo's reaction. She supposed he was used to being the bogeyman for most children. His usual expression certainly would daunt anyone over the age of two.

He looked so bewildered that she wanted to stretch up and kiss him. He had apparently overpowered a group of gunmen, taken their guns with only one shot, and now he looked terribly disappointed that he was taken so lightly by two eight-year-old boys.

"They like you," Willow said consolingly.

He scowled. That answer did not reassure him.

It was Brady who brought them back to the matter at hand, now that the children were gone. "What happened?"

Lobo explained, then said, "You two know Newton better than I do. Will he come here himself or will he just send men?"

Brady returned his look steadily. "He'll come. He'll bring men with him. You've challenged him now. I've never known him to back down on one. What about the dam?"

"I think it's safe for a while. I told them there would be someone waiting in ambush."

Brady shook his head. Lobo's audaciousness apparently had few limits. "They know there's only you and me."

"Don't be too sure about that," Lobo said laconically. "They might think we've picked up someone else, that Canton might have joined us. It's no secret he's been offered to Willow."

Willow's eyes widened. "Did you . . . ?"

"I just gave them somethin' to ponder," Lobo drawled innocently.

Brady's astonishment turned to admiration. A large group of men might charge one gunman, but two with reputations like Canton's and Lobo's? Lobo had just bought them time. "I'll get something to eat and go relieve Chad," Brady said, looking at the sun, which was falling quickly in the west.

Lobo nodded. He was only a little startled at how easily he was coming to depend on Brady when he'd never allowed himself to trust anyone before. His contempt for the ex-lawman had faded in the past days as he realized how hard the man was trying, how far he'd come, and how difficult each step must have been. His trust increased when Brady had enough sense to obey his orders and stay put when he'd heard the one shot.

"What about the river?"

Lobo knew instantly what Brady meant. There were two ways to the house, the road and by way of the river. The latter was the long way from Newton's place, meandering as it did through the two ranches. "They believe someone's covering it," he said. "They'll come by road."

Brady nodded. "Two shots," he said.

Lobo's mouth relaxed slightly. "Two shots," he agreed. The eyes of both men met for a moment before Brady headed for the house and Lobo moved toward the barn. Willow watched them separate, noticing the surprising ease between them, and she followed Lobo.

The twins had completed hauling the weapons to the barn, and now Lobo asked them to fetch some rags to dry them.

Willow stood at the door. "What are you going to do with them?"

"Clean and reload them. Stack some here and some in the house in case we need them."

"Do you really think Alex will attack?"

"I don't know what he'll do. We've pushed him in a corner now." He studied her face. "You sure you want to go through with this? I can tell him you'll sell, or that you won't let Morrow use your land."

"I promised Jake," she said stubbornly.

"I doubt he knew what he was askin'."

"I think he did. He knew no one in town would stand up to Alex."

"It's not your battle."

"It is now," she said. "It's my land."

He sighed. "At least take the kids and go into town."

She hesitated and looked at the darkening sky. "I'll send them with Estelle in the morning. I have a small house that goes along with the school."

"What about you?"

"Do you think I would leave you and Brady to fight my battle alone?"

His face tensed, and Willow thought how strong it was, how indomitable he looked. Was she being fair, asking this of him? She didn't even know why he was there.

"I can talk to him, I know I can," Willow added, almost desperately. "If Alex comes . . . ?"

"What if he doesn't?" Lobo said. "What if he just sends his men to burn you out?"

"I'll rebuild."

"How many times?"

"As many as it takes."

"It's just a piece of land."

"No." She shook her head. "It's more than that. It's . . . home." Willow met his gaze. "I never had one until now, not one of my own. My father was a teacher at a boys' school, and we lived in one of its buildings and ate in the big dining room. Nothing was really ours. Nothing . . . was permanent." There was a wistful note in her voice. "This is the only home I've ever had, and the only one that Estelle and Chad . . ."

Lobo was silent. The idea of home was foreign to him. The idea of actually wanting to own land, to stay in one place, had never occurred to him, though he was very aware that people killed for land. They'd hired him to do it. But he didn't want to think about that. "Your mother?"

"She died when I was born." Willow looked up at him, at the eyes that had warmed and deepened into a color even more startling than their usual coldly bright blue-green.

"And so you've adopted your own family," he said.

She had never thought of it that way. She'd just seen need, and tried to help. But perhaps that's exactly what she'd done.

The twins returned with the rags, and the warmth, the closeness, suddenly disappeared as he stepped back and lit an oil lamp. His eyes, when they returned to her again, were once more curtained.

Willow shook her head to try to rid herself of the sense of loss she felt. He was staying for now; that's what mattered. She watched as he focused all his attention on the weapons and then the twins as he sat down cross-legged with them, showing them how to dry and clean the weapons. It was as if he'd blocked her out.

"You'll eat with us tonight, won't you?" Her voice was low, but the plea was undeniable. Indecision crossed Lobo's face before he nodded curtly.

Brady cast glances at Estelle as she ladled out the stew she'd been preparing for dinner. He was damned if he knew what was different about her, but something was.

She turned and looked at him, and he realized what it was. There was life in her face again, life and hope and even perhaps eagerness.

"I saw . . . the water," she said tentatively. "It seems like a miracle."

"You can thank Lobo for that," Brady said. "I didn't think of it."

"But you did so much of the work."

"So did he."

"You both did," she replied softly. The fear he'd always heard in her voice was gone, and so was the hesitancy.

Brady didn't know what to say. He felt awkward at the praise, and undeserving. He should have thought of a dam long ago, but he'd been too befuddled with drink and regret and self-pity.

Self-pity. His gaze went up to her. If anyone had a right to self-pity, it was Estelle. Willow had told him Estelle's story, and somehow she'd survived a lot better than he had.

Admiration flooded him, admiration and a stronger emotion. He suddenly wanted to touch her, but he was afraid to. He'd noticed the way she flinched around men, the way she hid when strangers came, except Lobo, and that puzzled him. Brady felt another emotion, something almost like jealousy, and the knowledge startled him.

In confusion he hurriedly finished his stew, mumbled something like thanks, and left to relieve Chad.

Marisa could hear her father roar like a crazed bull. "Dammed the river? By God, she can't do that."

She slipped down the steps and listened at the door of her father's office. The other voices belonged to that new man she didn't like and Herb Edwards.

She heard snatches of conversation. Curses. The name Lobo. Canton. Threats.

"By God, I'll teach her who owns this territory." Her father.

"I want Lobo." Keller, the new man.

"Damming the river can't be legal. We should contact the sheriff." The voice of reason was Edwards's.

"Hell no. He's no more use than a worn-out mule."

"The only way is to kill Lobo." Keller again. "And burn them out for good."

"I don't want the woman and children hurt." Her father.

"They won't be," assured Keller.

"Hell, you can't guarantee that," Edwards said, his dislike of Keller evident in his voice.

"I want them out of there," her father roared again.

"I'll get them out," Keller assured them. "Just give me enough men."

There was a pause. "Edwards, call all the men in. We'll ride out in the morning."

"You, Mr. Newton?"

"I'll talk to her. If talk doesn't work, then . . ." The threat hung in the air, and Marisa felt sick. She crept back up the stairs, and an hour later, when she was called to dinner, she pleaded illness. She wasn't surprised when her father didn't come to inquire. She thought bitterly of how he had other things to consider.

Well, so did she.

She waited until very late, her glances going continually to the front of the house, which was busy with cowboys coming in. Marisa rifled through some old clothes, finally finding what she was looking for: a pair of trousers that she'd worn several years earlier, before her father insisted she wear only dresses.

Her body had changed, and they were tight around her hips, too tight, she knew, for her to pass for a boy. She needed a jacket that would fall below the telltale curves, and she remembered seeing one long ago in a trunk of her father's old clothes up in the attic.

It took her several moments to find what she wanted: a lightweight jacket that fell below her hips and a hat that, when the brim was down, would disguise at least part of her face.

Back in her room, she quickly pinned up her hair and tucked it under the hat, and waited until the area in front of the house cleared. Several horses, some of them still saddled, were tied to hitching posts. She slipped down the steps and out the back, and then tried to put some saunter into her footsteps as she walked around to the front. There were numerous new hands now, and she didn't think she would be recognized.

Marisa stopped beside one of the saddled horses. No one approached her; no one questioned her. She could hear bits and pieces of conversation, and the click-clack of weapons being cleaned. Now or never. She lifted her left foot into the stirrup, swung up, and started down the road to the gate.

She received only mild stares of curiosity from two riders coming in. She touched her heels to the horse and felt the animal's surge of speed.

Marisa looked up toward the western sky. A faint glow was rising from the mountains far in the distance. Less than an hour to dawn.

*   *   *

Lobo barely tasted the stew. He was restless in the small kitchen. At least, that was what he told himself.

Damn, but he felt strange as part of a group. It was confusing, unnerving. Awkward, dammit.

There was something else too. A curling of warmth at the unquestioning acceptance, at Chad's excited face, the respect of the twins, the brightness in Willow's eyes. He would remember this on clear, starry nights, on lonely, storm-battered ones. He would remember.

He suspected he would no longer be needed after tomorrow. The thought made his gut constrict, and he felt the same emptiness, the same stark terror he'd felt as a child tied alone outside a wickiup. He thought he had conquered that fear long ago, the fear of loneliness.

He was almost completely undone when Sallie Sue left her chair, worming her small body up on his lap and leaning her blond head against his chest, thrusting a tiny hand into his large, blistered one. Willow had wanted to bandage it, but he'd said no, afraid that even the thinnest bandage might slow his gun hand. The pain of using it, even to eat, reminded him of why he was there, and he needed that.

"Thtory," Sallie Sue lisped, and the twins echoed the request. Willow looked toward Lobo, and it was all he could do to keep his face guarded. She looked so pretty, the light of the oil lamp setting the auburn of her hair aflame and adding mystery to the pure blue of her eyes.

"Je—Lobo?"

He couldn't quite stop the jump of his heart of her surrender to what he'd demanded, and now he wondered whether he wanted it. For moments in the past several days he had felt like Jess. Jess the farmer, Jess the rancher, Jess the protector. And it had felt good, even satisfying.

Don't, he told himself now. Don't torture yourself about something that can never be.

The moment this was over, he was going to make tracks. As fast and as far as he could.

But Willow's eyes were searching his before she answered the children's request. He nodded curtly and started to remove Sallie Sue.

"No," she protested, clinging tightly to him. She felt good in his arms. He surrendered momentarily, and relaxed although he knew he should be outside and alert for trouble. But Brady was there. Perhaps a few minutes more, a few minutes of being in this charmed circle.

"Odysseus," Jeremy said. "He's just gotten away from the one-eyed monster."

Willow looked apologetically at Lobo. "Odysseus," she explained, "is the hero of a book written hundreds of years ago. He wandered for almost twenty years."

"He killed lots of people." Jeremy said with blood lust shining in his eyes.

"He tricked the Trojans," Jimmy chimed in.

"And outsmarted monsters," Jeremy added.

"Just like you." Jimmy beamed triumphantly.

Lobo wasn't sure whether he liked the comparison. He didn't know a thing about Trojans or monsters or people with strange names like Odysseus, but Willow was eyeing him with amusement, and her lips were formed in a smile so sweet he ached all over.

"Now," Willow said in voice low and compelling, "Odysseus is sailing toward home, but he has to pass the Sirens."

"What are Sirens?" Jimmy asked.

"Irresistible women who attract unwary sailors with their beautiful songs and lure them to their deaths," Willow explained.

"Aw, girls," Jeremy said. "I liked the monster best."

"These were very special girls with magic powers," Willow said, bringing back their attention.

She grinned suddenly at Lobo. "But Odysseus had learned his lesson with other women," she said, "and he was very wary. He'd heard about the songs that wrecked ships, so he made all his men plug their ears.

"Odysseus, though," she added, "wanted to hear the song himself, so he had himself lashed to the mast. When the song of the Sirens became audible, he strained and strained to free himself, but he couldn't, not until the ship passed."

Lobo sat back, one hand resting lightly on Sallie Sue's shoulder, and sympathized with the unknown Odysseus.

Christ knew he'd heard his own siren's song; only he hadn't had the good sense to take precautions. He listened with half an ear as Willow continued, feeling the warmth of Sallie Sue's body as she moved and stretched and finally fell asleep. Sirens. Just the feel of Sallie Sue's body, the soft measure of Willow's voice, the sound of excited small boys were his siren call.

He recognized it, and it scared the damn fool out of him.

Moments later he forced himself up, taking Sallie Sue to bed. He laid her down and watched as the child gave him a sleepy, trusting smile, and the eyes closed again.

He didn't stop back in the kitchen, he just slammed out of the house.

Odysseus and Sirens. Monsters and faraway lands. Stars shaped like animals. Warm babies and curious boys. A woman with eyes so blue they made the heavens jealous.

His cold, practical world had no room for any of them. None at all.

Twenty-five

Lobo watched the first glow of dawn spread its fingers over the distant mountains.

He had slept several hours and then relieved Brady on the hill. He'd always liked this time of morning, silent and golden and pure.

But now premonition crawled around in his belly like a snake. All his instincts told him this would be the day hell would break loose.

Ordinarily such feelings wouldn't affect him. A showdown had never bothered him before. Part of the job. Part of his life. Now he wondered whether he just hadn't given much of a damn about the outcome. He'd never known the excitement he knew many other gunfighters felt. He'd seen the glittering fascination, like the trance of loco weed, in the eyes of so many others like him, yet he'd never anticipated that moment when life and death hovered in the balance. He'd accepted those moments as part of his life, but he'd never relished them. Hell, he'd never enjoyed anything except his freedom.

Now even that didn't send the usual surge of satisfaction through him.

He'd have all the freedom he wanted after today—if he lived. And now that freedom didn't mean a damned thing. Christ, it even depressed the hell out of him.

Lobo looked back out at the road and saw a distant rider. His hands tightened on his rifle as he strained to see more in the first gray light of dawn.

It wasn't the doc, he knew that. Sullivan Barkley was taller, and Lobo remembered the man's horse. Who else would be coming alone at this hour in the morning?

As the rider moved closer, Lobo's puzzlement rose. The body was slender, a hat pulled down over his face. He sighted his rifle, and his finger curled around the trigger. Lobo judged the distance, then pulled the trigger and watched a bullet spit the dust just a few feet in front of the rider.

The horse reared, but the rider kept his seat, finally calming the horse, and bringing the animal under control. Lobo stood so he and the rifle could be seen clearly. "Ride up this way. Slowly," he ordered.

The rider obeyed, and Lobo squinted his eyes as his hands held the rifle steady. "Get off the horse," he ordered curtly as the rider and animal came within twenty feet of him. There was something odd about the intruder, something different.

He watched carefully, his finger still on the trigger as he was obeyed, and his surprise mounted as he saw the graceful way the figure slid from the saddle, at the hand that went up to the hat and took it off. He saw the profusion of dark hair.

"Christ," he exploded. "Newton's kid. What in the hell are you doing here?"

She very carefully held out her hands. There was fear in her eyes and her hands shook, yet her mouth was rigid with determination. Lobo felt a moment's admiration for her.

"I came to warn you."

Lobo loosened his grip on the rifle and let the barrel shift slightly toward the ground. "Now, why would you do that, Miss Newton?"

She glared at him, and he realized she was angry at being

ambushed. He leered at her. "Little girls shouldn't be out this time of the morning."

Suddenly she remembered their first conversation, and she smiled slightly. "I know. You eat girls for breakfast."

He looked surprised for a second, then his grim mouth softened. Apparently his ability to frighten was going to hell in a handbasket. "You're lucky. I already had breakfast."

She stared at him for a moment, realizing at last what Willow saw in him. When he relaxed, there was something incredibly charming about him. He looked younger and handsome and very appealing. But the hard look quickly returned, and the mouth tightened. "I asked why you wanted to warn Willow?"

She stiffened. "I just have to talk to her."

"Why?"

"It's none of your business."

Her defiance mixed with a trembling of her lips, and Lobo felt a weakening. He shouldn't. She could just be a decoy. She was Newton's daughter.

Yet her bravado was affecting. He knew she was scared. He could see it in her eyes and in the tense way she held herself, yet she stood her ground.

"You might just be a diversion, Miss Newton," he said, studying her reaction.

"My father doesn't need a diversion. He'll be here just after dawn." She hadn't meant to tell him, only Willow, yet those fierce, compelling eyes seemed to force the words.

"How many?"

"More than fifty. They've been rounding up cowhands all night."

"And why are you telling me this?"

She was silent, only too aware of her betrayal of her father. "Because . . . because he's wrong."

Lobo remembered his meeting with her when he'd first come to Newton, when she'd asked him to leave. He had thought little of her then, a curious child playing grown-up games. But now he found himself admiring her. He knew this act hadn't been easy for her.

His voice softened although his words were hard and un-compromising. "You've delivered the message. Go home."

"No," she said.

"No?" he echoed, drawing his eyebrows together in a way that usually intimidated.

She stood her ground, although she bit her lip, and his admiration increased. "No. I want to see Willow."

"Why?"

"Are you going to try to stop me?" The trembling was a little more pronounced.

He narrowed his eyes. "Try?"

"Do you have to repeat everything I say?"

He regarded her with amusement. "You would be wise to go home."

"I want to stay with Willow. If I'm there, perhaps Father won't do anything."

"Perhaps?"

She gave him a frustrated look. Did he never say anything but echo a piece of her sentence in such a wry, amused way? He made her feel five years old.

"I don't know," she said honestly. "I don't know him anymore."

He didn't want to let her pass. She could be lying. But other than tie her hand and foot, he didn't know how he could stop her. And it was really Willow's decision.

Lobo took a last look at the trail. If Newton's men were coming, there was no reason to wait out there. He should go back to the ranch and prepare a welcome, a welcome he knew Alex Newton didn't expect.

He nodded to her curtly. "I'll go with you," he said.

Lobo didn't offer her a hand. He didn't want to do anything that might make her stay at the ranch. Right now he wanted them all to go: Willow, Estelle, the children, all but Brady and himself. The two of them could protect the ranch better without innocents to worry about. He didn't think Willow would see it quite that way.

They rode at a trot, neither speaking to the other. Smoke was already curling from the chimney of the house, and the ranch looked inviting and hospitable. He wondered how it would look in the next few hours, if Newton's daughter was correct. His mind was already preparing a battle plan. Fifty men. But most of them would be cowpokes with little appetite for a battle, particularly against a woman.

Keller and his group presented the problem. Lobo had already seen how little regard the man had for women and children. And he knew that Keller had lost face during their two past encounters and needed some way to regain an image of strength.

The trick was going to be separating the cowhands from the hired guns.

And then what? If by some miracle or trick he could dissuade Newton from any more attempts on Willow's ranch, then what? He would have to leave. There was no choice, none at all. He couldn't saddle Willow with his reputation or the potential danger it represented. Neither could he inflict on her a man who could neither read nor write. She looked up to him now, looked at him with respect. He couldn't endure the possibility that eventually the respect would turn to contempt, or, worse, pity. She had lightly dismissed his lack of an education the other day, but he couldn't. It was a deep, frustrating anguish that had been with him much too long.

His hands tightened on the reins of his pinto, and the horse tossed its head in confusion. Lobo's hand soothed the animal with a touch along its neck just as the door to the house opened, and he saw Willow standing there.

The gray dawn was split now by a slash of sun cutting its way toward the mountains, and the brightness touched Willow, bathing her in a golden light. Her face looked so fresh and young and eager, and the blue of her eyes shone pure and deep.

Agony, so strong that it threatened to bend his body in two, rooted in his heart and branched out to his loins. So little time. So very little time.

He scrutinized Willow's expression, welcoming and joyful at the sight of him. He saw it change slowly when she saw Marisa slightly behind him. Worry started flooding a face so hopeful seconds earlier.

She walked down from the porch just as Brady emerged from the barn.

"Marisa?" Willow's voice was puzzled. It was very early for a visit.

Both Lobo and Marisa dismounted and walked over to Willow. Brady joined them. "My father's men are coming this morning, fifty or more," Marisa said. "He said . . . he said he would do anything necessary to get you out. I wanted to warn you."

Willow's slender body stiffened. "I was hoping—"

"I know," Marisa said. "I was too."

"Thank you," Willow said softly.

Marisa hesitated. "What are you going to do?"

"Stay," Willow said flatly. "I'm not going to let them burn this place."

"You can't. My father's . . . I don't know what he'll do."

Lobo broke in. "I'll stay. Willow, you take the young ones into town."

Brady moved closer to him. "I'll stay too."

Willow looked from one man to another. "I'll not run and let you fight my battles for me."

"If you don't think of yourself, then think of the kids," Lobo said roughly.

"Alex wouldn't hurt the children."

Lobo's face turned to pure exasperation. "Didn't you just hear what she said, for God's sakes?"

Willow stood undecided for a moment. "Chad can take them in."

"And if they run into Newton's men just as you did the other day?"

Willow flinched as she remembered the runaway horses. "I won't leave," she said stubbornly. "Perhaps Marisa . . ."

Everyone turned and looked at Marisa. She nodded slowly. She had intended to stay, but perhaps she could get some help in town and return. Perhaps Sullivan would know what to do.

The wagon was quickly hitched to the horses, the protesting twins and Sallie Sue loaded quickly, with Chad and Marisa on the front seat. Lobo hitched her horse behind the wagon. Estelle came out and watched, but also refused to go. "I can help load guns," she said with a determination that surprised the other adults.

They all watched as the wagon slowly wound down the road, then Lobo turned to Brady. "Let's get ready."

Lobo had plans, and now he discussed them with Brady.

Once Newton's men approached the ranch, Lobo would set off one of the charges in the ground. He hoped the explosion would be enough to make some of Newton's men wary of coming closer. If they continued to approach, Brady, from a position in the hayloft, would discharge a second round, while Lobo exploded a third. Hopefully, the attackers would believe there were more than two men at the ranch.

Lobo and Brady agreed on the tactics, then divided the guns collected the day before, making sure each was loaded. Estelle followed Brady into the barn, and Willow followed Lobo into the house. Both women knew how to load and use a gun; such knowledge was essential in an area with rattlesnakes, wolves, and other predators. Neither, however, had ever aimed at a man.

Lobo took up his post at the window. He thought about breaking the glass but hesitated. Perhaps it wouldn't be necessary.

His eyes went to Willow, who stood by his side as if she were a part of him. And she was. No matter what happened in the next few hours, the memory of her standing there, her eyes so clear and blue they could make a man cry, her lips trembling slightly but her chin set and determined, would always be with him. His hand went to her cheek, feeling its softness, and he ran his fingers along the fine lines of her face, etching it in his mind, his memory, his soul. The need— the dream—was so strong, so overpowering that he felt himself trembling.

Her hand went to his, pressing it gently against her face with tenderness, with aching possession, with wordless promise. His breath caught in his throat, and his heart beat erratically as he leaned down and kissed her with a haunting sweetness and longing that stilled time.

Willow felt tears gather behind her eyes. It was a kiss of

farewell. She sensed it. No matter what happened in the next hours, this was his good-bye. Her eyes met his, and she knew there would be no reprieve, not this time.

A mist had fallen over his eyes, not the curtain she was used to seeing, but the mist of tears that glistened like so many bright pieces of glass.

He withdrew, moving away slowly, like an old man, turning back to the window.

Twisted by a sorrow so deep she didn't know how she stood upright, Willow stood beside him and waited.

Alex Newton had his men lift him onto the seat of the buckboard and strap him there with a rigged-up buckle. It had been a long time since he'd ventured from his ranch, but he wanted to be at Willow's Taylor's ranch to make a final offer. And he wanted to be there in case Gar Morrow appeared.

He hadn't been able to sleep all night. His thoughts had gone to Mary, to Mary and Gar, and that day when he'd lost everything. It was time Gar Morrow lost everything.

He thought of his daughter upstairs. She had been the one good thing in his life these past years, but even she didn't understand. Part of the reason, he knew, was that he'd never told her the truth about what had happened. He hadn't wanted her to bear the burden of an unfaithful mother.

He looked around him, at the men mounting, and he thought he would give up everything to sit on a horse again and ride proud, as he had so many years ago. He and Jake and Gar had run their herds together, fought Indians and outlaws, built their ranches out of nothing. He, Mary, Jake, and Gar. The pain, the pulsing pain that never left him, ran deep and hot as he lifted his hand in signal to go.

Marisa took her charges directly to Sullivan's office. The town was just barely coming alive, the storekeepers preparing to open their establishments. But to Marisa, the town of Newton seemed abnormally quiet, even for this time of day.

She told Chad and the children to wait until she discovered whether Sullivan was home.

She banged impatiently on his door and heard a sleepy reply, some shuffling, and the sound of a twisting doorknob. Then Sullivan was standing there in trousers but no shirt. Circles were under his eyes, and she guessed he'd had a late-night emergency, but his eyes cleared instantly as his gaze rested on her. "Marisa?"

"Father's men are on their way to Willow's ranch," she said. "I have the children with me."

"Willow?"

"She refused to come, said she had to stay. Lobo and Brady are there with her."

"Brady?"

"He's . . . different," Marisa said. "Like he used to be. I don't know why, but I think that gunman trusts him."

"Two men against—how many?"

Marisa's eyes clouded. "I don't know. A lot. Men have been coming in from the range all day, and then there are those new men Father hired." Her face twisted with dislike.

Sullivan's gray eyes went cold. "Brady and Lobo don't have a chance against that many. Wait here."

He disappeared into the other room and returned within seconds, buttoning up a shirt. "We'll take the children to Mrs. MacIntyre."

"Then what?"

"I think I may call a town meeting of my own," Sullivan said thoughtfully.

Marisa stared at him, her impatience fermenting. She wanted to get back to Willow. If she was there, perhaps her father would retreat. But she wasn't even sure of that.

"I'll take them," she said breathlessly. "You see what you can do."

He looked at her suspiciously. "You'll meet me at the church?"

She hesitated, then nodded. She knew he wouldn't go otherwise. Her lie, she justified, was for a good cause.

Mrs. MacIntyre was only too willing to take the children, though her face creased with concern when she learned why the request was made. "Sullivan's trying to get some help," Marisa announced as a church bell started pealing.

"I'll make sure Mr. MacIntyre goes to the meeting," his wife said, "and that he does the right thing."

Marisa smiled gratefully, eager to be off. "I have a few people to see," she said, just in case Sullivan asked where she was.

"I'll take good care of the young 'uns," Mrs. MacIntyre assured her as Marisa turned and ran down the steps.

Moments later, Mrs. MacIntyre heard the church bell. Determined to speak her piece before her husband attended the meeting, she turned to Chad. "You take care of the younger ones for a few moments."

Innocence cloaking his eyes, Chad nodded, his mind already working. He couldn't leave Lobo and Brady and Willow alone. The ranch was his home too, his responsibility. Feeling every bit of the man he aspired to be, he watched Mrs. MacIntyre leave.

The wagon was in front, the horses still hitched up. Chad cast a warning look at the twins. "I'm going back. You two stay here and take care of Sallie Sue."

Jeremy shook his head. "We want to go back too."

"You can't," Chad pronounced.

"We'll tell if you don't take us with you."

"Me too," Sallie Sue chimed him.

"Holy goosefeathers," Chad swore.

"We have as much right as you," Jeremy said in a contentious voice.

"Me too," Sallie Sue echoed herself.

Time was a-wasting, Chad thought. He knew Jeremy and Jimmy would indeed tell on him and he'd be stopped. And Sallie Sue? No one would hurt little Sallie Sue, and he certainly couldn't leave her alone.

"All right," he said ungraciously. "But you have to do exactly what I tell you."

The younger ones shook their heads vigorously, Sallie imitating the others more than actually understanding what was happening.

Chad peered out the window. The street was full of people

moving toward the church and its beckoning bell. He waited several seconds until the way was almost clear, then lifted Sallie Sue in his arms and took her quickly out to the wagon. The twins followed and climbed in. Chad took the front seat, dislodging the brake and gently slapping the horses with the reins.

The wagon moved off at a fast clip. Chad kept expecting someone to holler at them, but no one did. He urged the horses into a faster pace, praying that nothing would happen until he arrived at the ranch.

The church was only half filled when the meeting started; there had been no time to contact people outside the range of the pealing bells. Those who filed into the building fidgeted with anxiety over what had called them out on a workday.

The meeting started with a prayer, as usual. Sullivan had already explained to the minister and mayor what was happening and had asked for their assistance. Both had demurred until they learned the wishes of the other townspeople.

Once the preliminaries were settled, Sullivan started to speak although his eyes kept looking for Marisa. "Willow Taylor's in trouble."

"Ain't she always?" came a voice from the back. Sullivan sent the speaker a baleful look.

"It's serious," Sullivan said.

"Ain't it always?" returned the unrepentant voice.

Sullivan ignored the speaker, the bartender at the saloon who regretted the loss of Chad's very cheap services. "Marisa Newton says her father's raiding the Taylor ranch this morning."

"How come she's tellin' you?" the sheriff, disgruntled at being the last to know, spoke.

"That doesn't matter," Sullivan said impatiently. "What does matter is that we do something."

"What can *we* do? We're just storekeepers and farmers," Mr. MacIntyre said.

"If we all go out there together," Sullivan said, "and show

Newton we're united and aren't going to tolerate this in our community, maybe he'll see reason."

"Old Alex ain't never goin' to see reason," the stable owner said. "We all know that. But mebbe Sully's right. Mebbe it is time we do something to end this damned feud, beggin' the ladies' pardon."

"Our ladies can't even walk the street anymore with all the gunfighters in town," Mr. MacIntyre added.

"And if they decide to stay, this town won't be worth a plug nickel. Lookit some of the other towns . . . Abilene and sech. Ain't fit for women and children."

"But we ain't gun hands," a doubter contended. "And Alex and Gar hired some of the best, according to hearsay. Why not jest let them go at each other, good riddance to both. Leave us in peace."

"And what about Miss Willow?" piped up Mrs. MacIntyre, who'd decided to stay and make sure that John did the right thing. The children would be all right for an hour or so, she reasoned.

"She brought this all on herself," the bartender said. "Besides, she has that gunslinger of her own now."

There was murmur throughout the crowd. "What about that, Dr. Sullivan?" said someone in the audience.

Sullivan silently groaned and damned Lobo. "There's two men, including Brady Thomas, against an army. They don't have a chance. Neither does Willow, and each of you know she won't give in to Alex Newton."

"What'll we do," complained a woman, "if we lose Miss Willow? Remember how much trouble we had getting a schoolteacher. Remember Abner Goodbody and Sam Morgan. I don't know 'bout you folks, but I want my Ethan to have some learning. He's been a different boy since Miss Willow came."

"My Hiram too," echoed another woman. "He's only eight, and already he reads the Bible."

Betty MacIntyre nodded her head fiercely, as did the other women.

Ethan's mother stood up again, a solid, rawboned woman

in her thirties. "You men here might be scared, but I'm not. I'm going out there to help her."

Another woman stood up. "I'm with you, Opal. I kin shoot as well as my man."

"I'm ain't going to let my kids go with no schooling," said a third. "Not like I did."

Before long, every woman in the meeting was striding determinedly out of the church as their men stared at one another with astonishment before scampering after them. Standing alone at the podium with a bemused Sullivan was Mayor Stillwater, who had watched his usually gentle, peaceloving Susan add her hue and cry to the proceedings. Too dumbfounded to speak, he slammed down the gavel to end the already disintegrating meeting and hurried after his warrior wife.

Those few moments of gentleness might never have happened, Willow thought as she studied Lobo. It had been nearly an hour now, and his face was expressionless, as if nothing had passed between them.

Lobo appeared at ease as he leaned against the corner of the window. But Willow knew that when he looked his most relaxed, he was at his most dangerous. Even if she hadn't learned that in the past few days, she recognized the wolflike glitter in those fierce turquoise eyes and what it meant.

She swallowed, wondering whether she was right in risking his life. But she had faith in him, complete conviction that he could make things right without anyone getting hurt. He had explained to her what he intended with the dynamite, and she'd marveled at his ingenuity. It was, she thought, as good a trick as even Odysseus could devise.

She couldn't take her eyes from him, from the tall, lanky body that she knew intimately, from its ridges and hard edges, its warmth and passion, the gentleness and violence. He was all violence now, all watchful, wary tension.

Willow wanted to say something to him, to beg him to stay after this was over. She knew that one victory here would mean only a greater defeat. She thought of the ranch without him. In so short a time he'd made such an impact on it, on everyone living here.

Willow forced her gaze from him, following the direction of his eyes. Jupiter was in his own section of the corral that Lobo had built. The other animals were milling around inside the larger corral. Lobo had not wanted to leave them inside the barn in case Newton's men did succeed in setting fire to it.

The chickens, including Brunhilde, had been chased out of the small henhouse for the same reason and the door locked against their return. Willow could hear Brunhilde's loud protest as she poked angrily first at the door of the henhouse, then at the gate.

Willow looked back at Lobo, whose gaze now raked over her slowly, lingering at her breasts and then returning to the road. She saw his eyes soften almost imperceptibly even if his hard mouth didn't, but the small flicker was enough. She reached out her hand and touched him, letting her fingers rest lightly on his arm. She wanted to do more, much more, but at the moment any contact was like a miracle. She saw him stiffen slightly, but he didn't draw away; instead, his gaze moved back to her face.

There was smoldering need in his eyes, and desperate fear for another person, and an anguished regret that made her blood run cold. For a moment she almost wished that his eyes were shaded, as they had been in the beginning, because she didn't know whether she could bear the message in them now. He was telling her that nothing had changed between them.

Suddenly she was in his arms, and his mouth was pressing hard against hers, as she sought with everything in her body to give to him whatever she could. Her hands went around his neck, drawing him into her world of sunshine and light and laughter. His lips softened for a fraction of a second. Then they both heard a shout, and his body stiffened, his hands thrusting her away and grabbing for the gun.

They both stared at the cloud of dust coming from up the road.

Twenty-six

Brady and Estelle saw the dust clouds at the same time.

"Godalmighty," Brady said. "There's a bunch of them."

Brady was lying belly down on the floor of the hayloft, and Estelle was stretched out beside him. For the first time in her life she didn't find it unpleasant to feel a man's heat next to her.

She strained her eyes to see. The dust eclipsed the riders, making it difficult to tell their number. She let out a small gasp as the haze drifted away, revealing an army of men approaching fast.

Brady put a hand on her shoulder comfortingly. "Lobo knows what he's doing."

"So do you," she said loyally, and Brady felt as if he'd sprouted another twelve inches. He looked down at his hands, and they were as steady as they had once been.

"If they start firing," he said, "you move back."

"No," she said steadily. "I'll stay here with you."

Part of him wanted to say no, but he realized it would do no good, just as it had done no good to ask her and Willow to leave. Estelle was a hell of a lot stronger than anyone gave her credit for, but then she'd had to be strong to survive what she had.

He smiled suddenly, a warm, sharing smile of approval and liking, and he saw Estelle glow like candles on the trees he and his family used to decorate every Christmas. He wondered only briefly at the memory; he'd tried for years to shut out images of his wife and son, but now he welcomed them. He had never thought he could have anything like it again, but now . . .

Brady heard the creaking of a wagon, and his eyes turned again to the gate. He saw a buckboard move slowly, the upright figure of a man sitting straight in front, and he recognized Alex Newton. His gaze moved to the men surrounding him, and he quickly identified Keller and the ones who had come the other night. Those were the ones to watch.

Suddenly a gunshot came from the house, and there was an explosion just outside the fence, sending rock and dirt high into the air. Some of the approaching horses reared in fear, two of them throwing their riders. The advance stopped, and a few of the men even retreated. Brady aimed at the red ribbon marking another group of buried dynamite.

"Don't come any closer," Lobo yelled from the house.

Brady hoped his hands would remain steady. He was to fire if Newton continued to approach.

"Lobo?"

The shout came from the wagon.

"What do you want, Newton?" came Lobo's reply.

"I want to talk to Willow."

"She doesn't want to talk to you."

"I'll give her anything she wants for the ranch."

"Sorry," Lobo yelled back.

"Lobo, damn you."

"Get out of here, Newton, and don't come back."

"Hell I will," Newton yelled. He lifted his hand to signal his men on.

Brady could barely see the small red marker, and there was a man near the buried charge. Close enough to be hurt? For a moment his hands trembled, and he murmured a brief prayer. He felt Estelle's hand on his shoulder, and strength flooded back into his fingers. He pulled the trigger, and there was another explosion. More men were dislodged from their horses, while several rode away.

It took minutes for the confusion and panic to subside. Then Alex roared again. "This isn't necessary, Willow. I don't want anyone hurt. I know you don't, but this land should belong to me. Tell me your price."

Another shot was fired and a third explosion made the ground rumble. The horses pulling the buckboard reared and were brought down only through frantic effort by the driver.

Newton signaled again with his hands, and some of the men remaining with him took out their rifles, aiming toward the source of the gunfire. A volley of shots rang out, and Brady covered Estelle's body with his own while Lobo did the same with Willow.

Canton was unsaddling his horse when a rider came galloping up to Gar Morrow's place. For lack of anything else to do, Canton had been prowling the edges of the Morrow property, his searching eyes studying the thirsty cattle bellowing their need. Morrow wouldn't be able to wait much longer, and that thought gave him pleasure. He was damnably tired of doing nothing.

He had partially amused himself by thinking of Lobo. The idea of his competitor defending the hearth and home of a schoolteacher had made him chuckle. As far as he'd known, Lobo had absolutely no weaknesses or attachments, which had made him very dangerous indeed.

He'd remembered the fury in Lobo's eyes when he had intimated that something was going on between Lobo and Willow Taylor. And Canton had not missed the flushed look of Miss Taylor or the leaves on Lobo's clothing. Nothing he'd been told about Willow Taylor had prepared him for the reality of the woman that day at her ranch, although he had seen her briefly at the dance. In just a few days time she had changed from a prim-looking woman into one most men would call beautiful. She'd had a glow that afternoon that was almost blinding.

He sorta envied Lobo.

The approach of the rider, however, quickly diverted his thoughts. There was an urgency about the man as he dismounted and ran up the steps of Morrow's house to the door. Canton strode quickly to intercept him.

"Newton's attacking the Taylor place," the man said breathlessly as Gar Morrow opened the door. "Heard it in town."

"Christ," Morrow said. "I never really thought . . ."

But Canton was no longer listening. This was why he was hired, and he was eager to earn his pay. Besides, it would be interesting to work alongside Lobo. If, he thought with another brief chortle, the man still had his senses about him. He heard Morrow order his men to saddle up, but Canton didn't wait. He hurried back to his horse, tightened the saddle straps which he'd just loosened, mounted, and galloped on ahead.

As Chad frantically whipped the horses toward home, a strange parade was beginning to snake its way from town. Led by the Sunday carriage of Mayor August Stillwater, a line of every kind of conveyance, from a lumber wagon to the town hearse, was also heading toward the Taylor ranch. Some were filled with whole families, while two had only one occupant each, both women. Several men rode on horseback and one boy was mounted on a mule. Sullivan was astride his horse, his hands much too tense on the reins. He'd looked everywhere for Marisa, but she wasn't anyplace to be found. Instinctively he knew she had gone to Willow. Yet he hesitated to leave the main party of Newton townsfolk. The mayor was too tentative by far, despite the stalwartness of his wife. And everything depended on the alliance—Willow's life and future, the peace of this area, the future of the town. Even, perhaps, his future. His and Marisa's.

He hadn't known exactly when he'd started thinking that way. Maybe the idea had been simmering in his mind longer than he thought; maybe only during the past hours when he witnessed the strength of this town, and especially of its women. He'd never expected it. He'd seen Willow's strength, and lately Marisa's, and now even the shy Mrs. Stillwater as well as all the other women in town showed more courage and determination than their men.

He had thought he was protecting Marisa, but now he realized he had been protecting only himself. Marisa had shown so much courage in the past few days; he'd been a fool to think she couldn't cope with occasional onslaughts of malaria.

Be careful, Marisa, he whispered. Be careful until I get there.

Marisa was almost at Willow's ranch when she heard an explosion, and her horse reared slightly and stumbled. When he came down, he took several halting steps. Marisa had heard many curses from her father's men, and now she borrowed several as she slid down from her horse and checked its hind legs.

Neither was broken, thank God, but the horse was lame and she didn't dare ride him farther for fear of permanently maiming the animal. She took the rifle from the scabbard and started walking, though she knew she would not reach the ranch in time to do any good. She heard another explosion, and her mouth went dry as she hurried her steps.

She was still trudging along the road when she heard the neigh of a horse and the sound of wagon wheels against the dry earth. She turned around, and what she saw made her want to swear again.

Coming closer was Willow's wagon. Chad was driving, and smaller heads were peeping fearfully over the front seat.

She started to wave when a third explosion came, followed several seconds later by the sound of rifle fire.

The wagon came to a stop, and Chad stared at her. "What are you doing here?"

She grimaced. "I could ask you the same question."

"We're not going to leave Willow there alone," Chad said stubbornly. "It's our home too."

Marisa thought rapidly. If she could get there, she might still keep her father from doing something he would regret the rest of his life. But the children . . .

It was as if Chad read her mind. "You can go with us, but you're not leaving us here."

Racked with doubts and indecision, Marisa finally nodded, and climbed up next to Chad. "Let me take the reins," she said.

Chad looked rebelliously at her.

"I've had more experience," she said, "and I heard they were spooked the other day."

Chad thought for several seconds. She was right. He hadn't driven a lot, and the team was difficult to control even at the best of times. He reluctantly handed her the reins.

Marisa slapped them against the flanks of the horses. The firing was continuing, and she had to stop it. She had to.

She slapped the horses again, and they sprang into a run. "Hold on," she told the children. They came over the hill and she saw the army arrayed in front of them. She slapped the horses again, her eyes intent only on the road in front of her, not on the riders who shouted and attempted to stop her. One leaned over to grab the traces, and she threw her quirt at him, knocking him off balance. She kept whipping the horses as she directed them around the buckboard where her father sat in astonishment. She went through the gates, slowing only as she approached the house, then brought the wagon to a halt just at the porch.

"Go," she yelled at the children. "Go inside."

Chad hesitated. "What about you?"

"I'm coming," she said, her gaze locked on her father.

The shooting had become sporadic, with seemingly everyone watching to see what would happen next.

"Marisa," her father roared.

Marisa turned to Chad. "Take the others in now."

The twins jumped down, and Chad helped Sallie Sue. They were just entering the house when a loud noise erupted from the henhouse. There was a frantic fluttering of wings, and one of the chickens flew out. Then a shot rang in the air.

Sallie Sue stopped and turned, her huge blue eyes fixed on the chicken, and she ran for it, with Chad right behind her. Lobo sprang through the door, immediately followed by Willow, and they both went after the children.

All of a sudden a million images swam in front of Marisa's eyes, so many she could comprehend none of them. Over a hill came a parade of some kind. The firing started again. Shots were ringing in every direction, along with shouts and curses.

Marisa screamed when she saw Sallie Sue go down. She jumped from the wagon and was nearly at the little girl's side when a burning flash of pain struck her leg, sending her to her knees. She saw Lobo throw himself over the child, and then he jerked twice before red spurted from his body. She looked down at the ground beneath her, and blood was puddling there as well.

Then pain turned everything into a red haze.

Keller had been baited all day, ever since his second humiliating confrontation with Lobo. His shame had turned into something close to insanity when they'd approached the Taylor ranch with old man Newton. The explosions had nearly upset him from his horse, and had done nothing to alleviate his rage.

Only two men were on the Taylor ranch, while Newton had fifty. There was no way Keller was going to let Lobo win this time. And then that damned Newton girl showed up, and her father ordered the firing to stop.

But nothing was going to stop Keller. If he fired at the stock, maybe Lobo would leave the house and the firing would start again. The henhouse was the closest. He aimed at it and fired, watching the chickens panic. One of the chickens escaped and ran across the yard, and then there was the little girl . . .

He aimed again, not at the child, but at a space right in

front of her, to draw Lobo out, but his horse moved suddenly and he saw the child go down.

When Lobo came running out, he aimed and fired, missing. Then Newton's daughter got in the way, but he fired nonetheless. Lobo wasn't going to escape this time. His gun barked and he saw Lobo fall while covering the child's body. Keller pulled the trigger again, watching as Lobo's body jerked and stilled.

Satisfaction and triumph darted through him. He looked around to see whether anyone had seen him take the notorious gunfighter, and his blood ran cold. Facing him was a man dressed entirely in black, and behind him, coming over the hill, appeared to be the entire town of Newton. He turned to his employer, and he saw hell in those eyes, hell and accusation and vengeance.

Keller's gaze went back to the man in black, who was reaching for his gun. Keller raised his gun toward the new danger, scarcely believing the speed of the man's hand as it moved. Before he could fire, he felt as if he'd been struck with a sledgehammer. He was falling, agony streaking through his body. His last thought, though, was that he had killed Lobo. He was the man who had killed Lobo.

I got Lobo.

Oblivious to the confusion around her, Willow knelt beside Lobo and Sallie Sue, her heart shattering at the stillness of the two bodies. Lobo was now lying on his side in a growing puddle of blood, his arms still protectively around the child. Willow became aware of others moving toward her, and she felt a moment of panic that perhaps they'd come to finish what they started, and she moved her body to shield the two wounded ones.

Fury and anger, but most of all grief, flooded her mind. Sallie Sue looked so small, so innocent, so incredibly precious as she was cradled by one of the most notorious gunfighters in the territory. Willow saw blood running from a hole in her arm when Sallie reached out a hand to the face of her protector.

"Thess," she cried, tears tumbling down her face. And Willow sensed that somehow Sallie knew that Lobo had saved her life.

Lobo didn't stir, and the child clutched at him in confusion and terror and pain.

Willow tried to take her, but the child wouldn't let go. Willow buried her head in Sallie's blond hair while she frantically reached out to search for signs of life in the prone figure. But he was so quiet, all the restless energy in his body stilled, the vibrant blue-green eyes closed.

She felt the wet stickiness of blood on her hands and then the hot flood of tears on her face.

"No," she cried out, her terrible grief silencing the noise and confusion around her. The parade on the hill stopped, the townsfolk stunned by the scene below them: Marisa twisting in agony, the child trembling and bloody, the gunfighter lying motionless, and Willow clinging to both the child and the man while defying anyone to touch or hurt them again.

It was Sullivan who broke the spell, who ran down the hill, disregarding the gunmen, disregarding the growing mumblings of outrage, disregarding anything but the figures on the ground.

Willow was barely aware of his presence, of his arms prying her away from Sallie. "Lobo . . . Jess," she whispered achingly, now touching him, seeking an answer, any answer, even the slightest movement, the smallest breath.

Blood was seeping from him in three places, the back of one shoulder, his chest, and his right hand, which was a mass of mangled bone and tissue. Willow leaned down, putting her lips to his, and she breathed sharply when she heard his ragged gasps for air. She took his undamaged hand, holding it tightly as if giving life to him.

Where was Sullivan? She looked around and saw him bent over Marisa while Mrs. MacIntrye held a crying Sallie Sue. After a few moments Sullivan returned to Lobo's side.

"Sallie Sue and Marisa will be all right," he said softly. "Sallie's wound is only superficial. Marisa's is more serious, and she's in a great deal of pain." He deftly examined Lobo, his face growing more and more grave.

"Sullivan?"

"It's bad, Willow, but I'll do what I can."

Willow felt a hand on her shoulder and she turned, her fingers still clasping Lobo's. She now saw the mass of people coming toward them. She didn't know who was touching her; she didn't care as she shied away. These were the people who had done this, who'd let this happen.

Fear for Lobo replacing her anger, she allowed her eyes to move warily around to make sure no one would touch or hurt Lobo again. She saw men taking down Alex Newton's wheelchair from the back of the wagon, and then helping him from the buckboard and placing him in the wheelchair. She saw Canton, still dressed in black, his hand holding a gun, walk over to a man lying on the ground just outside the fence. The atmosphere of menace was gone. Only shock remained. Shock on the faces of Newton, of his men, of the townspeople, of Brady and Estelle, who were emerging from the barn. Brady, who had his rifle ready . . .

All were fleeting images that barely registered in Willow's mind, once she understood the danger of more violence was gone. Now there was only the need to keep Lobo alive. She leaned down and whispered to him, loving words, pleading words, demanding words.

Sullivan was busy taking off Lobo's shirt, his eyes intent on the wounds.

"I won't let you die," Willow said. "I won't."

From a distance she heard Alex's voice. "Sullivan! My daughter!"

Even while Sullivan's hands continued their work, trying to staunch the bleeding in Lobo's hand, he looked up quickly.

"My daughter needs you."

"This man needs me more," he said, and Willow saw the agony on Sullivan's face at the choice.

Alex's face tightened, but he visibly controlled himself. "How is she?"

Sullivan looked steadily at Alex. "A bullet hit a bone. She's in a lot of pain, but she's not in any immediate danger." His gaze went back to Lobo. "No thanks to you," he added bitterly.

Lobo slowly opened his eyes, but no sound came from him, not even the slightest groan when Sullivan knew he must be in agony. One of his ribs, possibly more, was shattered and his breathing was ragged, indicating damage to at least one lung. His hand was also a mess, and Sullivan knew several bones had been hit. As a gun hand, it was probably ruined forever.

But the most immediate problem was loss of blood, and he did what he could to slow the flood as he prayed there was no internal bleeding. Lobo lay still during Sullivan's examination, although his questioning gaze moved toward Sallie Sue.

"She'll be all right," Sullivan said. "So will Marisa."

"Willow?" It seemed to take every ounce of his strength to ask.

"I think that depends on you," Sullivan said dryly. He turned around and called out to several townspeople while studiously ignoring Newton and his men. "Take him inside. Willow will show you where."

He turned back to Sallie Sue, who was now being held tightly by Estelle. They were both surrounded by a group of women wearing shocked and sympathetic faces. He pushed through them, and looked at the child.

"Thess," Sallie Sue demanded again, and Sullivan's heart hurt as he saw the anxiety in the tiny, drawn face. She was a gallant little thing, and he couldn't help but envy her devotion to Lobo. Envy but no longer wonder. He, like everyone else in the town, had seen Lobo risk his life for the child, perhaps even give it. His throat tightened as he felt a certain helplessness. But perhaps he could perform a miracle of his own with God's help.

"I'll take her inside," Estelle said, tenderness written all over her face, a new strength in her voice.

Sullivan nodded, then he went back to Marisa and started to gather her in his arms.

"No," Newton said. "I'll take her home."

Sullivan ignored him and picked Marisa up. "No, you

won't. I have two other patients here, and she needs medical attention. She stays here." There was a hardness in his voice that no one had heard before, and even Alex faltered, his eyes looking to the ground.

Then the rancher seemed to summon his nerve. "Do you think Willow will let me stay here with her?"

Sullivan glared at him. "*I* wouldn't. *She* probably will," he said with disgust and, ignoring Newton, took Marisa inside to Estelle's bedroom.

Willow watched as the men carrying Lobo carefully laid their burden down on one of the twins' beds. They looked at her awkwardly, embarrassed they had not done something sooner to prevent this, and backed away toward the door as they saw her touch the wounded man tenderly.

She didn't notice them leaving. All her attention was focused on Lobo. How many times had he risked his life for her and hers? And now he might die.

She heard the noise of Alex's wheelchair entering the next room. She heard his words to his daughter. "I'm sorry, Marisa. I'm so sorry."

"Is it over now?" was Marisa's strangled reply.

"It's over, Marisa," Newton said. "It's over."

Willow swallowed as she looked down at Lobo. His lips were clenched tight against the pain, his lungs gasping for breath, his eyes closed. At what price was it over?

Dear God, at what price?

Willow bowed her head and saw her tears fall on his face, mixing and joining with the beads of blood and sweat suffered in her defense.

And she knew the true measure of agony.

The whole town attended the funeral five days later despite a pouring rain.

A drifter who had had to wait three hours to get supplies asked John MacIntyre why all the stores and saloons had been closed.

"Funeral," came the short, clipped answer.

"Who in the hell is so important you close the saloon?"

"Ain't every day you bury a notorious gunslinger," MacIntyre said.

The man's interest suddenly increased. "Who?"

"Lobo. Was involved in a range war. Died of gunshot wounds two days ago."

"Lobo," the stranger said with awe. "Who got him?"

MacIntyre sighed. "Man named Keller. But we just buried him too. Gunfighter by the handle of Canton killed him."

"Gol dang," the stranger said. "Canton, huh? I heard of him too. Must have been mighty excitin' 'round here."

"Well, they're all gone now," MacIntyre said. "Town's getting back to normal. Real peaceful. Just like it used to be. Expect it to stay that way too, since we got us a real good sheriff again."

The drifter wanted all the details. The story would make good conversation at the next stop, the next campfire. "Who's that?"

"Brady Thomas. Used to sheriff here, but got sick. He's doing real fine now. Real fine. Even thinkin' of gettin' hitched again."

The man rubbed his chin. "I think I heard of him. . . . Didn't he catch the Lassiter gang couple years back?"

MacIntyre nodded.

"Well, don't that beat all. Think I might go visit that Lobo's grave. Sure be something to talk about."

John MacIntyre shrugged. "Sure would," he agreed as he packaged the man's meager purchases and gave him directions to the cemetery.

The drifter wrapped himself in his rain slicker and made his way to the cemetery several minutes later. There were two new graves, both covered with mud. One wooden cross read *Ed Keller*, the other simply *Lobo*. There was a sprig of flowers, looking lonely and beaten down by the rain, on the latter's grave, and the drifter wondered briefly who mourned a gunslinger whose reputation was as bad as any he knew. He finally shrugged and turned his horse north. This tale was going to earn him some drinks as well as campfire dinners.

Twenty-seven

Alex Newton and Gar Morrow, standing bareheaded in the falling rain, attended the gunslinger's funeral.

Gar was there because he thought it the least he could do. A woman and child were paying for his bullheadedness.

And the man named Lobo.

Alex was there because his daughter threatened never to speak with him again if he wasn't.

They stood on opposite sides of the grave while Reverend Cecil Mooney dispatched Lobo to wherever he was heading. He did it in eloquent style, borrowing heavily from Corinthians.

" 'Behold I show you a mystery. We shall not all sleep, but we shall all be changed.

" 'In a moment, in the twinkling of an eye, at the last trumpet; for the trumpet shall sound, and the dead shall be raised incorruptible and we shall all be changed.' "

Reverend Mooney's eyes pierced the two enemies as the words rolled off his tongue.

Gar stood awkwardly. He knew much of the trouble during the past few days had been his fault as much as Alex's. His pride, his honor, his friendship, had been attacked and he'd struck back blindly. Mary would have been appalled.

When the words were finally said, and the earth fell on the plain pine casket, Gar made his way over to Alex. "I have something that belongs to you. I would like to bring it to you this afternoon."

Alex glared at him. He was about to say he wanted nothing from Gar Morrow, but a glance at his daughter's face, as she sat in a carriage, her leg bandaged and splinted and resting on top of pillows, changed his mind. He nodded curtly.

Marisa had come home the day before. She had been at Willow's four days, and had agreed to return only if her father ended his feud with Gar Morrow. It had been an easy promise to make then, for he had suffered, afraid that he'd lost Marisa forever.

Alex looked at Willow's bowed head as she stood in the rain, her gaze fixed on the gravesite while the casket was lowered and dirt shoveled into the hole. He felt regret that he had been responsible for so much that had happened.

Hell, the least he could do was talk to Morrow.

Sullivan drove Willow home in his buggy. Brady rode solemnly alongside.

She sat tall, her shoulders back, her eyes only slightly teary. Mrs. MacIntyre had given her flowers to lay on Lobo's grave, and as she'd bent over the mound of dirt, Willow had said good-bye forever to the renegade.

She was grateful to the town. After showing up the day of the raid, they made Alex Newton very aware that Willow and all her charges were under their protection.

Not that it was needed. Alex was a changed man. He had come too close to losing Marisa because of his own hatred. He had stayed at Willow's house the day of the shootout, sitting beside his daughter's bed. He left the following morning, only after being assured that Marisa was recovering but could not yet be moved. The bullet had broken a bone, and a jolting wagon ride would bring not only pain but the possibility of further injury.

Alex had returned later that day and said he'd dismissed all the gun hands. He also said that he no longer objected to Gar Morrow's benefitting from the river. Willow hoped, and so did Marisa, that the two men would heal the bitter wounds between them. But that was yet to come. They were still separated by pride and distrust, but at least they would keep the quarrel between them now, and not drag others into it.

And Brady? After all the confusion, Brady had promptly taken charge. He had mediated between Alex and the towns-people and had ordered Canton out of town. Since the town sheriff had decided he wanted no part of the affair and had declined to accompany the trek to the ranch, August Stillwater took one look at the new Brady, conversed quickly with the town council, and offered him his old job back, on proba-tion, of course. Brady had said he would think about it. Two days later he told August that he might consider the position if the town would accept his fiancée, Estelle.

The citizens of Newton had received so many shocks re-cently that this condition didn't seem particularly odious. Their values in the past few days had changed radically. Ac-tions rather than appearances had suddenly become very important. After all, hadn't they all seen the once most re-spected man in town attack a woman? Hadn't they seen a notorious gunfighter offer his life for that of a child? Hadn't they seen the town drunk, together with one other man, fight off an army? Hadn't they seen the eccentric Miss Willow bring together the town in a way no one else had?

Even the womenfolk held their tongues when they'd seen Brady and Estelle emerge from the barn the day of the shootout, and watched as Estelle ran to the wounded on the ground. There'd been more than one tear in a few eyes.

So, Willow thought sadly, everything was turning out well for nearly everyone. Even Marisa and Sullivan seemed to have come to an understanding.

She'd walked in on their conversation on the day Marisa left for home. Marisa was glaring at Sullivan. "You must hate taking care of me," she said. "Watching me lie here."

Sullivan had looked confused. "Of course not." His hand had touched her gently. "I wish—" He'd stopped abruptly.

"You wish what?"

"That I could always take care of you."

"It's not that terrible, then?"

"Of course not!"

"Then you must think I'm a much lesser person than you are."

There was a silence, then protest. "How can you possibly think that? You're the bravest, most loyal—"

"But you don't think I love you enough, or am strong enough to take care of you the few times you get malaria."

"Marisa . . ."

"Well, you don't, do you?"

"Of course I do."

"But you don't love me?"

"I do," he protested.

"Good," she said. "Then it's settled."

Willow had to swallow a chuckle before backing out of the room.

And, sure enough, it had been settled. Marisa and Sullivan planned to get married in a month.

That left Willow.

Her hands clenched as they drove up to the ranch house. A strange horse was hitched in front, and Willow wondered idly whom it belonged to, and then she remembered!

Brady, who had been riding alongside the buggy, dismounted and strode over to the buggy. He offered his hand to Willow and helped her down. Estelle came out, a soft smile on her face for Brady.

"How are the patients?" Sullivan's question was gentle.

"Sallie Sue's as good as gold. The other, intolerable," she said. "As bad-tempered as a wounded bear."

Brady's face hardened as he continued to study the horse. He recognized it. "Canton?"

Estelle nodded.

"Dammit to hell. I told him to leave town."

"He says he's on his way," Estelle said.

"Christ, he could ruin everything."

344 •   PATRICIA POTTER

"I don't think so," Estelle said, her voice soothing. "He says
he was sent for."

Brady's gaze turned to Willow, who suddenly looked
sheepish as she nodded.

Brady grimaced. "Why?"

"I don't know, but he was almost desperate to see him."

Brady glowered and moved quickly inside the house.

The door to the twins' room was open. They could hear
Canton's lazy voice from within. "Never thought I'd be accepting a job from you. I'll take care of it, just like you said."
There was a short silence, then a cold chuckle. "Won't do any
harm to my reputation, killing the man who killed Lobo."

There was a grunt from within.

"I'll miss Lobo though. Always thought I would eventually
face him. I'll always wonder who was the fastest."

There was another grunt, something like a guttural oath.

Canton emerged from the room, stopping when he saw
Brady. He held up his hands in surrender. "I'm on my way,
sheriff." He smiled pleasantly.

"Canton . . . ?"

"You don't have to worry about me, Sheriff," Canton said.
"I'm just as glad to have Lobo dead and buried. Less competition for top dollar, you understand." He nodded to each of
the women and left.

Willow was the first to move. She went to the bedroom door
and looked in. Jess was sitting up, his face in a deep scowl as
he stared at his bandaged right hand.

"The whole town attended Lobo's funeral," Willow said.

Ice was in his eyes as he glared at her. He had not liked the
idea. He had fought it desperately. It was like killing himself,
like denying a vital part of who and what he was.

It was not until Sullivan made it very clear what his options were that he'd finally agreed. "You will never be able to
use that hand as you have," he said. "With time and effort
you'll have some use, but you'll never again have the dexter-
ity or speed you once did."

He had glowered at the doctor, as if doing so would cancel
the words. Gunfighting was all he knew, his one talent.

"You won't last a week out there with that hand," Sullivan had persisted. "You have a death wish? Go try."

Lobo knew he was right. He'd looked at his heavily bandaged hand with bleak eyes, and an emptiness filled him. For a while, during the past few days, he had hoped . . .

He hadn't known how he might reconcile his reputation with Willow's safety. But he had thought perhaps he could try. But then he had had a good right hand. He could protect her. Now he couldn't protect anyone. Even without a reputation, even as a plain rancher, he couldn't protect her.

His ability to defend himself, to provide for himself, had always been his one strength. Now he didn't have that. He was less than half a man. So he glared at her, wanting to frighten away that soft look in her eyes. Another day, and he'd have enough physical strength to ride away. He didn't know where he would go or what he would do.

But Lobo did have something he could leave Willow Taylor. Ever since his "death" had been proposed, he'd tried to find a way to help Willow fulfill her dream of a safe home, and Chad's of running cattle. He had money, but now that he was "dead," the problem was getting it.

And then he'd thought of Canton. He trusted Canton's professionalism. Willow's friends might try to change his mind about his plan, might try to interfere, but Canton wouldn't. And Canton had agreed readily enough to do what Lobo requested.

Burying his pride, he asked Canton to write him a will, giving most of his savings to Willow. The remainder would be left to Canton, who would then, for a fee, transfer the money to a bank in San Francisco under the name of Jess Martin. Lobo signed the will with the signature he used at the Denver bank, and the will was predated six days earlier.

At least he would leave Willow something. He didn't worry about Canton stealing the remainder of the money. Canton had his code of honor, and that included loyalty to one's employer. Lobo was, however briefly, Canton's employer.

Now that this particular business was completed, Lobo could leave. If he weren't there, Willow couldn't refuse the money, especially when it would give her and Chad the funds to start stocking the ranch.

His body still hurt like hell, and he felt as weak as a newborn wolf cub, but he was ready to ride. And the sooner the better, before he started getting damn fool ideas again. Soft ideas. Hurting ideas.

So he glowered during Willow's account of his funeral, liking nothing about it; not even the fact that the entire town had joined in a conspiracy of silence to save his life lightened his mood. Lobo was gone, and there was damned little left.

He tolerated Sullivan's ministrations, his changing of the bandages, in sullen silence. He saw the worry and fear in Willow's eyes before she left the room, and he felt his heart lurch with love. But he was no good for her. Lobo or Jess, he'd always been trouble, always would be. She deserved so much more.

He tried to move the fingers in his hand and received only agony for his trouble. Damned but he welcomed it; it reminded him of the loss he could expect. It strengthened his resolve.

Tomorrow, he swore to himself. Tomorrow he'd leave.

How many times in the past few weeks had he said the same thing? How many times had he ignored his own warnings? But tomorrow he couldn't. He had to go. For Willow, he had to go.

Although he knew it would break the heart he so recently and so painfully had discovered.

Gar Morrow didn't miss the hostile looks given him as he drove his buckboard onto the Newton spread. He had come alone, without any of his own hands. He didn't want any more trouble.

The rain was continuing, and it ran off his wide-brimmed hat. A large oilcloth covered the item in the back of the buckboard.

He drew up to the porch, so much like his own, and felt a regret for the past and present. He and Jake and Alex had once had something very rare together. Perhaps he should have told Jake long ago what had happened, but his pride hadn't allowed it. His best friend in the world had thought he betrayed him, had shot without giving him a chance for explanation, had turned him away after so many years together. The betrayal had blinded him to reason, just as it had blinded Alex.

Because of it, others had suffered. A child. A young girl. A man who had tried to protect them. Gar could find no justification now in his own actions. He was as guilty as Alex. His silence had been as responsible as Alex's rage.

He knocked, and the Newton foreman opened the door. "Mr. Newton's expecting you," he said. The foreman's gaze had searched him quickly, finding no weapons, before he led Morrow to Alex's office.

Alex was sitting in his wheelchair behind a desk. His expression was anything but welcoming, but Gar ignored it. He turned to the foreman. "There's a saddle in the buckboard. Please bring it in."

When the foreman disappeared, the two men studied each other. Until the funeral it had been years since they'd seen each other, despite the fact that they lived only miles apart. Age had favored neither of them: bitterness and loneliness lined both faces.

They were silent, watchful, as the foreman returned, carrying a heavy saddle.

"This belongs to you," Morrow said. "Mary meant it as a gift."

Alex's mouth gaped open.

"It was why she was at my place that afternoon," Morrow said heavily. "It was a gift for your birthday. One of my men was skilled as a silversmith. I helped her obtain what she needed. She'd planned it for months."

Alex grasped the arms of his chair and tried to rise, only to fall down again. "A gift?"

Morrow sighed heavily. "You never gave me a chance to tell you. You shot, and then I did."

Alex closed his eyes, trying to remember that day, the rage that had filled him. "A gift?" he said again.

"There was never anything between Mary and me, although I'd once hoped there would be . . . before you and she married. I loved her, but you were my friend, and she loved you very much. I was even glad that if it wasn't me, it was you."

"But why . . . all these years."

"You betrayed both of us that day." Gar said slowly. "Me, perhaps I could forgive, but Mary . . . Christ, she loved you and you dishonored her, made everything so damned dirty." He hesitated. "I suppose I wanted to punish you for her by letting you continue to believe . . ." His voice trailed off.

"Christ, Gar," Alex cried out. "I was crazy that day. And when you never denied it—"

"I didn't think I should have to . . . nor Mary," Gar said. "I was wrong." He swallowed. "She would have been . . . so damned . . . angry at both of us."

Alex buried his head in his hands.

"She loved you, Alex. She loved you as much as I've seen any woman love. She wanted something very special for you." He hesitated. "Neither of us deserved her, not you her love, nor me her friendship."

Gar Morrow stared at the man across from him, his friend, his rival, his enemy, and he felt an infinite sadness for both of them. He turned and left.

Twenty-eight

After the funeral, Jess Martin reverted back to his old ways. Even Willow became wary of his temper. Only Sallie Sue seemed to penetrate the armor he'd rebuilt around himself.

Two days after the funeral he started walking, far sooner than Sullivan advised, but he was like the restless wolf for which he was named, and if he felt pain, his shadowed eyes showed no sign.

At first the rain kept him inside, and then he ignored it. Willow watched him roam outside, watched him try to flex his bandaged hand. His ribs were also bandaged, and Sullivan had told her he could not ride for weeks, not without causing great damage.

She knew he had no intention of staying that long. He flinched each time she came into his room, and his replies to her questions or words were monosyllablic at best, silence at worst.

She asked if he wanted to take this time to learn to read, and he glared at her. She was terribly afraid that he blamed her for the destruction of his hand. And it *was* her fault. If she hadn't hung so stubbornly to this land, none of this would have happened.

So Willow had own her guilt to live with, and it was so deep that she hesitated to crowd him, to invade his privacy, no matter how much she wanted to touch him and love him and convince him that injured hand or not, he was more man than anyone she'd ever known.

Jess had made no secret of the fact that he would leave as soon as he was physically able to do so. He had already asked her to take him to the hotel in town, but she'd refused, and made sure he had no way to get there. With his hand he couldn't saddle his horse, nor hitch a team to the wagon, and with his ribs he certainly couldn't walk the miles into town.

He had, however, insisted on moving into the barn. Brady had moved into town to retake his job as marshal, although he frequently came out to the ranch to see how Jess was, and to do any needed chores.

She was doing nothing less than holding Jess hostage, and he stalked like a prisoner, trying to regain his strength, doing far more than he should. He was trying so hard, Willow knew, so he could leave her.

Because Sallie Sue coaxed him, he would sometimes stay after dinner for the stories. Despite his ribs, he allowed an insistent Sallie Sue to curl up in his lap, and his good arm would rest easily on her chubby good one.

On the fifth night after the funeral, Willow finished the story of Odysseus. He had returned home after twenty years of hardship and killing. Wary after years of misadventure, he decided not to announce his presence before entering the kingdom, and he quickly discovered betrayal. His nobles were quarreling among themselves and stealing from his kingdom.

"Like Mr. Newton," Jeremy said.

"Maybe," she conceded, "the quarreling part."

"But why didn't Penelope recognize Odysseus?" asked Chad, who, despite his grown-up denials to the contrary, was just as interested in the story as the others.

"He was in disguise. No one suspected who he was," Willow

said in a low, conspiratorial voice. "Only his old dog recognized him." Willow glanced over at Jess, who couldn't conceal his interest, though he tried.

"And then what?"

"All the nobles wanted to marry Penelope, but she said she would only marry the man who could string and shoot from the great bow of Odysseus. All the nobles tried, and none could do it. Finally this old beggar tries. Everyone laughs and mocks him. . . ."

Big eyes fastened on her as they all imagined the scene, the big hall, the beautiful Penelope, the bragging gunse—nobles.

"And he strings the mighty weapon and slowly lets fly an arrow."

"Odysseus!" Jimmy said.

Willow nodded, deciding not to tell the rest of the story, how Odysseus then killed all the nobles. Once again she silently asked Homer to forgive her.

"And they lived happ'ly ever after," Sallie Sue recited contentedly. That was always the end to Willow's stories.

Jess cast her a suspicious look, as if he knew she was withholding something. But in his current mood he wasn't offering any comments. He gently set down Sallie Sue, said a hasty 'night, and left.

Willow wanted to go after him very badly, but Sallie Sue pleaded with her to say her prayers, and by the time Willow finished and went to the barn, Jess's door was closed. Tomorrow, she thought to herself. Tomorrow.

The next day was gray and droopy and filled with rain. Willow knew she should be rejoicing. This was the rain everyone had been praying for, the rain that would fill the river. But she couldn't be happy.

She'd seen the determined look in Jess's eyes that morning when he came in for breakfast. He was still obviously in severe pain, but nothing she or anyone else could say would still him. He had eaten awkwardly with his left hand, and his lips had twisted into a grimace meant to be a smile only once, when Sallie Sue, sporting a sling on her arm, cuddled up to him. But even that smile, slight and wistful and fleeting, disappeared quickly.

Everything about him seemed to scream he was planning something, and she wasn't at all surprised an hour later when he stalked out to the barn. She went after him and watched helplessly as he tried to saddle the pinto and failed. He had managed to pull on the blanket, but now he stood defeatedly, frustration etched all over his face as his left hand held on to his saddle, which partially lay on the ground.

"Sullivan said you shouldn't ride so soon."

"He's an old woman," Lobo replied tersely. "I've ridden with worse injuries."

"But now you don't have to."

"Don't I?" He tried to lift the saddle again as Willow mentally started counting to ten.

"You are the most stubborn, pigheaded, unreasonable . . ."

The saddle fell again, and he swore in frustration. "I don't suppose you'd help . . ."

"No," she nearly screamed at him.

Lobo looked at his hand with such disgust and frustration and hopelessness that she wanted to cry.

All the anger drained from her, and she bit her lip. "I'm sorry."

He spun around to face her, something he'd been avoiding. "Sorry? Why?"

"It was my fault . . . your hand, your injuries, and now . . . going before . . ."

She hated the tears clouding in her eyes. She turned, not wanting him to see her weakness. He didn't tolerate weakness. Not in himself. Not in anyone.

Willow felt his left hand touching her cheek just as it had weeks before.

"Don't," he said. "Don't cry for me." He remembered another time she had cried. He had felt her tears on his cheek. It had been the first time he'd ever known her to cry. It had been the first time anyone had ever cried for him. It had been humbling and aching then. It was even more so now.

"I don't want to lose you," she said.

"I'm nothing but a mirage," he said softly, awkwardly, trying hard to put his reasoning into words. He was so afraid that Willow still didn't see him as he was, and that one day she would be bitterly disappointed in him. He couldn't stand to see her love turn to disgust. "A picture in the sky, something that doesn't really exist. I'm not your Odysseus. No matter what I call myself I'm still Lobo." He hesitated. "I've never known how to love. I don't know now," he added flatly.

"You know better than anyone I've ever met," she said. "Because you never ask for anything in return."

"Don't," he said roughly. "I know what I am, what I'll always be."

Willow stood on tiptoe, her hand going to his face. He hadn't been able to shave, and he looked now like a desperado, like the man he was trying to convince her he was. Her fingers touched the rough blond bristles and traced his clenched jaw.

"I love you," she said. "You're . . . not a mirage or a legend. You couldn't be, not with all your stubbornness and bad temper and . . . and . . ."

Despite himself, Lobo was unable to move, lost in the intensity of her eyes, in the need to touch her one last time.

He leaned down, his lips caressing the soft skin. "And . . . what?"

Willow felt hope bubbling up inside her at his sensual tone.

"Obstinacy," she said, but her voice teased him. "Like a mule."

"A mule?" There was an encouraging challenge in the words.

She blushed suddenly. "Well, maybe not exactly like a . . . mule."

His lips crushed down on hers then, with need and demand and want.

Fire erupted between them, as it always did, but now desperation made it glow white-hot. His lips possessed and loved and devoured, his good arm drawing her body close to his until they were nearly one again. Willow relished the stinging scrape of his beard against her skin, the clean, soapy, male scent, the angular plane of his bones, the firmness of his lips as he seemed to reach inside her and extract her very essence.

She prayed, silently and hard. She prayed that her love would communicate itself to him, would make him believe, would make him understand that he was good for them all, that he brought out the best in them all, that he'd made them all grow and take responsibility and stand tall.

Just as he had.

She tried to tell him that with her lips and her mouth and her body. But just when she thought she might succeed, just as his lips started to yield, he backed away, his eyes shaded and dark.

He studied the rough red marks on her cheek made by his beard, and the fingers of his good hand touched them very gently. "I always hurt you," he said in a low voice.

"No," she denied.

But his hand didn't stop the soft probing. "You see," he said, "I can't even shave myself."

"But I can do that," she said. "And you will again."

"The sawbones isn't so sure."

"That old woman," she scoffed, finally bringing a faint smile to his lips.

"Don't make this so hard."

"And what will it be for Chad and Sallie Sue . . . and even Estelle? They all love you."

"They'll forget soon enough."

"They will never forget. I'll never forget. You can't just walk in and out of people's lives."

"I'm a danger to you, especially now." He looked down at his hand.

"No," she said, the tears coming faster. She had to convince him.

Lobo looked back down at the saddle. "The longer I stay, the harder it will be," he said. "For all of us. Help me." It was an agonized plea.

"Where will you go?" she asked.

He shrugged.

Willow felt her heart crumble as she tried one last time. "We need you."

"A cripple?"

"You. Everything you are. Everything."

"I'm no damned good for anything. Not anymore."

"You're damned good at everything," she said, and he looked at her in shock. He'd never heard her utter a profanity before, not even at the worst of times. His brows came together.

But Willow went on, disregarding his deep scowl. "No one thought of the dam until you came. No one could have finished the barn so quickly, no one could have held off an army—"

He started to speak, to say he could no longer do that, but she wouldn't let him. "It was the intelligence, not the gun," she continued desperately as he started trying to saddle his horse again. "And what about Brady and Estelle?"

"What about 'em?"

She sighed in exasperation. "Surely you've noticed the changes."

He gave her a bittersweet smile. "Brady was already changing. Alex just speeded up the process."

"Not Alex. You."

"Don't let Brady hear you say that."

"He would be the first to admit it."

"Then he would be wrong. No one really changes. They just wander off a trail now and then. Like I did here. It's time to get back on it."

"You are the most stubborn, pigheaded, unreasonable—"

"You've already said that," he reminded her.

"Because it's true," she replied waspishly.

He clenched his teeth together. "Dammit, Willow, you're better off without me. You may have buried the name, but you didn't bury the man."

"The *man* is what I want," she said, the waspishness gone, replaced by softness.

He tried again to reason with her. "Even a stubborn, pig-headed . . . ?"

Willow suddenly smiled through the tears. "Odd, isn't it. But that's exactly what I want . . . what we all want. Even the town. Why do you think they did what they did at the funeral? Everyone."

The saddle dropped from his hand, and he swore softly before adding his most telling argument. "They didn't think I would be staying. That was just their way of getting shed of me."

"I think Brady made it clear that you might stay."

A strange look flitted over his face. No one had ever wanted him before, much less a whole town. Even less a sheriff, for chrissakes, even an ex-drunk one.

"I still can't read," he argued in a low, shamed voice.

"You will," she said, sensing victory.

"I'm restless."

"Not for long."

"I'm not a farmer."

"What about a rancher?"

"Dammit, Willow, it won't work."

"Why?"

"Someone will recognize me."

"What, a peace-loving rancher with a large family? With the respect of a whole town. Lobo?"

"The town will get over it quick enough. Tomorrow. The next day."

"Everybody in town saw you take that bullet for Sallie Sue," she said. "Everyone saw how you avoided killing any-one. Everyone knows what you did for Brady. There was even a town meeting—"

"A what?"

"A town meeting. When they decided to bury Lobo."

"A town meeting, for chrissakes . . ."

"They're usually about me," she said with that serene smile that drove him crazy. "It's time they had someone else to meet about." She looked thoughtful for a moment. "Just think," she said dreamily, "the two of us . . . we'll keep them busy for the next twenty years."

"Willow . . ."

"Thirty years?"

"Willow . . ."

"And you promised to show Chad some horse tricks."

"Willow . . ."

"And I think you and I have some unfinished business—"

"Willow . . ."

"I love you, Jess."

"Willow . . ."

"And Sallie Sue, Chad, and the twins . . . they love you."

"Willow . . ."

"Of course, you may not want such a large family—"

He leaned down and kissed her hard. It was the only way to shut her up. But some of the words caught fire in him. Maybe, just maybe it could work, he thought as her lips parted under his. In the past few weeks, more and more of Lobo had been eclipsed by Jess, by the boy who'd once dreamed about a home, by the man who'd taken pleasure in the simple acts of building, of plowing, of holding a child. Perhaps Jess could make it work.

There would still be Lobo in him. There would always be Lobo, but there was also the dreamer again. He looked at Willow and knew that anything was possible. She had brought Jess back to life, Jess, who'd loved his brother, who'd looked at a cinnamon sky and saw beauty, and who'd craved a family like others had.

And now a town had made that possible. A whole town of people, people who could have turned their backs to him.

The whole town?

He chuckled, and Willow couldn't decide whether she was offended. She'd never heard him chuckle before. "The whole town?" he asked as if he'd just comprehended her words. "The whole town wants me?"

She looked up at him delightedly. He looked so perturbed, so bemused by the thought that all his masks were suddenly gone, all the guardedness. She closed her eyes at the wonder of it.

"Maybe," he said thoughtfully, even wistfully, "maybe I could try. I did promise Chad . . ."

"Gar said he would even give us some stock . . . because we let him use the water."

Lobo . . . no, he thought suddenly. For the first time he thought of himself as Jess. He felt like Jess. Thoughts tumbled in his head as he considered her last words. His will. Willow had a surprise coming. But that could wait until later.

His good arm went around her suddenly, squeezing her tightly, and he didn't feel the pain in his ribs. He felt only elation.

Elation and hope.

"Lady," he said caressingly, "you're plumb crazy."

"Everyone says so," she agreed happily as his mouth pressed tightly against hers, and even the gentle sound of rain outside was lost in the legendary magic of what both knew was a homecoming.

Epilogue

The entire town of Newton attended the christening of Penelope Taylor Martin.

It reminded some of the frequent town meetings of what seemed like several years earlier. There had not been one for eighteen months. Peace and tranquillity had been restored to the small town nestled in the rolling plains.

Reverend Cecil Mooney officiated. Mayor August Stillwater and his gentle wife looked on with indulgent satisfaction.

Sheriff Brady Thomas and his wife, Estelle, were the proud godparents. Sullivan and Marisa Barkley beamed happily behind them with their own eight-month-old son.

Jess Martin stood tall during the ceremony, and bent over only slightly to sign his and his child's names in the church register. He did it with difficulty, not because he couldn't write, for he did now, but because two of his fingers remained stiff. Still, he knew the most complete joy in his life. All the nights he had worked so hard to learn, all the frustration, had finally given him the one thing he wanted most after his family.

His family. It didn't even sound strange anymore. Chad. The twins. Sallie Sue. They all stood as proud as he felt. And Willow. His infuriating, remarkable, strong-willed but incredibly gentle Willow. Her face was soft and loving as she looked down at their child, the newest addition to their family.

He looked around the church and saw all the other children there, even some young adults. They had all been Willow's children, were still her children. They looked at her with something akin to devotion. She had affected all their lives, was still affecting many of them, since she continued teaching, and Jess could no more try to dissuade her than he could stop breathing. He didn't want to. Her love for the children, and theirs in return, had made his new life possible.

The love and affection the town had finally given Willow also enveloped him. Gar Morrow had helped him choose and buy cattle; other ranchers had helped him learn the business; the local banker had protected his identity when funds were transferred by Canton. Willow had been incredulous at first at the sum of money, then quietly accepting, not so much for herself, but for him, because the money made it so much easier to build the dream her husband had, that of making a secure place for them all.

Strangers, gunslingers trying to make a reputation, had come at first, but they were quickly convinced by everyone that the man named Lobo had indeed died. They were all shown the grave, which usually had fresh flowers at the headstone. Willow took them often. It was Lobo, after all, who had given her Jess.

After the signing of the register, all the participants and guests went to a reception at the mayor's home, even Gar and Alex. The two men spoke cordially, but they did not have the friendship they once had. Too many years of bitterness lay between them for trust. But Willow had hope.

Willow always had hope, Jess knew. Willow would always have hope. And, by God, she somehow managed to turn hope into reality. He hadn't seen her fail yet. For chrissakes, look at himself.

His thoughts were interrupted as person after person came up and looked at the baby.

"Why Penelope?" one asked. "Is it a family name?"

Willow looked up at Jess with laughter in her eyes—and a secret message. By now Jess knew all about Odysseus and Penelope. He knew about a lot of things, including love and happiness and belonging, and pictures in the sky.

"Goes a long way back, a very long way back." He grinned with a wry warmth that made Willow tingle with love and anticipation. "But yes, it is a family name."